SUNLIGHT ON THE MERSEY

Following recent heartbreak, seventeen-year-old Rose is sent to work in rural Wales, where she is enchanted by the 'big house' and by David, its tragic young owner. Sister Iris can't escape so easily, especially when an accident has devastating consequences for the family. Meanwhile ex-soldier Charlie is keen to secure a brighter future for himself ... even if it means putting ambition above his own happiness. There is romance in store for each of the family. But can love blossom amidst the challenges that lie ahead?

SUNLIGHT ON THE MERSEY

by

Lyn Andrews

Magna Large Print Books
Long Preston, North Yorkshire,
BD23 4ND, England.

British Library Cataloguing in Publication Data.

Andrews, Lyn
    Sunlight on the Mersey.

    A catalogue record of this book is
    available from the British Library

    ISBN   978-0-7505-3931-9

First published in Great Britain in 2012 by
Headline Publishing Group

Published in Large Print 2014 by arrangement with
Headline Publishing Group

Magna Large Print is an imprint of Library Magna Books Ltd.

Printed and bound in Great Britain by
T.J. (International) Ltd., Cornwall, PL28 8RW

Prologue

Liverpool 1918

'Mam, how will we ever find our Charlie in this crowd?' fifteen-year-old Iris Mundy cried impatiently, holding tightly to her mother's arm. Weak late-November sunlight filtered down through the great glass domed roof of Lime Street Station to fall on the heads of the dense crowd milling about below on the concourse. It picked out the pitted brass fittings on the engine that had slowly come to a halt amidst clouds of hissing steam and the strident sound of grinding brakes. The first train bringing the troops back home had finally arrived.

The municipal band immediately burst into a rousing version of 'The British Grenadiers' and, simultaneously, a deafening cheer erupted from the waiting crowds as Liverpool welcomed home its surviving sons after four years of bitter and bloody conflict on the fields of France and Belgium. The atmosphere was electric, infused with pride, relief and overwhelming joy.

Kate Mundy's reply was drowned out by the noise but her expression was a mixture of grim determination and happiness as she began to push her way forward. It looked as if the entire population of Liverpool had turned out to welcome the boys back, she thought, although she did not intend to let that stop her being the first to embrace her son. Every day and night for the past year she'd spent worrying that he would be badly wounded or, even worse, killed, but now he was safely home. Although she was small and wiry her eagerness gave her the strength she needed to edge steadily forward towards the platform where the first passengers had begun to alight. 'Just hang onto me, Iris, and we'll get through this crowd somehow,' she shouted to her daughter above the din. 'Is our Rose with your da?'

Iris, who was a good deal taller and sturdier than her mother, managed to half turn and caught sight of her father with her younger sister, Rose, hanging grimly on to his arm. She grinned at him. 'There's no stopping Mam now, she'll steam-roller her way through regardless!' she called as the cheering gradually died away.

Bill Mundy grinned back, pride and happy anticipation in his eyes. He'd worried about his son just as much as Kate had although he'd tried not to show it too much; someone had had to bolster the family's spirits through those dark days. He was a big man, over six feet tall and well built, so the crowd of people in front of him presented little problem, but his fourteen-year-old daughter was slight and slim like her mother. 'Rose, luv, whatever you do, don't let go of my arm,' he urged. 'You might get lost in this crowd.'

Rose looked up at him, her dark eyes full of trepidation. 'I won't, Da, but I'll be glad when we can get out of the station. I didn't think it would be as bad as this. I've never seen so many people!'

Bill nodded. 'It's only to be expected, luv, it's

been a long, desperate and heart-breaking time for everyone. But as soon as we find Charlie we'll be out of here.'

Kate and Iris had almost reached the front of the crowd as more and more men and boys, still in uniform and with kitbags slung over their shoulders, jumped from the carriages and pushed their way towards the barrier, eagerly searching the crowd for loved ones, relief at being home at last plain on their faces. Too many of those faces looked so much older than their actual years, Kate thought sadly; the result of the horrors they had witnessed and lived through.

Iris suddenly caught sight of her brother in the front rank. 'There he is, Mam!' she cried, pointing and then waving madly. 'Charlie! Charlie, it's me, Iris! Over here, we're over here!'

Charlie's dark eyes lit up and his face creased in a grin as he pushed his uniform cap back revealing thick, short-cropped brown hair.

Kate half ran the last few yards, tears of joy streaming down her cheeks as she held out her arms to him. 'Charlie! Thank God! Oh, thank God, you're home safe!'

Charlie hugged her and then for the first time caught sight of his father and Rose over the top of her head.

'Welcome home, son! We've all missed you and we're proud of you,' Bill said in a choked voice, taking the kitbag from his son and patting Charlie affectionately on the shoulder. 'How's the arm now?' he added, noticing the lad wince slightly as Iris hugged him.

'Almost good as new, Da. Just the occasional

twinge,' Charlie replied off-handedly. He'd been fortunate to come through that bloodbath with just a flesh wound and a fairly mild case of trench foot. He turned his attention to Rose, who was bobbing up and down with excitement, her cheeks flushed, her eyes bright. 'Rose, you've certainly grown since I last saw you!'

Rose hugged him. 'I'll be fifteen next birthday, I've left school and I'm hoping to get a job soon! And now the war is over I won't have to work in munitions either. Oh, we've got so much to tell you, Charlie, and there are all kinds of celebrations being planned!' she blurted out. She really *had* missed him.

Iris smiled: Rose's enthusiasm was infectious. Her sister was fortunate not to have to go into a munitions factory as she, Iris, had had to do this past year. The work had been hard, dirty, tedious and dangerous and Rose would have found it backbreaking; Rose had always been what her Mam termed 'delicate'.

The little family reunion was being replicated all around them as wives, mothers, sisters and sweethearts embraced their menfolk with tears and cries of joy.

Bill took the situation in hand. 'Right, let's make our way out to the tram stop before the queues get too long. There will be more trains arriving soon and the traffic is already heavy,' he said, guiding them towards the still crowded entrance.

As they finally emerged into the pale winter sunshine, Kate clinging tightly to Charlie's arm, Rose still close by her father's side and Iris just behind them, Charlie stopped and stared at the familiar sight of St George's Hall, which dominated the opposite side of the road. The massive façade with its classical columns, the huge crouching bronze lions that guarded the plateau and the long flight of shallow steps that led up to it were blackened with soot but it was still an imposing sight – and one that epitomised 'home', just as much as the buildings on the Liverpool waterfront and the river itself did. There'd be sunlight sparkling on the turgid grey waters of the Mersey today, he thought.

'That's a real sight for sore eyes, Mam!' he said with a catch in his voice. And one he'd often wondered if he would ever see again. Many of his mates wouldn't, he'd left them behind in the mud of Flanders. He pushed the thoughts away. It was over now. He was home and he was determined he wasn't going to waste his life. He'd been spared and he was going to make something of himself.

Bill had been watching him closely and noticed the hardening of his son's expression with regret. Charlie had changed in the year he'd been away but it would have been a miracle if he hadn't. He could only try to imagine what the lad had been through and he was still only eighteen, he thought as he followed his wife and son down the steps and towards the nearest tram stop.

'Da, do you think our Charlie is ... all right?' Rose asked quietly. She too had noticed the change in her brother's demeanour.

Bill tucked her hand through his arm and patted it reassuringly. 'Now don't you go worrying any more about him, luv. He's home, he's fine, he'll settle down – just give him time.'

'Mam will be in her element now, fussing over him and fattening him up,' Iris added, grinning at her father. 'And there's the street party and everything to look forward to. That will cheer them all up.'

Bill smiled happily at his elder daughter. 'And then there's Christmas to look forward to and it will be great to have the whole family together this year.'

Rose's momentary anxiety disappeared at her father's words. Charlie was home and her da was always right. Their close and loving family was complete again, there was nothing to worry about.

'We've got a lot to look forward to now, haven't we, Da?' Iris added, linking arms with her father.

Bill nodded. 'We have indeed, luv. The future has got to be better than the last four years – and here's the tram. Let's go home.'

There had been a celebratory family supper that evening although Kate bemoaned the fact that the food shortages meant she could not provide the kind of meal she had envisaged for Charlie's homecoming.

'Mam, after what I've been used to, it's a feast fit for a king,' Charlie had laughed, tucking into the tiny portion of meat and potatoes while his sisters had fussed over him, pouring both himself and his father a glass of pale ale.

When the meal was over, the toasts drunk, the dishes cleared away and washed and Rose and Iris had gone up to bed, Bill urged Kate to follow them. 'You've had a long, tiring day, luv, and you've to be up at the crack of dawn in the morning to go to the market.'

Kate nodded, although she was loath to let Charlie out of her sight. At least she would sleep easily tonight, knowing he was safe, and she was also aware that Bill wanted some time alone with his son. 'Well, goodnight, luv. Sleep well,' she said, smiling.

'I will, Mam, you can be sure of that,' Charlie replied. It felt a little strange to be once again sitting in the so-familiar kitchen with comforts he'd not had for many months. He'd been away a year, not long compared to some of the lads, and yet it had seemed infinitely longer.

When Kate had gone Bill got up and extracted a small bottle from the back of the cupboard in the base of the dresser. 'I've been saving this for a special occasion,' he informed his son, pouring a small measure of the whisky into two glasses.

'This is certainly better than pale ale,' Charlie said appreciatively after taking a sip.

'Finest malt and not easy to come by. I'm glad you've come through it safely, lad, so many didn't, but it's been the longest year in my life and most probably yours as well. It's going to take you a while to ... adjust to life now.' He paused as Charlie nodded. 'I'm not going to ask you about what you went through, but if you want to tell me I'll be only too glad to listen and ... help ease your mind, if I can.'

Charlie shook his head as he stared down into the amber liquid in his glass. 'I ... I don't think I can talk about it, Da. Not yet anyway. Maybe ... maybe in the future, maybe never. It was a ... a

15

living nightmare. Sheer hell on earth. Too ... horrific to dwell on. I want to forget it; I don't want to think about it.'

Bill nodded slowly. The newspaper reports of the hundreds of thousands killed and wounded had been bad enough. Every city, town, village and hamlet had lost men. 'Then put it all behind you and think about the future,' he urged firmly.

Charlie shook off the oppressive feelings that were threatening to overtake him. 'That's just what I intend to do, Da. I look at it like this: I was just so fortunate to have been spared. Now I've got the rest of my life ahead of me and I'm not going to waste it. We ... we had an officer, a Captain Summerhill; he was a good bloke. Not an upper-crust, toffee-nosed snob as some were. He used to talk to me. He used to say, "If by some bloody miracle you come through this in one piece, Private Mundy, aim for the very best you can get out of life, for by God you'll have both earned and deserve it. You all will." So that's what I'm going to do. Aim high. Make something of myself. I'm not sure how I'll manage it but ... but I want to end my days a respected middle-class man with a position in society and a healthy bank balance. Is that too much to ask for, Da?'

Bill looked dubious but he slowly shook his head. 'No, the world has changed – is still changing – but not that quickly, Charlie. For the likes of that Captain Summerhill it wouldn't be hard to achieve all that – he'd have the right background, the right connections – but you're just a working-class lad from a poor area of Liverpool. I don't want to put a damper on your hopes and ambitions but it won't be easy.' It might be well nigh impossible, the class system was so rigid, he thought, but he didn't say so.

Charlie didn't reply. Getting the best he possibly could out of the future seemed the only thing that made any sense of the carnage of the past – and his da was wrong. It wouldn't be easy for Edmund Summerhill to achieve anything; he was buried in a shallow grave in Flanders.

Sensing his son's mood Bill tried to be optimistic. 'Still, it's something to aim for, Charlie, and don't forget you'll inherit the pawnbroking business one day, just as I did. You'll soon settle back into life now the war's over; we all will. I'd see if you can get your old job back – that will be a start. And remember, son, you can always rely on me for help, advice and a sympathetic ear. We can all look forward now with hope.' He poured the remaining whisky into their glasses. 'Here's to peace, happiness and prosperity.'

Charlie smiled. 'To all that – and to the future.'

Chapter One

Liverpool 1921

'It's rheumatic fever, I'm afraid, Mrs Mundy. I've examined her thoroughly and I know the symptoms well enough, unfortunately,' Dr Mackenzie informed Kate who stood beside him looking worriedly down at her daughter. Rose, now seventeen, was flushed; her eyes were fever bright, her skin clammy with perspiration. Wisps of her dark hair were stuck to her cheeks and forehead and there was fear in her brown eyes.

'I will be all right, Mam, won't I? I feel terrible now but I *will* get better?' Rose's voice held a note of panic. Rheumatic fever was serious; she knew that much. She had pains in her arms and legs and her head was throbbing.

Kate tried to hide her own anxiety. Rosamund, or Rose as she was always called, had been rather spoiled. As a baby she'd always seemed to be ailing and there had been times when Kate seriously wondered if she would succeed in rearing her to adulthood, but when Rose had turned seventeen and it seemed as though her fears for the girl were over, she'd come down with this. And rheumatic fever she knew could leave Rose with a weak heart.

'As long as you rest, Rose, you'll be fine and hopefully suffer no lasting effects,' the doctor assured his patient firmly. 'Take the medicine I've prescribed, drink plenty of fluids and stay in bed. I'll call in and see you in a day or two.'

Kate nodded, relieved at his words as she ushered him towards the door of the small, neat but rather sparsely furnished bedroom. 'Thank you, doctor. You know she's always been a worry to me so I'll take good care to see she does as she's told. And I can tell you this, too: she's not going back to that hotel to work. I swear that's where she picked it up. You get all kinds of people in those hotels and you never know where they've come from or who they've been mixing with,' she remarked darkly.

Dr Mackenzie smiled at her kindly. He'd known the whole family for years but he doubted she'd understand it was an inflammatory disease that often was the result of a severe throat infection and Rose could have contracted that anywhere. Rheumatic fever was seldom fatal in adults but the young were often left with serious heart, joint and eye conditions. In this area of Liverpool children were weakened by malnutrition and dire poverty, the privations of the war years hadn't helped. The Mundys were far better off than many of their neighbours for they ran two businesses, he mused. Kate had a greengrocer's shop and her husband Bill was a pawnbroker, both very necessary establishments in this dockland community. 'I think it will be a while before she's fit for work of any kind, Mrs Mundy, but if you are worried about her before my next visit, don't hesitate to send for me.'

Kate thanked him and showed him downstairs and out through the shop, which she had closed for half an hour as business had been slow that morning. They lived above it but she certainly wasn't going to let him out the back way through the yard with the privy, the tin bath tub hanging on the wall, the small wash house and the stack of empty wooden fruit crates which would go back tomorrow, not a man of his position.

She'd been up very early as usual, but it had been Bill who had gone to the market this morning. She glanced around the shop and frowned. He'd got everything she'd put on the list but she preferred to choose the produce herself. Most of the blokes at the market were decent and honest but there were a couple who would try to palm you off with stuff that was past its best. She had wiped and polished up the fruit and stacked it in neat piles in the window, the potatoes were in sacks on the floor but resting against the front of the counter and the vegetables were arranged by variety and size on the wide deep shelves on the opposite wall. Bunches of fresh and dried herbs were suspended from a rack behind the counter. It all looked neat and tidy. Things now were slowly improving, she thought. At the end of the Great War there had been serious shortages of food and real hardship. She shook her head sadly as she remembered the terrible loss of life those four years had resulted in. Tragedy and hardship indeed for so many of her friends and neighbours but at least Charlie had come through with nothing more than a flesh wound in his arm and a fairly mild case of trench foot, which had quickly cleared up. It had taken Charlie a while to adjust to life at home and during the first months he'd had nightmares and bouts of moodiness, although lately he seemed more settled and at ease, especially with his sisters. Now she was worrying about whether this fever would leave Rose with a weak heart, despite Dr Mackenzie's reassurances. At least Iris enjoyed good health.

She had a bottle of Robinson's Barley Water in the pantry, she remembered; she'd get it out and make up a jug and take it up to Rose. Drink plenty of fluids, he'd said.

Bill came into the shop and smiled affectionately at his wife. Despite the fact that her hair was no longer the burnished copper colour it had been when he'd met her and there were now fine lines at the corners of her grey eyes, to him she remained a very attractive woman. She was still small and slim and he often wondered where she found her boundless energy; time certainly hadn't slowed his Kate down much. 'I saw him leave, luv. What did he say is wrong with her?'

'Rheumatic fever, Bill, but he says we're not to worry, that with medicine, rest and plenty of fluids she should recover and have no after-effects. But you know as well as I do that it can do lasting damage. Have you closed up or have you left someone reliable in charge?' she asked as an afterthought.

'I just put a note on the door: "Back in ten minutes",' he replied. 'I'm sure she'll be fine, luv, try not to worry too much.'

'She's not going back to that hotel, Bill. I swear that's where she picked this up, mixing with all and sundry. I never thought she was really strong enough to cope with the work of a chambermaid anyway. Changing beds, cleaning and carting bundles of linen around is heavy work and she's always been a bit on the delicate side.'

He said nothing; jobs were hard to find these days, especially for young, unskilled, untrained girls like Rose and Iris. Iris had worked in munitions in the last year of the war but Rose had been too young to join her sister. The lads who had survived were back and so many of them were now without work. Unemployment was rife and getting steadily worse. He was seeing more and more items being brought in to be pledged and the number of them remaining unredeemed was rising. 'Well, we'll talk about that when she's feeling better, luv. Is there any chance of a quick cuppa?'

Kate nodded. 'I'll put the kettle on. You take this barley water up to her and tell her she's to drink a full glass of it whether she feels like it or not,' she instructed as she bustled about with the kettle, teapot and tea caddy. She wouldn't mind a quick cup of tea herself before she opened up as there would be no closing for lunch today. She couldn't afford to turn any business away even if it did only amount to a few pounds of potatoes or carrots for a pan of 'blind' scouse – most of her customers couldn't afford any meat to go in it. She thanked God daily on her knees for her good fortune. They all had work, even if her children weren't exactly enthusiastic about their various occupations and Bill had always worked hard to provide for them. Unlike quite a few in the same occupation, he was a kind and compassionate man, always treating the women who came in with their bundles on a Monday morning with respect. His 'ladies', he called them, although most of them had never owned a decent coat and hat in their lives, but wore shawls instead. He made sure they kept their dignity.

Kate and Bill had been married for twenty-five years and she could count on the fingers of one hand the times he'd lost his temper with anyone. She smiled to herself as she spooned the tea into the pot. She would never forget the evening the tall, well-built, handsome young man with the dark hair and eyes had asked if he could escort her home from the social evening she had attended with friends at a nearby church hall. She'd found out that he was the son of Arthur Mundy, a respected pawnbroker, that he helped his father and hoped to take over the business when the old man retired. Also that he was teetotal, which had pleased her mother no end for her own father had been overly fond of the drink, often to the detriment of the household budget. Yes, she had a great deal to be thankful for and if she could live long enough to see all her children married and settled she'd be a happy woman.

Rose had been dozing fitfully, the pains in her joints making restful sleep impossible. She'd had a very sore throat a couple of weeks ago and had been off work for a day, but it had gone and she'd thought nothing more of it until two days ago when she'd begun to feel really awful. Her head ached, she felt sick, she'd had no energy and then the fever had overtaken her. At least she now knew what it was and that she would get well again. And she'd overheard what her mam had said to the doctor about her not going back to Black's Commercial Hotel. For that she was really thankful. She hated the place, but it had been the only job she could get. She hated having to clean rooms, change beds, empty chamber pots and she knew it would be years before she would be promoted to something better, such as head chambermaid or housekeeper. She had enquired if she could be trained to wait on in the dining room – she wouldn't have minded that – but she'd been told very firmly that there were no vacancies and that should one occur then they would employ someone already trained in silver service. There was another reason why she had no wish to return there. Jimmy Harper. She'd been foolish enough to believe that he had really cared for her. He was the first lad who had ever asked her out. He'd started working at the hotel a few months ago as the boy who cleaned the guests' boots, brought them their morning papers and sometimes ran errands for them. He was the same age as her and they'd quickly become friends. She'd really, really liked him and had believed him when he'd said she was the only girl for him. They'd been courting for almost two months when one afternoon she'd caught him kissing Mavis Smythe, who had only been working there as a chambermaid for two weeks. He'd tried to laugh it off, saying Mavis had led him on, but she'd never felt so hurt and let down in her life before and having to see him every day and studiously ignore him made working at Black's intolerable.

'How are you feeling now, Rose?' Bill asked gently as he set the jug and tumbler on the beside table. She certainly still looked feverish. 'Has the medicine helped at all?'

Rose tried to sit up but the effort made her grimace. Bill took her hand in his. 'You just lie there, I'll get you another pillow and help make you more comfortable. Your mam said you were to drink a full glass of this.'

He found another pillow and placed it behind her and then filled the glass and held it for her as if she were seven years old instead of seventeen.

Rose managed a smile; she loved her father dearly and knew he was worried about her. 'I feel a bit better knowing exactly what's wrong with me but it will be a while before I get back to normal.'

He nodded his agreement. 'Take things easy and you'll be fine. Perhaps when you feel better you could read, that would help to pass the time. I'll ask Iris if she'll go to the library and get you some books. I'd go myself but I think she will have a better idea of what you enjoy than me. With everyone at work and your mam in the shop you'll need something to occupy you, once you're on the mend.'

Rose leaned back against the pillows and nodded. If she hadn't been feeling so ill the idea of lying here reading all day would have been heaven. She loved reading, especially romances whose heroines lived far more interesting and pampered lives than she did and always married a handsome, adoring and often wealthy man. It also helped to take her mind off Jimmy Harper. She dozed off, comforted by the doctor's assurances, her father's presence and the knowledge that her days at Black's Commercial Hotel were in the past.

'Did the doctor come, Mam? What did he say? How is she?' Iris fired the questions at her mother as she came into the kitchen at the back of the shop, put her bag on the dresser and took off her jacket and hat. She ran her hands through her thick auburn hair, which she'd recently had cut in the new short style, something of which her mother had strongly disapproved. They'd had words over it. She had dark eyes like her father but she also had his height and build, something

25

she frequently complained about, bemoaning the fact that she wasn't slender and petite like Rose.

'Don't just leave your hat and bag on the dresser, Iris; I'll be needing those dishes off it soon. She's a bit better. It's rheumatic fever but she'll get over it,' Kate informed her, handing his the offending cloche hat and clutch bag and shaking her head at the sight of her daughter's shorn locks. Iris was far too self-willed and independent in her opinion and working in that munitions factory appeared only to have increased those traits. It seemed as if all the changes in society could be blamed on the war.

'That's a relief! Shall I go up and see if there's anything she needs or wants, Mam?' Iris was genuinely relieved. Rose had been really ill these last twenty-four hours. Although they were very different in temperament and sometimes bickered, she was closer to her sister than she was to her brother Charlie; for the past few years she had found him somewhat difficult to live with, although she did sympathise with him after what he had been through.

'Don't be too long up there, Iris. I need you to help me with supper,' Kate instructed. 'Your da will be in a bit later tonight, he's trying to sort out his stock, and when our Charlie comes in I want him to give your da a hand or we'll be having our meal when it's time to go to bed.'

Iris smiled fondly at the sight of her sister propped up by pillows and looking far better than she had done that morning. 'You'll go to any lengths not to have to go to work, Rose, although I have to say this is a bit drastic!'

26

Rose grimaced. 'Don't torment me, Iris. I still feel awful.'

Iris sat on the edge of the bed. 'Poor you, but you will get better, Mam said so. Is there anything you want? I've not to stay up here gossiping. Da's staying on late and when our Charlie gets in he's going to get roped in to help.'

Rose managed a smile. 'He won't be very happy about that, knowing our Charlie.'

'He's never really happy about anything these days, unless of course it's counting his money,' Iris replied scathingly. 'Mam is always saying she doesn't know where he gets his miserly streak from.'

Rose nodded. 'Mam says I'm not going back to Black's and that's a huge relief, and for more than one reason.'

Iris nodded sympathetically; she knew how hurt Rose had been by Jimmy Harper's betrayal.

'I think it's going to be ages before I can even get out of bed. When I'm feeling better, would you go to the library for me, Iris?'

'Aren't you the fortunate one?' Iris joked. 'Lying up here with your head in one of those terrible romances you love so much while I'm stuck behind the counter at Frisby Dyke's measuring out knicker elastic and other such bits of finery. Of course I'll go and get you your books but only when Mam thinks you're up to reading. Now, I'd better go back down before she starts yelling up to me. I'm still not in her good books for having my hair cut! Mind you, if I'd asked her before I had it done she'd have forbidden it.' She grinned, taking in her sister's long, dark locks, which were now very tangled. 'You should have yours cut, Rose. This style would suit you and it's so easy to manage.'

'I might think about it,' Rose replied. At that precise moment she didn't really care how she looked. She just wished all the aches and pains would disappear and she could sleep.

It was nearly half past eight when they finally sat down at the table, much to Kate's annoyance for it had been a very long and trying day and she was worn out.

'You should get rid of half the stuff you have in the loft over the shop, Da. It's never going to be redeemed now and it's just old clothes and rubbish,' Charlie stated, helping himself to more boiled potatoes to accompany the large slice of meat and vegetable pie already on his plate. He was now twenty-one and strongly resembled his father in looks and build if not in nature.

'I don't think it's very charitable to call people's belongings "rubbish". They paid good money, for that stuff and it's unfortunate that they haven't been able to redeem it. Besides, what am I supposed to do with it?' Bill asked.

'Give it to a rag-and-bone merchant, at least you'd get a few bob for it. Better than having to burn it,' Charlie answered with his mouth full.

Kate glared at him 'Where are your manners, Charlie Mundy?'

Charlie shrugged but refrained from replying until he'd swallowed his food. God, but Mam was so picky sometimes, he thought irritably. Didn't she understand that after you'd spent a year in the stinking trenches, standing knee deep in filthy muddy water, deafened by the incessant pounding of the heavy guns, your guts turning to water with sheer terror and the horror of seeing your mates being blown to bits around you, things like 'manners' seemed pretty unimportant? 'I just thought it would be easier to get rid of as much stuff as you can. Make life easier. You'd be better able to keep track of things and turn that rubbish into hard cash. There's no point in working if you don't make a decent profit.'

'None of us earns what you would exactly call a fortune,' Iris stated succinctly, knowing her brother didn't earn much more than either herself or Rose. 'Hardly anyone makes what you call a "decent profit".'

Charlie glared at her. In his opinion Iris had far too much to say and mainly on matters that did not concern her. He decided to ignore her remark 'If you'd let me work with you, Da, I'm sure with your experience and my organisation we could really make a difference.'

'We've been through this time and again, Charlie,' Kate said firmly. 'You have a steady, decent job with the Blue Funnel Line. Granted as a clerk it's not well paid yet, but in time if you work hard you'll get promoted and then your pay will improve. You are very fortunate they took you back after the war. How many lads of your age have a good job – or any job for that matter? There isn't enough to be made from that business to employ you as well, especially as times are so desperately hard.'

'Your mam's right, lad. The way things are going folk will have nothing left to pawn and I'll be seriously out of pocket. We are more fortunate than so many around here, thank God, but we still need all of you to be earning a wage,' Bill added quietly.

'What's our Rose going to do when she's better, Mam? She said you won't let her go back to Black's,' Iris asked.

'We'll cross that bridge when we come to it,' Bill stated firmly.

'I hope you're not thinking of letting her stay at home doing nothing? You've just said we all need to work,' Charlie said quietly. That certainly wouldn't be fair on either him or Iris but then Rose had always been the spoilt one.

'Like your da said, we'll wait until she's over this and then see what she's capable of doing. I never thought that job was suitable for her constitution,' Kate said firmly. In fact an idea had already formed in her mind; she had been thinking about it all afternoon and intended to discuss it with Bill later, when they got a moment to themselves.

Charlie continued his meal in silence, thinking that he would make a far better job of running the pawnbroking business than his father did. He'd make it pay better than his da, who was too disorganised and far too soft with a lot of his customers. If he'd learned one thing during the time he'd spent in the army it was that you looked after yourself first and foremost because nobody else would. He'd come through it but he'd grown up and learned some hard lessons. Charlie Mundy was going to look after number one and he had vowed that somehow he would obtain a healthy bank balance and a position of respect in society, neither of which he would achieve as a humble shipping clerk. He was careful with what money he earned and was saving hard, but at present he could see no way of gaining a foothold on the ladder to prosperity.

Iris, too, finished her meal in silence wondering just how long it would be before Rose would be well enough to work again. She didn't particularly enjoy working in a shop but knew perfectly well she was fortunate to have a job at all. What would her sister be able to find in the way of future employment?

Chapter Two

Kate didn't get the chance that evening to discuss with Bill the idea that she'd been mulling over. After supper, when the dishes had been washed and put away, Charlie – after having read the headlines in the *Liverpool Echo*, which proclaimed that there seemed to be increasing industrial unrest and unemployment but also that the Prince of Wales was to open the newly refurbished Town Hall – engaged his father in a discussion about the merits of Liverpool Football Club over those of their rivals Everton. Kate knew from experience such a debate would be long and heated, so she had decided to go up and settle Rose for the night and then retire herself. She was exhausted and would have to be up again at four next morning to go to the market.

Rose had a more peaceful night. When Kate looked in on her next morning, she told her mother the pains in her limbs had abated somewhat and she felt a little better in herself. It appeared that the worst was over, Kate thought thankfully as she went down to open up the shop.

The morning was fine and the bright May sunlight that bathed the street lifted her spirits a little. She arranged the stock and swept the floor and as she brushed the dust off the doorstep she leaned on the broom handle for a few seconds looking down the street. They all looked exactly the same, these streets of dilapidated two-up, two-down terraced houses, she thought. They should have been demolished years ago. Their brickwork had been eroded by time and the elements and was blackened by the soot from the factories, domestic chimneys and those of the Clarence Dock Power Station; their paintwork was scuffed and peeling; the stone steps were cracked and broken. The women who occupied them broke their backs in an effort to keep their homes clean, even scrubbing their front steps daily. They had no modern facilities to make the task easier either, she mused. No electricity, only gas light; no hot water – some had no piped water at all and had to use standpipes; no bathrooms and only a tiny, dark scullery to serve the whole household, which frequently numbered ten or more. Washing had to be taken to the public wash house and then carted home and hung to dry on the lines strung across the street or on a rack suspended from the kitchen ceiling. It was no wonder in such conditions all manner of diseases were rife.

Yet again she contemplated her good fortune. They did have electricity and water; she had a copper boiler in the wash house; she had a large kitchen-cum-living room which was comfortably furnished, even though sometimes it did seem cramped, especially when they were all in there together. She would have liked a proper parlour but you couldn't have everything. In fact she didn't know of anyone who did have a parlour that was used solely for entertaining; space was at a premium and they were often used as bed-rooms. Her scullery wasn't a bad size and it had a window, a large stone sink and shelves and they didn't have to share the privy in the yard with three or four other families. Yes, she was fortunate but she wanted a better life for her children: a better future, better living and working conditions, better wages. Yet she was realistic enough to know that for the present they were fortunate to have a roof over their heads, food in their bellies, decent clothes on their backs and jobs.

She sighed and turned back into the shop, having caught sight of Maggie Connolly making her way up the street, a hemp bag over her arm. First customer of the day, she thought.

'Morning, Maggie. How's your Fred today?' she greeted the woman pleasantly.

'Said 'e felt well enough to go down ter the stands and see if there was a half a day's work on offer. Give us two pounds of carrots, a swede and two pounds of potatoes, Kate, would yer? And if yer 'ave a few fades I'd be glad of them fer the kids,' Maggie replied, leaning on the counter.

'I'm glad to hear he's up and about again. Let's hope he gets a morning's work.' Kate began to weigh out the vegetables and then tip them into Maggie's bag. A hard life spent working in all weathers, without good warm clothing or enough nourishing food, had taken its toll on Fred Connolly's health. Like everyone else, she deplored the system used on the docks where men were forced to congregate twice a day in pens and wait to be picked by the foreman for a half-day's work – if they were lucky. It was humiliating and degrading but it was how it had been done for years. She picked out four apples from a wicker basket behind the counter. They were well past their best but rather than throw them away she sold them as 'fades' to her customers at a tiny fraction of their cost. 'There you go, luv, they're not too bad but I wouldn't keep them longer than today.'

Maggie grimaced. 'Fat chance of that in our 'ouse, Kate. The kids are always starvin' when they get 'ome from school. 'Ow's your Rose? I 'eard the doctor 'ad been yesterday.'

'Much better this morning, thanks, Maggie. She's got rheumatic fever though.'

Maggie sucked in her breath and shook her head. 'Yer got ter be careful with that, Kate. It can be serious, leave her an invalid, it can. Look at Dora Foster's youngest. Poor kid, 'e can 'ardly get up the stairs now, gaspin' fer 'is breath an' his knees all deformed, like.'

Kate nodded, thinking of poor little Billy Foster. The child was fortunate that he had survived but now he was virtually a cripple. Dora hadn't been

34

able to afford to pay for a doctor and so the child had been left in a terrible state. Thankfully Rose had received medical treatment and the best care. 'I know but Dr Mackenzie said she should make a complete recovery and I'm going to make sure she doesn't overtax herself. I've got plans for our Rose when she's on her feet again.'

Maggie held out the coins to pay for her purchases and looked very interested. 'What kind of plans would they be then, Kate?' she asked. Rose Mundy had always been far more spoiled than Kate's other two.

'I've got to discuss them with Bill first, Maggie, but you'll be the first to know after I've done that,' she informed her neighbour.

Maggie nodded but before she could comment further two other customers arrived, Ada Marshall and Sal Appleby, both of whom she knew well.

''As your Rose got the scarlet fever, Kate?' Ada asked bluntly, nodding to Maggie by way of a greeting.

'No. Why?' Kate demanded.

'Well, I 'eard she was took bad and I 'eard there's at least four cases of it in Blackstock Street and that's just round the corner, so ter speak.'

'And yer know once these things get goin' it'll turn into an epidemic before long,' Sal added.

'She's on the mend now, thank God,' Kate replied. 'Now, what can I get you, Ada?' she asked, determined that she wasn't going to show how much this latest piece of news had worried her. Sal was right, these things usually resulted in an epidemic and Rose was in no state to combat yet

35

another disease. She resolved to speak to Bill tonight.

Thankfully she managed to get supper over early. Charlie went out with a couple of his mates for a pint and Iris had made arrangements to meet her friend from work, Florence Taylor.

'She seems a lot brighter today, luv,' Bill remarked as he brought down the empty jug to be refilled with barley water.

'She is and she's slept quite a lot so that's a good thing. Dr Mackenzie is calling in the morning so we'll see what he has to say. Now, there's something I want to talk to you about, Bill. I heard today that scarlet fever is raging again and our Rose isn't in any condition to contend with that too.'

Bill frowned as he sat down opposite his wife. 'I'd heard that quite a few kids in Blackstock Street have come down with it but how will that affect Rose? She's confined to bed; she's not going to be in any danger of catching it.'

'But we're both in contact with so many folk from around here and who knows how these things are spread? No, as soon as she's well enough I want to get her away from this neighbourhood, Bill. The weather is getting warmer now and you know what that means. Flies, rotting rubbish in the gutters and ashcans, people falling prey to all kinds of illnesses. I want to send her to stay with Gwen Roberts for a couple of months. She'll be delighted to have Rose, I know.'

Bill stared at her, a bit confused. 'You want her to go to Tregarron?'

Kate nodded. Gwen Roberts was an old friend

36

who lived in a small village in Denbighshire. Granted she didn't see her very often, usually only a couple of times a year when an omnibus trip was organised from the village to Liverpool for shopping purposes, but they wrote regularly. As a young girl she had gone on a very rare holiday with her mam and sister to a farm in Tregarron. Gwen had been the farmer's daughter and the same age as herself and they'd become firm friends. Her sister Molly had been recovering from a severe bout of measles, which had given her the idea to send Rose. Gwen's parents were now dead and her brother ran the farm. Gwen, who had never married, lived in a small cottage adjacent to the village post office where she was the postmistress.

'A few months in the country with fresh, clean air and good wholesome food will do her the world of good, Bill, you have to agree with that,' she urged.

'It will, but will she want to go, Kate? Will she be happy living in the middle of nowhere?' he asked. 'She's a city girl, she's used to all the shops, public transport and other amenities Liverpool has to offer.' He wasn't at all sure that his daughter would think this was a good idea.

'Like dirt and disease!' Kate added scathingly. 'Thankfully she'll get over this but it might leave her weakened and then she will pick up everything that's going around. No, Bill, we've had enough worries over our Rose's health to last a lifetime and I feel this will help her to get over that Jimmy Harper too. She's been really cut up about the way he treated her, although if you ask me she's better off without him, the little toe-rag seems to have the morals of an alley cat. A few months with Gwen will stand her in good stead, build her up, and when she returns we'll think about her helping me in the shop. I'm going to suggest it to Dr Mackenzie and I'm sure he'll agree with me.'

Bill nodded slowly. 'But we can't expect Gwen to keep her free of charge, Kate. And what will Rose do all day?'

'I've already thought about that. I've a few pounds saved, I won't send her there empty-handed and I suppose she could give Gwen a hand in the post office at busy times. It's not as if it's going to be for ever.'

Bill sighed as he picked up the newspaper. 'Well, the doctor can tell you when she will be fit to travel but I think you'd better see what she has to say about the whole thing first. She might well flatly refuse to go.'

Kate got up to put the kettle on, thinking that when she'd finished telling Rose about the gloriously happy time she'd spent in Tregarron the girl would raise no objections. She'd hint, too, that it would help Rose to get over the upset she'd recently suffered.

The following morning before she opened the shop Kate went up to see her daughter and outlined what she had in mind for Rose's convalescence, putting great emphasis on the pretty, peaceful countryside, the benefits of clean air and good food and the possibility that if Rose were to find things a bit too quiet then she could help out in the post office.

'It would be far, far better for you than staying here in Liverpool and going back to work in that hotel. You must find it quite a – a trial now, luv, having to see ... certain people every day, and you know how hot the summer months can be and how the stench from the ashcans and privies would turn your stomach. You'll love it. You know Aunty Gwen and a few hours helping her wouldn't seem like work at all, would it?' she urged.

Rose had listened to the description of the village and the countryside with some trepidation but it was the thought of going back to Black's and seeing Jimmy Harper again combined with the images and smells of the city in summer her mother's words had evoked that won the day. She smiled. 'It would be wonderful to get away from all that, Mam, and I do like Aunty Gwen.' In fact she had only met the small, dark-haired, energetic Gwen Roberts – on whom Kate had bestowed the honorary title of 'Aunty' – a few times, but she remembered her as being a rather pleasant gossipy person, and her mam always talked about her affectionately.

Kate smiled back with relief. 'I knew you'd agree. Now, let me tidy you up a bit and change those pillowcases before the doctor comes and we'll see what he says about the idea and when he thinks you will be well enough to go.'

Dr Mackenzie thought it was a very sensible idea and assured Kate that Rose would be fit to travel in about two weeks, depending upon how quickly she recovered, and Kate determined to write to Gwen that very evening asking would she be kind enough to have Rose to stay for the summer months.

That evening the news of Rose's proposed convalescence in Wales was received with astonishment by Iris and a little resentment by Charlie.

'And she's quite happy to go, Mam? For the whole summer? Won't she get bored stiff after a couple of weeks?' Iris asked, wondering just what her sister would find to keep her occupied for months in a tiny village with the nearest town over ten miles away.

'She's delighted with the idea,' Kate replied firmly, folding up the gingham tablecloth and putting it away in a drawer of the dresser. 'And I'm sure she has no wish to see that ... that Harper lad again.'

'Oh, I'll bet she is! She'll be spending her time getting waited on and reading those penny dreadfuls she's always got her nose stuck into,' Charlie muttered, wondering who was going to pay for Rose's extended holiday – for that's what it appeared to be to him. He did feel some sympathy for Rose, she was ill and she had been hurt by that young fool, but surely she had to learn to take the knocks life dealt? He certainly had.

Kate rounded on him. 'Charlie! You know our Rose has always been delicate. She won't be getting waited on and she'll be helping in the shop.'

This information did nothing to mollify Charlie. 'And who is going to pay for her keep? Miss Roberts can't be expected to foot the bill and I don't think it's very fair to either me or Iris if we have to contribute to this ... this ... holiday of Rose's.'

Kate pursed her lips, annoyed by Charlie's

words. 'It's *not* a holiday and no one is expecting you or Iris to pay a penny towards it. *I* will make the financial arrangements with Gwen. Now, I don't want to hear any more of your complaints, Charlie. And, Iris, don't you go upsetting her by telling her what he said or putting her off the idea. It's for the good of her health.'

Iris nodded her agreement whilst casting her brother an annoyed glance. 'I won't, Mam. I think it's a great idea as long as Rose is happy about it. I have to admit that it would drive me mad living in the country – all that *silence* – but she might enjoy it and Aunty Gwen's nice and she knows everyone in that village.'

Kate smiled at her eldest daughter. There wasn't a jealous bone in Iris's body but she wished Charlie could be a bit more sympathetic. He'd changed, she thought sadly, he'd never been as moody or self-centred before. It was the fault of the war. Would they never be free of its shadow?

Chapter Three

Iris discussed her sister's visit to Wales in detail with her best friend Florence Taylor, who worked in the accounts office of Frisby Dyke's. Florence's father was a successful coal merchant and they lived in a far better area of the city than the Mundys; her friend had received a far better education than herself, which was why Florence had a responsible job in the office and Iris was just a counter assistant. They had become friendly when Florence had asked her advice on some lace she wanted to purchase and after that they'd begun to spend all their breaks together and walked to the tram stop each evening. Florence was much quieter and more reserved than Iris was; she'd been almost as shocked as Iris's mam when she'd had her hair cut short.

'Oh, I just wouldn't have the courage, Iris. What if it doesn't turn out right and looks awful?' she'd exclaimed when Iris had informed her of her intention to visit Marcel's, a very modern hairdressing establishment in the city centre. 'And I dread to think what my father would say!' Florence had long fair hair which she wore in a neat chignon for work and her blue eyes had been wide with amazement at Iris's drastic decision.

Iris had shrugged and laughed. 'It would always grow again, Florence,' she'd replied. 'And, you never know, your dad might like you with short hair.' But Florence hadn't been persuaded.

'So, Rose is quite happy with the idea of spending summer in this ... Tregarron? I have to say, Iris, from what you've told me it sounds lovely – very peaceful and quaint.'

'It's only what Mam has told us about it. We've never been there and it was years and years ago when Mam went. It might well have changed beyond all recognition now. What have you got in your sandwiches today?' Iris asked, peering at the nicely wrapped package Florence had taken from her lunch box. It was a warm sunny day and they were sitting in St John's Gardens at the back of St George's Hall where the flowers in the ornamental beds were coming into bloom.

Florence smiled; it was a question Iris asked each day. 'Ham. What have you got?'

'Potted meat paste – again. Mam's not very imaginative.'

'I'll swap you two of mine for two of yours, I don't mind meat paste,' Florence offered generously.

'Thanks. Would you like to come to our house on Sunday afternoon so we can talk about this trip with Rose? I could get an atlas or something from the library and we could look it up. I've promised to get her some books for when she's feeling better. She's very fond of romances.'

'Is she? So am I but you don't sound very keen on them.' Florence hadn't failed to notice the rather disparaging note in her friend's voice.

'Oh, I don't mind some of them, as long as they're not too far-fetched, but I don't read as much as our Rose does. I prefer to be out and about more.' Iris bit into a ham sandwich with relish.

'You're more active than Rose then?'

Iris nodded, her mouth full. 'When I do read I prefer newspapers or journals. I like to know what's going on in the world so I can form my own opinions about people and things. I mean, isn't it great that now finally some women can actually vote and are able to run businesses and even become doctors?' she said when she could speak.

Florence frowned. She wasn't too sure about some of the changes taking place in society. 'I think I'll be quite happy just to get married and have a family, when I'm older of course. I'll leave things like politics and business to the men.'

Iris tutted. 'That's rather a staid view, Florence. Mind you, our Rose seems to prefer to live in a dream world.'

'I'd love to come and see her; will she be up to having visitors by then?' Florence asked. It was the first time Iris had invited her to her home.

'I expect so. She seems to be a bit better each day and she's always said she'd like to meet you. I talk about you quite a lot, you see,' Iris said. 'So, it's settled then. Come about three. With a bit of luck our, Charlie will have gone for a walk with Da, they usually do after dinner as they're both stuck inside all week.'

'I'll bring her some flowers to cheer her up,' Florence suggested. It was something her mother always did when visiting friends whether they were ill or not.

'I'd better make sure Mam has got a decent vase to put them in although if she hasn't Da's bound to have at least one in the shop she can borrow,' Iris replied cheerfully.

When she informed her mother of her invitation to her friend Kate had frowned. 'I hope she's not expecting anything fancy like afternoon tea?' Kate was aware that Florence Taylor lived in a far grander house than they did. 'And did you not think to ask your sister first if she wanted a visitor?'

'She's only coming to meet Rose and have a chat about her visit to Aunty Gwen's. She's not expecting afternoon tea, Mam, and she's not a snob,' Iris assured her mother, which mollified

Kate a little.

Rose was delighted when she learned that Florence was coming to see her and wanted to get up for a few hours on Sunday afternoon.

'You most certainly are *not* getting up, Rose! I'll get our Charlie to bring a couple of kitchen chairs up here for Florence and Iris. They'll just about fit in here beside the bed,' Kate replied, glancing around at the limited space in the room. The bed, a chest of drawers, a washstand, a single wardrobe and a bedside table took up most of it but both Rose and Iris were lucky to have their own rooms. Granted, the rooms upstairs above the shop were all small – they had been built as storerooms – but there were four of them, which meant everyone had a bedroom of their own, something unheard of in this area.

Although curious to see what this Florence Taylor was like Charlie agreed to go with Bill on their usual Sunday walk and Iris heaved a sigh of relief. The last thing they needed was Charlie breathing down their necks and uttering snide remarks about how fortunate Rose was to be going on this 'holiday' as he insisted on calling it.

Florence arrived very punctually at five minutes to three looking very out of place in the dismal, run-down neighbourhood dressed as she was in a pale blue and white linen two-piece, a small blue cloche hat trimmed with a white ribbon rosette over her fair hair, white cotton gloves, white shoes and bag and carrying a posy of late spring flowers. Her appearance had caused quite a stir for such finery was seldom seen in the area. She had been acutely aware of the curious and envious stares as

45

she had walked down the street and was embarrassed. Of course she had known where Iris lived but she had never ventured into the dock area before and the sight of such obvious deprivation disturbed her. In Cedar Grove there were no thin, pale, barefoot children dressed in ragged clothes playing in the gutter, their faces, hands and feet filthy. No women, also poorly dressed, standing on their doorsteps. No curtainless windows, some of which had missing panes covered by cardboard or stuffed with rags. No peeling paintwork and cracked steps.

'I think I'm a bit early but I wasn't sure how long the tram would take,' she explained to Iris, who had been standing at the shop door waiting for her friend.

'Come on in. Rose is dying to meet you and I must say you look very smart, Florence. I love your hat – it's gorgeous.' Iris guided her through the shop and into the kitchen where Kate, wearing her good navy dress with the white collar, was setting out the cups and saucers.

'Mam, this is Florence,' Iris announced proudly.

Florence smiled shyly and held out a white-gloved hand. 'I'm really pleased to meet you, Mrs Mundy.'

Kate smiled back, thinking what a pretty girl she was, so well mannered and with obviously expensive clothes. 'You are very welcome, Florence. Rose has been getting herself into a right state because I said she couldn't get up and come down to meet you.'

'Oh, no! She mustn't get up yet. My mother said it's quite serious and she must have rest and

46

not get over-excited, so I was instructed not to stay too long and tire Rose. I brought these for her, I thought they might cheer her up,' Florence indicated the posy.

Kate nodded, reflecting that women in this area usually only had flowers given to them on two occasions in their lives: as a wedding bouquet and the wreath that was laid on their coffins; but it was thoughtful of Florence to bring Rose a gift. 'I'll find a nice vase for them. Iris, take Florence up before our Rose takes it into her head to come down.'

Although still feeling weak and rather listless Rose immediately brightened at Florence's appearance and was delighted with the flowers. Taking in – a little enviously – her sister's friend's very smart outfit, she decided Florence was the best-dressed girl she'd ever seen; she was pretty too. Iris had brought a book on the history and geography of North Wales from the library along with a novel and they poured intently over a detailed map of Denbighshire.

'It doesn't look to be too far from Denbigh, which is the county town, so it says here,' Florence remarked, pointing to where it was marked.

'And it has a castle, which might be interesting to visit,' Rose added, entering into the spirit of things.

Iris privately wondered what could possibly be interesting about a pile of old stones but kept her thoughts to herself.

'You'll love it, Rose. My father and mother went on a day trip once to Llandudno which is ... there on the coast.' Florence indicated it on the

47

map. 'You can get a boat that sails around the coast directly from the Pier Head; they said the scenery was quite lovely. It will really do you good and I'm sure you'll make some friends, just like your mother did.' Florence was beginning to wish that she could go on an extended trip to the countryside, although she certainly would not want it to be convalescence.

'It says here there are quite a few "country houses and estates of note",' Iris remarked, studying the text closely. 'There's actually one listed near Tregarron, Rose. Mam never mentioned that, did she?'

'Where does it say that?' Rose asked and Iris pointed the lines out to her.

'"Plas Idris was built in 1846 by Sir Richard Rhys-Pritchard, a prominent industrialist and mine owner, and lies two miles from the village of Tregarron,"' Rose read aloud. 'Now, I'd like to go and see that,' she added enthusiastically. I wonder why Mam never mentioned it?' she mused, trying to imagine what Plas Idris was like. Was it similar to the big Georgian houses in Rodney Street but set in beautiful grounds, or was it more like a castle?

They chatted on about what else Rose could do to occupy herself until Kate appeared with a tray on which she'd set out her best cups and saucers and side plates, plus a plate of digestive biscuits, as a reminder that it was time the visit was brought to a conclusion. To Rose's questions concerning Plas Idris she answered that she'd heard it spoken of as 'the big house' but she'd never seen it during the time she'd spent there; there had been so many

48

other new experiences to savour and she didn't think Gwen or her family had much to do with the Rhys-Pritchards, they being, she supposed, the gentry in those parts.

When they'd finished their tea Florence said her goodbyes to Rose, asking her to write when she got to Tregarron, and Iris ushered her downstairs. Her father and brother had just arrived back and so she had to introduce her friend.

Florence smiled at Bill and said how pleased she was to meet him and how much she had enjoyed her visit and then rather shyly extended her hand to Charlie, thinking that Iris had never said how handsome her brother was. 'It ... it's very nice to meet you ... er...' She hesitated, unsure whether to address him by his Christian name or not. Would that seem too forward?

'Charlie. Call me Charlie, and it's nice to meet you too, Florence. Our Iris is always talking about you.' Charlie was quite taken with her. Oh, Iris was always going on about her and about what a good job she had, the big house she lived in and how successful her father was, but she'd never mentioned that she was a very attractive girl. She was small and slightly plump but with wide blue eyes, a perfect pink and white complexion and fair hair that seemed to wave naturally, showing beneath a very smart and, he deduced, expensive hat.

'I hope everything she says is ... good, Charlie,' Florence replied, acutely aware that he was still holding her hand, which made her blush.

'It is indeed. I hope Rose didn't bore you to tears going on about this ... trip of hers?' He tried to keep the note of resentment from his voice.

'Of course she didn't and we all enjoyed reading about it, didn't we, Florence?' Iris interrupted.

Florence nodded, not wishing to offend anyone. 'I think I'd better be going now and thank you again for the tea, Mrs Mundy.'

'I'll walk you to the tram stop,' Iris offered. She hadn't missed the admiration in her brother's eyes or the length of time he'd held Florence's hand and she hoped he wasn't getting any ideas about her friend. Florence was far too good for Charlie.

'Perhaps you'll come and visit us again?' Charlie pressed.

Florence smiled. 'Perhaps, but it's only good manners to wait to be invited.'

Kate smiled at her. 'You are very welcome to visit any time, Florence.' From the little she had seen of the girl she judged her to be thoroughly nice and with no side to her at all.

Charlie bestowed one of his rare smiles on his mother. Well, there was the invitation Florence had requested so he hoped she would come again to visit. He too thought she was well mannered and very ladylike, and he wondered why she had chosen someone as outspoken and strong-willed as his sister as a friend – although he was glad she had. Yes, Florence Taylor had made quite an impression on him and of course she was the only child of a successful businessman...

On the way to the tram stop their progress was slowed down by all the introductions Iris was obliged to make as the girls in the street, whom Iris had known since childhood, went out of their way to pause and chat. When they finally reached the corner Florence was quite relieved.

'You didn't mention that Charlie is so handsome,' she ventured.

Iris shrugged. 'He's my brother so I don't suppose I've ever really noticed if he was handsome or not,' she replied vaguely.

'Well, he is and I ... I thought he was rather ... nice,' Florence said firmly.

Iris grimaced. 'You wouldn't think that if you lived under the same roof as him. Ever since he came out of the Army he's been moody and very tight-fisted over money. He's not a bit thankful that the Blue Funnel Line took him back on. No, he wants to order Da around in the shop.'

'Well, you can't blame him for being moody, Iris. They all went through so much, it must have been horrific for them. My dad says the experiences will scar them for life.'

'I know and we were all really worried sick when he was away and especially when he was wounded,' Iris replied repentantly. 'But he wasn't like that before. You could always have a laugh and a joke with him and if you had a problem you could talk it over with him. Now ... now he's quieter, more withdrawn and sometimes I think he's really only interested in his own problems.' They had all indeed been desperately afraid that he would be killed as so many had been, or gassed, or blinded or badly wounded, but there was no denying Charlie had been different before he'd gone away. Always that bit more serious than herself or Rose ... but she didn't wish to dwell on this. 'Here's the tram now. See you tomorrow in work, Florence,' she said, relieved, for the conversation had disturbed her a little.

'See you then and thanks for asking me, Iris. I did enjoy meeting everyone. Will you come for tea next Sunday to meet my parents?'

Iris smiled as the tram drew to a halt and Florence stepped aboard. 'I'd love to. Let's talk about it tomorrow,' she called as Florence paid her fare. She waved as the tram trundled away.

Chapter Four

Charles was a little disappointed to learn that Florence would not be visiting next Sunday but very interested to hear that his sister would be meeting her parents. 'Where exactly do they live, Iris?' he asked when she told Kate about the impending visit.

'Why are you so suddenly interested in Florence and her parents?' Iris asked sharply.

Charlie shrugged. 'It was just a question. There's no need to get on your high horse over it.'

'Cedar Grove. It's in Aintree,' Iris replied cautiously.

'That's a fair way to go on the tram, Iris. I'd give yourself a good half-hour if you don't want to be late and I think you should take something for her mam. I think it will be expected,' Kate said, thinking she had no wish for her daughter to appear to lack manners. After all, Florence had brought flowers for Rose.

'What on earth can I take her, Mam? They've

52

got far more money than we have and you know I don't have much left after I've turned up my keep money to you,' Iris protested.

'It doesn't have to be something expensive; it's just the thought that counts. I'll make a Victoria sponge and we'll put it in a proper cake box. I'll get one from Madge Jessup – she works in Black-ledge's and I've done her a few favours in the past,' Kate said firmly.

'No doubt you'll come back and give us an item-by-item account of everything they've got,' Charlie muttered from behind his newspaper even though he would be very interested to hear all about this house in Cedar Grove.

Iris glared in his direction. 'Of course I won't! I'm going to meet Florence's mam and dad, not to inspect their home. She certainly wasn't pok-ing and prying into everything when she was here.'

'That's enough from the pair of you and I just hope you won't go doing or saying anything to show us up, Iris,' Kate said sharply.

Iris dressed with more care than usual the fol-lowing Sunday. Just what she would wear had been discussed at some length between the sisters and Rose, who was feeling much better and who was allowed up for a few hours each day now, was sorry she couldn't accompany Iris.

'You really think this jacket looks better with this skirt?' Iris questioned as she held up her only summer jacket, which was of navy blue cotton twill. 'What if it's very warm? I'll be all hot and flustered by the time I arrive.'

'It will look smarter. It goes nicely with that

navy skirt and white blouse.'

'But it looks so plain and boring. I thought I'd wear just the skirt with my pink hip-length top and get some dark blue glass beads to dress it up a bit,' Iris said. She did like to dress fashionably but on her very limited budget it wasn't easy. She could just about afford the beads she'd seen in Woolworth's in Church Street.

Rose considered this and finally nodded. 'That would still look well with the jacket. And wear your navy hat,' she advised.

On Sunday afternoon Kate inspected her daughter's appearance as she handed her the cake box tied neatly with fine twine. 'Don't forget to thank Mrs Taylor for everything and don't go bolting any food you might be offered.'

Iris raised her eyes to the ceiling. 'I won't, Mam. Honestly, you'd think I was going to tea in the Mayor's parlour!'

'I just don't want them to think you've not been brought up decently. Off you go now. Rose and I are going to start to sort out the things she's going to take to Gwen's.' Kate had received a reply from her friend by return post, stating that she would love to have Rose to stay and that Kate was definitely doing the right thing. Rose would be very welcome and there were numerous small tasks she could do to help at busy times in the post office – when she was up to it, of course.

When she alighted from the tram on the corner of Cedar Grove Iris was surprised by the size of the houses. She'd known Florence's home was much bigger than her own but she'd not realised by how much. The house was in a wide, tree-lined street and despite the fact that it was a very warm, sunny day the street was deserted. There were no children playing, no women and girls gossiping on their front doorsteps, no men standing on the corner discussing everything from football to politics. There were even motor cars parked outside a couple of houses. As she took in the neat, walled front gardens, the pristine paintwork of gates, doors and windows and the equally pristine lace curtains at the deep bay windows she thought how affluent the people who lived here must be.

She lifted the highly polished brass knocker of number ten and let it fall once, wondering now if the blue glass beads looked a bit tawdry.

'Iris, come in,' Florence greeted her, smiling broadly. 'Isn't it a gorgeous day? I think we'll sit out in the garden, it's much nicer than sitting in the living room which gets the sun all day and is rather hot and stuffy.'

Florence led her down the wide, carpeted hallway, which was decorated in shades of cream and eau-de-nil, and into a room at the back of the house: obviously a dining room, boasting French doors opening on to a garden. A plump fair-haired woman, fashionably dressed in a cream crêpe-de-Chine dress embellished with coffee-coloured lace inserts, was arranging flowers in a vase. She felt a little nervous, but as Mrs Taylor looked up and smiled warmly the feeling disappeared.

'Iris, how lovely to meet you! Florence is always talking about you and she's fortunate to have such a good friend. My husband is out in the garden, arranging the chairs so you can sit in the shade. Come through and I'll introduce you.'

She was introduced to a tall, heavily built man; he was probably the same age as her da, she surmised, although his hair was grey and receding and deep lines were etched in his forehead as if he frowned a great deal. However, he shook her hand and greeted her warmly enough and then went back into the house leaving the girls alone. Iris had given her jacket, hat and the cake to Florence's mother and she sat down beside her friend on one of the wrought-iron chairs that matched the small circular table. 'This is a real treat, Florence, to be able to sit in such a lovely garden, it's so ... peaceful,' she marvelled, thinking of their small, cramped back yard and the ever-present noises of the neighbourhood.

'It was really thoughtful of you to bring a cake, Iris, I know Mother is delighted. Homemade too. She hardly ever bakes, she says it's so time-consuming and she spends enough time in the kitchen preparing and cooking dinner. She has our bread and cakes delivered from the bakery.'

Iris nodded; it was just another example of the difference in their circumstances. 'You have a really gorgeous house, Florence, so big compared to ours, but I suppose your father's business is much bigger and more ... profitable than my da's.'

Florence looked concerned. 'It's not bothering you, is it? I don't want you to think... Well, it doesn't make a bit of difference to me, Iris, what kind of houses or jobs people have. You're my friend, that's what matters. I have never found it easy to make friends, not even at school, but from the first time I spoke to you I liked you.'

Iris smiled at her. 'I liked you too and no, it doesn't bother me that we come from different backgrounds.'

'Good. Now, when is Rose going to stay with your Aunty Gwen? Has it been decided yet?'

'At the beginning of the week after next. Mam is going to close the shop on the Tuesday and take her. Our Charlie made some enquiries and found that there's a bus that goes to Denbigh twice a week; you have to change at Mold though. Aunty Gwen's brother is going to meet them and take them out to Tregarron. Apparently he's just got a tractor, the first in the village, so they can ride on the cart.' She giggled. 'I don't know how happy either Mam or Rose are about that, it's not exactly arriving "in style", is it?'

'What's the alternative? Would they have to walk?' Florence asked, thinking that it would be a very long walk for Rose, who wasn't exactly strong yet.

'No, it's too far. Someone from the village would have met them with a pony and trap or something like that. I think if it were me I'd sooner travel like that than on the back of a farm cart. I've advised them both not to wear anything too good in case it gets dirty but Mam's having none of it.' She grimaced. 'She's already fussing about getting all Rose's stuff washed and ironed and packed.'

'Is she looking forward to going back to Tregarron after all these years?' Florence asked.

'She is. Da's trying to persuade her to stay until the next bus comes back to Liverpool, it's only a couple of days, but she says she can't close the

57

shop for so long. She'll only be there a couple of hours.'

'And is Rose getting excited? Too much turmoil won't be good for her, Iris,' Florence reminded her friend.

'So Mam tells her but she keeps asking Mam things like is there a library in Denbigh? What kind of shops are there? Are there any events going on in the village in summer? She'd drive you mad with her questions.'

'And are there any "events"?' Florence was curious.

'Mam says she thinks there is some kind of agricultural show or flower show, though what Rose would find there to interest her, I don't know. And as for the shops in Denbigh, I think they're all small and sell mainly food and household stuff. I hope she's not going to expect anything like Frisby Dyke's or Bunney's or Blackler's.'

Mrs Taylor appeared carrying a tea tray and both girls got up to help her set the table. There were small sandwiches, minus their crusts, laid out on top of a lace doily on one layer of a cake stand, some small fancy cakes on another and in pride of place the Victoria sponge, which had been cut into neat slices. It all looked very appetising and Iris made a mental note to tell her mam about it all.

'Tell your mother this is the lightest sponge I've ever tasted, Iris. I had a small piece as I cut it up, it's delicious! How is your sister now?'

'Oh, she's so much better and looking forward to her trip,' Iris replied.

'She just might enjoy it so much that she won't want to come back. I think I could settle quite

58

well in the country. I've been talking to Mr Taylor about moving somewhere away from Liverpool when he retires but he says he doesn't envisage doing that for a long time yet.'

'I don't know if I'd enjoy living somewhere like Tregarron permanently,' Florence added, thinking it was the first she'd heard of this. 'But it would be lovely for a change.'

'It would drive me mad! No, Rose will have to come back home whether she wants to or not. She can't stay with Aunty Gwen for ever. Even if she doesn't go back to work in that hotel, she'll have to get some kind of a job,' Iris said firmly, sipping her tea.

'Perhaps she could help your mother in the shop, Iris?' Mrs Taylor suggested.

Iris nodded, wondering if this was something her mam had thought of already.

'Before you go, Iris, I've some magazines I've finished with; perhaps you could take them for your mother?' Mrs Taylor offered.

Iris nodded but privately wondered just when her mam, between running a home and a shop, would get the time to read them. Maybe her mam and Rose could look through them on the bus to Denbigh.

When she arrived home she deposited the magazines on the kitchen table thankfully; they'd been a bit of a nuisance to carry and also rather on the heavy side. 'Florence's mam sent these for you to read on the bus,' she informed Kate.

'What, all of them? How long does she think it takes?' Kate asked, eyeing the pile and thinking there must be at least a dozen of them.

Iris shrugged as she took off her jacket and hat. 'She also said your cake was delicious, the lightest she'd ever tasted. According to Florence they only ever have shop-bought bread and cakes.'

Kate raised her eyebrows. She didn't know anyone who didn't bake their own bread for a large shop-bought loaf cost sixpence and didn't go very far in a big family. Surely a woman in Mrs Taylor's position had plenty of time to bake? But she was pleased by the compliment just the same.

'She seems quite taken with the idea of moving to somewhere like Tregarron when Florence's da retires,' Iris went on.

'Is he thinking of doing that? He can't be all that old,' Bill asked.

'I think he's about the same age as you, Da, or perhaps a bit older. At least he looks it, but I don't think he's about to retire. I think it's just wishful thinking on Mrs Taylor's part. I did enjoy myself though; we sat out in the garden at the back of the house and had our tea there. It was so quiet, Mam, and they have a small front garden too.' Iris sat down opposite her mother.

'Oh, wouldn't that be a treat? You certainly wouldn't want to sit out in that yard. Now, tell me all about the house and Florence's mother,' Kate pressed, wanting to learn more about this woman who didn't work or run a business, who lived in a house with two gardens and who didn't bake.

Charlie appeared engrossed in the article he was reading in the Sunday newspaper but he was listening intently to everything Iris was saying, remembering too how she had said Florence's father looked older than his da. Running a business on the scale of Taylor's Coal Merchants must be quite worrying, he thought, and with no sons to either help or leave the business to – only Florence and what would a young girl like her know about business? The wife didn't seem to be all that interested in it either. If Iris was to be believed she wanted him to retire and move out of Liverpool and maybe in time he would, providing there was someone he could trust to run the business for him ... a son-in-law perhaps?

An idea was taking shape in his mind. Why not? Florence was pretty enough, well brought up and probably not as strong-willed as Iris. It could be just the opportunity he was looking for to become both successful and well off and as far as he could see opportunities like that were as rare as hens' teeth. He'd survived the war and he'd sworn that he wouldn't waste the rest of his life, which was just what he would do if he remained a clerk with the Blue Funnel Line for ever, slaving away for a pittance to put money in someone else's pocket. No, he hadn't endured the horrors of the trenches just to come back to a menial position and a hand-to-mouth existence. He wanted something far better than that.

Chapter Five

Rose watched through the window of the bus as the Cheshire countryside slipped by: green fields dotted with trees in the shade of which rested black and white cattle. She'd bade a rather bitter-sweet farewell to her da and Iris and Charlie. Her emotions had been torn between the exciting prospect of a stay in Tregarron and the fact that she would miss them all. There had been tears in her eyes as her da had hugged her and said how he'd miss seeing her every day and Iris had said she'd have no one to relate the events of her day to; even Charlie had said it wouldn't be the same without her chattering on at suppertime. But it was only for a few weeks, she'd reminded them.

The fields gradually gave way to gently rolling hills grazed by sheep as they travelled on and into the Vale of Clwyd. Kate had taken this rare opportunity of some leisure time to read one of the magazines Mrs Taylor had sent her and they were both quite surprised at how soon the bus stopped in the small town of Mold. Kate helped Rose with her case as they transferred to another vehicle.

After an hour they reached the market town of Denbigh. Rose stepped on to the pavement outside the pub where the bus service terminated and looked eagerly around. In front of her was an open cobbled space where a tractor and cart had pulled up; the narrow street they'd come down was steep and lined with small shops and there seemed to be plenty of people about. Of course it was nearing lunchtime, she realised.

Kate was eyeing the farm cart with some apprehension as Gwen's brother Bob climbed down from the tractor and came towards them, smiling broadly.

'My, but you've grown up a fine woman, Katie Fairfax!' he said in his musical voice, taking her hand.

'It's a long time since anyone called me that, Bob. It's good to see you again. I hope the family are all well?'

'Megan is looking forward to meeting you and those lads of mine can't wait to meet young Rose but don't worry, I'll keep my eye on them,' he laughed, turning to Rose. 'She must take after her da, Katie, but you're a fine-looking girl just the same and very welcome, Rose.'

Rose blushed as she smiled at him. He took her case and effortlessly stowed it on the back of the cart.

''Cause quite a stir in the village with those looks, she will, Katie,' he said quietly to Kate. 'Now, I'll give you a hand up. There's clean straw and a rug over it so you should be comfortable. We'll get back quicker than you would if old Glyn Morgan had come to fetch you in that little trap of his, the pony's nearly as old as he is and can't even manage a trot these days.'

To Kate's relief they were both quite comfortable and as they drew out of the town and into the countryside she began to look forward to

63

seeing Tregarron and Gwen again. Meanwhile Rose clung quite happily to the side of the cart, eagerly anticipating her first sight of the village.

When finally they reached the place where the road forked Kate pointed left. 'Down there is Bob's farm. They call that part of the road the "Garn", it more or less goes in a complete circle around the village.'

'So we're here?' Rose asked, noting a fine house with a yard behind it and a board which proclaimed it belonged to 'Jenkins's Builders & Carpenters'.

'We are. There's the school and chapel over there and beyond that is the forge, then over there is the lane that leads to the mill,' Kate informed her gaily, thinking the place had hardly changed at all over the years.

Small cottages lined the road and then there was a butcher's shop, a general store and finally the post office. 'That must be Gwen's cottage, just beside the shop,' Kate said as the tractor slowed down and finally stopped. Bob jumped down and came to help them down.

Rose looked curiously at the small stone cottage; it looked just like something you saw on the lid of chocolate boxes, she thought. It wasn't thatched though, the roof was of slate, but the windows were small and there was a miniscule garden in front full of flowers and a climbing rose around the front door, laden with deep pink blooms.

Gwen Roberts appeared in the door of the post office, a neat navy shop coat over her white blouse with its cameo brooch pinned at the neck, her brown hair confined tidily in a small bun, her dark, bird-like eyes full of delight. 'Kate! Ah, isn't it lovely to see you,' she exclaimed as she hugged Kate and then turned to Rose. 'And you too, Rose, how are you feeling now, *cariad?* Come on into the shop till I finish sorting out Mrs Davies's parcel, then I'll close up for lunch and we'll get Rose settled and have a bite to eat.' She turned to her brother. 'Bob, will you wait for a cup of tea?'

'No thanks, Gwennie, luv. Megan will have the dinner ready for us. No doubt I'll be seeing you again soon, Rose, and it was a real pleasure, Katie, to see you. Megan said be sure to tell you to call in if you're passing by.' He waved as he climbed back on to the tractor and Kate and Rose followed Gwen into the shop.

Rose was introduced to old Mrs Davies who inspected her closely from head to foot. The whole village was aware that the girl from Liverpool who had recently been poorly was arriving today and she was pleased she was the first to see her. Then Gwen put the 'Closed' sign on the door and they went next door.

'Oh, it's lovely, Gwen! Haven't you got some nice things? I remember that clock, didn't your mam have it in the hall at Bryn-y-Garn?' Kate asked, looking around the small living room with its chintz-covered sofa, gate-leg table and chairs, bright rag rugs and many highly polished brass and copper ornaments and utensils above the black-leaded range and the grandfather clock.

'She did! Fancy you remembering it, Kate. Most things in here were Mam's; Bob kept a few bits after she died and I got the rest. Now, I'll put the kettle on and while it's boiling I'll take you upstairs and show you where Rose is to sleep.'

Rose followed her mother and Gwen up the very narrow stone staircase set beside the range which led to the two small bedrooms above, one either side of the tiny landing.

The room seemed smaller than her room at home but she deduced that was because of the much lower ceiling and small, low window. There was pretty flower-patterned wallpaper on the walls, a comfortable-looking bed with clean white sheets and pillowcases and a patchwork quilt, an old-fashioned marble-topped washstand with a china bowl and jug set and a fresh white towel, a wardrobe and a chest. As Kate complimented her friend on the comfort and cleanliness of the room Rose looked out of the window, kneeling on the cushion placed in the deep embrasure. There was a small garden at the back and beyond that fields stretching away for miles, bounded by dry stone walls, and in the distance she could see a copse of trees.

'We'll leave you to unpack, Rose. I'm going to help Gwen, then before I have to go back for the bus, we'll take a walk around the village,' Kate said before following Gwen downstairs where Rose heard them chatting and laughing happily.

She pulled the sash window down further and breathed deeply. She could smell the perfume of the flowers in the garden and the only sounds were birdsong, the buzzing of the bees amongst the flowers and the faint, far-off lowing of a cow. It was so quiet, so peaceful here and she had immediately loved the cottage and felt at home. Yes, she really believed she would be happy here, just as Mam had been all those years ago, and she was looking forward to seeing the rest of the village.

Their progress on their walk was rather slower than Kate had envisaged for people called to them over garden walls or stopped to chat, a few remembering Kate but most only knowing what Gwen had told them about her friend and her daughter. When they were stopped by the minister's wife, Kate remembered her as Bethan Jones who had been a friend of Gwen's since they were at school.

'It's a very long time since I last saw you, Bethan. Quite a tomboy you were then if I remember rightly,' Kate remarked.

'Not an attribute that suits a minister's wife, Kate, doesn't go down too well with the parishioners,' the woman laughed. 'No, thankfully I grew out of all that. Since I married Owen Williams I've been dignity personified. This must be Rose. I hear you've been ill, dear?'

'I'm much better now, thank you, Mrs Williams,' Rose answered, wondering if everyone knew absolutely *everything* about everyone in this village.

'I hope you won't find it too quiet here? There's not a great deal for the young ones to do, although there is the occasional barn dance.'

'I'm sure I won't,' Rose replied. Was the dance actually held in a barn or was it just a name?

'Of course there's the Denbigh Show next month, that's always a great occasion: people come from all over the county and it's on for three days. We have our own village flower show at the end of next month too. I'd be very grateful for some help with that. I've helped to organise it ever since I came back to the village when Owen was sent here after the old minister died – apart from the war years, that is. We didn't hold it then, things were just too ... dreadful and everyone was far too busy. We have it in the grounds of the big house with marquees set up for various classes, and refreshments of course.'

Rose had been listening politely to all this, wondering what on earth she would be expected to do at a flower show, but at the mention of the 'big house' her interest increased. 'You mean it's held at Plas Idris?'

Bethan Williams was surprised. 'You've heard of it, Rose? Not many people here ever refer to it by its full name.'

'Yes, I read that it's the home of Sir Richard Rhys-Pritchard's family.'

'It is. What's left of them. Their grandfather built it, made his money from mining, he did, and a fine house it is. I've only ever been inside a few times. Lovely grounds too.'

'I'd be delighted to help you out at the flower show, Mrs Williams, really I would,' Rose offered enthusiastically. She would love to see the place. Maybe she too would get to see inside it?

'We'd better be going, Bethan. I've to get back to town for the bus but I'm sure Rose will be useful and it's lovely to have seen you again.' Kate thought how much she would have enjoyed staying longer, but she had a business to run and a home and family to attend to. It would be a relief to know that Rose was well and happy and ready to get involved in village life; she'd even been quite enthusiastic about helping at this flower show. That had greatly surprised her.

Kate was tired when she at last arrived home late that evening and was thankful that Iris had a hot meal waiting for her.

'Sit down, Mam, you look worn out. Do you think Rose liked the place? Do you think she'll be happy there?' Iris asked as she poured her mother a cup of tea.

'I have to say it is tiring travelling but I enjoyed seeing Tregarron again and meeting everyone. And yes, Rose seems to like it there. Everyone made her very welcome and she's already been asked to help out at the village flower show.'

'Really? Help out how?' Iris asked, wondering what on earth Rose could do. As far as she knew her sister's only interest in flowers was in receiving them as a gift.

'I've no idea, Iris, but she seemed quite taken with the idea. Mind you, I think it has something to do with it being held up at that big house.'

Iris nodded slowly, remembering that when they'd read about it in the book Rose had said she would like to go and see it. 'I expect she wants to see how the "gentry", as you called them, live.'

'Well, she seemed happy enough when I left her and I know Gwen will look after her. She's going to write regularly. Gwen very kindly offered to let her use the telephone in the post office once a month, until I reminded her that we don't have a telephone or even know anyone who does.'

'Florence's da's got one, I saw it in the hall,' Iris informed her.

'Well, you can't go asking him to let our Rose call them. The man probably has it for business purposes. Besides it would be downright hard-faced to make a convenience of them like that. No, she can write and we'll write back,' Kate said firmly.

'Is it all right if Florence comes again on Sunday? We won't want tea or anything. If the weather is still good we'll go out somewhere seeing as we haven't got a garden to sit in.'

Kate nodded, suddenly too tired even to comment on Iris's last remark. She would have to be up at the crack of dawn in the morning and she had been having twinges in her back all afternoon. Probably it was due to sitting for hours on that bus, she thought: she wasn't used to long periods of inactivity. And of course she wasn't getting any younger either.

Chapter Six

Over the following weeks the two girls took it in turns on a Sunday to visit each other's homes, much to Charlie's satisfaction. The more he saw of Florence, the more his interest in and liking for her grew. It was becoming clear to him that she had all the qualities he considered desirable in a wife. She was quiet, amenable, refined, generous and sweet-tempered and, he suspected, very loyal. His re-

70

solve to court and, he hoped, marry her strengthened and he determined that the next time Florence came to visit he would take the opportunity to go and see her father. He'd given it a great deal of thought and had decided it would make a good impression if he were seen to be doing things 'properly'. He'd introduce himself to Mr Taylor and ask his permission to take Florence out. It would definitely be the best way, he told himself, and it would give him the opportunity to see for himself what kind of a man her father was and just how well off they were.

On the following Sunday Iris and Florence decided to spend a few hours in Stanley Park, which had a boating lake and glass houses containing exotic plants.

'If you're going wandering around in that oversized greenhouse you'd better come back here for a cup of tea, you'll both be parched. It's not exactly the weather for that kind of thing,' Kate said, for the afternoon sun was streaming in through the window, making the kitchen hot and stuffy.

'Wouldn't a trip on the ferry be cooler on a day like this? There's always a bit of a breeze on the river. You could always go to the park when it's not so hot,' Charlie suggested. A trip to New Brighton and back would take them longer than a stroll around the park.

'With the rest of Liverpool? We'd be packed like sardines in a tin on that ferry,' Iris retorted. Her brother had already announced he wasn't going for his usual walk but was meeting some of his mates; she'd thought it was unusual but had said nothing. 'No, we'll go to the park, but I'll bring

71

Florence back for tea, Mam, thanks. See you later.'

Once Iris had gone Charlie checked his appearance in the mirror on the scullery wall before he too left. His Sunday suit had been brushed and he was wearing the watch and chain his parents had given him for his twenty-first birthday in his waistcoat pocket. A freshly ironed handkerchief was tucked into the breast pocket of his jacket, his shirt was clean, his collar starched, he'd polished his boots. Setting his cap at what he hoped was a becoming angle, he called to Kate that he'd be back just after the girls and went out through the yard.

When he alighted from the tram on the corner of Cedar Grove his reactions were the same as his sister's had been. Yes, he could picture himself living in an area like this, he thought. It was indeed a far cry from the dirty narrow streets of the decrepit dock area, but you had to have a fair bit in the bank to live here, he mused, feeling a bit apprehensive for the first time.

He fiddled nervously with his tie before knocking and took a deep breath as the door was opened by Edward Taylor himself.

'Mr Taylor, I'm Iris's brother, Charles... Charlie Mundy. I'm sorry to disturb you but I was hoping to speak to you – if it's convenient, that is?'

Edward Taylor was surprised, to say the least. He'd been enjoying an hour of peace and quiet, reading the Sunday newspaper, for Ethel had gone to visit a friend for tea and Florence was of course out somewhere with Iris. 'You'd better come in then. Do I call you Charles or Charlie?'

72

'Charlie, if that's all right,' Charlie replied, following the older man down the hallway, his glance taking everything in. He was ushered into a large room decorated in shades of cream and beige, well furnished, carpeted and with expensive china and glass ornaments.

'Sit down, lad. Can I offer you a drink?' Edward asked, feeling it was the hospitable thing to do even though it was a bit on the early side for himself. The lad didn't resemble Iris, he thought, except in his height and build, but he was handsome enough and very neatly turned out. He had no idea what it was Iris's brother wanted.

'Thank you but no, I ... I don't drink a great deal,' Charlie replied, trying not to show how on edge he was.

'Glad to hear it. Now, what is it you wanted to discuss with me?'

'Well, as you know, sir, our Iris and Florence are great friends and ever since I met Florence I...' He paused briefly. 'The thing is ... I'd like your permission to ask Florence out, sir. I haven't said anything to her yet, I ... I wanted to do things correctly, ask you first if it would be all right.'

Edward Taylor was taken aback. It was the last thing he had expected to hear. He'd begun to wonder if it was a job the lad had in mind and had already begun to formulate his reply. 'So she doesn't know about this visit and you don't know if she will agree?' He frowned, wishing Ethel were here. 'She's very young, you know.'

'I'm aware of that, she's the same age as Iris, but I don't want to rush things or anything. I'd just like to get to know her better, sir.'

The older man nodded slowly. He'd always known the day would come when Florence would start walking out but she'd never given any indication that she was interested in anyone. She might well turn the lad down. 'I can't see that there's any harm in asking her. What do you do for a job, Charlie?'

'I'm a clerk in the offices of the Blue Funnel Line. I started as an office boy at fourteen, after I left school, but I'm hoping that I'll get a better position in the company soon. They did take me back when I returned at the end of the war.'

'You were fortunate to have come through that bloodbath. Which regiment were you with?'

'The Eighteenth Battalion, the King's Liverpool Regiment.'

Edward Taylor looked grim. 'The Pals' Regiment. Slaughtered like cattle at Montauban. Three men from this road died in the trenches there. I've the greatest respect and admiration for everyone who fought and died. Were you wounded?'

'Just a flesh wound in the arm but it was certainly no picnic, sir, and I find it ... difficult to talk about it. But it's over now and I'm trying to put it all behind me and look to the future. As I said, I'm hoping to be promoted soon and then ... well, I suppose if and when my father decides to retire I'll take over from him.'

'Ah, yes. He has a pawnbroking business, I understand.'

Charlie smiled. 'Inherited from my grandfather.'

'As was my own business. My grandfather started with a handcart, then progressed to a horse and cart. Backbone of the economy, Charlie, small family businesses, and I imagine in these hard times your father's is essential,' Florence's father commented approvingly. 'Well, I can't see that either my wife or myself have any objection to you asking Florence out, Charlie, but I suppose you have considered that she may well refuse?'

'I have but I'm hoping she'll agree.' Charlie stood up and held out his hand. 'Thank you, sir, both for your permission and for your time.'

Edward Taylor shook his hand warmly. 'Then we might be seeing more of you in the future, Charlie.'

Charlie smiled back, feeling very relieved. 'I certainly hope so.'

When the lad had gone Edward went back to his newspaper but he couldn't concentrate. It was disconcerting to think that Florence – his little girl – was growing up.

He relayed the reason and details of Charlie's visit to his wife when she returned.

'He wants to ask Florence out? You mean he wants to court her? They hardly know each other, Edward,' Ethel said, frowning.

He sighed. 'That's the very reason why he wants to ask her out, Ethel. To get to know her and vice versa. He seemed decent enough and I thought he was exceptionally well mannered to come and ask me first.'

Ethel wasn't at all happy. 'Yes, well, but ... but I always thought that when she started courting it would be someone with ... excellent prospects.'

'You mean you wanted someone better for her than a shipping clerk? He's ambitious, his father has a business and the lad has only asked that they be allowed to get to know each other better, Ethel. He hasn't asked to marry her. It might come to nothing; she might even refuse him. Let's not start worrying over Florence's future yet, she's only eighteen.'

'Nearly nineteen and I was engaged to you at the same age, don't forget,' his wife reminded him sharply. She hoped that Florence would marry well, a bank manager or owner of a large, thriving business, certainly not a lowly working-class clerk, even if he did have good manners and stood to take over a pawnbroker's shop in time. She wanted better than that for Florence. 'You have to take into consideration that she is used to certain ... standards, Edward.'

'I've enough to worry about as it is, Ethel, with all the violence in Ireland and mass unemployment here, and I've just read in the paper that there are now two million workers involved in disputes over pay and with the miners on strike supplies of coal are getting scarce and that will force the price up. I'm worried about what impact it will all have on the business and therefore our "standards",' Edward reminded her.

She sighed heavily. 'Let's hope the strike ends soon then,' she said and wisely let the subject of Florence drop.

As Charlie got off the tram and began to walk down the street towards home he caught sight of Iris and Florence coming out of the shop together. He frowned, wondering how he was going to ask Florence out with his sister seemingly always at her side. He'd have to choose his moment carefully. As they drew closer he realised that neither of them was looking very happy. 'Is something wrong?' he asked.

'Iris is insisting on walking me to the tram but she's not well, Charlie. I think it's the sun, we spent rather a long time sitting in the park,' Florence told him, looking anxiously at her friend.

'I've got a splitting headache, that's all. I suppose it's my own fault for taking my hat off but it was so hot,' Iris replied irritably. Her head was throbbing and even though she did feel awful she had refused to let Florence walk on her own, saying she'd never get there because everyone would waylay her, seeing as now everyone in the street knew her friend.

Charlie at once became solicitous; Iris couldn't have picked a better time to be suffering from the sun or the heat. 'You go back, Iris, you've probably got sunstroke. I'll walk Florence to the tram; it's no trouble at all.'

Iris nodded, grimacing at the pain the movement caused her. He could be right about sunstroke. Mam had said the same thing, although Kate had added that she hoped Iris wasn't sickening for something. 'I'll see you tomorrow, Florence, in work.'

'If you don't feel well enough, stay off tomorrow,' Florence advised.

'And lose a day's pay and have Mam moaning that I've brought it on myself? No, I'll be in work. I'll be fine after a night's sleep,' Iris insisted.

'What on earth made her take her hat off? It's so ... common to be seen in public without a hat,' Charlie commented.

Florence sighed. 'You know Iris, she's so impetuous and she doesn't care what people say or think about her. It's one of the things I like about her; I often wish I could be more like her.'

Charlie shook his head in amazement. 'Florence, you don't want to go taking too much notice of our Iris, you're ... fine as you are. Very ladylike.'

Florence smiled at him. 'Thank you for walking with me, Charlie. Did you enjoy your afternoon with your friends?'

'I have a bit of a confession to make about that, Florence. I wasn't with friends. I went to see ... someone. In fact I went to see your father to seek his permission to ask you if you'd like to come out with me one evening or maybe at the weekend?'

Florence stopped and stared up at him, her blue eyes wide. 'You went to see Dad?'

Charlie nodded. 'We had quite a chat; he's a very nice man, Florence.'

Florence had regained her composure and felt a stirring of pleasure and excitement. He liked her and wanted to take her out! And he must be serious if he'd gone to the trouble of going to see her father. 'What ... what did he say, Charlie?'

'He said it was fine by him, so ... would you?'

Florence put her hand to her cheek, which was flushed with both the sun and the emotions she was feeling. 'I ... I'd love to, Charlie.'

He beamed at her, thinking how pretty she looked. 'Then shall we say I'll call for you on Tuesday evening and we'll go for a walk? I don't want to keep you out too late, not on a weekday. Then maybe on Saturday evening we could go into town and have a meal somewhere ... nice.' He wouldn't mind spending money on a meal, as long as she didn't expect it every week. 'I know you like to spend Sunday afternoons with our Iris.'

'That would be lovely, Charlie,' Florence replied, suddenly feeling very grown up.

'Then I'll call for you at seven o'clock,' Charlie suggested and when she nodded her assent he offered her his arm, studiously ignoring the curious stares of the neighbours who were sitting or standing on their doorsteps trying to escape the heat of the small, over-crowded houses.

Why not? she thought. She had her father's permission, they were now officially walking out and as she took it she smiled happily at him, albeit a little shyly.

Charlie felt a huge sense of satisfaction. He'd take her mam a little gift on Tuesday; he hadn't met Mrs Taylor yet and he wanted her approval too. He'd have a word with his mam about it, see what she could suggest, for he'd have to announce to them all that he and Florence were now courting. He was sure his parents would approve, but he wondered how well Iris would take the news.

Chapter Seven

Kate had urged Iris to go and lie down after giving her two aspirins but Iris had refused, saying the bedroom would be like an oven having had the sun on it all day.

'I'll wait until later, Mam, when it's cooled down a bit.'

'All right, luv, but I can't open the window any wider or we'll be inundated with flies. I'll have to get some more fly papers tomorrow. At least our Rose won't be tormented with them like we are.'

'I wouldn't bank on that, Kate. They get plenty of flies in the country too,' Bill had remarked.

'Yes, but the houses all have plenty of space around them and no stinking, overflowing ashcans a few yards away in the jigger,' Kate had replied, thinking of the rubbish in the entry that ran behind the houses.

'Did Florence get her tram all right?' Iris asked as her brother arrived home.

'Of course she did. One arrived almost straight away,' Charlie assured her, taking off his jacket and tie and loosening his collar. 'Isn't it warm? I can't remember the last time it rained. I have to say I'd prefer it to be cooler than this.'

'Wouldn't we all?' his father remarked tersely.

'I'd prefer not to have the damned range lit but we'd have nothing to boil the kettle on or cook on either,' Kate added.

Charlie sat down at the table opposite his mother while Iris leaned back in the armchair, holding a damp cloth to her forehead. 'I've got something to tell you all,' he announced.

'What? What have you and your mates been up to now?' Kate demanded, pouring him a cup of tea.

'Nothing and it's got nothing to do with my mates either, it's to do with Florence,' Charlie replied quietly.

Iris sat up and Kate stared at her son. 'Florence? You mean Iris's Florence?'

Charlie proceeded to tell them of his visit to Cedar Grove and his conversation with Florence as he'd escorted her to the tram.

As Iris listened the throbbing in her head increased. She couldn't believe this. The nerve of him! He'd taken himself off to see Mr Taylor and then ... then he'd asked Florence out! And Florence had accepted. She must be mad!

'Well, I never thought you were that interested in her, Charlie. You've never said anything.' Kate too was astonished. 'And you hardly know the girl.'

'But I *want* to get to know her, Mam. I ... I liked her the very first time I met her. I like her a lot,' Charlie replied firmly.

Iris found her voice. 'I can't believe she agreed to go out with you. She must be mad!'

'Why? What's the matter with me?' Charlie demanded, annoyed by her attitude. 'She likes me. She said she'd love to go out with me.'

'She's far too good for you, Charlie, and you know it,' Iris cried furiously and then groaned as

81

the drumming behind her eyes increased.

'Now, that's enough!' Kate instructed sharply, although Iris did have a point, she thought. Florence came from a very different background and while she didn't object to the girls being friends, for Charlie to start to court Florence was a different kettle of fish altogether. 'And what did her mother have to say?'

'She wasn't in. I only saw her father and he seemed happy enough. Don't tell me you're going to object too, Mam?'

Kate shook her head. 'No, you're old enough by law to do as you please but I wouldn't bank on her mother being very happy. Florence is used to a much better home and lifestyle.'

Bill now added his thoughts on the matter. 'I agree with you, Kate, to an extent but don't let's get carried away. He's only taking her out to get to know her; no one is saying they're going to end up getting married. They're both still very young.'

Kate sighed; if that's what Charlie had in mind she could see plenty of obstacles ahead, but she did care for her son, and wanted to see him happy.

The situation had troubled Iris all night and she determined that before she went to work next morning she would have a talk to her mam. Charlie had already left by the time she went through into the shop.

'Mam, I don't know what to say to Florence about our Charlie. I don't know whether to say I think she's mad or–'

'Say nothing, Iris!' Kate instructed firmly as she placed the last bunch of carrots on the appropriate shelf. 'I wouldn't even bring the subject up unless she does. Right or wrong, she's agreed to go out with him. It's her decision.'

'But she's my friend, I don't want to see her get hurt or anything,' Iris protested.

'Of course you don't but who says she will? Our Charlie isn't much of a ladies' man – thank God, and he's obviously been thinking seriously about asking her–'

'So you don't mind?' Iris interrupted.

Kate sighed. 'I like Florence, she's a kind, generous, well-brought-up girl. All that worries me is the different backgrounds. If ... and it's a very big "if", they eventually got married Florence wouldn't have half the things she takes for granted now. Charlie doesn't earn enough to provide them. At the present time he doesn't earn enough to keep himself, never mind a wife; she'd find it very hard and that's when the cracks would start to appear. There's an old and very true saying: "When poverty comes in the door, love flies out of the window." But it might all come to nothing, Iris. They don't know each other very well and in time they might find there isn't that spark between them. And Mrs Taylor might well influence Florence because, as I said last night, I have a feeling she's not going to be happy. Now, you'd better get off or you'll be late.'

Iris decided to take her mother's advice but if Florence asked her opinion then she'd certainly tell her friend that she considered she was too good for Charlie.

In the event Florence had only said she was looking forward to Tuesday evening and she hoped Iris didn't mind her walking out with her brother. Iris had shrugged and had said if Florence was happy to go then that was all that mattered. Florence had smiled happily, feeling relieved. She had wanted her friend's approval for she had the distinct feeling that she certainly didn't have her mother's, although she had overheard her father saying that she shouldn't judge the lad before she'd even met him.

She was ready and waiting on Tuesday evening. She had changed after supper from the plain dark skirt and white blouse she wore for work into a light summer dress of lilac voile with short cape sleeves, a V-neckline and a dropped waist circled with a white sash. Her hat was a white cloche trimmed with lilac satin ribbon. The colours suited her, her mother had remarked when they'd bought the dress, and she hoped she looked her best. She had to admit as she gazed at her reflection in the long mirror on the outside of her wardrobe door that she felt a little nervous. After all, it was the first time she had ever been out with a young man and the first time she would be alone for a few hours with Charlie. You couldn't really call that short walk to the tram stop being 'alone'.

He arrived on time, looking very smart in his best suit and bearing a small bottle of Yardley's Lavender Water for her mother.

'I'm very pleased to meet you Mrs Taylor. I ... I thought you might like this. Mam says a few drops on a handkerchief are very refreshing in the weather we've been having,' Charlie said politely.

What Kate had actually said, when he'd asked her advice about what to take, was that when the smells from the back yards and the jigger got too much a bit of scent on a handkerchief always helped but he'd rephrased it.

Ethel thanked him courteously, not knowing quite what to make of him. He was a handsome lad, quietly spoken, and obviously he came from a decent, hard-working family, but she couldn't rid herself of the feeling that he just wasn't what she wanted for Florence. And there was something else that she couldn't put her finger on.

Florence smiled happily at him as she picked up her gloves and bag from the mahogany half-moon table in the hall. It was so thoughtful of him to bring a gift for her mother, she thought.

'I won't keep her out late, I promise. We both have work in the morning so we'll be back by nine thirty,' Charlie informed her parents as he ushered her out.

The nearest park was in Walton Hall Avenue so they got a tram. It was a beautiful summer evening and the perfume of the flowers that filled the ornamental beds and flanked the pathways filled the air and the leaves on the trees and bushes rustled gently in the light breeze. There were quite a few people taking advantage of the weather and the fact that the park was open until sunset to walk in the comparative coolness of the evening after being cooped up in hot, stuffy offices and shops all day.

'I'm sorry I didn't bring you something too, Florence, but–' Charlie started to explain.

Florence squeezed his hand and shook her head.

'Don't be, Charlie,' she interrupted. 'I didn't expect you to. After all you are taking me out for supper on Saturday.' She was aware that he didn't earn much; Iris had commented on the fact once or twice in the past.

'I would if I could, Florence. I want you to have ... nice things.'

'The nicest thing you can give me is your company, Charlie.'

They rounded a bend in the path and sat down on a bench that was surrounded by laurel bushes, which afforded them a little privacy.

'Did our Iris say anything to you, Florence, about ... us?' he asked, thinking of his sister's outburst.

Florence shook her head. 'Not really. I told her we are walking out together and she just shrugged and said if I was happy then that's all that mattered. Why?'

'She seemed a bit annoyed, but maybe I'm wrong. Maybe she was just surprised,' Charlie answered.

'Probably that was it. Don't forget, she wasn't very well although she said she was fine next day,' Florence reminded him.

Charlie relaxed; at least Iris hadn't repeated her derogatory remarks. Privately he thought his sister was a bit jealous; after all, as far as he knew there was no one special on Iris's horizon. 'I thought we'd go to the Stork Hotel on Saturday, Florence. I've been asking some of the older men in the office where would be best. I wanted to take you somewhere quiet and refined and where the food is good.' Various places had been suggested, most of them far too grand and expensive, particularly the Imperial which was next to Lime Street Station.

'That was sensible of you and it would be lovely. I've got to admit that I've never been there but then I've never been to any hotel for supper,' Florence admitted.

Charlie hadn't either. 'That makes two of us but I hope it's something we'll both enjoy. I want us to enjoy things ... together. Do you like going to the music hall and the moving pictures?'

Florence nodded enthusiastically although she had never been allowed to go to the music hall – her mother considered it to be far too rowdy. She'd often been to the theatre, however.

Charlie smiled at her and tentatively put his arm around her shoulder, thinking that future excursions to both places would be less expensive than hotel suppers. He could just about manage a visit to one or other of them once a week after all, you had to 'speculate to accumulate' and he had high hopes that in time they would become engaged. He had not missed the admiring glances her appearance had drawn as they'd strolled along the pathways. She was always beautifully dressed and in colours that he considered very becoming. She really was very attractive. He leaned towards her, catching the scent of rosewater and realising that he enjoyed her company. 'Florence, would you think me very forward if ... if I kissed you?'

Florence pushed the thought of what her mother would say from her mind as excitement filled her. Her very first kiss! What would it be like? She would remember this moment all her life! 'Oh, not at all, Charlie,' she breathed, closing her eyes and slipping her arms around his neck.

True to his word, Charlie had her back at Cedar Grove by half past nine and when he bade goodnight to both Florence and her parents he felt the evening had gone remarkably well.

'I'll see you on Saturday, Charlie,' Florence said, wishing he wouldn't go so soon. She felt elated and so very happy. Surely she was falling in love? That was an exhilarating thought.

'Shall I call for you?' Charlie queried.

'There's no need for you to drag out all the way here, Charlie. Ethel and I are going to the theatre so we'll drop Florence off outside the hotel,' Edward Taylor said firmly. He hadn't particularly wanted to go but Ethel had acquired the tickets some weeks back and now it seemed opportune.

'Thank you. I'll be waiting outside for you, Florence, the table is booked for seven thirty,' Charlie informed her as he took his leave.

Ethel nodded curtly and managed a fleeting smile. Her daughter's flushed cheeks and the light in her eyes told her that the evening had gone well – perhaps too well, she thought with a sinking feeling.

Chapter Eight

Rose peered out of the small bedroom window and frowned. Tomorrow was the day of the Tregarron Annual Flower Show and both she and Aunty Gwen had worked hard alongside Mrs Williams and the other volunteers getting everything organised. For weeks the weather had been very warm and mainly sunny but looking at the ominous dark clouds that were now gathering she hoped it wasn't going to rain. There were times when she missed her family but since she'd been here she'd hardly thought about Jimmy Harper at all. In fact now she reckoned she'd had a lucky escape and wondered what she had ever found attractive about him. She felt she had grown up a little and even Aunty Gwen said she was far more confident now. She went back downstairs, hearing Gwen calling her for supper.

'I hope it's not going to rain, Aunty Gwen.'

Gwen nodded as she poured the tea. 'It doesn't look too good out there, Rose. Mind, we do need it. Bob was only saying yesterday that there's been no rain for nearly a hundred days now – must have been counting – but then he's a farmer and no rain isn't good for either crops or animals. Let's hope that if it does it clears up by morning. Now, sit down and have your supper. You must be as tired as I am. Bye, but I'm tired of hearing Mrs Llewellyn-Jones complaining her floral arrangement isn't being displayed to the best advantage. She's moved it four times already and I still don't think she's satisfied!'

Rose smiled conspiratorially as she tucked into the cold ham and pickle, accompanied by thick slices of homemade bread and butter from the dairy at Bryn-y-Garn Farm. 'She is a real fuss-pot, I have to agree, but weeks ago I would never have had the nerve to say so.'

Gwen smiled at her. Spending time away from her home and family had been good for Rose, and she had grown fond of the girl.

'Her arrangement is gorgeous though. Do you think she'll win?'

Gwen raised her eyes to the ceiling. 'She has for the past two years so if she doesn't we'll never hear the end of it! But the judge's decision is final,' she ended firmly, watching Rose eat with satisfaction. Rose had grown much stronger over the weeks. She had a good appetite and had even gained a little weight, and the sun had put the colour back into her cheeks. She now looked the picture of health.

Rose had taken to country life like a duck to water. She'd made some friends amongst the girls in the village and Bob's two boys were quite smitten with her but Rose said although she liked them, it was just friendship, nothing more. She was unfailingly polite and obliging when she helped out in the post office and was well spoken of by everyone. She happily made the journey into Denbigh once a week with old Mr Morgan in his archaic trap with its equally archaic pony to visit the library and do whatever shopping was needed and she'd worked untiringly and uncomplainingly to help organise the show.

'Well, there are only a few little things left to do in the morning, Aunty Gwen. As long as it doesn't rain, that is. It would really spoil the day and it would ruin the lawns at Plas Idris too,' Rose remarked, thinking of the wide stretches of green sward that surrounded the house upon which marquees were now dotted.

'You're really taken with the big house, aren't you?'

'I love the gardens, they're beautiful, it's like being in a park,' Rose replied. It must be wonderful to be able to look out on to such a scene each day, she mused. She'd been quite excited and a little apprehensive the first time she'd gone there with Gwen. She had stared in amazement at the house as they'd got off their bicycles at the end of the long, tree-lined driveway. It was the biggest private house she'd ever seen, built of local stone. Parts of it resembled a castle: crenellated walls, Gwen had called them. There were long sash windows overlooking the grounds and wide steps leading up to the front door, which was huge and made of thick oak. The whole area in front of it was gravelled but large stone urns filled with flowers stood at intervals along the walls of the house.

They'd been shown into one of the smaller sitting rooms, which was furnished in shades of blue, and she'd noticed then that the brocade curtains were a little faded as was the material that covered the sofa and various armchairs. The sunlight streaming in through the window had drawn her attention to the layer of dust covering the glass domes of the numerous displays of dried flowers and stuffed birds that were set on tables around the room.

She'd been introduced to Miss Rhys-Pritchard, whom everyone called Miss Olivia, and her younger sister Miss Elinore, both of whom she judged to be in their late twenties or early thirties, both unmarried and dressed in obviously expensive but decidedly unfashionable clothes. She had been rather overawed, particularly by Miss Olivia, and had said little during the discussion about the show that had followed but Gwen had enlightened her on many things when they'd left.

'It's a shame really, see, the house going downhill like that,' she'd said as they'd cycled down the drive towards the road that led to the village. 'They used to have a big staff there when their parents were alive but since the war people don't want to go into service any more.'

Rose had nodded. 'I noticed that the place needed a good dusting and that things were looking a bit ... worn.'

'They still have money though. Own most of the farms around here, they do – Bob is one of their tenants – but the two mines were sold off after the tragedy,' Gwen had said gravely.

'What tragedy? Was there a mining disaster?' Rose had asked. She knew such things happened.

'No, not for years in any of the ones their father owned. One weekend the parents went off to visit friends in England – somewhere in the Wye Valley we heard – but they never got there. Terrible accident there was, see. Their motor car overturned on a steep stretch of the road after colliding with a farm cart and rolled down the side of the hill. Both killed, they were. Tragic, it was.' Gwen had shaken her head sadly remembering the big funeral for the Rhys-Pritchards. 'Folk say Miss Elinore never got over it. She was her father's pet, see.'

'I thought she was a bit vague but after a shock like that you would be. Was it very long ago? How old was she then?'

'About the same age as you are now, Rose. Must have been nine years ago now.'

Rose had felt very sorry for Elinore Rhys-Pritchard; she couldn't envisage losing both her parents like that.

'And then of course young Mr David, or Dai as they call him, was badly wounded in the war,' Gwen had continued.

Rose had been surprised. 'I didn't know they had a brother.'

'Oh yes indeed. Shrapnel in both legs. Terrible! He can walk but only a few steps and it's so painful that he spends most of his time in a wheelchair now. Such a shame when you think of how you used to see him galloping around on that big bay hunter he had. Sold the horse, those girls did. Took him a long time to get well and I've heard that it's affected him in other ways too. Very down he gets. Sad, isn't it?'

'I think it affected a lot of the boys like that. I know our Charlie didn't come back the same person,' she'd told Gwen.

After supper she'd helped Gwen clear away and wash up and had then read for half an hour but she didn't stay up and finish her book, knowing they had an early start in the morning.

Thankfully the overnight rain had cleared next morning and the sun was shining, giving the promise of another hot day.

'Much better after that rain, isn't it? Everything looks and smells fresher,' Gwen commented, breathing in deeply as she and Rose mounted their bicycles and rode to Plas Idris.

The place was a hive of activity when they arrived and Gwen smiled. 'Get a good crowd today, we will, I shouldn't wonder. Now, there's only an hour before we open to the public. There's at least four busloads coming from Denbigh and some from Mold and Pentrefoelas and the judges will be starting their inspection soon. You go and find Miss Olivia and see if there's anything urgent she needs doing. I'll make sure that Mrs Llewellyn-Jones isn't still causing a fuss,' Gwen directed.

Rose found Miss Olivia in the small marquee reserved for the judges. She looked well, she thought. Her wide-brimmed straw hat decorated with pink artificial flowers was reminiscent of the style worn before the war, as was her blouse. High-necked and pale pink, it had inserts of white lace in the leg-o'-mutton sleeves which matched the white skirt she wore and from under which white buttoned boots could be glimpsed. The outfit made her look every inch the lady she was. Gwen had said she was twenty-nine but Rose thought that she looked older and would probably appear younger if she adopted the more modern styles now fashionable.

She herself was wearing a blue and white cotton dress with a drop-waist, short sleeves and a fluted hemline which she'd bought in Denbigh and which looked fresh and cool. She'd trimmed her blue cloche with some white ribbon which had brightened it up.

'Miss Olivia, Miss Roberts sent me to ask if there's anything needing to be done.'

Olivia turned, a frown creasing her forehead. 'Ah, Rose! Yes, there is something you can do,' she said. She was feeling slightly harassed and thankful to have another pair of hands. She had met the girl on several occasions and had found her a pleasant, willing worker although her accent grated a little. 'Would you go over to the house, please? Elinore has forgotten to bring the "Best in Show" cards over and the judges will be starting any minute now. They're on the sideboard in the dining room, so she informs me. Do you know where that is?'

Rose shook her head. 'No, but don't worry, I'll find it.'

'It's at the back of the house, the last door on the left before the baize door to the kitchens and would you hurry, please? I don't want any complaints about tardiness or bad organisation.' She sighed, thinking she could well do without her sister's forgetfulness on days like today, before turning back to the group of elderly gentlemen who comprised the panel of judges.

Rose quickly covered the distance to the house and made her way down the wide hallway, finally reaching what she hoped was the dining room. She breathed a sigh of relief when she opened the door to see a long, highly polished table and matching chairs. Floor-length, mulberry-coloured velvet curtains held back with gold-coloured cords graced the large windows but the internal shutters had only been partly folded back and so the room was rather dark. She found the cards in a neat pile on the heavily carved sideboard that took up most of one wall but as she turned to leave she was startled to see a young man sitting near the window furthest from her.

'Oh, I'm so sorry! I didn't think there was anyone here. I ... I suppose I should have knocked first. I was sent to fetch these cards for the judges. Miss Elinore forgot to take them over with the others,' she blurted out awkwardly. To her relief he smiled.

'Poor Ellie, she often forgets things and I think sometimes she finds all Livvie's instructions rather confusing,' he said with a note of affection in his voice as he moved towards her.

Rose could now see that he was sitting in a wheelchair. 'Well, I have to agree that things have been a bit hectic these last couple of days,' she said shyly, realising that this must be David Rhys-Pritchard.

She could see him quite clearly now and she thought he would have been a very handsome young man if it hadn't been for the scar on his left cheek and the signs of suffering deeply etched on his features. She judged him to be about as old as her brother Charlie.

'What's your name?' he asked, knowing from her accent that she wasn't local.

'Rose. Rose Mundy. Well, Rosamund actually but everyone calls me just Rose. I'm staying with Miss Roberts, the postmistress.'

'Rose – Rosamund. Rosa mundi,' he repeated. '"The rose of the world". Did you know that?'

Embarrassed, she looked down at the cards she was clutching, not knowing if he was mocking her. 'No, I don't know why Mam picked that name. I ... I think I'd better go now, the judges are waiting,' she replied. Then she looked up but he had turned away and was staring out of the window, lost in a world of his own, seemingly unaware that she was even there. Quietly she let herself out, closing the door gently behind her, and ran down the length of the hall and out into the gardens, heading for the marquee. The experience had unsettled her.

She had no time over the next few hours to dwell on her encounter with David Rhys-Pritchard as she accompanied Gwen and Bethan Williams around the many exhibits, which included vegetables and craftwork as well as flowers and floral displays, but when they finally arrived home, late that afternoon, she remembered it.

'Aunty Gwen, when I went over for those cards I met David Rhys-Pritchard and he said something ... odd.'

Gwen looked concerned. 'What? Nothing ... inappropriate, I hope?'

Rose shook her head. 'He said my name means "Rose of the world". I don't know if he was making fun of me or not.'

Gwen smiled. 'I don't think he was, *cariad*. There is a rose called "Rosa mundi" and that's exactly what it means. I think it was meant as a compliment.'

Rose was still a little puzzled. 'He asked me did I know that but when I answered he'd turned away and it was as if ... I wasn't there.'

'Ah, don't take that to heart. I told you he can be a bit ... strange. It was the war, luv,' Gwen assured her.

Rose nodded. 'He must have been very handsome before he was wounded. I felt sorry for him, it must be awful to be left crippled like that.'

'He was indeed a handsome lad. Terrible, it is. Terrible, but those girls look after him well enough and there's nothing either of us can do to help or change things,' Gwen replied.

As she began to set the table for supper Rose thought that Charlie had been lucky, very lucky indeed not to have been as badly wounded as David Rhys-Pritchard.

Chapter Nine

Charlie was feeling very fortunate indeed for as the weeks passed his romance with Florence blossomed and he was becoming quite fond of her. They saw each other twice a week, every week, and it was becoming quite clear that he wouldn't have much trouble persuading her to agree when he asked to marry her, which he intended to do at Christmas. He got on well with her father so he didn't expect any opposition when he went formally to ask for her hand. Her mother was a different kettle of fish though. Even though she was unfailingly polite it was quite clear that she neither liked him nor thought him good enough for her only daughter. He hoped that when the ring was on Florence's finger her attitude would soften.

She wasn't the only one who thought Florence was above him. He'd had a few rows with Iris too and so now relations between them were decidedly cool. He'd become really angry the last time she had voiced her opinions, he remembered. 'You're jealous, Iris, that's what you are. You just can't stomach the fact that Florence really cares for me and prefers to spend time with me rather than you,' he'd shouted at his sister.

Iris had laughed cuttingly. 'Jealous! That's a laugh! Doesn't she come almost every Sunday? No, I just think she is making a mistake and I don't want her to get hurt.'

'I'm sick to death of hearing what *you* think, Iris. It's what *Florence* thinks that's important.'

'For heaven's sake! Shut up, the pair of you.' Kate was exasperated.

'He's up to something, Mam, I know he is!' Iris had cried.

'Like what, may I ask?' he'd demanded angrily, wondering if she really did have some inkling of his plans.

'Like courting her just to get your feet under the table with her da–'

'Oh, for God's sake, Mam, will you tell her she's going off her rocker!' he'd interrupted furiously.

'Iris, that's a terrible thing to say!' Kate had upbraided her. Any fool could see that Florence genuinely idolised Charlie and he seemed to think the world of her, treating her always with affection and respect. She'd wondered if he did have a point about Iris being jealous though.

'I don't want Florence to get hurt, that's all,' Iris had explained, which made him even more angry.

'She won't get hurt! I suppose the fact that I spend every spare penny I have making sure she enjoys herself when we go out counts for nothing?' he'd said cuttingly. 'Or that I often get off the tram two or three stops early to save a few coppers?'

Kate had intervened then and firmly told them she didn't want to hear another word on the subject. She had resolved to speak to her daughter later: a conversation he'd heard part of through the scullery door.

'Iris, luv, you must stop accusing Charlie of being devious. You're just going to have to accept that, whether you like it or not, Florence and Charlie seem to love each other,' Kate had said gently but firmly.

'Mam, I can't help it. He wasn't in the least bit interested in Florence until the day she came here to meet Rose,' Iris had protested.

'He hadn't met her until then. He'd only ever heard you talk about her,' Kate had reminded her.

'Yes, well, but after that he wanted to know where she lived and then after I'd been for tea and I'd described their house to you, doesn't he take himself off to see her father and the next thing is they are courting,' Iris protested stubbornly. She just couldn't rid herself of the feeling that Charlie had some kind of ulterior motive.

'I think you're making something out of

nothing, Iris,' Kate had sighed.

'Her mother doesn't like him. Florence has told me that,' Iris had persisted.

'She obviously wanted better for Florence. If they do eventually get married, Florence is going to have to accept that she's not going to be able to live in the style she does now, but if she loves him, they'll manage. She's got a decent enough job. Now, let the subject drop, Iris, please. I hate to see you and Charlie at loggerheads.'

He hadn't heard clearly what reply his sister had given, but then the conversation had turned to Rose and he'd moved away from the door.

He'd left the office and had walked down to the Pier Head to catch the tram home and was deep in thought about his sister's animosity towards his courtship of Florence as the vehicle made its way through the streets of the city centre and out towards Scotland Road. As it reached St Anthony's Church there seemed to be some sort of hold-up, which brought him out of his reverie. Passengers asked the conductor what was wrong. Was there a problem with the overhead trolley? How long did he think they would be stuck here?

'I'll have a word with the driver, hang on a minute,' the man replied. He went to confer with the tram driver and was back in a few seconds. 'Looks as though there's been an accident. My mate up front says he can see an ambulance, a bit of a crowd and plenty of bobbies but he hopes we won't be held up for long.'

'Probably another bloody horse that's bolted. Cause mayhem they do, stupid animals, you've only got to sneeze and they're off!' someone remarked caustically.

It was fifteen minutes before the traffic began to move again but as he alighted at his stop Charlie thought that at least the women would be busy getting the evening meal organised and wouldn't be on their doorsteps gossiping, so at least he wouldn't get waylaid and have to stop and be asked questions, the answers to which they most probably already knew. They did it just to make certain they had the facts right before passing on any information they'd gleaned.

Iris was already home and his mam was shutting up the shop so his sister was setting the table.

'What's for tea?' he asked, taking off his jacket and cap.

'There's a pie in the oven,' Iris answered curtly.

Charlie noticed the envelope on the dresser. 'I see our Rose's weekly letter has arrived. No doubt full of gossip about what's going on in Tregarron, as if we're really interested.'

'Speak for yourself. I think her letters are very interesting and often amusing and so does Mam.'

'What is amusing?' Kate asked as she came into the kitchen, catching the end of Iris's conversation.

'Our Rose's letters,' Iris supplied.

'I have to say I really look forward to them. When she wrote about the flower show it brought back some memories, I can tell you,' Kate said.

'When's she coming home? Or does she intend to stay there for ever?' Charlie asked.

Kate sighed. 'Reading between the lines I think she'd like to but I'm going to suggest she comes home next month. Gwen can't keep her much longer, it wouldn't be fair to ask her to. No, she can come back before the end of August.'

Iris nodded; she missed Rose. 'Is Da staying open late, Mam, or will he be in soon?'

'He closed a bit earlier today, luv, he had some business to attend to. I don't like him keeping too many pieces of jewellery in that old safe he has in the shop. Gold is too valuable and times are hard, it's safer in the bank, but he hates going.'

Charlie looked perturbed. 'I wouldn't have thought there was that much, Mam?'

'It mounts up, Charlie. It's awful really, the number of poor souls who've had to pawn their wedding rings and other bits just to make ends meet and haven't been able to redeem them. No, I told him it was best to take it to the bank for safekeeping.'

'He shouldn't be long now though, they close early enough,' Iris stated, glancing at the clock on the mantel over the range.

Half an hour later Kate decided that rather than let the pie dry up they would eat and she'd plate Bill's up; he'd probably met someone and been delayed. They had almost finished when the sound of someone banging hard on the shop door interrupted them.

Kate got up. 'If that's Mary Duncan wanting more potatoes because she's run out I won't be very happy! If she spent more time in her kitchen and less jangling on her doorstep, she'd be more aware of what she needed.'

Iris got to her feet. 'Sit down and finish your meal, Mam,' she said firmly. 'I've finished mine.

I'll go and I'll serve her.' Quite often people called after they had closed. Hilda Jarvis who ran the corner shop said she was tormented every night by people who'd run out of things. She never seemed to get a meal in peace.

As she opened the door Iris's hand went to her mouth and her heart dropped like a stone. A police constable was standing there looking grim.

'Is your mam in, luv?' he asked.

She could only nod as panic swept over her. It was Da! Something had happened to her da, she knew it!

'Then I think I'd best come in,' he said gently, noting her obvious distress. She led him through the shop and into the kitchen and when Kate saw him she uttered a cry of distress.

'Mrs Mundy? Mrs Kate Mundy? I think you'd better get your coat, luv.'

'Oh, my God! It's Bill! What's happened to him?' she cried.

'He's in Stanley Hospital. I'm afraid there was an accident, a lorry skidded and went out of control. It's not good, they say. I'm very sorry. Is there anything I can do?'

Charlie, although white-faced and shocked, reached for his jacket. 'Can you try and find us a hackney or something? If we have to go on the tram it will take ages.'

'I can but it will ... er ... cost. Cabs don't come cheap,' he reminded them. People in this neighbourhood never travelled in such style. They couldn't afford to.

'I know, but don't worry, we've got the fare,' Charlie assured him. This was one time he wasn't

104

going to quibble over a few shillings.

On the way to the hospital Kate blamed herself. 'If I hadn't nagged him to go to the bank, this wouldn't have happened.'

'Mam, stop it! It's not your fault, you were only doing what you thought was best,' Iris had said and Charlie had agreed but it hadn't helped, Kate couldn't stop fretting.

When they arrived, Kate was immediately taken off by the sister in charge, who instructed Iris and Charlie to wait as the doctor was still with their father.

'Oh, I hope it's not too bad, Charlie,' Iris said, biting her lips as they sat on one of the long wooden benches.

'So do I but that copper wasn't giving much away, was he? Just said it didn't look too good. What exactly did he mean by that, I ask you?' Charlie too was worried but he'd already started to wonder when his father would be able to return to work and how they would manage in the circumstances.

The minutes seemed to drag by but then they were both startled to see a doctor, accompanied by the sister who'd told them to wait, appear and beckon to them. Their sombre expressions made Iris tremble with a growing fear. 'Can we see him now, please? Is he going to be all right?' she pleaded.

'Of course you can see him, but ... but I'm afraid he has succumbed to his injuries, which were serious. He died a few minutes ago. I'm so sorry.'

The tears that had been welling in her eyes

began to slide down Iris's cheeks as she clung to her brother for support. It couldn't be true! Da couldn't have *died!* He'd been fine that morning – his usual good-natured self.

'Mam...?' Charlie said, his voice cracking with grief. He'd seen hundreds of men die and die horribly, but this was his father!

'Naturally very upset and shocked. Would you take them to her please, sister?'

Iris didn't remember that short journey down the white-tiled corridor but when she saw her mother cradling her father's head in her arms and sobbing brokenly, the sheet covering him covered in blood, she too broke down. Charlie, too, was fighting back tears as he gently put his hand on Kate's shoulder.

'Mam, he ... he was so badly injured. He must have been in great pain. It ... it's for the best,' he tried to comfort her.

Kate raised a tear-blotched face. 'What am I going to do without him, Charlie? He was the love of my life, my best friend and I sent him off to the bank! I sent him to his death!'

Before he could answer the sister took charge. 'Now, Mrs Mundy, you must not think like that! Accidents happen and that's exactly what they are. Tragic accidents. You are shocked and over-wrought but you must not blame yourself. You are all shocked and overwrought. I'll get one of the student nurses to bring you some sweet tea while the formalities are taken care of.' She turned to Charlie, who was obviously more in control of his emotions. 'Young man, could I ask you to accompany me to the office?'

Charlie nodded grimly and followed her out while both Kate and Iris tried to stop crying.

'He ... he looks peaceful now, Mam,' Iris at last managed to say. He did, she thought. If it weren't for the bloodstained sheet he'd look as if he were just asleep. Her mind and emotions were in turmoil but she had to try to help calm her mam and stop her blaming herself.

Kate's sobs were diminishing. 'It ... it's just such a ... shock, Iris. I ... I always thought we'd grow old together. He ... he wasn't even fifty-five.'

Iris clung to her. 'I know, Mam.'

A young nurse arrived and asked them to follow her as she'd organised some tea and they needed to attend to Mr Mundy now. Reluctantly they left, holding tightly to each other, and when they entered the small room adjacent to the matron's office they found Charlie waiting. The details of the accident had been relayed to him. A lorry had skidded, mounted the pavement and crushed Bill against the wall of a building. His injuries both external and internal had been so serious that there had never been any doubt that they would prove fatal.

'I've got the death certificate, Mam, and I'll attend to all the other formalities tomorrow. You're too upset.'

Kate nodded slowly. A funeral would have to be arranged but she couldn't think about things like that now. She just *couldn't*.

'Rose! Charlie, we'll have to get word to Rose, she'll have to come home,' Iris cried, suddenly remembering her sister.

Charlie nodded. 'I'll go and see Florence's

father after I've got you both home.'

Iris stared at him in some confusion.

'He's got a telephone, hasn't he? If Mam's got the number for the post office in Tregarron we can phone. She can get the next bus home.'

'I ... I think I've got it somewhere but I'm not sure...' Kate couldn't think straight.

'Don't worry, Mam. I'm sure we can find out,' Charlie reassured her. He was certain that Mr Taylor wouldn't object under the circumstances and he would be able to inform Florence of the tragedy at the same time.

By the time they'd got home and he'd given his mother and sister a drop of brandy each and had one himself it was getting quite late. He wondered if he should leave it until tomorrow, but then decided no, it had to be tonight.

Edward Taylor was surprised to see the lad when he opened the door but given the lateness of the hour and Charlie's expression he realised something was very wrong. 'Come in, Charlie. What's happened?'

He listened in silence as Charlie told him of the accident and then, giving the lad a tot of brandy and a pat on the shoulder, went to fetch his wife and daughter.

Florence immediately went and sat next to him and took his hand, tears welling up in her eyes.

'Oh, Charlie, I'm so very, very sorry. Your mother and Iris...?'

Before he could answer Ethel spoke, moved by his plight. 'Heart-broken, I imagine, and no wonder. The shock.' She shook her head, thinking of young Iris.

Charlie finished his drink but still felt shocked. 'It's our Rose, you see. We've got to let her know and tell her to come home. I've the number for the post office in Tregarron and I was wondering if I could possibly...'

'Of course you can use the telephone, but isn't it too late? Will there be anyone to answer it? Does your mother's friend live on the premises?' Edward Taylor asked, thinking of the practicalities.

'She lives in the adjacent cottage,' Charlie replied. He hadn't given a thought to whether Gwen would hear the phone.

Florence's father stood up. 'Right, we'll try and if there's no reply you can call again in the morning. I take it there is public transport of some kind your sister can use to get home? The train?'

'There's a bus service twice a week,' Charlie informed him.

'Not exactly regular,' the older man commented as they went into the hall. When they managed to get hold of Rose he'd arrange something, he thought, even if he had to drive there himself. The poor girl would be distraught and if she had to wait for days to get home it wouldn't help.

They had some difficulty getting through to the exchange and when the operator suggested that as the number wasn't answering they should try tomorrow, Edward explained that it was an emergency and that she should let it continue to ring.

Finally Gwen answered and Charlie told her what had happened. She gasped, 'Oh, my God! I'll go and get poor Rose now!' but he stopped her, asking that she just tell Rose and say she must get the next bus home. At length she agreed, after he'd said it would be better, for Rose if she heard the terrible news from Gwen personally, rather than over the telephone.

As he replaced the receiver he thanked Florence's father. 'I do appreciate your help. I ... I'd better get back now to Mam.'

'These next few days are going to be pretty grim for you, Charlie, and if you need to use the telephone again don't hesitate to call. We are all very, very sorry, please tell your mother that.'

'I will,' Charlie replied as Florence kissed him on the cheek and promised to come and see Iris after work tomorrow.

'And if there isn't a bus either tomorrow or the day after, I'll go and bring Rose home myself. Can't leave the poor girl there waiting, she'll be frantic,' Edward offered as he showed Charlie out.

As he closed the door Florence went to him and hugged him, thinking how upset poor Charlie must be and knowing how she would feel if anything terrible happened to her father. It was a very sobering thought.

Chapter Ten

Rose couldn't take it in. Gwen had woken her and told her the tragic news as gently as she could and had then sat with her as she'd sobbed brokenly. Later that morning before Gwen

110

opened the post office she ran up to tell Bethan Williams what had happened and ask her to sit with Rose as she had to go into the shop.

'Of course I will, Gwen. I'll try and give her what little comfort I can. She'll be going home then?' Bethan asked as she hastily took off her apron and reached for a cardigan.

'As soon as possible, Bethan, but I can't see a way of going with her myself and I don't want her to have to go alone, she's in no fit state. Broken-hearted she is, poor love.'

'Don't worry about that, we'll think of something. Maybe I could go with her.'

'I'm distracted with it all, Bethan, I really am. And poor, poor Kate: how must she be feeling?'

'At least she's got Iris and Charlie with her, we have to thank God for that.'

Bethan spent the rest of the morning making cups of tea and trying to comfort Rose but she felt very helpless. All Rose kept saying was that she should have gone home earlier than this and she'd regret it all her life that she'd not been there when her poor da was dying. She couldn't believe that she would never see him or hear his voice again.

'But you will, Rose, you have to believe that. He'll be waiting for you in heaven, *cariad*,' she comforted her.

Gwen came in at lunchtime, looking anxious and flustered. 'How is she, Bethan? I've been so distracted that I've had to tell people why and then I've spent most of the morning trying to persuade them not to knock and offer their condolences. It's too soon.'

As she again put the kettle on Bethan nodded. 'It is. I've persuaded her to go and lie down but I doubt she'll sleep. She's sort of dazed but that's only to be expected. Has there been any more news from Liverpool?'

Gwen took the cup of tea her friend offered. 'Just before I closed up a gentleman telephoned: a Mr Taylor. He said he was the father of Charlie's "young lady", who is also a friend of Iris's. He said he'd drive over tomorrow in his motor car and take Rose back as there won't be a bus for three days and Charlie is arranging the funeral.'

Bethan nodded. 'That's very kind of him.'

'It's a great relief to me too. She couldn't go on the bus in the state she's in. I'll get her things together tonight after supper.'

'Don't you worry about that, Gwen. I'll do it this afternoon.'

Gwen reached over and patted her hand. 'It's times like this when you need good friends and you've always been there when I needed you, Bethan. I just wish I could go over and see poor Kate.'

Bethan nodded as she sipped her tea. 'Go on the next bus, Gwen. I'll cover for you. You'll never forgive yourself if you don't,' she urged.

Edward Taylor arrived mid-morning the following day and, putting a note on the shop door, Gwen took him into the cottage where Rose was sitting waiting, her case packed. She was a little calmer but her eyes were swollen and red and she was very pale.

'Rose, I'm Florence's father and I'm so very

112

sorry about what's happened. I've come to take you home,' he greeted her gently. He felt very sorry for the whole family but young Charlie was proving to be a sensible and reliable lad. He hadn't gone to pieces the way both his mother and sisters had and that was a real blessing, although he'd confided that he'd miss his father terribly.

Rose nodded, unable to dispel the numbing mist that was clogging her mind. She had slept fitfully, exhausted by grief, shock and the tears she'd shed. She just wanted to get home to her mam. 'Thank you. I don't know if I could have faced ... the bus,' she replied.

He took her case out to the car while Gwen hugged her tightly.

'I'll miss you, Rose, I really will. I've loved having you here but now your mam needs you. I'll see you soon though, I'll be over on the next bus to see you all. Bethan is going to stand in for me. Tell your mam that.'

Rose buried her head in the older woman's shoulder. 'I ... I'll miss you too, Aunty Gwen. Everyone here has been so kind to me. I felt so ... settled here.'

'Maybe you'll come back one day, *cariad*. You'll always be welcome. Now, let's not keep Mr Taylor waiting.'

Rose waved as the car drew away, wondering if she would ever come back to Tregarron where she had been so happy – until this terrible thing had happened.

When she finally arrived home she found her mother and Iris sitting in the kitchen and she could see from their red and puffy eyes that they had had as bad a night as she herself had.

Iris ran to her and hugged her and Rose broke down and sobbed for the room, so familiar from babyhood, seemed so empty and alien without her father.

Kate tried to comfort them both, making a huge effort to pull herself together. 'Now, try and calm down, both of you. Rose, come and sit down, luv, and I'll make a pot of tea.'

'I don't want any. I've drunk so much of it that just the thought of it makes me feel sick,' Rose said, wiping her tears away with the back of her hand. 'Where's our Charlie?'

'Gone to Brougham Terrace to ... to register the...' Kate fought down a sob, unable to bring herself to say the word 'death'.

Iris spooned the tea into the pot. She really didn't want any either but she had to do *something*, she thought miserably. 'Even though he's terribly upset he ... he's been very good, seeing to all the formal things,' she told her sister.

'Everyone has been so kind. The Taylors and all the neighbours. Mrs Taylor sent a lovely card, it arrived in the first post, and Mr Taylor insisted on going to Tregarron and doing all the telephoning,' Kate added.

'Florence came straight from work yesterday, she was very upset, and she's promised to come again tonight. I put a notice on the door of the shop but Mrs Marshall and Mrs Connolly have offered to take over until Mam feels up to it again, if we can sort out supplies with the market people,' Iris continued.

Kate nodded wearily; she was thankful for their offers of assistance. In this neighbourhood when tragedy struck everyone knuckled down and helped out as best they could and they'd all called, every woman in the entire street, and all with sincere words about how much Bill would be missed.

''E was a proper gentleman, Kate. Kind, pleasant – treated us all as if we were somebody when we went into the shop and was always delighted when we could afford ter redeem our stuff. "'Is valued and regular ladies" 'e always called us. Aye, 'e was the salt of the earth, luv, and we'll miss 'im,' Ada Marshall had assured her. And there had been cards and messages from the proprietors of other businesses, particularly other pawnbrokers, including Cookson's down on Scotland Road.

'Aunty Gwen is coming on the next bus, Mam, though not to stay. Mrs Williams is going to cover for her in the post office,' Rose said, thinking that she really must make an effort to find the energy to unpack.

'That's good of her – good of them both,' Kate replied, the tears again threatening to overwhelm her. She really didn't know Bethan Williams all that well; people were so kind and thoughtful and she drew comfort from it, knowing that there were dark days ahead.

The funeral was arranged for the end of the week and they were all dreading it. 'It ... it will seem so ... final. I know Da's ... gone ... but it doesn't seem *real*,' Iris had said to Rose, who had agreed but who repeated what Bethan Williams had said and confided that it was something that she was clinging to.

The church was packed to capacity that summer morning for Bill Mundy had been well liked and respected in the neighbourhood and everyone who could spare an hour had come. As the hearse had travelled slowly through the streets people had stopped what they were doing and stood in silence. Men had taken off their caps and women had bowed their heads, a policeman had even saluted and, although grief-stricken, Kate had felt a rush of pride in the man she had loved and been married to for all those years. She would never forget all their gestures of sympathy.

Iris, desperately fighting back her tears, was holding Rose's hand tightly as both girls slowly followed their mother and brother up the aisle. Charlie, dry-eyed but pale, felt that at least the war had taught him how to hide his feelings and appear dignified although inside he felt bereft. He knew he would struggle to hold back his tears, but he was pleased and moved to see Florence, accompanied by both her parents, in the congregation. They stood out being far better dressed than everyone else, wearing the full black of mourning and not just an armband as most people were.

The whole day had passed in something of a blur, Rose thought as the last of the neighbours left having tidied up after the funeral tea.

'I'm exhausted,' Kate said, sinking into a chair. It had been the hardest day she'd ever lived through. Not even when Charlie had been away in the

116

trenches had she endured such a trial but she'd had Bill by her side to help her through that ordeal.

'We all are, Mam. Why don't you go on up? Rose and I will put these last few bits away,' Iris urged.

'Mam, there's something I have to discuss with you,' Charlie said tentatively. 'I know it's not exactly the best time but, well, it's a bit pressing, like.'

'What?' Iris demanded, wondering just what was so pressing that it couldn't wait until tomorrow.

'What do you want to do about the shop? Da's shop. It's Friday tomorrow and you know people always come in to redeem their clothes for the weekend.'

Kate nodded. It was a custom that had been adhered to for decades. The women brought all the decent clothes in on a Monday and redeemed them on Friday when the men were paid. It was a way of borrowing a few shillings that would help to tide them over the week and everyone had what passed for their best clothes back for the weekend.

'We'll have to open up. I can't let them down like that, your da wouldn't have wanted that,' Kate said. But how could she stand behind that counter in Bill's place and face everyone again?

'I'll do it, Mam. It will be too harrowing for you,' Charlie said firmly. He didn't mind that much about letting people down. If they chose not to open people would have to understand, bereavement was a valid enough reason, but if the pledges weren't redeemed they'd be out of pocket and it might set a precedent too and that was something he definitely wasn't prepared to let happen.

'Thanks, Charlie. Are you sure you can cope?'

'Of course I can. Now go on up and try to get some sleep,' he urged.

She managed a sad little smile. 'You're a good lad, Charlie.'

Iris had to agree. For the first time it occurred to her to question how they would manage to run both businesses now. As Kate went upstairs and she and Rose folded the tablecloth and put the condiments back on the dresser she wondered just how they would all face the future without Da.

Chapter Eleven

The days that followed were indeed dark and hard and nerves were stretched as they all tried to come to terms with their grief and loss. Charlie realised that the sooner they all tried to get back to some kind of normality the better; he also concluded that the welfare of the family was his responsibility now. He was concerned about his father's business for the shop had been closed for a while now and he knew that out of desperation people would take their custom elsewhere; they weren't the only pawnbroker's in the area by any means. He decided to broach the subject with his mother and sisters sooner rather than later.

'Mam, we've got to try to get back into some kind of routine,' he said when supper was finished that evening. 'It will be better for us all. Things won't ever be the same but we've got to think of the future. All our futures.'

'Can't we leave it for a bit longer, Charlie?' Rose pleaded. She was feeling so miserable; being at home wasn't the same without Da and every single thing in the place reminded her of him.

'Rose, we can't go on doing that or we'll wake up one day and find we don't have an income of any kind and we'll be out on the street. Iris and I are the only ones who have been going to work,' he reminded her. Left to Rose no decision would ever be made.

Kate sighed and pushed her plate away from her. She was struggling to adjust to life, her days seemed so empty without Bill, but she knew she had to think about the practicalities sometime. 'Charlie's right. We have to decide what we're going to do.'

'I've been thinking about it, Mam, and it makes sense for me to take over Da's shop and you and Rose run the greengrocer's,' Charlie suggested.

'And I'll keep my job at Frisby Dyke's? Wouldn't it be better for me to run Da's shop?' Iris put in.

'No, I don't think you're old enough or have the right ... attitude, and both are important. People like to feel comfortable and confident,' Charlie replied flatly.

Kate frowned. She wasn't sure about this. 'I think it would be better if you stayed with the Blue Funnel Line, Charlie. It's secure and there are chances of promotion. Your da was always in

119

favour of you working outside the business. I'll take over his business – I think you're right about confidence and comfort and I know most of them very well indeed – and Iris and Rose can run the greengrocery between them. That way we'll keep our options open.'

Charlie wasn't very pleased by this but kept his feelings to himself. 'Will you be able to manage it, Mam? It's quite a responsibility.'

Kate nodded. 'I'm sure I will.'

'At least it will save you having to get up at the crack of dawn each day, Mam. You're not getting any younger, and the work will be easier,' Iris added. She thought it was a great idea; after all she was used to shop work but now she would be working for herself – more or less – and she'd save on tram fares and lunches. The idea of going to the market early each morning didn't bother her and if need be she could also help out in the pawnbroker's. 'I won't mind going to the market.'

Rose nodded her assent, relieved that she wasn't going to be told to go and find a job somewhere else like Black's or in a factory. She wouldn't mind helping Iris.

'Keeping your job will give you a bit more independence, Charlie. You'll be able to save up for ... for the future. I'm sure Florence will agree with me.' Kate smiled wryly at her son. 'I can't see Florence living happily over the shop.'

'It was good enough for you, Mam!' Charlie pointed out for he and his sisters had been born in the bedroom above the pawnbroker's. It had been years before his parents had saved enough to start up another business and acquire the lease on the greengrocer's.

'I know. And I don't want you to think I'm shutting you out or anything like that. In time you might want to run the business instead of working for someone else and that would be fine with me, as long as you had some savings behind you and a decent home of your own as well. I ... I always wanted good, secure, comfortable lives for you all. We both did, your da and I.'

'I know, Mam. Well, let's see how it goes and if it gets too much for you we'll have to think again,' Charlie agreed. He wasn't sure it would work. His father's business needed completely reorganising: the place was a shambles, what he'd seen of his father's records left a lot to be desired and he knew his mother wouldn't change things at all. He also wondered how Iris would get on for he deduced she would be doing most of the work. Rose had always been prone to day-dreaming and did not seem to have changed.

Iris duly gave in her notice the following day and Kate and Rose went into the shop with Charlie for the first time since Bill's death.

'I've got to say it's a bit of a mess, Mam. I didn't really have the time to sort much out that Friday,' Charlie said, frowning as he looked around.

'It's just as he left it. He expected to be back in the following morning. And he had his own system,' Kate replied sadly.

Charlie placed the two ledgers his father had used on the top of the counter. 'We'll start by having a good look at these and I'll see if I can come up with a simpler and clearer system of working. Then we'd better go through the stock. Rose, could you start by dusting and giving the floor a sweep? Tidy things up a bit? We'll open for business in the morning, Mam, before all our customers desert us entirely.' He wasn't going to let his sister spend the time just peering curiously at the various objects displayed on the shelves and in glass-fronted cases as she was now doing. She'd have to get used to doing a day's work from now on instead of spending her time fiddling around occasionally in a post office or at some flower show, he decided as he ran his finger slowly down the list of names entered in the ledger, the items described and the amount paid out. Some of the sums his da had lent were, in his opinion, too high for the items pawned, he thought grimly. He'd have to have a word with Mam about it but he'd wait until she'd been open for at least a week. Let her get settled in first, he thought.

Ada Marshall and Maggie Connolly agreed to open the greengrocery while Iris worked out her notice. Charlie had said he would go to the market but Kate had insisted she would do it, one more week would make no difference and she wanted to inform her regular suppliers that they would be dealing with Iris in future.

They had all been very sympathetic and said they would miss dealing with her but would be pleased to see Iris and would make sure her inexperience wasn't exploited. As she left for home on the Saturday Kate felt a pang of regret it was as if a door was closing on part of her life, but she had to admit that it would be something of a luxury not to have to get up so early, especially now that summer was over and the darker, colder mornings of autumn were approaching. She would make one last trip the following Monday with Iris, to introduce her.

Iris was looking forward to the change in her working life. She would be her own boss, there would be no Miss Hepworth, the departmental supervisor, watching everything she did and no Mr Fowler, the floor walker, prowling between the counters raising eyebrows if she seemed to be chatting for too long with customers. She'd asked her mother were there any basic rules to the buying and Kate had advised her to stick to the staples and not get tempted by anything 'exotic' as they'd never sell such items. 'We're not in the same league as Cooper's in Church Street. We're just a small shop in a poor neighbourhood.' Iris had nodded her agreement, thinking of the displays of exotic fruit and vegetables that graced the counters of Liverpool's biggest and most expensive delicatessen.

It was chilly at this hour of the morning and barely light, she thought as they entered the huge covered market. It was already busy. Fruit and vegetables were stacked in wooden crates and outside horses and carts and the occasional van stood waiting to be loaded. Kate introduced her to her three usual suppliers, one of whom had always delivered her goods to the shop.

'So, this is Iris. Nice to meet you and I hope we'll get along fine,' Bert Bradshaw said amiably.

Iris judged him to be in his late fifties; he was well built if a little round-shouldered, with grey eyes and a shock of iron-grey hair. 'Nice to meet you too, Mr Bradshaw. You're quite happy to go on delivering to us?'

'Aye, I don't see any reason to change the arrangements now. I have to pass the end of your street on my way home so it's no trouble to drop the stuff off. Your mam's always been a good customer.' He nodded and smiled at Kate. 'Mind you, she's a bit on the fussy side.'

'I have to be, Bert, you know that. My customers are more than a bit on the "fussy side". Even though they haven't got much in the way of money, they still want value for it.'

He nodded. 'Right then, what will it be this morning?'

Kate showed Iris what to look for and how to pick the best items. 'A lot of it is seasonal but if there's no stock in don't be tempted to buy something else to replace it. Ada's going to serve alongside you for a couple of days and believe me she's a mine of information on just exactly what our customers expect.'

Iris nodded, peering at boxes of carrots and thinking it couldn't be *that* hard to buy and sell fruit and veg.

Kate picked out what she wanted and Bert Bradshaw called out to a young man to come and stick a label on each of her purchases.

'This is Tom Morrissey, just started with me this morning. He's been out of work for a while. Couldn't get anything regular since he left the Army,' he informed Kate and Iris.

'Nice to meet you Mrs Mundy and ... er ... is it Miss Mundy?'

Iris nodded, smiling. He seemed a pleasant

enough lad, about Charlie's age, she deduced. He had thick, curly brown hair and blue eyes and was as tall as Charlie but more wiry. 'It's my first morning too. I'm taking over the shop from Mam,' she informed him as he effortlessly lifted the boxes and stacked them neatly, placing a label with the numerals '49' printed on them on each one.

'You're lucky to be running a business at your age and I'm lucky Mr Bradshaw took me on. It's almost impossible to get any kind of steady work now but my granny's a friend of his wife's.' His expression changed. '"A land fit for heroes" we were promised,' he said bitterly.

'I know. It's not right, not after everything you went through. Our Charlie was in the Pals' Regiment.'

'So was I, the Seventeenth Battalion,' he replied and then he smiled again. 'But it's over and now I've got a steady job and I've met you, so things are definitely looking up.'

She smiled back; she liked him.

'I'll drop these off later, that's another of my duties. Driving the horse and cart. You never know, if things pick up sufficiently I might be able to persuade the boss to trade the nag in for a van.'

Iris thought this was being a bit too optimistic but she didn't say so. 'So, I'll be seeing you later then?'

'You'll be seeing quite a bit of me, Miss Mundy, if you're taking over,' he replied, thinking she was a fine-looking girl.

'Call me Iris. "Miss Mundy" makes me feel so

old!' she laughed. Being addressed in this manner reminded her of how much responsibility she'd taken on.

He grinned. 'And I'm Tom.'

'Well, I'll see you later on, Tom. I'd better be off. Mam's beckoning me so I think it's time to go,' she replied, feeling for the first time in weeks that there was a little brightness in her life. She looked forward to seeing Tom Morrissey again.

Chapter Twelve

As the days of Autumn slipped by and September turned to October and then November, life began to take on a semblance of normality again, although the loss of Bill was still raw. For Kate there were days – at quiet times – when she could almost feel his presence in the shop. Her sense of loss would then overwhelm her and she would break down. She missed him so much and always would.

She did admit that although running Bill's business was rather more complicated than she had at first envisaged, at least it wasn't quite as physically demanding as running the greengrocery had been. She was still providing a necessary service for local customers but since she was dealing with her neighbours' financial dilemmas they often divulged things they wouldn't have mentioned when buying vegetables. At first she had found this rather embarassing but gradually she had

126

come to see why Bill had been so liked and respected. He'd offered advice and tried to help,
often in cases where the only answer would have
been a steady, decently paid job for at least one
member of a family, and he had been scrupulous
in keeping their confidences to himself. Her customers included wives of men who squandered
what little they earned on drink or illicit gambling
like pitch and toss or the horses. She had on more
than one occasion seen women in tears, driven to
desperation at how to put food on the table when
most of a pitifully small wage had gone over the
counter in one of the hundreds of pubs along the
Dock Road. Mary Duncan was one such wife: she
had confided that it had been Bill who had found
a solution, suggesting she go and meet Ned from
work on Fridays to deter him from stopping at the
first pub he came to and that generally it worked.
Kate was determined to honour Bill's memory by
serving his customers as loyally as he had. For
that reason she'd remained firm in her decision to
stick to Bill's rates, despite having several arguments with Charlie over the amount she lent on
pledged items. She was the one who had to deal
with desperate customers, not him, she'd told her
son, thinking that he was becoming obsessed with
making money and saving.

Over the weeks Iris had got to know Tom Morrissey quite well and he had finally asked her out
to the music hall on the first Saturday in November.

'Aren't you too tired to go out? You're both up
so early every morning and then you're on your

feet in the shop all day and we were really busy today. I'm worn out,' Rose had enquired as she watched her sister brushing her short auburn hair before placing the small black felt cloche over it.

Iris had shaken her head as she contemplated her reflection in the mirror. 'No, and it's not as if we're going to be doing anything as energetic as dancing. We'll be sitting down enjoying the show. But I wish I had something a bit brighter to wear. Black doesn't suit me.' They were still in mourning of course.

'You suit it better than I do, though I don't mind wearing it for ... Da,' Rose had commented. 'You really like Tom Morrissey, don't you?'

Iris had nodded, a pink tinge creeping across her cheeks. She did like him, she liked him a lot, and she'd been wishing he'd ask her out for a long time. They got on well together, they liked the same things, and they had a similar sense of humour and optimistic outlook on life. He was now the eldest of a family of four. His older brother had been killed in the war and his two sisters were younger than him. His father had worked on the docks all his life and up until recently his mother had cleaned at the 'Immigrant House': a building owned by Cunard where the immigrants waiting to embark on one of the company's ships were housed until they left for a new life in America. Florence had commented that that must be a very hard way indeed to make money and she'd agreed; Mrs Morrissey had given it up for that very reason and the fact that her arthritis was getting worse.

'So, that's you and Charlie walking out,' Rose had said, feeling dispirited.

Iris had turned to her. 'Rose, this is the first time. You can't say we're "walking out" – not yet – but I hope ... well, I hope it won't be the one and only time he asks me,' she'd confided, feeling a little apprehensive. Of course she saw him every day but this was *different*.

He was waiting for her outside the Rotunda, peering into the window of one of the shops that constituted most of the building's ground floor. He turned and grinned. 'I was just wondering what kind of sweets you'd like? Fruit Pastilles or Everton Mints?' She looked very smart, he thought admiringly. Her black coat was trimmed on the collar with black braid and she was wearing a small hat that suited the shape of her face. A white scarf was tucked into the neck of her coat.

'You don't have to go buying me sweets, Tom. I brought some nuts for us to eat.' She held out the small paper bag. Bert Bradshaw didn't pay him very much, she'd already surmised.

He took her arm and guided her towards the theatre lobby. 'Well, if you won't let me buy you sweets I'm going to get a programme,' he said as he bought their tickets, which she noted were not for the cheapest seats up in the gods.

They both enjoyed the show for there was a wide variety of acts, not all of which were appreciated by the audience, who didn't hesitate to make their feelings known.

'Oh, don't you feel sorry for that poor man! All that shouting and booing!' Iris laughed as a magician whose last trick had gone spectacularly wrong was jeered and booed off stage.

Tom laughed too. 'You've got to admit he wasn't much good. At least no one started throwing things. I've seen that happen in the past.'

'That's why Florence isn't allowed to come to the music hall. Her mam says it's too rowdy,' Iris said. She'd often mentioned her friend to him.

'It can be but it's good fun. Sounds a bit too straight-laced, her mam,' Tom remarked, helping himself to the nuts Iris had brought along.

There wasn't time for further conversation as the next act was announced and they settled back to enjoy 'Arthur Delaney, King of Comedy'.

Tom took her hand as they walked to the tram stop at the end of the evening. 'Have you enjoyed yourself, Iris?' he asked.

She nodded enthusiastically. 'I have and thank you but I'm glad I can have a lie-in in the morning.'

He smiled at her. 'So am I, although I don't really mind getting up early. Will we go out again next Saturday?'

'I'd like that, Tom,' she replied, feeling quite elated and also relieved that he'd asked.

'You know I liked you the very first time I met you at the market, Iris, and since then ... well, we get on, don't we?' He felt a little embarrassed at revealing his feelings on a crowded street.

'We do get on well together, Tom,' Iris replied, thinking of what Rose had said. 'Our Rose said I suppose now I'll say we're "walking out",' she added a little hesitantly, wondering if she was being a bit forward.

'Well, we are, aren't we?' he asked questioningly.

'Oh, yes, Tom!' Iris replied happily. 'I just hope Rose isn't going to feel a bit left out what with Charlie and Florence and now ... us. She's only ever been out with one boy and that ended in disaster.'

He nodded. 'She'll find someone, Iris. One day her "Mr Right" will come along.'

'Just like you did.'

He squeezed her hand, wanting to take her in his arms and kiss her but not in front of all these people waiting for the tram. 'Have Charlie and Florence been courting long?'

'Months now and I have the feeling that he's going to ask her to marry him soon,' Iris replied with a sharp edge to her voice. She still didn't approve.

'Do I get the feeling that you won't be too happy to have her as your sister-in-law? I thought she was your friend – isn't that how they met?'

'She is my friend and I'd love her as a sister-in-law but I just don't think it will work. You should see the house she lives in. Her father is really well off. He's even replaced his three delivery carts and the teams of horses with motor lorries – Florence said he finds them quicker and more economical and hopes they will increase his business. If she marries our Charlie she can't expect anything like the comfort and luxuries she has now. Her mam doesn't even expect her to contribute anything, she can spend all her wages on herself. That's what she used to do, but lately she's been telling me she's saving, so I think she's actually hoping they'll get engaged.'

'Well, if they love each other I don't suppose she'll mind having to do without things. I wouldn't – in her shoes,' Tom said.

Iris wanted to say that she thought Charlie had an ulterior motive for marrying Florence but she didn't. She still couldn't get the thought that he was just using Florence to get his hands on her father's business out of her mind.

Charlie had been saving hard but it wasn't easy and the rings he'd been looking at cost a small fortune. He wanted to get Florence something good – a decent-sized diamond – but realised that his savings wouldn't stretch to that, not in the jewellers' windows he'd looked in so far. At the end of the month he had determined to ask her father formally for his consent and he'd hoped to be able to provide an acceptably sized ring.

He pushed his hands deeper into his pockets as he walked along Scotland Road towards home on the Monday evening, having got off the tram three stops early. He was pondering asking his mother for her advice when a thought occurred to him. Did the ring really have to be a new one? What if he were to buy an unredeemed pledged ring? He'd get more for his money but would Florence or, more importantly, her parents frown on that? There was a big pawnbroking establishment a bit further down the road, Cookson's; they'd been there for years and years. He'd have a look in the window and maybe ask for some advice.

He studied the rings they had in the window but saw nothing that impressed him so decided to go in.

Mr Cookson looked up irritably as Charlie entered, he was just ready to close up. 'Yes? Can I help you?' he asked curtly.

'I'm sorry it's late, I'm on my way home from work, but I wanted to ask your advice. I know you have a great reputation in the trade and my father was a pawnbroker, sir,' he added to mollify the man, who was obviously impatient for his supper.

'Really?'

'Bill Mundy,' Charlie supplied.

The older man's expression immediately changed. 'Ah, yes. Terrible tragedy, that was. So, you're his son. What can I help you with, lad?'

'I'm hoping to get engaged at Christmas and I'd like to get Florence a really good ring; she comes from a far ... better ... background than me, you see,' he began.

Mr Cookson smiled and nodded. 'Don't want the young lady to be disappointed or the future in-laws to look down their noses.'

Charlie nodded enthusiastically. 'You've hit the nail right on the head, but I can't afford what they're charging in T. Brown's or Boodles or the like. I was thinking of something second-hand.'

'So you've decided on an unredeemed pledge? It's a wise decision, er...'

'Charlie. Charlie Mundy, sir. I think I'll get more for my money that way. I've been saving hard and that's not easy to do on a mere clerk's wages.'

'You will get a better deal, Charlie. How much can you afford to spend?'

Charlie knew to the penny. 'I think I can stretch to six guineas but that's my very top limit.'

The older man nodded slowly. 'That's not a bad amount. I don't have anything suitable in at the moment but trust me, I'll find you something before Christmas. Times are hard and getting harder, you'd be surprised at the type of people who are having to pawn or sell things these days and I have contacts amongst the big jewellers.'

'I'd be so very grateful to you. I knew asking your advice was the right thing to do.'

'And of course I'll give you a bit of a discount, your father having been in the trade. How is your mother getting on? I don't know her personally of course but it must be hard for her.'

'She's slowly coming to terms with it. She's taken over his shop but...' He shrugged not wanting to say that if he was running it he was certain they'd make more of a profit. 'Well, I'll let you close up. Thanks again, sir. I'm really grateful.'

'Call in again in about a week or ten days, Charlie,' Mr Cookson advised as Charlie left.

He walked the rest of the way home in a far happier frame of mind. If he could provide a really nice ring then what did it matter if it wasn't new? And he'd been promised a discount. Why hand his hard-earned money over to one of the fancy jewellers in town and get something far smaller and less ostentatious in return? That wouldn't be a very wise thing to do. Not good business sense at all.

'You're late, was there a hold-up?' Kate asked when he finally arrived home.

Iris came in from the shop where she'd just finished serving Mrs Duncan, who had again run out of potatoes.

'That woman would drive you mad! What does she do all day? Doesn't she realise that people have got other things to do?'

Kate managed a wry smile. 'No, I don't think she does. Sit down and get this while it's hot. Charlie has only just got in,' she informed her daughter.

'Get held up?' Iris asked without much interest.

'No, not really. I just walked halfway home,' he replied offhandedly.

Kate pursed her lips. He certainly was saving hard, she thought. Any day now she expected him to tell her that he'd proposed to Florence.

'You going out with Tom Morrissey again on Saturday?' Charlie asked, helping himself to a slice of bread to accompany the thick meat stew his mam had served.

'I am. Any objections to that?' Iris asked. She was tired; it had been a long day and Rose hadn't been much help. She was aware that her sister didn't like working in the shop, finding the hours long, the conditions at this time of year cold and the customers irksome. Often at quiet moments Rose resorted to reading, which irritated Iris for she could always find something that needed attending to.

'No, seems like a decent enough bloke to me. Can't say it's much of a job he's got though.'

'He's very thankful he's got a steady job. Not everyone can work in an office!' Iris snapped back.

'Oh, don't start, you two! I've enough on my mind,' Kate said crossly.

'What's the matter, Mam? Has someone been upsetting you – in the shop, I mean?' Charlie asked.

Kate shook her head. 'No, nothing like that. Oh, I suppose I'm just tired,' she replied. In fact she was worried about Rose, who lately seemed very down and uninterested in everything, except the novels she read, and she wondered if it was because she was missing Bill. Well, they all were of course, there was a huge gap in her own life, but maybe Rose wasn't coping as well as Iris and Charlie seemed to be. Or was it something to do with his now courting? Did Rose feel left out? Perhaps she should have a talk to her youngest daughter. Then there was the pain in her back which had gone from being a twinge to a constant dull ache. She *was* tired and she was getting older, too old for all this bickering between Charlie and Iris.

Her opportunity to talk to Rose didn't arise until the following Saturday evening when Iris had gone to meet Tom Morrissey and Charlie had gone to Florence's for supper.

Rose had helped her to clear away after their supper and had then gone upstairs to fetch her book.

'Rose, luv, before you get engrossed in that I want to talk to you,' Kate started.

Rose looked at her apprehensively. 'What have I done wrong now, Mam? Has Iris been complaining that I'm not chatty enough with the customers?'

'Of course not! You haven't done anything "wrong", Rose,' Kate replied, stoking up the fire in the range for the evenings were getting much colder now.

Rose sat down in the chair near the range and looked expectantly at her mother.

'I'd be a very poor sort of a mother if I didn't know that you're not happy, Rose. What's wrong, luv? You know you can tell me. Is it ... losing your da?'

Rose bit her lip; it was impossible to hide much from Mam. 'It is and it isn't, Mam. I still can't get used to the fact that he ... he's ... gone. I still look for him when I come into the kitchen and it's still a shock that he isn't here.'

Kate nodded, struggling to keep her composure for Rose's words were probing the deep wound of her own grief. 'I know, luv. I find that too. Sometimes I turn to speak to him; to tell him something, and then it ... it's awful to realise he's not there,' she confided. 'Or is it something to do with both Charlie and Iris courting? Are you feeling left out?' she pressed.

Rose shook her head. 'No, Mam, I don't feel like that. I'm happy for them both and I know that someone will come along for me one day and then...'

'Then what is it, luv? What's making you so ... down and dispirited? You were never like this before you went down with rheumatic fever. You don't feel ill, do you?' Kate fervently hoped Rose wasn't sickening for something else.

'No, I feel fine in myself, Mam, honestly, but...'

'But what? You have to tell me, Rose, or I'll

worry myself sick,' Kate urged.

Rose felt utterly miserable. How could she tell Mam that she hated working in the shop? It was so cold now and she had little interest in the conversations of their customers, which usually centred on how hard their lives were, how little money they had, their children's ailments and a hundred other insignificant details of their lives. The time dragged and so whenever she could she would read, immersing herself in the life and loves of the heroine, although she knew Iris strongly disapproved. 'It ... it's working in the shop, Mam. Oh, it's much better than working at Black's but...' She twisted her hands together, not wanting to continue.

Kate looked at her closely. 'It's more than that isn't it, Rose?'

Miserably she nodded. 'Mam, I ... I ... wish I could go back to Tregarron. I miss it so much, especially now that Da isn't here. Of course I love you and Iris and Charlie but...' Rose struggled to put her feelings into words. 'Having lived there I find I can't bear the way everyone lives on top of each other here, all the noise from the street, the traffic, the crowds, the dirt and litter, people coming into the shop full of moans and complaints...'

Kate sighed deeply. 'You worked in the post office at Tregarron too, Rose.' She hadn't realised that Rose had become so disenchanted with city life.

'But it was different, Mam! It ... it wasn't all the time and the people there were different too.'

'It was summer then, Rose. It wouldn't be the same place in the winter,' Kate mused.

Rose summoned up as much courage as she could. 'Mam, can I ... can I go back, please?'

Kate stared into the flames. She didn't want Rose to go away but she didn't want her to stay here pining either. Tregarron offered a very different kind of life to the one Rose now lived but she obviously wanted that. What could she say? There were all kinds of problems to be overcome. Rose would have to find work to support herself – Gwen couldn't possibly be expected to keep her. But what could she do? As far as she knew, apart from maybe working in a shop, there were few opportunities. She might be fortunate enough to get a job in a shop in Denbigh but transport would be a problem. 'I'll have to think about it, Rose. It's a huge decision to make. It would be a very big ... change for you and for me. I'd miss you so much and I know Iris would too.'

'But you *will* think about it at least, Mam?' Rose pleaded, thankful that her mother hadn't dismissed the possibility of her return out of hand. If only she could make her mother understand just how much she missed the tranquillity, the open spaces, and the slower pace of life that had afforded her time ... time to herself.

'I'll think about it, Rose, I promise,' Kate reiterated, thinking she would have to discuss it with Iris too, for if Rose were to go back Iris would have to run the shop by herself. Could she cope with that?

Chapter Thirteen

Kate had given the matter a great deal of thought over the following days and she had watched Rose closely, noticing for the first time that the girl didn't eat very much and seemed very listless and disspirited at the end of each day. She had been so wrapped up in her own grief and the worry of everyday life that she hadn't realised how unhappy her youngest daughter was, which disturbed her. She felt guilty and upset at the same time. Guilty that she hadn't noticed and upset that Rose wanted to leave both home and family.

'Mam, you've not been listening to a word I've been saying,' Iris said sharply. She'd been outlining what extras she intended to stock in the shop for Christmas and had been seeking Kate's approval. Charlie was out with Florence and Rose had gone up, saying she would have an early night but would read for a while.

'I'm sorry, luv. I was thinking about Rose,' Kate replied.

'Has she said anything to you, Mam? I know there's something bothering her but I don't know what it is. I can hardly get a word out of her these days.'

'She wants to go back to Tregarron. I asked her myself what was wrong. She's not been herself since–'

140

'None of us has,' Iris interrupted.

'I know but, but lately she's been so quiet and ... down and she eats like a bird. I just didn't realise that she was missing the place so much until she told me and the last thing I need is for her to be pining.'

Iris frowned. That was true: Mam had enough to worry about without Rose moping. 'I know she's not happy working in the shop, Mam. She won't make an effort to hold a conversation with anyone and you know how much the customers love a good gossip. What did you say to her about Tregarron?'

'That I'd think about it and I have been, Iris. I hate to see her so miserable but if she goes she'll have to find a job to support herself and that's not going to be easy. And, as I reminded her, she was there in the summer; it might be a very different place in winter. Too quiet, too isolated.'

'And she wasn't grieving for Da then either,' Iris added.

Kate nodded. 'If she went, Iris, how would you feel about it? You'd be in the shop on your own. Would you be able to manage at busy times?'

'Oh, that wouldn't bother me, Mam, of course I'll manage. You ran it on your own and really there are times when Rose is a bit ... superfluous, but coming up to Christmas I might need her help.'

Again Kate nodded. 'It does get busy.' She sighed heavily. She wasn't looking forward to Christmas this year. She would miss Bill even more.

Iris smiled. 'I just hope there won't be too many

like Mary Duncan or we'll be open until midnight.'

Kate had come to a decision of sorts. 'I'll write to Gwen and see what she has to say about it. She might not want Rose there permanently; just visiting for a few months was a very different thing. Now, don't mention anything to Rose.'

'I won't, I promise.'

'If Gwen doesn't mind and we can sort something out job-wise and I decide to let her go it won't be until early next year. I won't leave you to struggle through Christmas on your own and besides ... this will be the first Christmas without your da and I'd like you all around me as I know it's going to be difficult.'

Iris reached over and took her hand. 'We'll get through it, Mam – together.'

Kate smiled at her. 'We'll have to, luv. Now, what were you saying about stocking holly and mistletoe?'

Nearly two weeks later Charlie again called to see Mr Cookson on his way home from work. He'd left it a little longer to give the man more time. This time his appearance at closing time was met with a warmer welcome.

'Charlie, just the lad! I've managed to get you a real bargain and it's a beauty.' He went into the back of the shop and reappeared with a small leather pouch.

Charlie leaned eagerly forward as a ring was drawn from the pouch and placed on the counter. It certainly was, or had been, a very expensive ring. The centre stone was a square-cut ruby surrounded by diamonds and the gold shoulders that held the stones were intricately and delicately carved with leaves. He whistled.

'That is certainly a beautiful ring, Mr Cookson! I bet it cost a good deal more than six guineas when it was new.'

'A great deal more, I'd say. I put the word out amongst my contacts and this came up. Belonged to a lady who is finding it difficult to maintain her lifestyle on what her late husband left her, so I was told. Of course I've given you the discount I promised, so for you, Charlie, it's six guineas.'

Charlie picked it up and examined it more closely. Yes, it was just what he'd wanted. 'Florence will be delighted, I'm sure, and I'm certainly very, very grateful. I'll get the money tomorrow and call in on the way home, if that's all right with you?'

The older man nodded and returned the ring to the pouch. 'I'll give it a good clean and put it in a proper ring box and you'll never know it's not brand new.'

Charlie was about to express his thanks when the man delved under the counter, searching for something.

'I saw this the other day and it took my fancy. Would you give it to your mother for me as a mark of respect? Tell her I thought that seeing as now she's one of us – so to speak – it's rather appropriate.' He held out a small gold brooch. It was circular and inside the circle were three balls of gold, the symbol of the pawnbroker's trade.

'That's very kind of you and I'm sure she'll appreciate it. I'll see you tomorrow evening then and thanks again,' Charlie promised as he left.

He was delighted with the ring – even Mrs Taylor couldn't look down her nose at it. It looked expensive and it had been. Sixteen or seventeen guineas he deduced, remembering the rings he'd seen in Boodles that were way beyond his means – and no one could cast aspersions on that amount of money.

He didn't give the brooch to Kate until just before she went to bed, his sisters having already gone up.

She was surprised as he held out the little box. 'What's this, Charlie?'

'A gift, Mam. Go on, open it,' he instructed. He'd been tempted to keep it and give it to her as a Christmas present but had thought better of it because when he brought the ring home tomorrow he wanted to show it to her and she'd ask where he'd got it. He was very proud of having obtained such a great bargain.

Kate opened it. 'Charlie, it's lovely! But it's not my birthday or anything,' she protested. He'd never bought her anything as expensive as this in the past, not even for birthdays.

'Mr Cookson gave it to me and told me it caught his eye and that he thought it was an appropriate gift for you, seeing as now you're "in the trade".'

Kate was puzzled. 'Mr Cookson? Who's Mr Cookson?'

'You know, that big pawnbroker's on Scotland Road, Mam.'

Kate was even more confused. 'But I don't know the man! I mean I know of him but I don't think I've ever met him, although I seem to remember we had a sympathy card from him.'

'He knew Da,' Charlie said.

She nodded; of course he would have known Bill. 'But when did you see him?'

'I called in a couple of weeks ago. I asked him about buying a ring. An engagement ring.'

Kate smiled. 'I've been waiting for you to tell me that you're going to ask Florence to marry you. All this scrimping and saving, it had to be for something.'

'I'm going to ask her father for his permission at the weekend. I'll have the ring then and you should see it, Mam. It's really stunning. Mr Cookson got it for me and he's giving me a discount too. I think it's because he thought well of Da, but he's letting me have it for six guineas.'

'Six guineas! You're spending *that* much on a ring for Florence!' Kate was astounded. Her own engagement ring had only cost a fraction of that and it wasn't a ring to be sneezed at either.

'Well, I couldn't give her something with stones so small that you'd have to get a magnifying glass to see them, now could I? New, I'm sure it would have cost more like sixteen guineas.'

Kate was even more astounded by that amount. 'It's not stolen, Charlie, is it?'

He was outraged. '*Mam!* What a thing to say! Cookson's don't deal in stolen goods, you should know that. They're very, very respectable. No, someone he knows bought it from a lady who has fallen on hard times. Stolen! Honestly!'

She nodded, thinking he was right. Mr Cookson wouldn't fence jewellery any more than she would. 'It was just my immediate reaction to the amount, Charlie. It's second-hand then?'

He nodded. 'You've got to agree, Mam, it's great value for money. Now, don't go saying anything to our Rose or Iris, especially Iris. I don't want her to spoil the surprise for Florence. I'm going to ask her at Christmas.'

Kate nodded, thinking he did have a good business head on his shoulders but wasn't buying a second-hand ring taking it a bit too far? She hoped Florence wouldn't be disappointed.

Charlie took the opportunity to ask Edward Taylor for a few minutes of his time after supper was over; he often had supper with them on a Saturday now. Florence was helping her mother with the coffee.

'Come on into the living room – or "parlour" as my dear old mam always insisted on calling it,' Edward informed Charlie as they left the dining room.

'I won't take up much of your time; we can't let the ladies think we've deserted them altogether. As you know, sir, Florence and I have been courting now for over six months and ... and I'd like your permission to marry her. I don't mean right away, it will be some time before I can find a decent house to rent, but I'd like to ask her at Christmas.'

Edward nodded slowly. He'd been expecting this. It was quite obvious that his daughter loved the lad, despite the fact that Ethel didn't consider him the ideal choice. 'You love her and will take good care of her?'

'Oh, yes! You can be certain of that, sir. You have my word. And she'll have the best I can afford,' Charlie assured him earnestly.

'Then I've no objections, Charlie. I like you. You work hard, you're honest, you don't waste your money. I admired the way you handled everything when your father was killed: that showed strength of character and reliability. And I've noticed that you ... respect Florence.'

'Oh, I do,' Charlie replied gravely. 'I ... I hope it won't seem presumptuous, but I've already bought the ring.' He brought out the small black box from his pocket and handed it to her father.

Edward Taylor opened it and was very surprised indeed.

'This is beautiful, Charlie! It must have cost you a fair bit?'

Charlie felt very pleased with himself. 'As I said, only the best I can afford will do for Florence.'

Edward nodded. The lad must have saved every farthing he could get his hands on to buy a ring like this. 'Well, I have to say I'm sure she will be delighted, Charlie.' He handed the box back. 'Now, we'd better go and have our coffee before Ethel comes in and demands to know what's going on.'

'You won't say anything to Florence, sir, will you? I want to surprise her at Christmas,' Charlie asked.

'Not a word,' Edward Taylor promised although he thought he should forewarn Ethel.

'I wish you'd discussed it with me first, Edward. You know I have ... reservations,' Ethel said with some annoyance after her husband imparted the news to her later that night.

'There wasn't time, Ethel, and he wants his proposal to be a surprise. He's going to ask her at Christmas and he's bought her a very expensive ring, so if I'd fetched you in to "discuss it" it would have looked very odd. Anyway it's traditional to ask the girl's father, not both her parents,' he finished irritably. He thought Ethel's 'reservations' were groundless.

'That's a very old-fashioned view to take, Edward,' she retorted. 'Florence is our only child and I want the best for her.'

He sighed deeply. 'So do I, Ethel, and it's obvious that Florence loves him. I like the lad, he's honest, steady and reliable, he's assured me that he'll take care of her and that she'll have the best he can afford, and judging by that ring I don't think we've much to worry about. The only thing you've got against young Charlie is the fact that he's neither a bank manager nor holds some other lofty position, but he's got ambitions. Surely, Ethel, you have to agree with me? You've got to know him better over the months – he's been here for supper often enough.'

Ethel bit her lip. Everything her husband said was correct but she just couldn't take to the lad. It was just a gut feeling she had – a mother's intuition perhaps. In her opinion he didn't seem to care as much for Florence as her daughter did for him. 'Of course I've been able to get to know him, Edward, but, well ... sometimes I think he could be more affectionate towards Florence. It's as if he's trying to impress us so much that he isn't...' Ethel was struggling to find the right words. '...isn't being himself. I wonder does Florence really *know* him? Does she feel that he truly loves her?'

Edward was exasperated. 'I just don't understand you at all, Ethel. If he was all over her like a rash you'd be horrified. Of course he loves her, he told me so, but he also respects her. He doesn't always have to be gazing into her eyes or kissing her. What more do you want, for God's sake? I think he'll make an excellent husband and that she'll be very happy with him and I've given my permission so let there be an end to all this "reservations" nonsense!'

Ethel Taylor pressed her lips tightly together. It was useless to argue with him when he was in this mood but she was far from happy at the prospect of having Charlie Mundy as a son-in-law.

Chapter Fourteen

As Christmas approached Kate was busier than she'd been for a while as people tried desperately to raise money to bring a bit of festive cheer into hard and difficult lives, even if it meant pawning their small treasures and even everyday items. 'Let's hope the New Year brings you better luck,' she said repeatedly to her customers, thinking that surely things *had* to get better soon. At least all the trouble in Ireland was over now that the Anglo-Irish Treaty had been signed, creating the Irish Free State. Maybe next year all the industrial unrest would be sorted out and there would be more jobs for those who desperately needed them. She'd had a letter from Gwen who had written that she'd given the matter of Rose's return a lot of thought. Of course she didn't want Kate to be parted from her youngest daughter and hoped she hadn't influenced Rose in any way, albeit unconsciously, but if Rose was so unhappy now in Liverpool then she would be quite prepared to give her a home. Kate knew she would be well looked after and of course Rose could return at any time if she changed her mind. The matter of a job was the stumbling block, of course. She couldn't offer Rose full-time employment in the post office, there were rules and regulations and there wasn't the call for an assistant postmistress in such a small village. The local shops had no vacancies and were not likely to have any either. She promised to ask in Denbigh but didn't hold out much hope; even if there were jobs Rose would have to cycle twenty miles each day and often the weather was atrocious and she was fearful that Rose's health wouldn't stand up to such rigours. But she urged Kate not to despair; she would go on trying to find work for Rose.

Kate had decided to say nothing to Rose and although Rose was aware that she'd had a reply from Gwen, for she'd seen the postmark on the envelope, she hadn't mentioned the matter again.

Iris hadn't had time to worry about her sister as the days seemed to fly by and they were much busier in the shop. She'd asked Tom if he was doing anything special for the festive season and confided that she would find it hard this year, without her father.

'No, nothing out of the ordinary. Da always

goes for a drink on Christmas Eve and Mam is always busy with the preparations. Our Lily and Madge will probably be going dancing though,' he'd informed her. 'Would you like to go somewhere special on Christmas Eve, Iris? Take your mind off ... things.'

She'd smiled but had shaken her head. 'We'll both be dead on our feet, Tom, but thanks. And Mam will be busy too, what with the shop and the preparations for Christmas dinner. Rose and I will help out as much as we can, of course. I haven't a clue what our Charlie is doing. Going to Florence's, I suppose.'

'Would you mind if I called in then? I wouldn't stay long, no more than an hour, but I'd like to see you, Iris.'

She'd nodded. 'I'd like to see you too, Tom, on our first Christmas together.'

'I'll call about eight o'clock then and maybe on Christmas Day we could go for a walk somewhere – to walk off all that food?'

'At least there is more food in the shops these days. During the war we could hardly get anything,' she'd replied, thinking that even though she would miss her da terribly at least she would have Tom to help her get through the day. Her poor mother wouldn't have such support, but she and Tom would do whatever they could to make it bearable for Kate.

On Christmas Eve Iris and Rose finally closed up at six o'clock; both were tired but Iris was looking forward to seeing Tom later. Kate had closed an hour earlier having decided that no one would

151

come in now. A few women had come in in the afternoon, wanting a few shillings to spend in St John's Market later that night when things were sold off cheap. She'd already plucked the goose, which was resting on the marble slab in the pantry, and intended to prepare the vegetables later, after supper. Iris had put them aside that morning after Tom had dropped all the produce off.

'Well, that's it for two whole days and I can't say I'm sorry,' Iris announced as she took off her brown shop coat and hung it in the scullery.

'I'll never understand why people leave things until the last minute. I'm worn out,' Rose added.

'Shortage of money, Rose. They get better bargains at the end of the day and they have to make what little they've got stretch a very long way. I know for a fact that Ada, Sal and Mary Duncan are going down to St John's at ten o'clock,' Kate replied, shaking her head. 'It will be midnight before they get home and then they'll still have things to do and you know what half the men around here are like on Christmas Eve, falling in dead drunk at all hours. I always thanked God that your poor da was teetotal, God rest him.'

Rose felt the tears prick her eyes. She was dreading tomorrow. There would be no seeing her father's face light up at the little gifts they'd bought him; no watching him as he presided over the table and carved the goose. 'I know it's a terrible thing to say but ... but in a way I'll be glad when Christmas is over.'

Iris nodded. 'I know what you mean, Rose, but we'll just have to try to make the best of it.'

Rose didn't reply, wondering what Christmas in Tregarron would be like. She was certain that there would be no drunken singing, shouting or fighting as there would be in this neighbourhood.

'Tom's calling later, Mam. Just for an hour. You don't mind, do you?' Iris asked, thinking her mother looked pale, tired and a bit tearful.

'No, I like the lad, Iris. He might well help to cheer us all up.'

Charlie came into the kitchen wearing his good suit, a heavy overcoat and carrying the new trilby hat he'd bought. He'd justified the extravagance by telling himself it made him look more respectable and as tonight he would – he hoped – officially become Edward Taylor's prospective son-in-law, a trilby was more suitable to that position than a cloth cap.

'You're done up like a dog's dinner! I know it's Christmas but a trilby? What's wrong with your cap?' Iris asked.

Kate smiled at her son, thinking he looked very smart indeed. 'It's an important night for Charlie. Go on, I think you can tell them now, son.'

'Tell us what?' Iris demanded.

'That I'm going to ask Florence to marry me tonight, before supper. I've bought the ring already,' Charlie revealed, drawing the box from the inside pocket of his jacket.

'Really? Oh, Charlie, can we see it?' Rose cried eagerly.

'I hope she accepts then,' Iris muttered under her breath although she knew her friend would. Florence had been dropping hints for weeks now.

They both gasped in astonishment at the ring

and Kate and Charlie exchanged happy glances.

'It's ... magnificent, Charlie! I've never seen anything like it,' Rose cried, thinking that Florence would surely be delighted.

'That must have cost a pretty penny. Now I understand why you've been acting like Scrooge for months,' Iris added, thinking that Rose was right. She'd never seen anything as fine either.

'It's true value is about sixteen guineas but I got it for six from Cookson's and not even her mam can look down her nose at it. Not when it's obviously an expensive ring,' Charlie announced proudly.

Rose thought this was very astute of him but Iris frowned. It seemed to her that it was more important to her brother that the Taylors were suitably impressed by this ostentatious ring than that Florence was pleased. She wondered how her friend would feel about having a second-hand ring. Cookson's was a big pawnbroking establishment and she hoped the name wasn't embossed on the inside of the box. Well, she wasn't going to mention that fact to Florence. She would sooner have something cheaper, smaller, less showy but chosen especially to delight her, rather than to impress her family and friends. That's if of course Tom ever asked her to marry him. She sincerely hoped he would, even though they'd only been courting a short while. She wouldn't even mind not having a ring at all. A plain gold wedding band would be sufficient.

Charlie felt very proud and confident as he walked up Cedar Grove that cold, frosty evening. In many windows brightly decorated Christmas trees, illuminated by dozens of tiny candles, could be glimpsed. Tasteful wreaths of entwined holly and evergreens were attached to front doors and the occasional burst of muffled laughter could be heard but little else. There were no drunks hanging on to the lamp posts or staggering along roaring carols in tuneless voices; no crowds hanging around outside the pub doors being closely watched by burly coppers, on hand for the first sign of trouble. No scruffy kids still out, begging passers-by for a penny. This was the kind of neighbourhood he wanted to live in and tonight would mark the beginning of his journey to that end.

Florence opened the door to him, dressed in a new midnight-blue velvet dress embroidered around the neckline with silver bugle beads. A headband of the same material, similarly embellished, encircled her shiny loosely waving hair, which she'd recently had cut short. He'd liked it at once; it suited her and made her look more grown up and elegant but he'd been surprised that it had been at her mother's suggestion.

'Charlie, don't you look smart! I do like the hat, it really suits you. Come in.' She took his coat and hat and hung them in the small cloakroom next to the front door that boasted stained-glass door panels.

Charlie lingered in the hall, noticing the display of Christmas roses and holly arranged in a vase on the table beside the telephone. 'Florence, before we join your parents, can I talk to you? There's ... there's something special I have to ask.'

Florence blushed as she felt excitement rush

through her. Oh, this had to be *it!* She'd been hoping and praying for months now that he'd ask her to marry him. 'Of course, come into Dad's little study.'

She ushered him into the small room and he glanced around, never having been in here before. It wasn't fancy; there was a desk half covered with papers, a chair and shelves on which reposed files and ledgers. A fire burned in the hearth, heavy velvet curtains covered the window and an electric reading lamp on the desk gave the room a cosy but subdued feel. This was obviously the hub of Edward Taylor's business, he mused.

'What ... what is it, Charlie?' Florence asked tentatively, her eyes cast demurely down but her flushed cheeks betraying her feelings.

Charlie took the box from his pocket and reached and took her hand. 'Florence, you know how I feel about you and we've been courting now for a while and so I'm asking you if you'll marry me? I have your father's permission.'

Florence raised her eyes and he was delighted and relieved to see the happiness shining in them. 'Oh, Charlie! Of course I'll marry you. I love you so much, you know that,' she cried. This was the happiest day of her life!

'I bought this for you, Florence, I hope you like it. I know we'll be happy.'

Florence gasped as he took the ring and slid it on to her finger. 'Charlie! It's ... gorgeous! Oh, I'm the luckiest girl in the world and I'm so very, very happy!' She threw her arms around his neck and kissed him. It was true, she thought, and he obviously loved her a great deal to have spent so much on her ring.

'Shall we go and break the news now?' he asked a few seconds later, gently disentangling himself.

'Oh, yes!' Florence cried joyfully.

Her parents were sitting beside the fire, her mother holding a crystal glass containing sherry, her father's a measure of finest Scotch whisky.

'We … we've got something to tell you. We're engaged, look at the gorgeous ring Charlie's given me,' Florence announced, holding out her left hand.

Edward immediately got to his feet and shook Charlie warmly by the hand. 'Congratulations! I didn't think for a moment she'd turn you down, Charlie.'

Charlie grinned at him. He was almost one of the family now, he thought smugly.

Ethel Taylor had also risen and had kissed Florence, trying her best to feel happy for her daughter, who was so obviously delighted. She was also quite astonished by the ring Charlie had bought. At least if he rose to a more affluent position in life – and she hoped he would for Florence's sake – Florence would have a ring she wouldn't be embarrassed to wear in public. 'Congratulations! It's beautiful, Florence,' she said, echoing her husband.

'Well, I think this calls for something a bit special to drink and in anticipation of the happy event I purchased a bottle of champagne. It's outside in the yard, in a bucket – chilling. I didn't want to put it in the larder in case I spoiled the surprise,' Edward announced.

157

'Oh, really, Edward,' Ethel laughed although wondering why the yard? She couldn't see what was wrong with the larder. Her daughter never ventured in there, and she had known that Charlie was popping the question this evening, so there had been no question of the surprise being spoiled. 'I'll get the glasses,' she announced, following her husband out but going into the dining room and to the china cabinet.

The table was already laid and if she said so herself it looked lovely: tasteful and yet festive at the same time. She doubted there would be a starched, lace-edged cloth, solid silver cutlery, fine bone-china dishes, cut-crystal glasses and a centrepiece of a thick church candle, the base decorated with holly and red velvet ribbon, on the table in the Mundys' home. She frowned. Well, they were officially engaged now so all she could do was try to put a brave face on it and pray that unless something happened to make Florence change her mind, it would all turn out well in the end. It certainly was an expensive ring he'd bought, she thought, and then stopped in the act of taking out the glasses. That ring! There was something familiar about it, she was sure. If she could just get a closer look at it she might remember. She shook herself mentally. Perhaps she was wrong. She should hurry: they'd be waiting for the champagne.

Tom had arrived on time and bearing a bottle of port. 'I thought a drop of this might be welcome, Mrs M.,' he explained as he handed Kate the bottle.

'That was very thoughtful of you, Tom. I think we could all do with a drop of "cheer". Iris, get some glasses.' Kate smiled, thinking how Tom's presence always seemed to lift her spirits.

Iris too smiled at him, glad he had come for his presence had lightened the atmosphere.

'I left Mam peeling a mountain of spuds that she's going to put into a bucket of cold water but I promised I'd do the carrots and sprouts when I get back. Da won't be in from the pub until later and neither will the girls. It's all go, Mrs M., isn't it, at Christmas?'

Kate smiled at him again. He'd taken to calling her 'Mrs M.' of late and she quite liked it. 'You can say that again, Tom.'

'I take it Charlie is out celebrating with Florence?' Tom enquired.

'He's having supper with her parents and they've got something to celebrate indeed, Tom. They're getting engaged. At least I hope they are although I can't see Florence turning him down,' Kate announced as she handed round the glasses.

'Are they? Well, that's something to drink to. So, she's going to be your sister-in-law after all, Iris.' Tom raised his glass and Iris nodded.

'And you should have seen the ring he's bought her,' Rose put in. 'It's gorgeous and very expensive.'

'But not new,' Iris added but, catching a glance from her mother, went on, 'not that that matters. Florence will love it and I'll love having her as my sister-in-law.'

'When's the wedding then?' Tom asked, not missing the note of disparagement in Iris's voice.

159

'I don't think our Charlie's got a date in mind yet,' Kate said as she sipped her drink. 'But I don't expect it to be any time soon. He'll have to save up hard again if he wants to find a house in a decent area to rent and to furnish. He can't expect a girl like Florence to live in a neighbourhood like this, even though she's far from being a snob.'

'Perhaps they could live with her parents? They've got a big house, haven't they?' Tom suggested. It wasn't uncommon.

Kate shook her head. 'They have but I can't see her mother being happy about that idea. I still think Mrs Taylor would have liked Florence to marry someone with a better job and better prospects.'

'You can't choose who you fall in love with, Mrs M.,' Tom said seriously, looking pointedly at Iris.

'That's true enough,' Kate replied, smiling. The lad was obviously in love with Iris and she with him and she approved. She'd be happy if they too were to become engaged but on what he earned they might well have to start their married life here with her. There would be room, she thought, for she'd decided to let Rose go back to Tregarron next month. She'd received a note from Gwen that morning, brief and to the point. Rose could start work as a housemaid at Plas Idris in the New Year. Miss Olivia Rhys-Pritchard had been very amenable to the idea when it had been mentioned by Mrs Mathews, the housekeeper, with whom she'd had a word. It appeared that finding good, reliable staff was getting to be almost impossible.

Later Tom reluctantly bade them goodnight and as Iris showed him out through the shop he stopped and took her in his arms.

'I'll see you tomorrow afternoon. I'll bring your present,' he promised.

'I hope you haven't got me something too expensive, Tom. I've only bought you–'

'Don't tell me! Surprise me! And no, it's not expensive – much as I'd like it to be.'

She smiled at him. 'I'm not Florence.'

He became serious as he kissed her forehead. 'I know. I ... I couldn't afford much of a ring, but...'

'Tom, what are you saying?' she asked, wondering if she'd heard right or if she had misconstrued his words.

'I'm trying to say that I love you and that if you'll have me ... we could be very happy together.' He bent and kissed her.

Iris clung to him, feeling such a surge of joy wash over her that it made her feel dizzy. 'Of course I'll have you,' she whispered when she was able.

'I can't promise you much, Iris. My wage is little more than a pittance and although I'm grateful for it there's no prospect of me getting anything else that would pay more. So it might well be years before I can afford ... anything, but I just wanted to let you know and sort of make you mine.'

'I *am* yours. There's never been anyone else and I don't mind waiting. I don't even want an engagement ring, never mind one as showy as Florence's. It's *you* I love and want to spend my life with. I don't need a ring to prove that.'

He kissed her again. He hadn't meant to ask her yet, it had just happened – probably prompted by the news of Charlie's engagement – but he was glad now he had.

When she at last drew away from him she smiled, utter bliss shining in her eyes. 'I don't think we should say anything to Mam yet though, it might all be a bit too much for her now. First our Charlie and now me, and Rose wanting to go off again, back to Tregarron and for good this time.'

Tom nodded. 'I think you're right. Let's keep it our secret for a while.'

Iris hugged him; she could hardly believe it. 'I'll see you tomorrow.'

'You certainly will, Iris. I love you. And Happy Christmas.'

When she'd closed the door after him she leaned against it, her hands pressed to her cheeks. They were going to get married – one day! Oh, she never thought she could feel this happy even though she missed her father so much. It was such a pity that Da had never met Tom – she was sure he would have liked him. Somehow she felt that he was looking down on her with joy and approval. This was going to be a much happier Christmas now than she had ever envisaged.

The day had proved to be far happier for them all, Kate had thought thankfully as she put her feet up at last on Christmas Night. Of course it had been painful to sit down to the meal without Bill, she'd had a hard time keeping back the tears, but Charlie had taken their minds off the situation by relaying the events of Christmas Eve at Florence's. He'd been full of Florence's joy that he'd proposed and how delighted she was with her ring, the real champagne her father had bought because he too was pleased, and how even her mother had at last seemed happy to accept the fact. He'd described how beautiful the table had looked and said the meal had been truly great, with roast beef and venison (which he'd never tasted before) and the trimmings, followed by a fancy meringue dessert and fresh fruit. To finish Florence's father had poured him a brandy and given him a cigar. Oh, it had indeed been a truly splendid occasion and Mrs Taylor had invited them all for supper on New Year's Eve. That, however, was something Kate was rather apprehensive about but she said nothing, realising that she would have to meet Charlie's future in-laws sooner or later.

Tom had called after they'd finished the dinner and he and Iris had gone for a walk after she'd opened her present. She'd exclaimed in delight at the lovely scarf he'd bought her, bemoaning the fact that she'd only got him socks, which were very boring and unimaginative. He'd protested that they were very useful, especially these cold mornings.

Rose had been a little quiet and Kate had caught her staring into space on occasions looking sad and wistful, but she'd been delighted with the novels both she and Iris had bought her and when Iris and Tom had gone, Rose had settled down to enjoy the one called *Treasured Dreams*, which had been Iris's choice.

Later that evening Kate decided she would put Rose out of her misery and despite feeling exhausted and loath to stir from the comfort of her armchair, she summoned up the energy to put the kettle on.

'Mam, sit down, I'll do it. You've done enough for one day,' Iris urged.

'It's just that I feel a cup of tea would be nice while we discuss your future, Rose,' Kate persisted, getting out the tea caddy.

Iris looked surprised. It seemed rather late to start discussing this but she said nothing.

Rose looked at her mother hopefully but a little frisson of fear passed through her. 'What ... what have you decided, Mam?'

'You know I had a letter from Gwen a few weeks ago, Rose.'

Rose nodded. She had so much wanted to ask what Gwen's letter had said but had been afraid to.

'Then I had another note yesterday morning,' Kate went on.

'And?' Iris asked.

'And Gwen is happy to give you a home, Rose, and she's managed to find you a job too.'

Rose felt relief wash over her. 'Oh, Mam!'

'She had a word with Mrs Mathews, and Miss Olivia Rhys-Pritchard is willing to take you on as a housemaid,' Kate informed her daughter.

'You mean she's going into service? Won't she have to live in?' Iris queried, wondering if Rose would like the idea. It certainly wouldn't suit her and Rose had hated being a chambermaid in the hotel. Everyone knew the hours were long, the

164

pay terrible, the time off almost non-existent and the work usually thankless and often heavy: all reasons why girls were not finding it very attractive these days, especially when they could earn more, work fewer hours and have more freedom working in shops and factories, where they were not subjected to the rigid hierarchy that existed in such households.

'No, Gwen told Mrs Mathews that she would prefer to have Rose live "out" and hinted that it would save them money as they would only have to pay Rose a wage, they wouldn't have to keep her as well. Apparently they have one other housemaid, a parlourmaid and a scullery maid to assist the cook. And of course the housekeeper and a butler and one footman.'

'So, Rose and one other housemaid will be expected to do all the housework? Didn't you tell me the house is huge, Rose?' Iris asked.

Rose nodded. It wasn't what she had expected but she had to have a job. She didn't mind housework but she knew it would be hard work, possibly as hard as being a chambermaid at Black's, and she felt a little apprehensive, but to be able to return to Tregarron would be compensation enough.

'Gwen has asked in various shops but there was nothing to be had and besides, both she and I doubted that cycling twenty miles a day in all weather would be good for you, Rose.'

Rose pushed the thought of the number of rooms at Plas Idris to the back of her mind together with the fact that she'd never been in service before. 'I won't mind working at Plas Idris,

Mam, as long as I can go home to Aunty Gwen each night.'

Privately Iris wondered whether cleaning a house as big as that plus cycling two miles from and to the village would be any easier than cycling twenty miles a day to Denbigh to work in a shop but she said nothing for Rose was looking far more animated than she had for months.

'So, I've decided to let you go, Rose, as long as you're happy to work there,' Kate concluded.

Rose got up and threw her arms around her mother. 'Oh, Mam! I'm so happy and thank you.'

Kate managed a tired smile. 'You know you can always come back if you want to.'

'I know, but I'm sure I'll be as happy there as I was last time. When...?'

'The second week in January, Gwen has told them you'll be starting. You can go over a few days before to settle in with Gwen, get your uniform and have your duties explained to you. That will give me time to get your things ready too,' Kate added.

'Time too to go to supper at Florence's on New Year's Eve,' Iris added, wondering if, after Rose had gone, she should tell her mother that she and Tom Morrissey had come to an understanding.

That night as she pulled the quilt up around her ears Rose felt happy for the first time in months. She was going back to Tregarron, to the tranquillity, to the cosy comfort of Gwen's cottage Y-Bythin and to the somewhat faded splendour of Plas Idris and its beautiful grounds, which she was certain would look just as lovely in winter as they had in summer. She determined that she would not complain no matter how hard she found the work; it was only housework, after all, just on a bigger scale. From what she remembered of Mrs Mathews, she hoped she'd find her fair and considerate. In about ten days she would be leaving Liverpool for ever but apart from leaving her mother and Iris, she would have no regrets.

The day after Boxing Day when Charlie arrived at Florence's for supper he thought he detected a certain coolness in her mother's manner towards him but it wasn't until the meal was over that he became fully and embarrassingly aware of the reason.

'Everyone has greatly admired Florence's ring,' Ethel remarked. 'Where did you say you bought it, Charlie, I've forgotten?' she asked casually.

Charlie was a little taken aback. 'I ... don't think I mentioned where I'd bought it.'

Ethel pursed her lips, ignoring the slightly curious look her husband was directing at her. 'You see, when I first saw it I thought it looked ... familiar,' she continued, watching him closely. She noticed the wary expression that crept into his eyes.

'Familiar? How can that be?' Florence asked, looking puzzled.

Ethel ignored her daughter. 'This morning I was speaking to my Aunt Emily on the telephone, something I often do as she's my late mother's sister and was widowed last year, and she was telling me how hard she is finding it to live on what Uncle Edwin left her, so much so that recently and regretfully she had to sell some of her jewellery – and then I remembered where I'd seen that ring before. I recalled it so clearly because the leaves that decorate the shoulders are ivy leaves and Uncle Edwin had it specially engraved for her, because her middle name is Ivy. She confirmed that it was one of the pieces she'd sold and for a fraction of its original price. And you bought it, Charlie, for Florence. You bought her a second-hand ring!'

Charlie's cheeks flushed with humiliation. 'I ... I only wanted the best for Florence.'

'You consider a second-hand ring to be "the best"?' Ethel's voice was full of scorn.

Florence looked from her mother to Charlie, biting her lip in confusion and disappointment.

'I ... I couldn't afford the prices they were asking in the big jewellers in town!' Charlie cried, seeing the hurt in Florence's eyes and feeling annoyed and a little guilty.

'So just where did you buy it?' Ethel demanded.

'In Cookson's. It's a very respectable establishment,' Charlie replied grimly.

'It's also a very big pawnbroker's on Scotland Road!' Ethel informed her bewildered daughter. 'And I think it's extremely underhand and ... penny-pinching of you, Charlie, to try to pass it off as a new and very expensive ring!'

Florence couldn't hide her feelings. 'Did ... did you get it in a ... pawnshop, Charlie?'

Charlie's humiliation was complete. 'Florence, I wanted to get you the very best ring I could afford, truly I did! I ... I asked Mr Cookson, who was an associate of my da's, to look for something for me. The rings in Boodles were way beyond my means...'

'So, you actually went out of your way to find a secondhand ring at a bargain price that you could pass off as new and very expensive without Florence ever knowing – in fact without any of us knowing! I think that is ... utterly despicable! And it makes me wonder what else you have been hiding from us?' Ethel added darkly.

Florence was now on the verge of tears and Charlie felt that he could quite cheerfully throttle her mother. 'Florence, I never intended to deceive you, I swear I didn't! I wouldn't do that! It's just as I've said, I wanted something special for you, I wanted the best, but I just couldn't afford it! I ... I thought that this way I could give you a ring you'd be proud to wear and even though it's not new you have to admit that it is a beautiful ring! I had no intention of hurting or disappointing you. That's the last thing I wanted.'

Edward had remained silent throughout the exchange but his anger had been growing and now he got to his feet, his expression grim. 'Ethel, I'd like a word – in private, if you please! And I think we should leave Florence and Charlie alone for a few minutes.'

Ethel hesitated for a second but as Edward took her arm firmly she had no alternative but to let him lead her into the hall.

'Just what do you think you are playing at, Ethel?' he demanded when he'd closed the dining-room door behind him.

'Well, isn't it obvious now, Edward? He's been deceiving us!'

'Don't talk rubbish, Ethel! Florence loves him and he loves her and he wanted the best for her but he couldn't afford it! I wouldn't call that "deception".'

'If he loves her he wouldn't let her think he'd given her a new and expensive ring!' Ethel retorted.

'He never said it was new, we all just assumed it was.'

'And we would never have found out if I hadn't thought I recognised it!' Ethel shot back.

'That was unfortunate but does it really matter that it's not new? He just wanted to please her. He was honest and open enough to admit that he couldn't afford a ring from the likes of Boodles. Well, neither could I when I bought your engagement ring. You were happy enough with that small diamond I bought, I seem to remember. I think this was all totally unnecessary, Ethel, and I hope you're happy now that you've upset our daughter. I just pray this doesn't cause a rift between them.'

It wasn't the reaction Ethel had expected and she glared at her husband. 'Well, I would have expected you at least to agree with me!'

'No, I don't, Ethel. You've caused a storm in a teacup over nothing of importance. Now, we'd better go back and see what we can do to patch things up.'

'I don't consider it to be "nothing" and I'm going to bed. All this has given me a headache!' Ethel snapped, heading determinedly towards the stairs, leaving her husband standing staring after her in annoyance.

As soon as her parents had left the room Florence had turned to Charlie. 'Why didn't you tell me it wasn't new, Charlie?'

He put his arms around her. 'I'm sorry ... I ... I don't suppose I thought much about it, Florence. I mean I didn't think you would get so upset. I really meant what I said. I wanted you to have something very special, I wanted the best for you but I just couldn't afford sixteen or seventeen guineas. I've been saving every halfpenny I could and I paid a good bit for it, Florence, every penny I had. I just didn't think you would be so ... upset about it not being new.'

Florence nodded slowly. He had been saving hard for a long time, she knew that, and he had wanted to buy her the best he could afford. Did it really matter that it wasn't a new ring?

'I just want you to be happy, Florence, and I want to marry you,' Charlie said, kissing her gently on the forehead. 'I never intended to deceive anyone.'

Florence believed him and felt a frisson of annoyance. Her mother had taken an irrational dislike to Charlie from the start and this episode had proved that her opinion hadn't changed. Well, she loved him and was going to marry him regardless of what her mother thought. 'I am happy, Charlie, and it is a beautiful ring.' She smiled. 'And ... and the fact that it belonged to Aunt Emily means that it's stayed in the family and I think that's a bonus.'

Charlie breathed a sigh of relief. The last thing he'd wanted to do was upset Florence.

171

Chapter Fifteen

This time Rose went alone on the bus for both her mother and Iris had to open their businesses. She didn't mind at all, she'd told Kate as she hugged her mother tightly and promised to write regularly and visit when and if she got a weekend off. Both Kate and Iris had said how much they would miss her but would look forward to hearing how she was settling in.

As the bus travelled on towards Mold through the pastureland of Cheshire, now devoid of cattle, Rose thought back to the day Edward Taylor had driven her back to Liverpool. She remembered very little of that journey, she'd been in a daze, unable to believe what had happened. In the months that had passed she had come to terms with her loss; she still grieved for her father but that grief wasn't as raw as it had been. When the landscape changed as they entered the Vale of Clwyd the hills now looked bleak, she thought, the heather and bracken brown and dry but the small, hardy sheep still grazed on their slopes.

The bus wasn't full and there was little conversation amongst the passengers and so Rose had time to try to analyse her feelings. In the time that had elapsed since her father's death she hadn't been happy in Liverpool and it hadn't just been because of the loss of her da. No, it had been something else. Something she had begun to realise in the days and weeks after the funeral, when life had again taken on a semblance of normality. She'd experienced a sense of not belonging any more and it had grown stronger every day, even though she loved her family. She had been born and brought up in a large, bustling city that was also the gateway to the world and the countries of the British Empire that lay beyond the Mersey estuary, and yet a few months in a small, quiet rural village had totally changed her and her outlook. She no longer felt happy and at home in the busy, noisy, crowded and often dirty streets. Things had somehow changed, or maybe it was she who had changed but hadn't realised it.

Charlie and Iris both had someone special in their lives now and were making plans for the future but she wasn't jealous in any way; she was glad for them both. She didn't envisage anyone coming into her life in the near future and she was content with that. She just hadn't been able to see a happy and fulfilled life for herself in Liverpool.

She was very unsure how she would feel working at Plas Idris for she had only visited on the few occasions connected with the flower show, but she had no choice and was grateful that Gwen had obtained a position there for her. Gwen was giving her a home and she could not expect more; she had to work to support herself. She was aware that there were customs and ways of working that were strictly adhered to in such houses and of which she had no experience; she had become vaguely aware of them on her visits. The way she and Gwen had gone to the back door and not the impressive front entrance; Mrs Mathews asking a girl in a maid's uniform to escort them to the Blue Drawing Room; the deference Gwen had exhibited towards Miss Olivia; and the slightly imperious way Olivia Rhys-Pritchard had treated both Gwen and herself. She remembered with embarrassment how she had just barged into the dining room without knocking the day she'd been sent to fetch the forgotten 'Best in Show' tickets. She wasn't averse to hard work – the work both at Black's and in the shop hadn't been exactly easy – but the world of the large country house was completely alien to her. Still, she hoped she wouldn't find it too arduous and she had loved the gardens and the grounds, and at least she could go back to the village each evening.

When she finally reached Denbigh and alighted it was to find Gwen's brother waiting but this time there was no farm cart hitched to the tractor.

'So, you've come back to us, Rose, then. We were all so sorry to hear about your da,' Bob Roberts greeted her as he took her case and helped her up. It was obvious that she was to sit in the cramped space beside him and as the vehicle was open to the elements she was glad she had on a warm coat, knitted gloves, scarf and hat. Her case had been stowed behind the seat. 'It's very good of you to come for me,' she replied as she tucked the rug he'd brought around her knees. 'It was a terrible shock for us all when Da was killed like that and I just couldn't settle afterwards. I wanted to come back to Tregarron. Liverpool just doesn't seem like ... home ... now.'

He nodded and they pulled out of Lenten Pool. The noise of the vehicle made conversation a little difficult but she seemed content, he thought, to just sit and watch as the houses gave way to fields.

Gwen heard them coming as they passed the school and came out to stand at the shop door. When Bob had helped Rose down she hugged her. 'Welcome back, Rose. I hope you're not frozen stiff, but I couldn't get Mr Morgan to pick you up in his trap. He's a martyr to his rheumatism and doesn't go out much when it's as cold as this. Go on in, luv, the door is open and there's a good fire to warm you up. I'll be in in half an hour.'

'No, I'm not too cold, Aunty Gwen. Mr Roberts brought a warm rug for me. Oh, I'm so ... happy to be back!'

Bob took her case as Gwen returned to the shop and as Rose entered the small, warm and cosy room she felt a sense of contentment envelop her. She felt utterly at home here. After Bob had gone, she took off her coat and hat and pushed the kettle on to the hob to boil. Then she went upstairs to the small bedroom where Gwen's brother had deposited her case. Everything looked just the same, she thought as she crossed to the small window and looked out. Of course there were no flowers in the garden now and the trees in the distant copse were bare, their branches black and skeletal against the grey January sky, but she felt happier than she had done since the morning she'd been woken with the tragic news about her father.

By the time Gwen came in she'd unpacked, set the table and had a pot of tea waiting.

175

'My, but it's cold today. Coldest it's been so far; I shouldn't wonder if we didn't have snow before long. Have you thawed out yet? It's a long, cold journey by whatever means you make it. At least with Bob it's quicker. Pour the tea, luv.'

Rose did so as Gwen cut slices of bread in the tiny kitchen at the back and then brought the plate through with the butter dish, a plate of home-cured ham and a jar of chutney, which she placed on the table. 'We'll just have a bite now. There's a good thick meat stew simmering in the oven for supper and I've an apple and blackberry pie ready to go in later, if you'll keep your eye on it for me. Then we can have a proper gossip over supper and I'll tell you all about what's been going on here and about your job at the big house.'

Eagerly Rose tucked into the food, suddenly feeling very hungry.

She learned from Gwen that evening that she was to start work at Plas Idris at six each morning, which meant she would have to leave the village at a quarter to, earlier if the weather was bad. During her stay in the summer she had borrowed a bicycle but Gwen now informed her that Bob had picked up a second-hand one in Denbigh for her for a couple of shillings and one of his boys had given it a fresh coat of paint and had fixed a small basket to the handlebars. Mona Mathews would instruct her on her duties and of course Nancy, the other housemaid, would be on hand as well. She was expected to stay until half past seven; fortunately the family did not dine late and never entertained these days, and Nancy and young Beryl, the scullery maid, managed the clearing away and washing up between them. She would have Wednesday afternoon off and each alternate Sunday afternoon off too.

Rose had ventured that the hours were long but that she didn't mind, sometimes she'd been in the shop for almost as long. When Tom Morrissey had dropped off the produce she'd often helped Iris to wipe it and stock the shelves before they opened and as Mrs Duncan (amongst others) was prone to leaving things to the very last minute they sometimes hadn't closed up until well after half past six.

'But you had more time to yourself, Rose, every evening and all day Sunday. One afternoon a week plus one afternoon every other Sunday isn't a lot but it's what the others get,' Gwen had informed her.

'I expect I'll get used to it. At least I'll be coming home each evening and in summer it doesn't get dark until late and people are out in their gardens or talking a stroll. And I'll have this Nancy and Beryl to talk to during the day,' Rose added. 'I take it they live in? And the parlourmaid?'

Gwen had nodded. It was unusual for maids of whatever standing not to live in but she had been determined that Rose wasn't going to. The fact that decent staff of any kind was difficult to get and that Rose was reliable and known to them had worked in Gwen's favour. She'd heard that those attic rooms allotted to the servants were freezing cold in winter and like ovens in summer. 'The parlourmaid is called Nora, she's from Ruthin. Nancy's home is near Wrexham, and

177

young Beryl is from a farm on the edge of the moors so it's too far for all of them to travel. I've no idea where Mrs Mathews or Mr Lewis, the butler, or Henry Jones, the only footman left now, come from. They've been with the family for years and don't have a great deal to do with the village folk. Of course the handyman and the gardeners are all local, none of them live in.'

Rose hoped that the other maids would not resent the fact that after dinner she wouldn't be available to help with the chores but would cycle the few miles back to the village at the end of the day.

When she awoke next morning she drew back the curtains and found that during the night it had snowed. Everything was covered with a pristine white blanket with the dark edges of the dry stone walls protruding sharply, but the sky was now blue and the sun was shining.

Gwen was already up, dressed and preparing breakfast.

'You should have woken me,' Rose said. She felt a little guilty for before she started at Plas Idris she intended to help Gwen as much as she could.

'I thought I'd let you sleep on, see. We've had quite a bit of snow overnight. After breakfast I'll have to get the shovel and clear it from in front of the shop.'

'I can do that, Aunty Gwen. I brought my wellington boots. I can clear the path in front of the cottage too.'

Gwen smiled at her. 'It's a good girl you are, Rose.'

'Then later I was thinking I could go up to Plas Idris. I don't mind walking. It's not that far and it's a lovely crisp, bright winter day.'

'Are you sure? I doubt you'd be able to cycle until that lane has been cleared a bit.'

'I'd like to see Mrs Mathews and meet Nancy, Nora and Beryl and see the house and grounds again. They must look wonderful in the snow,' Rose mused aloud.

'Like something on a Christmas card, I should imagine, though I've never been there in winter myself. You make sure you wrap up well and don't leave it too late before starting back. It goes dark early and it will start to freeze once the sun has gone and then it will be very treacherous underfoot,' Gwen advised. 'And I don't want you falling or getting lost in the dark. You're used to street lighting.'

Rose set out mid-morning and called and waved to the people who were clearing their paths as she passed by. She was welcomed back cordially by everyone. When she reached the lane she saw that a few vehicles had obviously ventured along it, judging by the tracks in the snow. The hedges rose on either side, the bare branches of the hawthorn and blackthorn now a white tracery and she marvelled at the silence, broken occasionally by the rasping cry of a rook or crow. The snow that covered the fields sparkled in the sunlight and as she trudged on she began to hum happily to herself.

At last she turned in through the huge wrought-iron gates and began to walk up the driveway, glancing up at the dense evergreen foliage of the yew trees standing like white frosted sentinels on either side of the path. Beyond them the grounds stretched away like a shining white sea. When she turned the bend at the end of the drive she stood and stared around her, breathing in the cold, sharp air. The branches of the rose bushes and the shrubs in the borders drooped under the weight of the snow; the stone urns that flanked the walls of the house were empty now but where the snow had adhered to them they looked as if they had been dusted with icing sugar. The snow had been cleared from the steps leading up the front door, she noticed, and the grey stone walls of the house rose steeply from the snow-covered gravel; they too seemed to shimmer, frosted like the urns. The long sash windows reflected the sun's rays and the heavy layer of snow that covered the roof glinted in the brilliant light; the icicles hanging from the guttering looked like slivers of silver. It was beautiful. Gwen had been right, she thought. It looked like a scene from a Christmas card and the resemblance was heightened by the stillness that enveloped everything. She'd been right to come back, she thought, as she walked on towards the house. She wouldn't mind the long hours or the menial work just as long as she could look out on such tranquil beauty each day.

After Rose had gone Iris determined that she would tell her mother of Tom's proposal.

'So you've come to an understanding,' Kate replied after Iris had imparted the news.

'On what he earns, Mam, it will be ages before we can think about getting married. I don't mind

180

though, I'm just happy to know that he loves me and that one day we will get married. You don't mind, do you? I suppose he should have spoken to you first but I don't think he intended to ask me so soon.'

Kate smiled at her. 'Of course I don't mind. I'm pleased, Iris. I like him. He's hard-working and you seem very suited to each other. I take it there is to be no official announcement or anything?'

Iris shook her head. 'You mean like our Charlie and Florence? No, he can't even afford a ring yet but I don't care. I'm not one for show, Mam, you know that. He wants to marry me and that's all that matters,' she said firmly.

Kate nodded, thinking of the evening she'd spent with Florence's parents on New Year's Eve. She had been a little over-awed by the size of the house and the furnishings; she didn't have anything in common with Ethel Taylor except Florence's friendship with Iris and her engagement to Charlie. In fact only Iris and Charlie had seemed at ease and she'd noticed that even Charlie didn't have much to say to Ethel. She and Rose had definitely found the evening rather strained. Of course she'd met Florence's father before and she liked him; he'd made every effort to make her feel welcome and at ease but his wife had been a different kettle of fish. Even though she seemed to have accepted the fact that Florence was going to marry Charlie at some time in the future, Kate could not forget that the woman didn't feel that her son was good enough for Florence. She had also felt that the serving of champagne in expensive crystal glasses, the effusive toasts, the silver cutlery and bone-china dishes on which the sumptuous, beautifully cooked meal had been served had been an attempt on Ethel's part to emphasise the differences in their backgrounds and status. She'd been very relieved when it had all been over but from the hints Ethel had dropped about the wedding and what she had in mind for that occasion, she knew she would have to come into close contact with the woman again in the future. 'Well, I'm delighted for you, Iris, and now that Rose has gone and will be earning a wage of her own, I think you should keep a little more of the takings from the shop. You'll need every penny if you are going to start saving up.'

Iris hugged her. 'Oh, thanks, Mam! I'll save as hard as I can from now on and I'll tell Tom that you're quite happy to have him as a son-in-law.' She grinned. 'I bet you'll get on better with his mam than you do with Mrs Taylor.'

Kate grimaced and then smiled. 'I'm sure I will. Well, I suppose now I'd better write and tell Rose the happy news – unless you want to?'

Iris shook her head. 'No, you know I'm not great at writing letters. I hope she's settled in with Aunty Gwen.'

'I'm sure she has but I hope she won't find working at Plas Idris too ... trying. She won't have much time to herself or as much independence as she's been used to. She'll have to mind her Ps and Qs too, they can be very particular and strict – hidebound, really – in these places and she's not used to that.'

'I'm sure in time she'll get used to it, Mam. She wanted to go back, she wasn't happy here and she had to have a job,' Iris reminded her although she felt that she wouldn't swap her life and work for Rose's, not for all the tea in China. She was enjoying running the greengrocery and was constantly looking for ways to increase trade.

Kate sighed. 'I hope so, I really do, but she isn't like you, Iris. You're like me, practical and level-headed; Rose has always been a bit of a dreamer and she certainly won't have much time for that now,' she replied, making a mental note to ask Gwen to write and report how her youngest daughter was getting on at Plas Idris for she wasn't certain that Rose would tell her the truth. She had wanted to go back so much that she might paint a very different picture in her letters to how, she was really feeling. Kate sighed again, wondering if she would ever stop worrying about all of them. Probably not. It was what mothers did.

Chapter Sixteen

As the flames caught the wood and paper Rose sat back on her heels with a nod of satisfaction. Nancy had drawn the heavy curtains and was folding back the interior shutters and peering through the window.

'I hate February! Look at it out there, dull, grey, misty and cold,' she complained. 'Still, there's one good thing about it,' she finished on a more cheerful note.

'What's that?' Rose asked, getting to her feet for the fire was burning up nicely now.

'There's not much of it, see. It's a short month and then winter is finally over.'

Rose smiled and joined her fellow housemaid at the window. A heavy mist hung over the grounds of Plas Idris and as it was barely light yet there was very little to see. Both girls turned away to resume preparing the dining room before the family came down for breakfast. At least before Miss Olivia came down, dead on the stroke of eight, Rose thought. Sometimes Miss Elinore didn't appear for breakfast and often David Rhys-Pritchard had a tray taken to his room. You always knew when he was having one of his 'difficult' days because a tray would be requested, Nancy had informed her.

Rose turned back to dust the long buffet and replace the lace runner and the condiments and Nancy began to set the table. Rose thought she would be very glad to see the end of this winter. She had found working here difficult to start with. She was unfamiliar with the routine of a big house and the tasks that were allotted to each member of staff, although these days the lines of demarcation were more blurred, according to the housekeeper, because the number of staff was greatly reduced. It was really one of Beryl's jobs to see to the fires but she was hopeless at it and so Rose had suggested to Mrs Mathews that she do it. It would be done far more quickly and with less mess, she'd said, and she didn't mind. And it was really the footman's task to set the table, overseen by the butler, but Henry Jones had been with the family for so long that Mr Lewis seldom bothered. Henry did it for lunch and dinner but she and Nancy had taken over breakfast for Henry was getting on now and suffered with rheumatism: movement was stiff and painful for him in the morning.

Nor had she realised that the house would be so cold and draughty despite the fires that burned in every room. She had had to stay one night in January when it had snowed heavily and it would have been foolhardy to try to get back to the village, she remembered grimly as she placed the guard in front of the now fiercely burning fire. Miss Olivia had telephoned Gwen to say she was staying and she and Nancy had made up a bed in one of the rooms in the attic. It had been freezing up there and she'd been so cold that she'd hardly slept and had vowed that snow or no snow the following night she would go back to her warm, cosy bed at Gwen's. Thankfully the thaw had set in next morning.

'What are you doing this afternoon, Rose?' Nancy asked, interrupting her thoughts.

'Nothing much really. I've a letter to write to Mam and I thought I'd spend a few hours catching up on my reading. I'm trying to finish my book,' Rose replied. She didn't get as much time as she liked to read these days. She surveyed the now cheerful and tidy room with satisfaction, glancing at the ornate clock on the mantel. Beryl would be bringing up the hot dishes any minute now and Miss Olivia would be down in a few minutes. 'Have the papers arrived yet?'

Nancy nodded. 'I think so, I saw Mr Lewis getting out the iron.'

It had astonished her at first when she had learned that the newspapers were actually ironed before being placed on the table in the hall; it had seemed such a trivial and unnecessary task. But Nancy had explained that it wasn't just to get rid of any creases as she had imagined but to ensure that the ink did not transfer itself to the hands or clothes of those members of the family who read them.

'I'm thinking of going into Denbigh, why don't you come with me?' Nancy asked as she went to help Beryl who was backing into the room bearing a large tray heavily laden with dishes. 'Put it down on the table, luv, before you drop it,' she instructed the kitchen maid.

Rose helped the two girls transfer the dishes to the buffet. 'Thanks, Nancy, but I really do want to finish my book and I'm trying to save up. If I go into town I'm bound to go spending money on things I don't really need.'

Nancy was about to ask what she was saving for but the appearance of Olivia Rhys-Pritchard curtailed the conversation.

'Good morning, Rose, Nancy,' Olivia said pleasantly and then frowned. 'Beryl, shouldn't you be back in the kitchen by now, helping Cook?'

All three girls nodded politely and left, Beryl looking flustered and irritable and muttering, once outside in the hallway, that she was always being picked on.

'Ah, take no notice, *cariad*,' Nancy said as she and Rose made their way towards the main drawing room where the family had spent the previous evening and which would need cleaning and tidying. 'What do you find to write to your Mam about each week, Rose? I can never think of anything interesting to put in my letters. After all, we don't lead very exciting lives, now do we? We get up, we work all day, we have supper and we go to bed – very boring! At least you get to go back to the village each night.' Nancy took out her frustration on the sofa cushions, repeatedly dropping them on the floor which she'd been taught was the best way of plumping them up.

'It's not *that* bad. If you worked in a factory you'd find the work just as boring and the conditions in some of them are awful. Our Iris said the work was tedious, heavy, dirty and sometimes dangerous when she was in munitions,' Rose informed her as she placed the dirty cups and glasses on a tray ready to be taken downstairs.

'That's as maybe but we'd get better wages and more time off,' Nancy reminded her. 'How is your Iris getting on?' Nancy always enjoyed hearing about Rose's family and Iris in particular who worked for herself in that shop. Nancy found that extraordinary. She envied her.

'She's fine. She's really trying to make a go of the greengrocery so she has to put in long hours. Mam said in her last letter that both she and Tom are saving hard, as is Charlie,' Rose replied.

'Any sign of a wedding date being set yet, with Florence and Charlie?' Nancy asked, replacing the last of the cushions.

'I think Florence is hoping it will be some time this year but with our Charlie, who knows?' Rose shrugged.

'He was very lucky, Rose, to come through the

war so well,' Nancy said seriously, 'unlike Master Dai,' she added, jerking her head in the direction of the rooms on the ground floor at the front of the house where David Rhys-Pritchard had his bedroom, bathroom, drawing room and small study, for he was unable to contend with stairs. His drawing room had French doors which opened on to the terrace and the gardens.

Rose nodded, thinking of their young master. When she'd encountered him for the first time as a servant in the house she had been very surprised that he remembered her.

'You're new, aren't you?' he'd enquired as he'd come into the hall to find her on her hands and knees dusting the bottom treads of the staircase. She'd hastily got to her feet, unsure whether she should dip a curtsy or not.

'I started work here a few days ago, sir,' she'd replied, dropping her gaze and feeling awkward at the intensity of his gaze.

'But I've seen you before. I remember ... the way you speak,' he'd continued. Before she had had time to say anything he'd exclaimed, 'Rose. Your name is Rose and you were here last summer. Rosa mundi. Rose of the World.'

She'd blushed, twisting the duster between her fingers. 'That's right, sir. I was staying with Miss Roberts and helping with the flower show. I ... I wasn't sure if you were ... teasing ... me about my name.'

To her surprise he'd smiled at her and she'd thought how different it made him look: quite handsome, despite the scar.

'No, Rose, I wasn't teasing you. I was just ... I

suppose I was just telling you what your name meant and ... and that it's a lovely name,' he'd replied.

'Thank ... you, sir,' she'd said, her cheeks flushed with embarrassment.

'And now you have come to work here? Had you grown tired of Liverpool?'

Haltingly she'd tried to tell him how she had been unable to settle back in her native city after her father's sudden and tragic death and at that he had nodded sadly and looked away.

'So we both have experience of how ... cruel life can be, Rose,' he'd said and she could have bitten her tongue.

'I'm sorry, really. I am, sir, for ... reminding...' she'd stammered.

He'd looked back towards her. 'There is nothing to be sorry for. I hope you will be happy here, Rose.'

She'd nodded and he had propelled himself down the hallway towards his rooms.

She'd spoken to him on a few occasions since, but only when he'd been inclined to stop and speak. There had been occasions when he'd barely acknowledged her and days when he never left the confines of his rooms. She'd told him a little of her family and of how she enjoyed walking in the countryside when the weather permitted and of her love of reading. He'd asked what books she enjoyed and seemed a little amused when she'd told him.

'I go to the library in Denbigh whenever I can,' she'd finished.

'I'm sure you would find it easier, more convenient, to use the library here, I'll speak to Livvie about it. I know we have copies of Jane Austen and the Brontë sisters' books which I think you might enjoy.'

'Oh, I wouldn't want to put you to any trouble,' she'd replied, wondering what Miss Olivia would think of one of her maids borrowing books from their library, but to her surprise Olivia hadn't objected. She had suggested *Jane Eyre*, which Rose had loved and ever since she had been working her way through the Brontës' others. In fact this afternoon she hoped to finish *Wuthering Heights*, after she'd written to Mam.

'Well, that's that finished. I suppose we'd better make a start on Miss Olivia's bedroom now while she's still at breakfast,' Nancy announced, breaking Rose's reverie.

'And find out whether Miss Elinore has made it downstairs yet this morning,' Rose added.

'You can't help but feel sorry for her sometimes, half the time her mind seems miles away, but the way she plays fast and loose with mealtimes plays havoc with our work and really annoys Miss Olivia. Mind you, I can't say I blame her for not wanting to get up, I don't myself these dark, miserable mornings. I'll really be glad when spring comes,' Nancy said firmly.

When Rose arrived at the cottage that afternoon she found Gwen in the middle of polishing the numerous brass ornaments old Mrs Roberts had collected over the years.

'I see you're very busy,' Rose greeted her, smiling.

'I've been meaning to do them for ages. Mam would have ten fits if she could see the state of them. She did them religiously every week but I just can't seem to find the time. If Mam hadn't treasured them so much I'd have got rid of them ages ago. No wonder Megan didn't want them – just more work and she's enough on her plate as it is. Everything all right up at the big house then?'

'Oh, fine, but both Nancy and I will be glad when the weather gets warmer,' Rose replied, taking the tin of *Brasso* and a cloth from beside Gwen.

'Now, *cariad*, put that down. You do enough polishing. It's your afternoon off. Put the kettle on,' Gwen instructed.

'I'm going to write to Mam first then if you don't mind, I want to finish my book,' Rose said, pushing the kettle on to the hob and taking the teapot down from the shelf.

'Good of them, it is, to let you borrow books. Never heard of them doing it before,' Gwen commented as she critically inspected the horse brasses she had just finished.

'I don't suppose anyone was very interested in reading before. Nancy and Nora aren't and I don't know if Beryl can read. She said she wasn't all that keen on going to school and her mam really didn't bother as long as she helped her out at home.'

Gwen tutted and shook her head. 'Shocking, that is, not giving the child a chance in life. Now, I'll clear this lot away and you can write to your mam and I'll put a note in too. I don't write as often as I should.'

Rose smiled at her as she got out the cups. 'And neither does Mam but you're both so busy.'

Gwen sighed and shook her head. 'But I don't have the excuse of having a family to look after.'

Rose put her arms around her and hugged her. 'Yes you do. You look after me and I couldn't be happier.'

It had been a long, cold and tiring day, Kate thought as she closed up the shop and drew her coat more tightly to her. What bit of cheerfulness there had been around at Christmas had long since evaporated with the onset of the bitter February weather. Many of her neighbours lacked the money to buy either food or fuel with which to heat their homes adequately and had resorted to burning the skirting boards, banister rails and even floorboards. Water froze in the pipes and without hot food and warm clothing people were suffering badly, especially the very young and the old. Her shop and the loft above were packed to capacity and she prayed that when the days got longer and warmer things would improve for everyone.

Iris was already in the kitchen and had a good fire burning in the range. 'Mam, you look frozen stiff. Sit down here while I get you a cup of tea. How's business been today? I can't say I've been rushed off my feet.' She herself was only just beginning to feel warm: standing behind that counter in the cold shop all day had turned her feet to two blocks of ice.

'Slow, luv. Very slow, there just isn't the money to redeem things,' Kate replied, easing herself down in the armchair for her back was aching badly. She seemed to be in constant pain these days but she put it down to the cold. 'Is Florence coming tonight?' she asked tiredly. The last thing she needed was a visit from her future daughter-in-law, who was always full of enthusiastic hopes and plans for her wedding – whenever that might be.

Iris nodded as she handed her mother a mug of hot tea. 'And there's a letter from our Rose.'

Kate sipped her tea gratefully as she took the envelope Iris handed her.

'I wonder if they've had any more snow?' Iris mused.

'I should think our Rose has had enough snow to last her a lifetime, it wasn't quite so "lovely" or "picturesque" when she couldn't get back to Gwen's,' Kate commented as she scanned the lines.

'That was only one night, Mam,' Iris reminded her. 'What's she got to say?'

'She's still enjoying being there, says Gwen has enclosed a note – I really *must* write to her – and is looking forward to spring.'

'Aren't we all?' Iris put in tersely.

'Asks about you and Tom and our Charlie and Florence,' Kate continued.

'As she always does,' Iris again interrupted.

'And is hoping to finish *Wuthering Heights* and intends to start on Jane Austen's books next,' Kate read.

'Well, I have to say her choice of reading matter has improved since they started to let her borrow their books.'

Kate looked thoughtful. 'I wonder if it is in the

hope of "improving" her?'

Iris laughed as she began to set the table. 'Mam, anything would be an improvement on the stuff she used to read.'

When Charlie arrived home and Iris had served the meal Kate decided it was time she brought up the subject of his wedding although she wasn't much looking forward to all the fuss that it would engender, especially on Ethel Taylor's part. If that woman had her way this wedding would be a very grand affair indeed. However, Kate was more than aware that Florence was becoming increasingly impatient to set a date.

'Charlie, I know I've asked this before but have you any idea in mind about a date for the wedding? It won't exactly be cheap buying outfits and wedding gifts and I'd like to have some idea so I can budget accordingly,' she asked.

Charlie nodded slowly; he'd known this conversation was in the offing. 'I think that by next February I'll have enough saved,' he replied, ever cautious.

'*Next* February' Iris exclaimed. 'It's not exactly the best time of the year to get married. It's always freezing and there could be a foot of snow and then our Rose might not be able to get back home. Why not make it next spring or even this autumn?' she asked, thinking that if he insisted on February she would have to buy not only a dress and accessories but a good winter coat as well, unless of course Florence asked her to be bridesmaid. And if she did in mid-winter she'd probably catch her death of cold in a dress of some unsuitable material.

'Iris's right, Charlie. Why not leave it until the spring? I'm certain Florence would be happier to have it then rather than in the depths of winter, to say nothing of her mother. Have you mentioned a date to Florence at all?' Kate asked.

Charlie could see the sense in their arguments. Delaying would mean he had more money in the bank for he intended to find a place in a decent neighbourhood for them to live and that wasn't going to be easy. 'She keeps hinting but I've said nothing definite. Maybe you're right about spring.'

'Well, for heaven's sake put the girl out of her misery and suggest it,' Kate urged. 'Tell her when she comes tonight and then she and her mam can start making definite plans. I know it's a good while off yet but these things take–' Kate suddenly groaned.

'Mam, is your back playing up?' Iris asked, concerned.

'It's just the weather, luv. I'll take a hot-water bottle up to bed with me,' Kate replied grimly.

'Florence's Dad hasn't been feeling too well lately either,' Charlie informed them.

'What's up with him?' Iris asked distractedly. She was still concerned about her mother. If Mam's back didn't improve soon she intended to insist she go and see Dr Mackenzie.

'Just working too hard, so Florence said. He's been told to take things easier but he says how can he? This is one of the busiest times of the year for him,' Charlie replied. He could see the man's point of view; a business was a business and wouldn't run itself. He'd been mulling over

195

in his mind the possibility of suggesting that he give Edward Taylor a hand with the paperwork at weekends. It would be a chance to get to know the ropes, he'd thought.

Kate nodded. 'None of us are getting any younger and when you work for yourself you can't afford to be ill,' she said, thinking that now both she and Edward Taylor had the additional worry and expense of a wedding in a little over a year's time. But she was glad Charlie wasn't sticking out for a winter wedding.

Chapter Seventeen

Florence wasn't exactly delighted when Charlie informed her later that evening that he felt they should set a date in April the following year for their wedding.

'I had been hoping that, well, maybe it would be sooner, Charlie. October is lovely. All the leaves on the trees turning to gold and red and russet. I could take that as a sort of theme, have the flowers and bridesmaids' dresses in autumnal colours and St Mary's-on-the-Hill has lovely grounds with lots of trees that would look great in photographs.' Florence had been looking forward to her wedding so much she really didn't want to wait so long.

'I'd originally thought about next February but Mam and Iris seemed to think–'

'Oh, not a winter wedding, Charlie! The

196

weather could be awful. I mean if we lived in a pretty village in the countryside and there was snow or ice it could be quite picturesque but in a city...'

Charlie nodded, ignoring her hints about October. He wasn't going to be rushed and he wanted some money behind him. 'Mam said it would be too cold so we'll set a date in April. That will give everyone plenty of time to get organised and for us to find a nice house in a good area.'

Reluctantly Florence agreed. 'There will be a lot to do,' she mused and then brightened. A spring wedding would be just as pretty with the new leaves and blossom on the trees and all the flowers emerging. 'We'll have to go and see the vicar first of course and see what he has in his diary and then we'll need to decide where we are going to have the reception. Goodness, there are so many things to think about but I'm so happy we've finally decided on a date, Charlie!'

Charlie nodded. There was a lot to organise and that would keep her happy and occupied. 'We'll go and see the vicar soon, Florence,' he promised although he couldn't see that there was any great rush, he doubted the vicar's diary would be that full so far in advance.

'And I'll start to make a guest list with my mother and see where she thinks would be suitable for the reception,' Florence added. 'Of course I'll have Iris and Rose as my bridesmaids,' she continued.

'I don't know how that will work, Florence, with our Rose living so far away,' Charlie reminded her.

Florence frowned, seeing the first obstacle to

197

her plans. Rose wouldn't be available for choosing colours and materials, or for dress fittings. 'I'll ask Iris what she thinks. I don't want Rose to feel left out but it could be a problem. Maybe if she were to give the people she works for some sort of advance notice that she will need time off to come to Liverpool...'

'Florence, luv, you can't expect the likes of them to be giving our Rose days off by the minutes. She's a servant and lucky to have the job; she's at their beck and call, not the other way around,' Charlie reminded her.

Florence bit her lip and nodded.

'And, Florence, don't go bothering your dad too much with wedding plans just yet. He's got enough on his plate. How is he feeling?'

Florence looked anxious. 'Mother is trying to make him rest more but it's not easy. The doctor is thinking about prescribing some tablets. It's his heart, he thinks, and too much stress and work.'

Charlie nodded sympathetically. 'When I see him next, Florence, I'm going to offer to help with the paperwork at weekends. He's running quite a big business you know and it can be very taxing.' If his future father-in-law's health continued to deteriorate then Ethel just might succeed in persuading him to retire and he wanted to be ready to step in and take up the reins. The best way to gain the necessary experience and Edward Taylor's trust was to have familiarised himself thoroughly with the business.

She nodded. 'That's good of you, Charlie, I'm sure he will appreciate the offer,' she replied but already her thoughts were returning to the arrangements for her wedding.

His opportunity came the following Friday evening when he arrived at the house in Cedar Grove to find Florence closeted with her mother in the dining room and her father about to go into his study. He had to admit that the man looked tired and rather drawn.

'Ethel has instructed that I sit in the living room and read the paper but I've a few things to attend to that won't wait. They're both engrossed in all the lists they're making and Ethel has been talking about the Imperial and the Adelphi Hotels as possibilities for a reception. I shudder to even think what those places charge for a bottle of wine let alone a meal; between them I think they intend to bankrupt me. If you can't face all that palaver, Charlie, go and sit in the living room. I'll join you when I've finished.'

'If you don't mind I'd like to join you in the study, I've a proposition to put to you,' Charlie said.

'If it's anything that will help to curb the excesses Ethel has in mind, you're welcome, lad.'

Charlie looked quickly around the small room he'd only been in once before and noted that it was far more untidy than it had been on that occasion.

'Things are in a bit of a mess,' Edward explained, sitting down and running his hands through his thinning hair.

'That's only to be expected,' Charlie replied, thinking this was just the opening he needed. 'I know you've been told to take things more gently and I also know that that's easier said than done in business, so I hope you won't take offence but I'd be more than willing to help you out with the paperwork at weekends. It can't be all that different to the stuff I deal with at work.'

Edward looked up. 'You'd be willing to give up your free time at weekends to help sort this out?' He indicated the piles of invoices and bills scattered on the desk and the half-open ledgers.

'I would, if it meant you wouldn't have as much to do and could take a bit of time off. I've also told Florence not to be mithering you with all these plans for the wedding. I'm sure she and Mrs Taylor are more than capable of organising everything,' Charlie said firmly.

Edward nodded slowly; it would certainly be a help. He indicated that Charlie sit down. 'I'd be glad of some help, lad. There's quite a bit to do though.'

Charlie took off his jacket, rolled up his sleeves and sat down. 'I'm a fast learner and don't forget I've reorganised Mam's way of working. Now, if you can show me your systems of ordering, distribution, expenses and payments – both in and out – I can make a start first thing tomorrow morning.'

Edward Taylor smiled. 'I have to say our Florence certainly did well when she picked you, Charlie. It will be a load off my mind to get this lot sorted.'

Charlie smiled back. 'And once we've got things under control again I can make sure they stay that way. It should only take a few hours a week then and give you peace of mind.' Organising the wedding would keep Florence content and occupied, he thought, for he certainly didn't want to spend his weekends being dragged around hotels and churches and the like, or to spend hours discussing the merits of roast beef over roast lamb or what flowers would be appropriate. Not when he had the opportunity of learning the ropes of her father's business and of being able to ascertain at the same time approximately how much Edward Taylor was worth.

When he announced to Florence that from now on his weekends would be spent helping her father to allow him to rest more she hadn't been too perturbed, remarking that as he would be here in the house he would be on hand to help make decisions. He'd concurred but he still did not intend to become too involved; such matters could be dealt with by the women.

When he'd announced casually to Kate the following week his intention to spend his time at Cedar Grove on Saturdays and Sundays sorting out his future father-in-law's paperwork he'd received a searching look from his sister.

'You're getting your feet under the table there all right, Charlie,' Iris had remarked.

'What's that supposed to mean?' he demanded.

'Just that you seldom do anything if there isn't something in it for you, some sort of ... reward,' she shot back.

Charlie turned his attention to his mother. 'Do you have any objections to me helping him out, Mam? He's supposed to rest more.'

Kate shook her head. 'No, lad, I've no objection.'

'You could help Mam out on Saturdays, take

over in the shop so she could rest,' Iris persisted, suspecting that he was only doing this to further his own ends but also realising that even if Mam were to have Saturdays off she would still find work to do in the house.

Charlie ignored her. 'And it's to stop Florence bothering him with all the wedding fuss and performance.'

This time Kate nodded: that she could understand. Florence was bound to be excited about her wedding, wanting everything to be perfect, but she could be over-enthusiastic about things at times and abetted by her mother they would try the patience of a saint. 'Even so I doubt he'll escape it entirely. I've already had her on at me wondering about our Rose being a bridesmaid and the nearer it gets the worse the fussing will become.'

Iris had to agree with her. Florence had broached the subject with her too, wondering if the Rhys-Pritchards might be persuaded to give Rose extra time off, which she thought was highly unlikely. In fact, in her opinion, it was downright fatuous of Florence to even think they would.

'No, lad. You go and give the poor man a hand and leave Florence and her mam to our Iris and me,' Kate said firmly.

'That's good of him but I have to say your Charlie seems to have an eye to the main chance, Iris,' Tom remarked as he manhandled the last sack of potatoes into place. The shop wasn't open yet, which had given Iris the time to inform him of

Charlie's latest plans. He was going to the football match that afternoon but had insisted on staying behind to help her in the shop after he'd delivered the produce.

'Far too much so. I'm certain he's determined to get his hands on her da's business one way or another, so he's sticking his oar in now,' she confided, shaking the loose soil off a bunch of carrots.

Tom grinned at her. 'By making himself indispensable?'

She nodded. 'He did say though that he'll be there to stop Florence from mithering her da too much and she's already started. Honestly, Tom, she and her mam seem determined to make this wedding into some kind of "Society" do. She's even mentioned the Imperial for the reception. I can't see what's wrong with a community hall myself. You can do them up to look really nice.'

He put his arms around her. 'Do I detect the green-eyed monster raising its head?'

She laughed and kissed him on the cheek. 'Not a bit of it! I'd hate all that fuss and palaver and it's a shocking waste of money. When we've saved up enough to get married, a nice costume and hat, a quiet service and a cup of tea or a drink and a few sandwiches back here will suit me just fine. It's hard enough to put money by as it is without wasting it on a big, fancy wedding. It will be bad enough having to wear some kind of frilly bridesmaid's dress for Florence. Mam will have to be done up to the nines too.' She frowned as an image of Kate holding her back in pain flashed into her mind.

'Now what's the matter?' Tom asked looking anxious.

'Mam's not at all well, Tom. It's her back but she is insisting it's due to the cold and damp. I want her to go to see the doctor – it's gone on too long – but I'll have the devil's own job to persuade her. Will you help me?'

He nodded; he was fond of Kate. 'Of course, luv,' he promised. It was probably just rheumatism, aggravated by the weather. His own mam had had to give up her job because of it but he could see Iris was worried. It would at least set her mind at rest if Kate saw the doctor.

Iris took the opportunity to raise the subject when Kate came home at dinnertime, looking cold and obviously in pain. They both closed for lunch and the pawnbroker's shop was only at the other end of the street. Iris had insisted that Tom stay and have some soup before setting off for Goodison Park. She'd made it with the vegetables she'd been unable to sell.

'You look as though a bowl of this soup wouldn't go amiss, Mrs M.,' Tom greeted her affably. 'Mam always says you can't beat it this weather.'

Kate nodded slowly, sitting down at the table after taking off her coat. 'She's right, Tom.'

Iris placed a bowl down in front of her. 'Mam, you don't look a bit well and it isn't just the cold.'

Kate was about to brush aside her daughter's comments but Tom looked at her with concern.

'She's right, Mrs M. I've been thinking the same thing for a while now. Why don't you go and see the doctor? You don't have to suffer in silence.

Mam doesn't. Our doctor gives her some powders to take; they seem to ease the pain a bit and help with the swelling in her joints.'

'You see, Mam, it's not just me who is worried about you. Maybe Dr Mackenzie can give you some of those powders,' Iris urged, flashing a grateful look at Tom.

'No sense in doing nothing, is there? Not when it might help,' Tom added.

Kate still wasn't happy about the idea. 'Do you think your mam would let me try one of those powders, Tom? Just to see if it works? There's no sense in bothering the doctor or paying out good money if it doesn't.'

Iris wasn't going to let her off the hook like this. 'Mam, you can't do things like that! What is good for one person may not be good for another. Only a doctor can make that decision. You might be doing more harm than good. No, go and see Dr Mackenzie on Monday.'

Kate shook her head. 'You know I can't go on Monday, I'm too busy.'

Iris had forgotten that Monday was when everyone brought in their Sunday clothes to pledge until Friday. 'Then you can go on Tuesday,' she said firmly. 'Honestly, Mam, sometimes I just don't understand you at all! You never thought twice about either calling him in or taking us to the surgery when Charlie, Rose or I were poorly and you know how often that was with our Rose.'

Kate could see she wasn't going to get any peace until she agreed. She sighed heavily. 'All right. I'll go and see him on Tuesday morning if it will keep you happy.'

Iris smiled at Tom, feeling relieved. 'Good. Now, get that soup down you while it's still hot.'

Tom winked at her as he got to his feet. 'I'd best be off or I'll not get a decent enough speck and end up with a stiff neck.'

Kate managed a smile. 'It's a good job Bill's not here to see an Evertonian sitting at his kitchen table.'

Tom nodded and grinned at her. The rivalry between the fans of Liverpool's two football teams ran deep.

Iris too smiled. 'Mam, my da wasn't that bad about football! It's only a game, after all.'

Tom adopted an expression of mock horror. 'Shame on you, Iris Mundy! Wash your mouth out! To some people it means more than their religion.'

Kate laughed. 'Get out of here with your blasphemous views, Tom Morrissey!' He was a good lad, she thought. She was sure he would make Iris an equally good husband.

Kate went to see Dr Mackenzie on Tuesday morning as she'd promised. She had to admit that she really wasn't feeling well. She'd closed the shop a bit early on Saturday and had sat beside the range with the stone hot-water bottle wedged behind her. She'd not slept well that night either and had been very grateful when Iris had offered to cook on Sunday. There had just been the two of them as Charlie was at Florence's house and Tom wasn't calling until the afternoon when he and Iris were going to give the greengrocery a fresh coat of limewash.

She'd dozed in the armchair that afternoon, glad of the respite for Monday was always a busy day.

She'd informed the doctor of her symptoms and how long she'd had them, he'd examined her and asked some questions, and then she'd mentioned the powders Mrs Morrissey took for her rheumatism.

'I do indeed know of them, Mrs Mundy, and they can help, but I'm not at all sure that it is rheumatism,' he replied, writing something down.

Kate felt a frisson of anxiety run through her. 'Then what is it, doctor?'

'I'm not totally sure but I've been reading a great deal lately, medical papers and the like, and I know there is a doctor who is similarly interested and so I want you to go to see him for some tests – at the hospital.'

'*Hospital!*' Kate cried in horror. She'd never been in hospital in her life. In fact the only time she had been inside one was when Bill had been knocked down and had died.

'Now, Mrs Mundy, don't be alarmed. There's nothing sinister about these tests. They are a minor procedure, I assure you. They will help to diagnose what's causing the pain and then once we know we can do something about it.' He tried to sound reassuring for he knew many of his patients viewed hospitals in the same light as the workhouse. In fact the Royal, where he was sending her, had started out as just such an institution. 'Modern medicine has moved on a great deal. Any association between a hospital and a workhouse is best forgotten. Now, I want you to rest as much as you can and take aspirin to help relieve the pain. They'll send for you.'

Despite his words Kate was filled with a terrible foreboding. In her experience hospitals were places which you usually left feet first – in a box.

'They're just tests, nothing to get excited about,' she repeated firmly to herself as she walked home but she decided that she wouldn't tell either Iris or Charlie about them. Although in her heart she was far from certain that there was nothing to worry about she wasn't going to have them fretting about her. No, she'd say it was just rheumatism and that the doctor had said it would get better as the weather got warmer and she was to take aspirin tablets for the pain. At least that wasn't a lie.

Chapter Eighteen

It was one of those rare late February days when pale winter sunlight bathed the grounds of Plas Idris and Rose decided that she would spend her afternoon off sitting in the gardens reading. The air smelled moist and damp but it was much milder than it had been of late and the first spiky leaves of the daffodils were beginning to appear. Under the trees in the pasture there were snow-drops and beneath the yews that bordered the drive purple and yellow crocuses were just ap-pearing. As she walked along the path towards the rose garden, which was protected by the wall of the kitchen garden, she smiled to herself. Spring was definitely on its way.

There was a rustic bench at the far end of the path, which was sheltered and in direct sunlight; she would be warm enough there, she thought, she was well wrapped up. She settled herself on the bench, listening to the birdsong and thinking that next month the bare branches of both the trees and the rose bushes would begin to shows signs of new growth. In summer the roses would be glorious but even now it was a tranquil, pleasant spot.

She became so engrossed in her book that she didn't see or hear David Rhys-Pritchard approaching. Glancing up she was surprised to see him.

'Oh, you startled me, sir! I didn't hear you,' she cried, jumping to her feet.

'I'm sorry, Rose, I didn't mean to intrude. Do sit down. I was tempted out of doors by the mild weather. Is it your afternoon off?' He manoeuvred the wheelchair around until he was sitting beside her.

'It is, sir, and I decided that I'd stay here as it's such a lovely day.' Reluctantly she closed the book and laid it on the bench beside her.

He smiled at her. 'You are an avid reader.'

'I do enjoy reading, sir. Do you read much?'

'I used to read a lot but now ... now I don't seem to have the same interest or ... concentration,' he confided. She was quite unlike any of the servants he'd known. She was quiet and seemed a little reserved – or maybe she was just shy. She'd looked so content and at ease sitting here reading, her dark hair tucked underneath a red tam-o'-shanter, she obviously enjoyed being out in the garden and seemed to have settled well, despite being a city girl.

Rose nodded, thinking she understood. It would be hard to concentrate if you were in pain and she knew he frequently was. 'What kind of books did you used to enjoy, sir?'

'Oh, travel, adventure, exploration, things like that,' he replied with a note of bitterness in his voice. Travel and exploration were things that were denied him now. He'd thought that going to war would be the greatest adventure of all but he'd quickly learned that it wasn't.

Rose hadn't missed the harsh note and thought that it was no wonder he didn't want to read such books now. 'What about murder mysteries, sir? Agatha Christie's book is becoming very popular although I don't know if I'd like it and I'm not clever enough to try to work out who would be the guilty person.'

He smiled at her kindly. 'I wouldn't say that, Rose.'

There was a brief silence and then he spoke again. 'Tell me about your life in Liverpool, Rose.'

'It was very ... ordinary, sir.'

'You have a brother and a sister or so I remember you telling me.'

Rose nodded. 'Charlie and Iris, they're both older than me. Our Charlie is a clerk in a shipping office and Iris runs the greengrocery for Mam. Charlie is the eldest, he's the same age as you, sir.'

He frowned. 'Did he ... fight?'

Rose nodded, not really wanting to talk about

the war, feeling it would only bring back memories she was certain he wanted to forget. 'He doesn't talk about it though. He was in the King's Liverpool Regiment.'

'I was in the Welsh Guards and I can understand why he doesn't want to speak about it, Rose. It ... it was sheer ... hell!'

She twisted her hands nervously in her lap. 'I ... know, sir, I'm sorry I said anything...'

'You have nothing to be sorry for, Rose. I brought the subject up.'

'Shall we change it then, sir?'

'Yes, it's too lovely a day for such dark thoughts. Don't you miss Liverpool at all? It's a fine city and a great port. I would have thought that at times you must find it rather too quiet here.'

Rose brightened. 'Oh, no! I don't find that at all. I always loved the river and all the ships and there are many grand buildings in Liverpool but ... but there is a lot of unemployment and poverty too. Where ... where my Mam lives people are really poor and the houses are terrible, the streets are narrow and crowded and very noisy. I'd much sooner live in the country. I love this house and especially the gardens, even in winter, and it is so good of you to let me borrow books. You have so many, almost as many as they do in the library at Denbigh.'

'But sadly nothing by Agatha Christie,' he said, smiling wryly.

'I wouldn't mind bringing you one from Denbigh, if you think you'd enjoy it,' Rose offered, thinking it was the least she could do and if it would help to give him a little enjoyment then she would be glad to. He seemed to be seriously considering it.

'Would you read it to me, Rose? As I said, I seem to lack the concentration these days.'

She was very taken aback and became flustered. 'Me, sir? I ... I don't know if I could. I mean, my reading might not be ... well...'

'You could try. It might take my mind off ... things and help to pass the hours. They can be long and rather ... bleak.'

Slowly she nodded. She felt sorry for him and it was little enough to ask 'I ... I'll try, sir.'

'Thank you. Don't worry about making a special trip into the library in Denbigh, Livvie often goes in in the car. I'll ask her to get one of Mrs Christie's novels from the bookshop.'

Rose nodded. It looked as though she was committed now. She didn't know what else to say and felt a little relieved when he said he mustn't take up any more of her free time and made his way slowly back down the path towards the house. As he reached the stone archway she caught sight of Olivia Rhys-Pritchard coming towards him and hoped she wasn't coming looking for her. But Miss Olivia stopped and seemed to be in conversation with her brother, so Rose picked up her book again.

'I've been looking for you everywhere, Dai,' Olivia informed her brother with some irritation.

'I decided to take advantage of the mild weather. I've been talking to Rose,' he said as she took the chair handles and began to push him back towards the house. That irritated him for he was quite capable now of propelling himself and he valued what little independence he still had. In fact he had started to make some enquiries about a motorised chair, a new invention that Mr Sandford, his consultant, had mentioned on his last visit. It would make life easier and would tire him less.

'Of course, it's her afternoon off although she usually goes into the village,' Olivia replied offhandedly. She had more serious matters on her mind.

'Today, like me, she is enjoying the weather. Or I *was*. What is so urgent that you came looking for me, Livvie?'

'Ellie is what is so urgent,' Olivia replied grimly.

David sighed. 'What's she neglected to do now?'

'It's what she *has* done that's the problem. I wanted to speak to you alone, away from the house and any possibility of ... eavesdropping.'

'Then why don't we sit on the terrace?' he suggested, wondering what it was that his slightly woolly-minded sister had done now. Elinore resisted all Olivia's attempts to 'organise' her, she had always been what he termed a 'free spirit' and since their parents' death had become more so.

Olivia sat down on one of the stone benches set at the edge of the wide paved terrace. 'She appears to have embarked upon an unwise and quite unacceptable liaison. I only found out about it because I came upon her reading a letter aloud to herself and with obvious pleasure. When I asked her who it was from she said, "My very dear friend Ernest Williams."'

'And who is Ernest Williams?' David asked curiously.

'Apparently he's some kind of farmer over near Pentrefoelas. She met him last year at the Denbigh Show and, unbeknown to me, they've been corresponding ever since.' Olivia was outraged that this had been going on under her very nose and she'd only just learned of it.

David frowned. He had a duty of responsibility towards both his sisters. 'Have you met him?'

'Of course not – well, I may have done at the show, but I don't remember. It's not as though he moves within the same circles as us.'

'And she called him her "friend"?' David persisted.

'Her "very *dear* friend". The Lord above only knows what kind of letters they've been exchanging, Dai!'

'I doubt she would say anything inappropriate. Do you know anything about him?'

Olivia frowned. 'Not really. Just that he has a large farm, which she says he owns – not rents – and employs people and that he's in his forties. Dai, she's far too young and impressionable...'

David sighed heavily. Elinore wasn't that young, he thought. 'Well, Livvie, I suggest we ask him over for dinner. At least that way we can see what kind of a man he is.'

'I don't think we should encourage him at all,' Olivia said firmly.

'At least if we meet him, Livvie, we can judge just how ... involved Ellie is. She's not a child, you know.'

Olivia was shaking her head. 'I don't know

about that, Dai, you know what she's like. She's very scatterbrained at times and can be stubborn and personally I think he's far too old.'

'I'll tell her to write and ask him over for lunch next Sunday,' he said firmly. 'Lunch would suit me better than dinner and I can't remember the last time we entertained.'

Olivia pursed her lips. She did not approve of inviting this stranger to lunch and he certainly wasn't of a class she considered suitable as a friend for her sister. She didn't want to entertain him at all and it would mean extra work for the servants. She shivered for the sun was now falling lower in the sky and it was turning chilly. 'I think we'd both better go indoors now. Neither of us wants to catch a chill.'

David assented but as they reached the French doors that led into his drawing room he stopped. 'Livvie, could you do something for me? Next time you go into Denbigh, would you call into Parry's and purchase one of Agatha Christie's crime novels, please?'

Olivia looked at him curiously. He'd never expressed any desire to read since he'd returned home.

'Rose informed me Mrs Christie is becoming very popular and she's promised to read to me. My concentration just isn't up to it these days,' he said as he propelled himself into the room.

Olivia stood staring after him, wondering had everyone suddenly gone mad. First Ellie dropping the bombshell of her clandestine friendship with this Mr Williams and now Dai telling her that Rose – of all people! – was going to read a crime novel to him.

Kate was very apprehensive when she next visited Dr Mackenzie after having had the required tests.

'Do they say what's the matter with me?' she asked tentatively as he studied the notes on his desk.

'They at least concur with me. Dr Redding is an eminent man in his field. He's had an interest in this condition for years, stemming from the fact that his own mother suffered from it. It has a long and complicated name but in lay terms it means that your bones are becoming very brittle and it's possible that one of the small vertebrae – bones – in your back has a hairline fracture, which would account for the considerable and continuing pain.'

Kate digested this is silence. It sounded ominous.

'I'm afraid it is something to do with your age and probably started some time ago. In the early stages there are no definite symptoms, so you wouldn't be aware you are suffering from it. Later there might be pain and tenderness in the bones and the likelihood of serious fractures.'

'What ... what can I do, doctor?' Kate asked hesitantly. She'd never heard of this before.

'Very little, I'm afraid, and it is progressive, which means it will get worse as you get older. You must get as much calcium as you can – dairy products are a good source – and avoid situations which involve the risk of falling and sustaining a fracture. The more brittle your bones become the more prone you will be to them breaking. I know it will be very hard for you, Mrs Mundy, but you really must consider doing less, both at home and particularly in the shop.'

'But ... but I've always worked, you know that,' she protested.

He nodded. 'But you don't want to risk breaking an arm or leg or rib or anything else and you might not even have to fall to do so. It is a serious condition.'

Slowly she nodded. 'And it will get worse?'

'I'm afraid it will. How rapidly we just don't know. It's only a fairly recent discovery. In the very worst case a fracture can occur by just moving a joint.'

'I'll have to think about ... all this, doctor,' she promised.

'And in the meantime rest more,' he urged kindly. He knew how hard it would be for her to change her lifestyle. 'And I think you should discuss your domestic and business arrangements with your family,' he advised.

As she walked home Kate realised he was right. She would have to talk to Charlie and Iris for this didn't just affect her: it looked as if she was going to have to give up working in the pawnboker's. She certainly had no wish to be breaking bones right, left and centre; the pain in her back was hard enough to contend with. She wished Bill were here to give her some support.

'I went back to see Dr Mackenzie this afternoon,' she informed her children after supper that evening.

'Is the rheumatism worse, Mam?' Iris asked sympathetically.

Kate shook her head. 'He asked me to go back after ... after I'd had the tests.'

'What tests?' Iris suddenly felt very anxious.

'I didn't tell you because I didn't want you to worry,' Kate stated.

'So, what did he say was wrong?' Iris demanded, praying that it wasn't anything serious. Having to have "tests" sounded ominous to her.

As simply as she could Kate told her what the doctor had said.

Iris looked worried. 'Mam, I've never heard of that before. You mean that as it gets worse you could break your arm or your collar bone just by doing something as simple as brushing the floor?'

Kate nodded. 'I'd not heard of it either but this afternoon I got to thinking and I remember Ada's ma-in-law, old Mrs Marshall, she was always breaking something and spent years in terrible pain before she died. Ada used to say her bones were like matchwood, that you only had to look at her and something broke.'

'Then you'll have to really take things easy now, Mam,' Iris urged.

'I know. It's not a pleasant thing to look forward to, running the risk of breaking something if I fall or knock myself. I'll have to give up working in the shop and turn the business over to you, Charlie,' Kate said reluctantly.

'And you'll have to do far less here in the house, but I can take over most of the heavy stuff,' Iris offered.

Charlie nodded. It seemed as though at last he

was going to be his own boss, which was what he'd wanted ever since his da had died. 'I'll give my notice in, Mam, first thing tomorrow. You can't be lifting and dragging things about now and some of the stuff that's brought in is quite heavy. It's no wonder your back is bad.'

Iris frowned. 'He said you could already have broken one of the little bones?'

'A "hairline" fracture, he called it, I suppose he meant I've sort of chipped it.'

'Then from now on you're going to take things easy. We'll manage and I'll write and tell our Rose,' Iris said determinedly.

'Do you think we should suggest she comes home?' Charlie asked. Rose wouldn't be very happy giving up her job and coming home to help out, he was certain of that. She enjoyed working in that big house and living with Gwen too much, her letters were always full of it.

'No, but at least she should know,' Iris replied firmly.

Kate said nothing. It was very disconcerting – not to say depressing – to realise that from now on she would have to rely so much on Iris and Charlie. She'd always been so active and it was hard to accept that there were so many things she would no longer be able to do. It was as though she was losing her independence. Inwardly she sighed. She was getting old and there was nothing she could do to avoid that.

Chapter Nineteen

In the weeks that followed Kate found it very hard to adjust to not working in the shop or doing nearly as much in the house as she'd been used to. Time dragged and she'd never been one for sitting and reading or knitting.

'I swear all this time on my own is driving me mad,' she complained to Iris one evening. Tom had joined them for supper, which she had prepared – something she could do at her leisure and mainly sitting down – but which Iris had cooked and would clear away after. 'If I were Rose I'd happily have my head stuck in a book but I'm just not used to doing nothing or gossiping with the neighbours for hours on end.'

'Why don't you invest in a wireless set?' Tom suggested.

Charlie frowned. 'That would be expensive.'

Iris shot him a reproving glance. 'But if it gave you pleasure, Mam, it would be worth it,' she urged.

'It's not just the cost of the set, you have to have a licence now and that costs ten shillings. I know that because Florence's father was complaining about it, it's a new thing they've brought in.'

'Ten bob over a year isn't that much, Charlie, less than a shilling a month,' Tom put in.

'Well, you don't get much for your money as far

as I can see. There's only one station: 2HT,' Charlie replied sharply. He didn't need Tom Morrissey suggesting such extravagances as buying a wireless set.

'At the moment, but once they get better established I'm sure there will be more choice. What do you think, Mrs M.?' Tom asked, looking to Iris for support.

'I think it would be a good investment, Mam, and you wouldn't feel as if you were on your own so much,' Iris urged.

Kate nodded. 'I'll think about it,' she said. 'It might help the time pass more quickly.'

Iris nodded her approval. 'Did our Rose have anything interesting to say?' she asked.

'Yes, she said in her letter that she's going to start to read to that poor young man she works for, he's crippled and said he can't concentrate well enough to read himself,' Kate informed them.

Charlie thought that Rose had a very easy life compared to both himself and Iris. Iris worked all hours in the shop and the house and he had his work cut out running the pawnbroker's. He didn't find it easy dealing with the people who came in. He knew times were hard and money scarce but they always had a sob story which annoyed him, and he was aware they didn't trust him the way they had his mam and before her his da. He'd heard the odd muttered comment to that effect. Also the fact that he had to be in the shop on Saturdays meant he could only spend Sunday helping out his future father-in-law, although he intended to make up for that by going to Florence's a couple of evenings a week.

No, Rose had it easy sitting reading to someone.

'She'll enjoy that and she's good-natured, is Rose, she won't mind giving up her time,' Iris remarked affably.

March had indeed 'come in like a lion', Rose thought as she, Nancy and Nora helped Henry to set the table that Sunday morning while the family were at church in the village. A fierce wind was tearing through the branches of the trees that surrounded the house and rattling the window casements, and the sky was an ominous shade of grey which threatened rain.

'I hope the gentleman arrives before the rain starts or he'll be soaked – if he's riding, that is,' Nancy remarked as Henry indicated that she move the claret glass more to the right of the wine glass. The best Crown Derby dinner service had been carefully unpacked and washed as had the cut-crystal glasses and all the girls had remarked that they'd never seen the dining table look so grand. Two large silver candelabra and the matching silver epergne – filled with tastefully arranged fruit – formed the centrepieces. Henry had remarked that when the old master and mistress had been alive the table was set like this almost every evening. There had been a great deal of entertaining in those days, he'd said sadly.

'If he's a farmer he'll be well used to the weather,' Rose replied, thinking of Gwen's brother Bob.

There was no further conversation as Mr Lewis entered to check that everything was in order.

'Right, you, Rose and Nancy, go back to the

kitchen and help Cook and Beryl. I'll be here to open the door when our visitor arrives and Nora be ready to take his hat and coat,' Mr Lewis instructed.

Nancy pulled a face as she closed the door behind them. 'I bet we won't even get to see what he looks like. I wonder will Miss Elinore end up marrying him? She looks really lovely, she asked me to fasten the clasp of her necklace when I took the fresh towels up. She's done her hair in a different style and she's wearing a dress I've never seen before and seems quite excited,' she informed Rose.

'Hush, you know Mrs Mathews said she didn't want to hear any gossiping in the servants' hall,' Rose reminded her companion, although she too would have liked to see both Miss Elinore and her gentleman friend.

'Well, at least you won't have to spend the afternoon reading to Master Dai,' Nancy whispered.

'You know I don't mind reading to him, Nancy, in fact I quite enjoy it now,' Rose replied. It was true, she thought. She'd been a bit hesitant and self-conscious at first when he'd presented her with a copy of *The Secret Adversary* – Mrs Christie's latest – but gradually she'd become more confident and indeed had become interested in the story. She'd willingly given up a couple of hours on Wednesday afternoons and now she was just as eager as he was to find out who the murderer was. 'Maybe when the gentleman has gone there will be time to read another chapter,' she mused aloud, thinking that it was almost as enjoyable to sit in his quiet drawing room that looked out across the grounds as it was to sit in the rose garden. It was certainly more comfortable for the weather wasn't very conducive to sitting outside.

'I wouldn't bank on that, Rose, luv. After the dishes and glasses and cutlery have been washed, they've all got to be put away again, see. Unless of course the gentleman coming to Sunday lunch is going to be a regular thing.' Nancy giggled and winked.

Rose shook her head but laughed all the same. Nancy loved a bit of excitement.

She was pleased when after tea David Rhys-Pritchard did indeed request that she go and read to him, although it would mean she would be later getting home to Gwen's for she still had chores to complete. As she entered his drawing room she thought how warm and welcoming it looked with the heavy curtains drawn over the windows, shutting out the cold blustery March evening, and a good fire burning in the hearth. The sofa and chairs were covered in a dark green brocade and the mahogany furniture gleamed softly in the light.

'I wasn't sure if you would require me, sir, not with the gentleman...' she said as she sat down in the armchair he indicated opposite him.

He smiled. 'Mr Williams left an hour ago, Rose, but he's coming again in a fortnight.'

'Mr Lewis said he drove over in a motor car,' she ventured.

'He did. Apparently he is what is termed a "gentleman farmer", which surprised Livvie,' he replied. 'And I found him a very agreeable man.'

Olivia had indeed been surprised to find that

Ernest Williams appeared to be quite a wealthy man, he thought. Her attitude to him had thawed considerably when she found out he had a motor car and that he owned his land and a substantial house and employed a dozen people. He had liked him and it was quite obvious that Ellie did too and that Ernest Williams – a widower but with no children – was quite smitten with his sister. It was early days yet but he hoped Livvie wouldn't put any obstacles in Ellie's path. She deserved a chance of happiness; she hadn't had much of it in her life so far.

'I ... I'm glad you liked him, sir. Miss Elinore will be happy and none of us minded the extra work,' Rose informed him.

He nodded. 'It was good of you to give up your time off; Livvie will make sure you are suitably recompensed. Have you heard from your family lately?' he added.

Rose nodded, but her face immediately filled with anxiety. 'My mam isn't too well, sir. She has something wrong with her bones, so my sister wrote. It's got a complicated name but it means they're very brittle and she could easily break something. And it will get worse as she gets older, so she's had to give up working in the shop.'

'That must be worrying for you, Rose,' he said quietly.

'It is, sir, but I've been thinking that maybe now she has more time to herself, when the weather gets better she might be able to come and visit Miss Roberts. They're old friends and I know she'd like that.'

He considered this. 'It might be beneficial but

she would have to be careful travelling, I think. Will she come by bus or train?'

Rose nodded. That was something she hadn't thought about and she remembered just how uncomfortable the journey had been. 'By bus and it can be a bit ... bumpy and I wouldn't want to put her at risk. Do you think I should even mention it at all, sir?' she asked.

'I'd wait for a while, Rose, and see how she progresses ... and, Rose, do you think that when we are alone you could stop calling me "sir"?'

Rose looked taken aback. 'What ... what should I call you?'

He smiled at her. 'Try "David", after all we are friends, aren't we? And having you call me "sir" makes me feel so old and decrepit when in reality I'm only a few years older than you. How old *are* you, Rose?'

'Seventeen, I'll be eighteen in June,' Rose replied, thinking it would be very peculiar to address him by his Christian name but pleased that he had said he considered her not just a servant but a friend.

'You see, I'm just three years older than you. Now, shall we try and find out a bit more about who this "Secret Adversary" might be?'

Rose smiled and opened the book. 'I've been looking forward to finding out too ... David.' She hesitated a little before she pronounced his name.

When Charlie arrived at Florence's on the Thursday evening Ethel Taylor was surprised to see him. 'I didn't know you were calling this evening,

Florence didn't mention it,' she greeted him as she opened the door.

'That's because she didn't know. I hope it's all right. Because I can now only help Mr Taylor on Sundays I thought I'd put in a few hours during the week, after work.'

Ethel nodded. She had grudgingly admitted that it was indeed helping Edward to have the lad's assistance and she sometimes wondered if she had misjudged him.

'How is your mother?' she asked.

'Getting rather fed up, she's not used to having so much time on her hands,' Charlie answered bluntly.

'I'm sure she will get used to it and she must follow the doctor's orders. Still, I'm sure that as the wedding draws closer she'll be glad she has more time to spare. We have things we must discuss together; guests from your side of the family, any favourite family hymns, what colour she is thinking of for her outfit – we don't want to clash or choose exactly the same colour. There is plenty to do. Perhaps she'd like to call one afternoon?' Ethel suggested as she ushered him towards Edward's study.

'Isn't it a bit early for things like that?' Charlie asked, thinking there were still twelve months to go and he was sure his mam wouldn't want to be bothered with Ethel Taylor fussing about colours and outfits just yet.

'It's never too early, Charlie. Good organisation is the basis for the perfect day,' she replied firmly. She thought he was showing very little interest in any of the arrangements so far; in fact they'd only been to see the vicar two weeks ago and then only because Florence had made a fuss about it.

Edward was equally surprised to see him but pleased; the lad was bright and quick to master things and seemed very capable.

'I'm very grateful, Charlie. You must be tired after being in the shop all day. How is it going?' he asked as Charlie sat down.

'Things aren't great, we're just ticking over. I can't see me making a great deal of money out of it to be perfectly honest.'

Edward frowned. 'I know you had little choice in the matter but do you think you would have been better off staying with the Blue Funnel Line?'

Charlie shrugged. 'I honestly don't know. I always wanted to work in the family business but I didn't realise that a certain ... temperament was needed or that times would continue to be so hard.'

'Surely that is to your advantage?'

'Not if people haven't got the money to redeem their pledges. It leaves me with a lot of stuff I have to get rid of at a loss and that's certainly not good business,' Charlie replied gloomily.

Edward nodded. 'How would it be if I paid you something for the work you do for me?' he offered. After all it would be to Florence's advantage. She certainly wouldn't want the wedding to be put off until the lad had enough money saved to provide her with a decent home.

'Oh, I couldn't possibly consider accepting payment! Things aren't that bad, just ... difficult. I hope you don't think I was hinting...' Charlie was concerned; tempting though the offer was he didn't want Edward Taylor to think he was scrounging or wasn't capable of making a success of his business. 'No, things are bound to pick up soon and I'm still learning the ropes. It's very generous of you to offer but I couldn't take payment for what is basically just "helping out". Anyway, I gain great satisfaction from the fact that you trust me with the knowledge of your business affairs.'

The older man nodded slowly, his estimation of his future son-in-law rising.

Chapter Twenty

The purchase of a wireless set brightened Kate's days considerably and, as the weather got warmer, with more rest the pain in her back gradually subsided. Iris too was thankful for the balmier days, light mornings and longer evenings. 'It's certainly easier getting up in daylight and not ending the day half frozen,' she remarked to Tom when he arrived to drop off her order. 'And Mam isn't in nearly as much pain now either and that's a blessing. Even our Charlie isn't moaning as much about business although Florence and her mam are starting to fuss, which is irritating him.' Florence had arrived the previous evening, bringing with her swatches of material for bridesmaids' dresses and she could see her friend was impatient for a decision.

'Mother said the choice is really mine but I wanted to discuss the colours with you, Iris. I just can't make up my mind between these two.' Florence had handed over two pieces of silk taffeta, one apple-blossom pink, the other a pale primrose-lemon. 'They're both colours I like and they're just perfect for a spring wedding.'

'They're both lovely, Florence, but I think I prefer the pale lemon, it goes better with my hair and if our Rose is going to be a bridesmaid, it will suit her too. I think the pink is a bit too pale,' she'd said.

Florence had nodded happily. 'That's just what I thought too. I think white and pale lemon with touches of green will be a really lovely spring colour theme. Now that's decided your mother and mine can choose what colours they'll have. All we need to do now is decide on the style for your dress,' Florence had continued.

Iris had sighed and had listened while Florence had outlined what she had in mind.

Now she rolled her eyes and grimaced at Tom. 'I told you she'd want us in something frilly, didn't I? You should have seen what she had in mind! We sort of compromised in the end as I said it was pointless having something I could never wear again – not that I'll have much call for pale lemon silk taffeta.'

'Oh, you never know, one day I might be able to afford to take you to a posh dance,' Tom replied.

'I don't know if I'd feel comfortable at a posh dance,' she laughed.

'Is Charlie getting more involved in all these

arrangements now?' Tom asked.

'No, he's managing to stay well out of it – so far – and I think Mam is glad she's going to stay with Gwen for a couple of weeks next month.'

Tom nodded. It would do Iris's mam the world of good, he thought, but wondered who would keep the peace between Iris and her brother for they frequently bickered.

When both Rose and Gwen had written suggesting that Kate go to Tregarron in June for the flower show she had been delighted. It would be wonderful to spend time in the country with her old friend and her youngest daughter, she'd thought, and she'd never been to the show. Gwen had suggested that she get the taxi from Denbigh to Tregarron for she certainly couldn't ride on a farm cart now, not with her condition. She would arrange it and try to obtain a special rate for her. Rose had written saying that not only would there be the entertainment of the show but that there was to be a party too as Miss Elinore was getting engaged to Mr Williams and the whole household was excited about it. Yes, with the prospect of a few weeks' holiday and her wireless set Kate felt her life was definitely better than it had been.

Gwen had all manner of things planned for when Kate came to stay and had discussed the travelling in detail with Rose.

'She should tell the bus driver that she has this medical condition so he should take it easy,' Gwen said firmly one evening in June as Rose was helping her to tie up the climbing rose beside the front door.

'I can't see her doing that,' Rose replied, breathing in the heady perfume of the deep pink blooms.

'Well, I intend to tell Mr Griffiths who has the taxi to take things very easy. Pass me those secateurs, *cariad*.'

'And she'll be here for my birthday, although it's just a normal working day for me and will probably be busier too with all the preparations for the party. Miss Olivia has been making lists for weeks and is always having long discussions with Mr Lewis and Mrs Mathews about taking on more staff.'

Gwen nodded. 'Quite an occasion for them, it is, see. There hasn't been a party up there in years.'

'I don't suppose there has been much to celebrate,' Rose replied. She was looking forward to it. Everyone was; both family and staff seemed far more animated and Miss Elinore had certainly blossomed since the news had been announced.

'Has anything been said about a date for the wedding? That will be a very grand affair, I shouldn't wonder. There'll be people coming from far and wide. I know there are aunts and uncles and cousins and family friends: I suppose they'll be staying at Plas Idris,' Gwen informed Rose, standing back to inspect her handiwork.

'I haven't heard a date mentioned yet but I should imagine it will be later in the year or early next year; these things seem to take a lot of organising. I know Mam will be glad to get away from all discussions on weddings,' she said, gathering up the gardening implements. 'Florence and Iris have already decided on the colour for Iris's dress.'

'What about you, Rose?' Gwen asked.

Rose shook her head. 'I've written and told Florence that it's just not practical for me to be a bridesmaid too. I don't mind, I'm sure they will give me the time off to attend the wedding, but I can't expect them to let me traipse back and forth to Liverpool for fittings and the like. And Iris was Florence's friend before Florence even met our Charlie and me.'

Gwen nodded. 'Just as long as you don't feel slighted.'

'Not at all. And I'm really looking forward to Mam coming,' Rose replied happily.

The weather was glorious when Kate arrived, tired and hot and relieved that the journey was over.

'Kate, come on in: I've some homemade lemonade in the kitchen. It's so lovely to have you to stay.' Gwen hugged her friend gently.

'I won't break, Gwen, luv,' Kate laughed.

'That's just what you might do, Kate,' Gwen said seriously. 'We'll have to take good care of you. Rose won't be back until after eight; they are all getting in a bit of a tizzy up there what with the show in a few days and the party. She'll be able to tell you all about it when she gets in. Now, I'll take your case up and we can unpack after you've had time to rest a bit. Bethan said she'd pop down later to see you.'

Kate settled back contentedly in her chair. She

was really going to enjoy this little holiday.

Rose arrived home later that evening and after leaving her bicycle in the outhouse found her mother and Gwen sitting in the small garden at the back of the cottage.

'It's such a lovely evening I thought we'd have supper out here. Bob called so I got him to bring the table out,' Gwen told her, indicating the table already set for the meal beneath the shade of the old apple tree in the corner.

Rose hugged her mother, feeling as if it had been a year instead of just months since she'd last seen her and noticing too that Kate had become thinner. 'Mam, I've really been looking forward to you coming to stay.'

Kate smiled affectionately at her, thinking the life here did seem to suit Rose. She had more colour in her cheeks and looked fit, healthy and happy, which was indeed a blessing. 'And I'm delighted to be here. You're looking really well, Rose. Working up there must suit you.'

'I do enjoy it, Mam, even though the hours are long and at the moment we're all really rushed off our feet,' Rose assured her, and then went to help Gwen to bring out the evening meal on two trays.

Gwen poured the tea and Rose handed her mother a plate of cold roast beef with cheese, tomatoes and chutney, accompanied by slices of crusty bread and butter from Bryn-y-Garn Farm.

Over the meal Rose informed them of the preparations that were going on at the big house and

234

Kate relayed all the news from Liverpool. They were about to start clearing away when Bethan Williams arrived.

'Bethan, how lovely to see you again,' Kate greeted her as Rose went into the cottage for another cup and saucer.

'I'm so glad you have come to spend a few weeks here this time, Kate, and not just a few hours,' Bethan said warmly, nodding her thanks for the tea Gwen poured.

'If I go home looking as well as Rose does, it will have been well worth the journey,' Kate replied.

Bethan nodded. 'She's a lovely girl, Kate, and is well liked, but she does have to work hard! Things are all at sixes and sevens at Plas Idris at present. That house is being cleaned and polished to death – I saw when I was up there this afternoon.'

Kate nodded. 'Helping organise the show, I assume.'

'I'll be spending a few hours there tomorrow myself,' Gwen put in. 'If you like you can come with me, Kate, but you're not to do anything at all strenuous – no helping to move tables or chairs or anything like that. Oh, I just hope that Mrs Llewellyn-Jones isn't going to create the usual fuss, we can do without it this year,' she added grimly.

'She will,' Bethan said flatly. 'Full of her own importance, she is, but with all the fuss over Miss Elinore's engagement I doubt anyone will take much notice of her.'

'He's a widower, isn't he, the man she's going

235

to marry?' Kate remarked. Rose had told her so in her letter.

Bethan nodded. 'Sad, it was. Only been married for two years, they had, she was one of the Davieses from Aberdaron. Lovely girl. She died in childbirth and the baby with her. Little boy, it was. He was very cut up over it, poor man. Kept himself to himself after that.'

'Until he met Miss Elinore.' Rose smiled. 'I've only seen him twice but he seems a nice gentleman and David ... er ... Mr Rhys-Pritchard', she hastily amended, 'says he likes him a great deal and thinks Miss Elinore will be very happy.'

The three older women exchanged glances. It was Kate who broke the silence. 'There seems to be a lot of tragedy surrounding that family.'

'There has been,' Bethan agreed.

'Let's hope that Miss Elinore's wedding marks a new beginning for them then,' Gwen said sagely.

'I doubt Miss Olivia will ever get married; after all, someone has to run that house and ensure that Mr David is well taken care of,' Bethan commented.

'He's much better these days. I can see an improvement in him from when I first went to work there. He doesn't seem to have nearly as many "difficult" days now and he's just got one of those motorised wheelchairs, which will make it much easier for him to get around,' Rose stated.

Gwen smiled. 'Is that so? That should be a big help. Maybe he'll start to take more of an interest in the estate now. I know he has a land agent but his father always kept a close eye on things, was always very interested in his tenants. You say he enjoys the time he spends listening to you read to him, Rose, I suppose that's a start.'

'He does and we often discuss who we think the killer is and why and the twists and turns of the plot. She really is a very clever woman that Mrs Christie.'

'Do you discuss other things?' Kate asked, thinking she would have a word with Gwen later on about Rose's attitude towards her young employer.

'Sometimes. He always asks about you and the rest of the family,' Rose admitted. 'He's very polite, Mam, but I am just a housemaid after all.'

'So he doesn't talk much about himself?' Kate persisted.

Rose shook her head, feeling a little uncomfortable and wishing she hadn't inadvertently called him by his Christian name. They were friends but she wasn't sure what her mam would think of that friendship. 'No, and he won't talk about the war at all, except that he was in the Welsh Guards and he only told me that after I'd told him what regiment our Charlie was in.'

Bethan nodded. 'None of them like to talk about it.'

Rose got to her feet. 'I'll start and clear away now, it's starting to get dark.'

Bethan too rose to her feet. 'And I'd best be getting back. I left Owen writing his sermon. I'd take the opportunity to rest tomorrow, Kate, get over the journey, while Gwen and I are up at the big house. You'll have plenty of time to see the place on the day of the show and of course nearly everyone in the village has been invited to the party – after the family and guests have all had dinner, that is. We're to be entertained in a marquee.'

Kate looked startled. 'You never mentioned that, Gwen. I don't know if I've brought a decent enough dress to wear.'

Gwen smiled at her. 'It was to be a surprise – the icing on the cake, see, and don't worry about a dress, we're not expected to wear anything fancy. After all, we're mainly just tenants.'

When the dishes had been washed and put away and Rose had gone up to bed as she had a very early start next day, Kate decided to sound her friend out.

'We all noticed that she called him "David", Gwen, and it's not like our Rose to forget her manners. I hope there's nothing going on there.'

Gwen frowned. 'I know she thinks highly of him, Kate, and perhaps she's even become ... fond ... of him but, in a sisterly sort of way. I think she feels sorry for him. I don't think there is anything "going on", as you put it. He's in a wheelchair and still endures a lot of pain. I suppose her reading to him takes his mind off things.'

Kate nodded slowly. 'Rose has always been ... impressionable, always lived in a sort of dream world. She's not as practical and down to earth as Iris and I don't want her to get herself into a situation where she might get hurt. We're working-class Liverpudlians, Gwen; he's from a very different background. The "gentry" I suppose you'd call him, wealthy, well educated and waited on by servants all his life.'

'I don't think Rose is as impressionable as you think, Kate. She can be quite level-headed and she knows her place; even though she spends time with him she doesn't shirk her chores. I wouldn't worry too much about her. If Mona Mathews thought there was anything amiss, she'd certainly bring it to both my attention and Miss Olivia's, I can assure you. Both Miss Olivia and Miss Elinore think highly of Rose, Mona told me so herself. Now, you get a good night's rest and stop worrying about Rose. You're here to enjoy yourself and it's her birthday tomorrow,' Gwen finished firmly.

Chapter Twenty-One

Rose was very surprised next day when after lunch she was summoned to David Rhys-Pritchard's drawing room. The French doors were open wide, flooding the room with sunlight and giving an excellent view of the gardens where the big marquees were being erected. There were to be five of them, the usual four for the flower show and a fifth where the villagers and tenants who had been invited to Elinore's engagement party would gather in the evening. A warm summer breeze wafted across the terrace and rustled gently through the thick green foliage of the surrounding trees. The stone urns, filled now with flowers, were a riot of colour as were the huge bushes of rhododendrons and hydrangeas that graced the shrub borders.

'Come in, Rose,' David instructed.

'There's a great deal of activity going on out there and don't the flowers look magnificent? I just hope this glorious weather holds,' Rose commented as she crossed the room towards him.

David turned away from the open doorway and moved back into the room, smiling at her. 'So do I, Rose. Ellie is so looking forward to everything. I've not seen her so excited or so happy in years.'

Rose smiled back wondering why he had called for her. They had finished *The Mysterious Affair at Styles* and Miss Olivia had been too busy to find the time to go into Denbigh to look for another crime novel. In fact she was going to suggest that she go into Parry's Bookshop on her next afternoon off.

'Happy Birthday, Rose. I ... I hope you like this.' David held out a small package.

'Oh! Thank ... you!' Rose replied, surprised and a little flustered. 'How ... how did you know?' She felt the colour flooding her cheeks.

'You told me your birthday was in June and I found out the exact date from Mrs Mathews,' he replied, indicating that she should sit down. 'Are you going to open it?'

Rose unwrapped the package to find it contained a slim box. 'I didn't expect... It's very ... kind of you ... David,' she stammered, not knowing what to say. Inside the box was a bookmark made of silver. From the top of the slender column was suspended an ornament delicately shaped in silver filigree as a fan, complete with a red silk tassel. Rose took it out and examined it carefully; it was quite heavy. 'Oh, it's beautiful! But it's *silver!*

I ... I've never had anything like this before in my life!'

'I wanted to give you something to mark the occasion, Rose, but I wasn't sure what you'd like. And then I noticed this in the silver collection and I thought it would be perfect as you enjoy reading so much. Pretty and useful,' David informed her.

Rose was at a loss for words. He'd given her a very expensive gift and one from the family's own collection of silver. She'd often seen Mr Lewis carefully cleaning the silver; no one else was allowed to do it. 'From the ... collection. Do you think...?'

'Rose, it is *my* collection and I want you to have this as a birthday gift,' he said quietly.

It *was* a beautiful and useful gift, she thought. 'I'll treasure it, David, I really will,' she promised shyly.

He smiled at her. 'But I hope you'll use it as well.'

She nodded. 'I will.'

'And are you looking forward to the party?' he asked to change the subject for he could see she was a little uncomfortable. He hadn't intended to embarrass her.

Rose carefully, replaced the bookmark in the box. 'Oh, I am! I can't remember the last time I went to a party. In fact I've never been to anything quite as ... grand,' she replied. The only party she had been to in her life was the street party that had been held to celebrate the end of the war and she wasn't going to bring that up. 'And I'm sure Miss Elinore will look absolutely gorgeous,' she enthused for the dressmaker had visited the house on several occasions. Miss Olivia had engaged agency staff from Llandudno, to help out and the cold buffet for the tenants and servants was being provided and served by caterers: no expense was being spared. She'd been delighted when Mrs Mathews had informed her that when the family dinner was over, she, Nancy, Nora and Beryl could join the villagers in the marquee for the rest of the evening. A musical quartet had been engaged to play for the family and guests in the Grand Drawing Room and some local musicians would play in the marquee.

'I'm sure she will too and it will be a busy time for everyone. I saw Miss Roberts here this morning,' he informed her, thinking of the day he'd first seen her when she'd accompanied the post-mistress here, almost a year ago now.

'She was coming about the show. My mam is resting today, she's tired after the journey but thankfully she arrived safe and sound.' Rose got to her feet; she still had plenty of work to do.

'Then she will be coming with Miss Roberts to the party, I presume?' David enquired, thinking he would like to meet her mother.

Rose nodded. 'Aunty Gwen told her last night and she was very surprised but delighted. I'd better get back now, David, and thank you again for such a truly beautiful gift.'

'I wanted to give you something special, Rose,' he said, wishing she could stay but knowing that there were other demands upon her time. Olivia had instructed that the whole house be cleaned from top to bottom and rooms were now being prepared for the guests.

Rose smiled. 'It's the most beautiful and *special* thing I've ever owned, David, you are so ... kind and generous to me.'

'You are my friend and you are very special to me, Rose. I mean that.'

'Thank you, that means ... a lot to me, David,' Rose stammered before turning and leaving the room in some haste, her heart beating in an odd jerky kind of way.

Outside in the hallway she leaned against the wall, her cheeks flushed. He had said she was 'special' and he'd gone out of his way to find out when her birthday was and had given her a beautiful gift, one he had put some considerable thought into choosing, to say nothing of its value. They were growing closer and she had become fond of him, but ... but was that wise? She had been fond of Jimmy Harper once and that had only led to heartache. Hearing Nancy's voice on the stairs she pulled herself together. She had no intention of telling Nancy or anyone else of David Rhys-Pritchard's birthday gift.

The flower show that year seemed to have attracted more interest than usual, Gwen thought as she and Kate got ready for Elinore Rhys-Pritchard's engagement party. It had been quite an exhausting few days for the weather had held and the heat in the marquees had been stifling – to the detriment of the flowers and vegetables, which had to be frequently sprayed with water – but the increased crowds and added interest very probably had been generated by the forthcoming event. Neither of

243

them had seen Rose during the day but they would see her this evening, she'd assured Kate. They were going to Plas Idris with Bob and his family and they were all looking forward to it.

'Doesn't it look ... splendid and very big!' Kate commented as they walked up the drive and the house came into view. 'I don't think I could ever get used to a house *that* size, even though our Rose seems to have. I'd keep getting lost.'

Dusk had barely begun to fall yet lights blazed from almost every window and little coloured lanterns had been strung between the branches of the trees and shrubs. The front door stood wide open allowing glimpses of huge vases and urns of flowers in the spacious hallway. From inside the house strains of music and laughter could be heard.

Gwen smiled and nodded. 'Just like the old days, it is, Kate. It's lovely to see the place looking so well again.' She lowered her voice a little. 'And the fact that two of her floral arrangements have pride of place in the Grand Drawing Room has made even Mrs Llewellyn-Jones quite bearable.'

There were many people making their way towards the marquee and they were joined by Bethan and her husband. Inside on long trestle tables covered with white cloths the 'cold collation' – as it was officially termed – was laid out.

'That looks very appetising,' Bethan said admiringly. 'They certainly know how to give a party. Mind you, when I was a child the old master always held a ball for the tenants every year with no expense spared either.'

'And we always had a wonderful time,' Gwen added as Bob was despatched to obtain drinks for them.

'Will we see the happy couple, do you think?' Kate enquired. She'd never been to anything like this in her life before.

'Oh, definitely,' Gwen assured her firmly.

Half an hour later, when everyone had arrived and the entertainment was in full swing, Kate spotted Rose accompanied by three other young girls, all still in their respective uniforms. Kate waved and Rose detached herself from her companions.

'Isn't this just *wonderful!*' Kate enthused, sipping a glass of sparkling wine. She had no intention of dancing but would be quite content to sit and watch and she was looking forward to the buffet.

'If you think this is very grand, Mam, you should see them up at the house. Oh, the dresses and the jewellery and the gentlemen in evening suits ... even we've got our best uniforms on.' Rose smoothed down the black skirt of her dress and tweaked the lace edge of her white apron. 'The house looks gorgeous too, everything polished up, flowers in every room and all the best china and crystal,' she added. Her eyes were sparkling and her cheeks flushed from both excitement and the warmth of the evening.

'We're hoping to see the happy couple,' Kate confided.

'Miss Elinore had just gone up to fetch her silk wrap when Mrs Mathews said we could come and join in so she'll be here any minute now,'

Rose informed them.

Gwen turned towards the open side of the marquee. 'You were right, Rose, luv, here they come!'

Everyone broke into spontaneous clapping as Elinore entered, looking quite radiant. She was accompanied by her fiancé and followed by her sister, brother and two cousins.

Rose was very surprised to see Olivia and particularly David. She'd only expected Elinore and Ernest to put in an appearance.

'Oh, doesn't she look ... gorgeous! There's just no other word for it!' Gwen exclaimed, thinking the girl had really blossomed. She had always been the prettier of the Rhys-Pritchard sisters but tonight she was radiant. Her light brown hair had been cut in a becoming bob and was encircled by a band of shell pink silk studded with pearls. Her matching silk dress had a skirt which floated in handkerchief points and a bodice heavily embroidered with seed pearls and silver bugle beads. She wore a necklace, earrings and bracelet of pearls and her eyes shone with obvious happiness.

'And doesn't Miss Olivia look well too,' Kate added, thinking she'd never seen dresses like these before, except perhaps in the windows of Liverpool's most expensive and exclusive shops. Olivia's dress was of black crêpe de Chine and silk chiffon, embroidered with gold thread and beads. She still refused to have her hair cut but it was swept up elegantly and held in place by gold pins which were decorated with sprays of delicate gold flowers with tiny jewels for centres. Rose had already seen all this finery but she concurred with her mother and Gwen, thinking that David too looked splendid and quite handsome in his black tailed evening suit and white waistcoat, shirt and bow tie. You hardly noticed the scar now, she thought and she, at least, barely noticed the wheelchair, she was so used to it.

The minister, Bethan's husband Owen, took it upon himself to speak for everyone and he wished Elinore and Ernest every happiness and thanked them and David and Olivia for inviting everyone to share the auspicious occasion and with such magnificent hospitality. Then, when everyone went to shake their hands and offer their personal messages of congratulation, Gwen reached over and took Kate's arm.

Kate hesitated. 'Oh, do you really think I should? I mean I'm not ... a tenant and I don't live in the village. I don't even know them and I'm not sure what to say.'

'Everyone was allowed to bring a guest and you're mine. Just wish them well,' Gwen stated firmly, urging her friend forward.

'They won't bite, Mam. They're really very nice,' Rose whispered for Kate was looking very ill at ease.

Gwen introduced her to Elinore and Ernest and Kate wished them every happiness and was thankfully turning away when Rose caught her arm.

'Mam, I'd like you to meet Mr David Rhys-Pritchard. Sir, this is my mother, Mrs Katherine Mundy.'

David looked up at the thin woman in the blue and white flowered cotton dress and smiled as he extended his hand. 'I'm very pleased to meet you, Mrs Mundy. Rose told me you were visiting Miss Roberts. I hope you are having a pleasant evening?'

'Oh, yes, indeed! It's all quite ... splendid ... sir,' Kate replied, overcome with embarrassment.

He smiled at Rose. 'Rose is very kind, she gives up quite a lot of her free time to read to me and we often have quite animated discussions, don't we, Rose?'

'We do, sir,' Rose replied.

David looked at Kate thoughtfully. 'Would it be impertinent of me to ask does Rose take after her father?'

Kate relaxed a little; he was a pleasant young man and it wasn't *that* hard to talk to him. 'She gets her dark hair and eyes from Bill, my late husband, but she takes after me in her ... build.' She smiled at Rose. 'But she has her father's nature. He was a kind, generous, hard-working and good-tempered man.'

'Then she definitely has inherited those traits. How are you feeling, Mrs Mundy? I hear you haven't been well,' he enquired politely.

'Oh, it's nothing too serious. I'm just getting older. A few weeks here in the country will perk me up no end,' Kate replied, thinking that considering what this poor young man had suffered and would continue to suffer for the rest of his life, she wasn't badly off at all.

He nodded. 'I'm sure you will benefit from it. Now, if you will excuse me, I must thank the Reverend Williams for his short speech. Enjoy the rest of your evening, Mrs Mundy. I'll see you tomorrow, Rose.'

Rose took her mother's arm as they turned away and followed Gwen towards the long tables where the buffet was starting to be served. 'You see, Mam, he's really very nice.'

Kate nodded. She was glad the interview was over but she hadn't failed to notice the expression in David Rhys-Pritchard's eyes when he'd looked at Rose. 'He is, luv, but don't forget *who* he is or that you are a paid servant in his house,' she said quietly.

Chapter Twenty-Two

Iris was tired but she wondered if she should wait up for Charlie who had gone to Florence's house after supper. When he was out she found it very strange being in on her own, it was very quiet even though she had the wireless set. Kate had been away for over a week now, and she missed her. She was used to seeing her mother in the kitchen when she came through from the shop and of chatting to her of the day's events. She'd had a long letter this morning which she decided to read again while she waited for her brother to return as she'd really only scanned through it, mainly to reassure herself that Kate was well.

She settled herself in an armchair and reread the letter, smiling to herself. Mam really seemed to be enjoying herself; she'd been tired after the journey but she'd soon recovered and both Gwen and Rose were in good form. Iris felt very relieved that her mother was well and that her sister was happy. Kate was full of both the flower show and the engagement party, which, judging from her mam's highly detailed and enthusiastic report, sounded like a cross between a rather posh street party and a very elegant Society event. They certainly had a lavish lifestyle up at Plas Idris, quite unlike her own, she mused, although she wouldn't have wanted to swap. Kate had loved seeing all the beautiful flowers and the marvellous fruit and vegetable exhibits at the show, particularly the spectacular floral arrangements created by someone called Mrs Llewellyn-Jones, who apparently got first prize every year but who was something of a fusspot, according to Gwen.

Mam had met the entire Rhys-Pritchard family, including the new fiancé and the servants, or so it seemed, and Iris wished she could have seen for herself the style of the gorgeous evening dresses and expensive jewellery and the engagement ring, which according to Kate made Florence's ring look insignificant. The food and drink that had been laid on sounded mouth-watering and very lavish.

She was reading the final paragraph, which contained the details of a picnic that Gwen had planned, when she heard Charlie coming in the back way.

'I was rereading Mam's letter. She sounds as if she's having a great time. What's the matter?' she finished, realising from his expression that something was wrong.

'It's Florence's dad, he's been taken into Walton Hospital, that's why I'm home later than usual.'

Iris was instantly concerned. 'What's the matter with him? Is he going to be all right? Is Florence all right?'

Charlie took off his jacket, sat down opposite her and ran his hands through his hair. It had been a very worrying evening. 'When I arrived there was utter panic. He'd collapsed, Florence was in tears and her mam was half out of her mind with worry, but she'd telephoned for the doctor and when he arrived he sent for an ambulance straight away.'

Iris's eyes widened. 'Oh, my God! What's wrong with him?'

'He'd complained of not feeling well, he had pains in his chest, then he collapsed. The doctor at the hospital said he's had a heart attack but that he was now "stable" – whatever that means – but they're keeping him in, so by the time I got Mrs Taylor and Florence home and calmed them down a bit...' He stood up, crossed to the dresser and took out the half-bottle of brandy Kate kept there for emergencies. He poured a small amount into a glass.

'But he *is* going to get better?' Iris was forcefully reminded of the terrible foreboding she had experienced that awful day when her da had been taken to hospital. No wonder Florence had been in tears; it must have been an ordeal for her friend.

Charlie nodded as he took a swig of the brandy. 'They're going to keep a close eye on him but they think he'll be all right as long as he has complete rest and takes the tablets they're giving him. He's not going to be able to do anything, and I mean *anything*, for quite a while and he's not to be worried or get upset over anything either.'

'But they will let him go home soon?'

Charlie nodded. 'When they feel he is well enough.'

Iris bit her lip. 'Do you think we should let Mam know?' she asked.

'No. There's nothing she can do, is there? And she'll only start to worry about Florence. But now that both Florence and her mother have calmed down they'll be fine. No, leave Mam to enjoy herself.'

'It's half-day closing tomorrow, I'll go and see Florence,' Iris offered, getting up to put the kettle on.

'She'll appreciate that; she's not going into work tomorrow. She'll telephone them in the morning.' Charlie paused. He was feeling calmer himself now but Edward Taylor's predicament had presented him with some problems. 'There is something I have to discuss with you, Iris, before you go to see Florence.'

She frowned. 'What?'

'Mr Taylor's business – it's not going to run itself.'

Iris was outraged. 'Oh, for heaven's sake, Charlie! Don't you ever think of anything other than business? The poor man is lying ill in hospital!'

'And if I know him he'll be worrying about his business and that's not going to help him get better, is it?' Charlie retorted.

Iris had to agree with this and she nodded slowly.

'So, what I'm going to suggest to Mrs Taylor is

252

that I take over the business until he's back on his feet again. I know enough about it now to keep things ticking over nicely.' Charlie had thought all this through on the way home on the tram.

'You'll have to close up the shop, I can't manage both businesses.'

Charlie hesitated, wondering how she would take his next suggestion. 'I know you can't, Iris, but I was wondering if Tom Morrissey would stand in for me for a few weeks?'

'Tom? But he already has a job,' Iris protested.

'He starts very early and finishes early, Iris. He needn't open up until mid-morning,' Charlie reminded her.

'But he knows nothing about pawnbroking.'

'And you knew nothing about greengrocery but you soon learned. I'll go over everything with him and he's no fool.'

Iris was considering this. 'We can't ask him to do it for nothing, Charlie.'

'I don't intend to but I can only afford to pay him the rate he gets now.'

That wasn't very much, Iris thought, but she was thinking of Florence's father's health and her friend's peace of mind. 'I'll ask him in the morning.'

'You will impress upon him how important it is for Florence's father and that it will only be a temporary arrangement? He'll be getting paid and doing us all a great favour at the same time,' Charlie urged.

But mainly you, Iris thought. Her brother had obviously worked all this out. He wasn't prepared to close his shop and lose business but he also intended to make sure that Edward Taylor's business didn't suffer either and she was certain that both Mrs Taylor and Florence would be greatly impressed by this show of consideration on Charlie's part. Still, for Florence's sake she'd ask Tom.

She asked him next morning and was surprised and somewhat relieved when he agreed, saying it would be an interesting experience and the extra cash would come in very handy.

'It's not going to be a fortune, Tom, in fact it's just buttons,' she reminded him as he went through to the kitchen to see her brother.

When she arrived at Cedar Grove after lunch that afternoon she found Florence pale and still a little tearful.

'Oh, Iris, I still can't take it in. Mother is at the hospital now but he's only allowed one visitor and only for half an hour; they're very strict. He has to have complete rest,' she said as she ushered Iris into the morning room.

'He's in good hands, Florence, so try not to worry too much. But I know it must have been a terrible shock for you.' She could fully understand her friend's emotions, remembering how she had felt when she'd learned of her da's accident. It wasn't quite the same – Edward Taylor hadn't died – but it was only natural that Florence was upset.

Florence nodded and dabbed at her eyes. 'It was. He's not usually ill. He ... he's always been ... here. I got very upset this morning when I realised he wasn't.'

Iris nodded sadly, thinking of her da. 'I know.

254

You never think anything ... awful is going to happen to them. But look on the bright side, Florence, he is going to get better and come home again and Charlie told me to tell you not to worry, he's got everything in hand.'

'Oh, Iris, he's so good. I just don't know what we would have done last night without him. Mother and I were in such a state but he took charge completely.'

'I'll put the kettle on. We'll have a cup of tea and I'll tell you what Charlie's organised.'

They had tea and Iris told her friend of the plans her brother had made. By the time Ethel Taylor arrived home Florence was feeling much better.

'How is he now?' Florence asked as Ethel took off her hat and Iris made a fresh pot of tea. Florence's mother looked pale, anxious and exhausted, she thought.

'He's had a comfortable night, the doctor said, and he does look a bit ... brighter, thank God. I've hardly slept a wink worrying about him.'

'Sit down and have this tea, you look as though you need it, Mrs Taylor.' Iris handed her the cup.

Ethel nodded. 'Thank you, Iris. It's very kind of you to come and I have to say Charlie has been very good, but Edward is his own worst enemy. He still works far too hard despite being warned to take things easier. Well, from now on things will have to change. We can't risk this happening again.'

'Iris has just been telling me that Charlie has organised everything so we're not to worry,' Florence explained.

Ethel looked questioningly at Iris.

'Charlie is going to take over the business until Mr Taylor is back on his feet again; he's familiar with everything having helped him out lately. And Tom Morrissey, my young man, is going to run Charlie's business. He's starting tomorrow. Charlie will be here this evening to see how Mr Taylor is progressing and he'll start first thing tomorrow. So, you see there is nothing for Mr Taylor to worry about – except getting better.'

Ethel nodded slowly. It seemed as if she had misjudged Charlie; he had ensured that Edward would have no cause to worry but she had plans for when her husband was well again. She was going to insist that he sell the business and retire. They would buy a nice bungalow either in the country or by the sea somewhere so he could relax more, maybe even take up golf. 'I'm very grateful for all this help, Iris, I really am, and I'll tell Edward when I visit him this evening. I'm sure it will put his mind at rest. Now, if you'll excuse me I think I'll go and have a nap, I'm exhausted.'

Iris and Florence washed the cups and then Iris tried to lighten the mood by telling her friend all about Kate's letter.

'You know I'd quite forgotten about my wedding with all the upset,' Florence said. 'I hope Dad is going to be fit and well by then...' she added anxiously.

'Of course he will be but, Florence, I wouldn't even mention anything about it for quite a while yet. The last thing he needs is to be reminded of all the ... arrangements,' she urged. She had been going to say 'fuss and expense' but had changed her mind; Florence really was genuinely upset.

When Ethel returned to the hospital that evening she was very relieved to see her husband sitting up and looking more like his old self.

'You look much better, Edward dear,' she greeted him, kissing him on the cheek.

'I feel it, my dear. I seriously had my doubts last night that I would pull through, I've never experienced pain like it.' Edward still felt ill and the attack had given him a nasty shock.

'They've been marvellous here, Edward. Now, perhaps you'll do as you're told. You are to have complete rest and are not to get anxious or upset about anything. Young Iris called this afternoon and between them she and Charlie have everything in hand. Charlie is going to take over for you and Iris's young man, Tom ... something or other ... is going to run the pawnbroker's. Charlie apparently thinks he's capable of doing so. They will both start first thing tomorrow.'

Edward nodded thankfully. He'd been trying not to think about what would happen but he was very, very relieved to hear this. Charlie too was very 'capable', in his opinion. 'That really is a weight off my mind, Ethel. And it's very considerate of them both to help us out. Iris is a very good friend to Florence and Charlie ... well, he has a good head on his shoulders and he'll make a fine husband.'

Ethel nodded in agreement. 'And when you are back on your feet, Edward, we'll talk about the future. I think you should seriously consider retiring. We can't risk this happening again and we neither of us are getting any younger,' she finished firmly.

Edward closed his eyes. 'We'll talk about it when I come home, Ethel,' he promised.

He was exhausted by even this brief visit.

Chapter Twenty-Three

Kate had arrived home looking and feeling rested, and was horrified to hear of Edward Taylor's illness. But she'd been pleased to learn that in the emergency Charlie, Iris and Tom had worked together to help the Taylors out. Mr Taylor had recovered slowly and was now back at work although he had taken on extra help, at Ethel's insistence. That meant that Charlie didn't need to spend his spare time at Cedar Grove doing the paperwork and was also now back in the pawnbroker's shop. Tom Morrissey had told her that he'd enjoyed standing in for Charlie; it had been an interesting and eye-opening experience and a sobering one too. He'd come to realise that he was fortunate to have a reasonably steady job and the prospect of a stable and happy future with Iris, when they had a bit more money put by.

As the days grew shorter with the approach of autumn Kate had a letter from Rose informing her that Miss Elinore was to marry Ernest Williams just after Christmas in a quiet ceremony to which just family were to be invited. It had surprised almost everyone that there wasn't to be a grand Society wedding but apparently it was what the couple wanted.

Iris relayed this news to Florence when the two girls met up in Lyons Tea Rooms one Wednesday lunchtime in early October. It was a beautiful autumn day now, Iris had thought as she'd alighted from the tram. It had been misty that morning but the sun had soon dispersed the mist and the leaves on the trees in the parks were a riot of oranges, reds and golds. It was quite a while since she'd indulged in the little luxury of having lunch with her friend, Iris thought happily as she walked up Lord Street.

Florence was already waiting and had ordered a pot of tea for two. 'I didn't order anything else, I wasn't sure what you'd like,' she greeted her friend.

'How about toasted teacakes?' Iris suggested as the waitress appeared. 'Rose has written with news of Elinore Rhys-Pritchard's wedding. It's to be a very quiet affair apparently, after Christmas.'

Florence looked disgruntled. 'You'd think with all their money they'd have splashed out, she being the first to get married.'

Iris shrugged. 'It's what Elinore wants. How are things going with your arrangements?'

Florence frowned. 'I sometimes wonder if we'll get to the church at all.'

'What's our Charlie been saying to upset you now?' Iris demanded.

'It's not Charlie, it's my mother! I've not to mention the wedding at all to Dad–'

'She's only thinking of his health and there's plenty of time yet,' Iris interrupted.

'I know that but recently she's started going on about wanting him to sell the business and retire to the country or the seaside and take up golf.'

Iris looked very interested. 'Is that so?' Well, that certainly wouldn't please Charlie, she thought. That would really scupper his plans for getting his hands on Edward Taylor's business. 'Does our Charlie know about this?'

Florence nodded. 'He doesn't seem very pleased either. I mean, honestly, Iris, why does she want to sell up and move, away, especially with the wedding planned for next April. Can you imagine the complete chaos it will cause? And *that* certainly won't benefit Dad's health.'

The teacakes arrived.

'What does your dad have to say about it?' Iris asked when the waitress had moved away. Florence was cutting her teacake delicately.

'I don't think he's in favour of it much either although he hasn't said so. I just think if they have to sell up and move they should at least wait until after I'm married and settled in a home of my own,' Florence stated pettishly.

Iris nodded slowly; that seemed the logical thing to do. 'Won't it be very hard for him selling a business that's been in the family for years and that he's worked so hard to build up, to say nothing of going to look for a new house?'

'Of course it will; that's my point exactly. I just don't know what Mother is thinking of even though she is insisting it's for his benefit. He should take the time now to relax and enjoy what he's worked so hard for, she says.'

'Where exactly is she thinking of moving to?

Somewhere like Tregarron?' Iris enquired, wiping a bit of melted butter from her mouth with the serviette.

Florence frowned. 'I think she's more inclined towards the coast.'

'Well, what about Southport? That's beside the sea and it's not that far away, Florence. You can get there by train in about three-quarters of an hour,' Iris suggested, thinking that as well as not being too far it was quite posh enough to suit Ethel Taylor.

Florence stirred her tea. 'Oh, I don't know, Iris. I just wish she'd stop going on about it. It's all quite depressing, shall we change the subject? Have you and Tom started to make any plans yet?'

Iris smiled wryly. 'Every time I mention it Tom says to wait until we've got a bit more money saved. On his wages we won't be able to afford a place of our own, we'll live with Mam, but it is convenient for me to go on living over the shop and I can make sure that Mam is all right too, so I'm not sure why he's being so cautious.'

'Have you asked him?' Florence probed. If they were moving in with Mrs Mundy then she couldn't see a reason for delay.

Iris nodded seriously. 'It's because he was out of work for so long when he came back after the war and still doesn't earn much, it's made him wary. I think he feels that if he loses this job and can't get another then he'd rather have a few pounds saved to tide him over. I can understand that.'

'But you'll still have the shop,' Florence remarked.

'And we'd have to live on the takings – Mam included. Tom's got his pride. If – God forbid – he was out of work he doesn't want to be seen to be living off his wife and mother-in-law.'

Florence raised her eyebrows. 'Is that what people would really think?'

'They would around our neighbourhood and they'd say so as well. No, I'm not rushing him, Florence. I don't want him to feel ... humiliated in any way.'

Florence could see her point. She sighed. 'Nothing seems straightforward at the moment, does it?'

Iris smiled. 'I suppose that's just life, Florence, and we have to make the best of it. Cheer up; perhaps your mam will see the sense in not moving until after your wedding.'

Florence managed a smile. 'I hope so.' Reluctantly she reached for her bag. 'I'd better be getting back to work now. You know what they're like if you're a few minutes late. You never hear the end of it.'

Iris grinned. 'I knew there were some advantages being your own boss. I'll see you later in the week, Florence,' she promised, pouring herself another cup of tea.

Iris spent an hour window shopping and then she made her way home, nodding to the women who were taking advantage of the fine weather standing gossiping – as usual – on their doorsteps.

'I'm back, Mam!' she called as she came through the shop, thinking how it looked bright and clean and tidy. She tried hard to keep it that way despite the surrounding neighbourhood becoming increasingly run down. When she entered the kitchen there was no sign of Kate and she frowned, wondering where she was. She called up the stairs and upon getting no reply she went into the scullery. The back door stood wide open. 'Mam!' she called. Then she caught sight of her mother sitting on the step, hunched over and clutching her right arm. The basket containing the wet washing and pegs lay on its side, the contents strewn on the flags of the yard.

'Oh, my God! Mam! What happened? What have you done?' she cried, kneeling down beside Kate, whose face was white and screwed up in agony.

'My arm ... and my shoulder. I ... I tripped... Oh, Iris, the pain!' Kate gasped.

'Don't move; I'm going for our Charlie! Just hang on, I won't be long,' Iris urged.

As she ran through the kitchen and the shop and then headlong down the street she blamed herself for going window shopping. She should have come straight home. But she'd told her mam to leave that bit of washing; that she'd put it out when she got back from town. Now the Lord alone knew what her mother had broken.

Charlie immediately closed the shop and ran up to the main road to find a taxi while she ran back home.

Kate was still sitting on the step but tears of pain were now sliding down her cheeks and she was shaking.

'Charlie's gone to get a taxi, we'll take you to hospital. Can you stand if I help you, Mam?'

Slowly and carefully she helped her mother to her feet and guided her inside. She eased her down on to a chair in the kitchen before running through into the shop to look for her brother. Thankfully as she opened the door a cab drew up and Charlie got out.

'I'll go and get her a jacket or cardigan to put round her shoulders. You help her into the cab,' Iris instructed.

There wasn't time to dwell on the fact that the last time they'd all been in this hospital had been the day Bill Mundy had died. Kate was in too much pain and Iris was too worried about her. Charlie, after paying the driver and following them in did recall it but his mother was his main concern.

Kate was dealt with quickly, efficiently and with great consideration. Kate had broken her arm in two places and the doctor decided that because of her condition, after they had set it and encased it in plaster of Paris, they would keep her in overnight. She wasn't very happy about it but Iris urged her not to make a fuss.

'It's for the best. You've had a shock, you're in a lot of pain and they'll look after you. I'll go home and get you a few things and bring them back. Oh, Mam, I'm so, so sorry for not coming straight home.'

Kate tried to smile but it resembled more of a grimace. 'Don't go blaming yourself, luv. I should have been more careful.'

'You should have had a bit more patience, Mam. She would have put the damned washing out when she got back,' Charlie added grimly.

Iris took back a clean nightdress and toiletries and made sure that her mother was settled and more comfortable. Then she returned home and, after gathering up the damp clothes and pegs from the yard, dumped the washing basket in the scullery and made herself a cup of tea. She felt weary and decidedly guilty. It was very clear now that Kate could do herself serious damage when she tripped or fell; her condition was obviously deteriorating and she would certainly need to be more closely watched. It was very worrying, she thought dejectedly.

She discussed it with both her brother and Tom when he arrived later that evening. 'She's clearly getting worse; it's just a single, shallow step that she's gone up and down a million times before. What if she falls down the stairs? Dear God, it doesn't bear thinking about! She could break every bone in her body!'

'That's a bit extreme, Iris. I don't think she's as bad as that ... yet,' Charlie said gravely. 'But we're going to have to watch her more carefully in future.'

'I can't be with her every minute of the day,' Iris reminded him, biting her lip, 'but I'll look in on her far more often in future. She's not going to be able to do much at all when she gets home.'

'It doesn't seem very fair that you should be solely responsible for making sure she's safe,' Tom said quietly.

'I can't be shutting the shop and running up and down the street all day,' Charlie protested, thinking it was all very well for Tom Morrissey to point this out without coming up with an alternative.

'I wasn't thinking of you, Charlie, you've a living to earn, the same as both Iris and I have. And you're getting married next year. We'll all be in a mess – financially – if we don't work.'

Somewhat mollified, Charlie nodded his agreement. 'Well, in that case I think it's about time our Rose stopped swanning about at that Plas Idris place and came home. She could help Iris both in the shop and with Mam. She's needed here now.'

'She hated working in the shop, Charlie, and she was as miserable as sin here!' Iris reminded him. 'And I wouldn't exactly call the long hours and hard work at Plas Idris "swanning about".'

'She appears to spend most of her time sitting reading to that Rhys-Pritchard feller. That's not what I call "hard work",' Charlie retorted belligerently.

'She does that in her own time,' Iris shot back. 'And how do you think Mam would feel if we drag our Rose back here? She would know Rose was only home under sufferance and she'd feel guilty and absolutely mortified, as if she wasn't fit to look after herself, like a ... child. Leave her with some dignity and independence, Charlie. She'd also hate to see Rose miserable, and Rose would be, and that would make Mam feel ten times worse. No, I'm not going to write and demand that our Rose comes home.'

Charlie glowered at her. 'Then what the hell are we going to do?'

Iris glared back but Tom got to his feet. He'd been thinking while this argument had gone on and he'd come to a decision. 'Write and tell Rose

266

about your Mam's accident, Iris, and ask her to request some time off in the very near future – to attend our wedding. If we get married, I can move in and I'll take over the running of the shop, which will leave you more time to devote to your mam. That will suit everyone. Rose needn't be forced to come home, your mam won't be made to feel she's in any way a burden, Charlie can devote himself to his business and Florence, and you will have peace of mind, Iris.' He smiled at her. 'And we were planning to get married anyway so why not sooner rather than later?'

'But will you be able to manage both jobs?' Iris asked, although everything he had said made sense.

'Of course. You'll be here while I'm at the market and then I'm sure between us we'll easily manage the shop. And if you need to go out shopping or to visit Florence, I'll be here to keep my eye on your mam.'

Charlie got to his feet and shook Tom's hand. 'I think we all need a drink. Not only have we all had a bit of a shock over Mam's accident but we should celebrate. Thanks, Tom. It's the perfect solution.'

Tom grinned. 'Keep everybody happy, but mainly Iris, that's my motto, Charlie.'

Iris felt the tension and worry that had gripped her for the past hours drain away. Tom had found a solution to their dilemma. His common sense and selfless consideration never failed. It was one of the reasons why she loved him. She knew without a doubt that her future and her happiness were safe in his hands.

Chapter Twenty-Four

Iris collected Kate from hospital the next day and after settling her mother comfortably in an armchair in the kitchen, she informed her mother that she and Tom were going to get married within the next couple of weeks.

'We've decided it's for the best, Mam. We'll never have enough money for a place of our own so we might as well make it sooner rather than later. You know I love Tom and I'll be so happy to get married. If you agree, Tom can move in here and he'll go off to the market and then help me in the shop for the rest of the day. And I'll be on hand to make sure you don't go falling down the back step again. Is it still very painful?'

Kate nodded, trying to digest Iris's news. 'But better than it was and I'm glad to be home. I didn't get much sleep in that place; what with the pain and them in and out by the minutes.'

'They were just making sure you were all right, Mam,' Iris reminded her.

'I'll be delighted to see you married, Iris, and of course it makes sense for Tom to move in here, so there's no point in putting it off. You'll be beating our Charlie to the altar then.'

Iris smiled. 'Well, the Register Office. We don't want any fuss and there will be no wasting money on fancy outfits. I'm going to buy a new coat and hat and we'll come back here for a drink and a bit of something to eat. We're just inviting Tom's mam and da and his sisters; Charlie will be Tom's best man and I'm going to write and ask Rose to stand for me. If she can't get the time off then I know Florence will. It will be just the kind of wedding I want.'

Kate nodded slowly. 'You'd better write to her, Iris. The more notice she can give them the better chance she has of getting home. I'm pleased, luv. He's a good lad, steady, hardworking and thoughtful. You'll make a grand couple and after the shock of this, well, it will be a bit of a relief for me to know that you're on hand if I need you – not that I'll be bothering you much. Once I get over this I can get back to running the house.'

'You'll just have to be more careful, Mam, especially with steps and stairs and the like.'

'I know. Now, you get started on that letter, I'll just close my eyes and see if I can catch a few winks of sleep.'

Gwen handed Rose the letter when she returned from work in the evening. She had a fair idea of what it contained for she'd had a note from Iris herself, explaining everything.

'It's getting quite nippy of an evening now,' Rose commented as she opened the letter while Gwen poured her a hot cup of tea. Then she uttered a cry as she read the first lines.

'It's all right, *cariad*, just keep on reading. Your mam is fine now,' Gwen reassured the girl.

Rose frowned as she read of Iris's fears for her mother's future health and wellbeing. Mam's condition was getting worse and that upset her.

Charlie had wanted her to go home and she wondered for a moment was he right but then she read that that wouldn't be necessary as Iris and Tom were getting married and would be living with Kate.

'I'll ask Mrs Mathews first thing in the morning about me going home for a day or so. I never thought Iris would be married before Charlie but it seems the sensible thing to do, in the circumstances, and I'm very relieved to know that Mam will be looked after. But she writes that I'm not to mention to Mam that our Charlie wanted me to go home to look after her or that Tom is going to spend more time in the shop than she will be doing.'

'That's sensible too. She doesn't want your mam to think she's becoming a burden in any way.'

Rose bit her lip. 'The doctors said it would get worse and it seems to be.'

Gwen nodded sadly. 'I'm afraid so, luv. I don't think we can risk her making the journey here again so you'd best stress that to Mrs Mathews when you ask her for time to go home. I think it will be us going to visit her in future.'

The housekeeper listened to Rose's request carefully and initially agreed. 'I'll have to consult Miss Olivia but I can't see that it will be a problem, Rose, not under the circumstances.' Then she'd reconsidered. 'However, there is the travelling to think about. The bus only goes to Liverpool twice a week which might mean you will have to be absent for up to a week.'

'I know and I've already mentioned it to Nancy, Mrs Mathews. I hope you don't mind but as the extra work will fall upon her I thought I should at least give her some warning.'

The older woman frowned. 'Thinking about it, Rose, it could present problems. Nora is a parlourmaid and would consider the work beneath her and it isn't fair to ask Nancy to undertake double the work for a week, now is it? In fact I don't think we could manage with just one housemaid.'

'No, I suppose not.'

'I'll speak to Miss Olivia and let you know Rose,' Mrs Mathews promised and Rose had no option but to agree.

Later that afternoon she encountered David Rhys-Pritchard in the hallway and acknowledged him politely if a little vaguely, which did not go unnoticed for usually she was very cheerful.

'You seem preoccupied, Rose. Has something upset you? You haven't received bad news from home, I trust?'

'I'm sorry. I have had news from home; my mam has had a fall and has broken her arm,' Rose informed him.

'I'm so sorry to hear that. It must be worrying for you.'

Rose nodded. 'My sister thinks her condition is getting worse and ... and there was some mention of me having to go home to help look after her, but they've sorted it all out so thankfully I won't have to leave here.'

David was alarmed by this disclosure. 'They *have* definitely sorted things out?'

271

'Yes. My sister is going to get married in a fortnight – she and Tom intended to at some point – and so they will live with Mam. Tom will help in the shop so Iris can spend more time looking after Mam. I've asked Mrs Mathews if I can go home for a few days for the wedding – and to see Mam of course – but...' She shrugged.

'But what? Has she refused?' David asked sharply.

'Not ... exactly, but you see there is a problem with the travelling. There is only a bus twice a week from Denbigh so instead of me just being away for two days, it will be almost a week and it really isn't fair to expect poor Nancy to do my work as well as her own. I don't think she could manage. Mrs Mathews is going to see what Miss Olivia has to say,' Rose finished. It she was honest she already wasn't holding out much hope of being able to go.

David smiled at her. 'It's very coincidental, Rose, and as it turns out very fortunate, but Livvie was telling me at breakfast that she and Ellie intend to go to Liverpool in the near future to shop for Ellie's trousseau and some Christmas gifts – the shops in Liverpool apparently being far superior to those in Llandudno or Chester – and Livvie is quite capable of driving there and back. I'll explain everything and suggest to her that you travel with them.'

'Oh, do you think she'll agree? I wouldn't want to impose or inconvenience her in any way, but I really would like to see Mam and stand for Iris. It's just a Register Office wedding but she is my only sister.'

'I can't see that she will object. They're staying for two days with Aunt Grace and Cousin Lionel at their house in Rodney Street. You remember Lionel from the engagement party?'

Rose nodded happily. 'I do but I didn't know they lived in Liverpool. I'd be very, very grateful, David.'

'Then write back to your sister and tell her and I'll arrange it with Livvie,' he promised, watching her as she hurried away and thinking that it was such a small thing to do and yet it had brought the smile back to her face. It had crossed his mind that had she been refused the time off, her family might become annoyed and try to persuade her to leave Plas Idris. The thought of not seeing her daily made him despondent. Life would be so bleak without her; he was growing very fond of her.

The next weeks were hectic for Iris and Tom as they made all the arrangements, redecorated Kate's old room and reorganised bedroom furniture. Tom moved his belongings in bit by bit; Iris went shopping for her wedding outfit as well as working in the shop and running the house, for Kate (to her chagrin) was unable to do very much and Iris insisted that she should not even try yet.

Florence had advised her to buy a good quality coat as not only would it look smart but would remain so for years to come. 'It will last, Iris, and if you choose something on the plain side it won't date. You have to splash out a little bit on your wedding outfit,' she'd urged. So Iris had asked her to accompany her on the shopping expedition.

The prices had horrified her in the first shops Florence insisted they visit, but in the more moderately priced Blackler's she had settled on a well-cut wool coat in what the sales assistant termed 'Baltic blue', which was a few shades lighter and brighter than royal blue. The colour suited her and the style, straight with a hemline ending just below the knee and with a wide shawl collar and cuffs edged in black velvet ribbon, made her look slim and elegant, or so Florence insisted. She'd also purchased a black velvet cloche hat which sported a rosette of royal blue ribbon, which wasn't exactly the same shade of blue as the coat but was near enough. She had black shoes and a black bag, she reminded Florence as they left the store, Iris feeling very satisfied with her purchases and their price.

'And you *must* have flowers, Iris. Leave that to me, I'll order and pay for them,' Florence insisted.

'That's really generous of you, Florence, but don't go getting the buttonholes for the men and the sprays for Mam and Mrs Morrissey, we'll buy those,' Iris informed her.

'Indeed you won't! Let me help out a little bit, Iris, please? You're my best friend and it's your special day and soon you'll be my sister-in-law.'

Iris nodded happily, smiling as she linked arms with her friend and they walked towards the tram stop. It would be a little strange but nice to think that soon she would be Mrs Tom Morrissey. Florence was happy too; even though it was going to be a very quiet affair compared to hers she still wanted Iris to have some of the trimmings and she'd ensure that the flowers were the prettiest available in late October. She'd also decided on what she would wear and it would be something very plain: her grey coat with a burgundy-coloured hat, for the last thing she wanted to do was outshine her friend on her wedding day.

Olivia Rhys-Pritchard dropped Rose off in Liverpool city centre on Tuesday afternoon, pro-mising to pick her up at the same time and place on Thursday, and then headed in the direction of Rodney Street. Rose caught a tram home. Iris and Tom were to be married at four o'clock on Wed-nesday afternoon as Saturday was Iris's busiest day. They'd arranged it for late afternoon so that Charlie and Florence, Mr Morrissey and Tom's sisters would only have to take a few hours off work. As the tram trundled through the streets Rose thought to herself that strangely now she didn't think of the city as 'home'. All these roads and buildings were very familiar, of course, but her feelings had changed. She was now used to fields and hills, Gwen's cottage and the spacious, elegant rooms of Plas Idris. As Olivia had driven – rather more quickly than Rose would have liked – towards the city, she had remembered the last time she'd come home: when Edward Taylor had come to Tregarron to drive her back after her father had died. She hoped that the sad, bereft atmosphere that had pervaded the house and shop had gone. She was looking forward to seeing everyone and in particular her mam again, and of course finding out what Iris had bought to wear for her wedding.

'It was very good of them to bring you with them, luv,' Kate greeted her youngest daughter.

'Yes. I didn't think at first I'd be able to come because of the bus times but when I mentioned it to David he arranged it all. How is your arm now, Mam? Still painful? Aunty Gwen sends her love and says she's coming on a Christmas shopping trip from the village that's been arranged for next month, so she'll call to see you,' Rose informed her mother as she took off her coat and hat.

Kate nodded, noticing that Rose had used his Christian name again, but delighted to hear of Gwen's impending visit. 'It's a lot better than it was but things have been a bit hectic since my fall. Both Iris and Tom have managed to organise everything though and Charlie spends quite a few evenings at Florence's house so he's not under my feet too much. Iris has a really smart coat and hat, Rose. I'm sure she'll show it to you later on.' Kate pulled a face. 'I'm going to look a bit of a fright, I can't get a coat or jacket on properly with this damned arm.'

'No you won't, Mam, wear your best dress and we'll drape your good coat over your shoulders. It will look very stylish,' Rose assured her, smiling.

'I've never achieved being "stylish" in my life yet but at least the plaster will be off and the arm healed for our Charlie's wedding,' Kate replied. She'd have to look smart for that occasion for Ethel Taylor most certainly would!

Charlie splashed out on a taxi to take the small wedding party to Brougham Terrace to the Register Office and proudly escorted Iris. She looked

276

very smart in her outfit. The colour and style of the coat suited her and the bouquet Florence had ordered was perfect. The flowers must have been expensive, Rose thought as she fastened the spray of small chrysanthemums to the lapel of Kate's coat. It lent her mother an air of elegance and made Kate feel more confident in her appearance.

Tom and his family were waiting in the ante-room all dressed in their best clothes, and Tom immediately crossed and kissed Iris on the cheek. 'You look absolutely gorgeous, Iris!'

'Florence has excelled with the flowers, hasn't she, particularly as they're hard to get? I ... I feel a bit nervous though,' she confided as her mother and future mother-in-law chatted amiably while Rose and Florence talked to Tom's sisters. Both Tom's father and Charlie were glancing around and thinking the place wasn't a very cheerful venue for a wedding. Charlie was remembering that the last time he had been here was to register his da's death but he shrugged the thought aside.

A few minutes later they were ushered into a larger wood-panelled room with a desk on which a small vase of flowers had been set to one side of the leather-bound register. Half a dozen chairs stood in a semi-circle. Florence thought it looked dreadfully bleak and far more suited to the mundane business of registering births and deaths than a wedding. She wished Iris had waited a few more weeks and had a church wedding; there was something far more spiritual and romantic about a church, even in winter and without music or masses of flowers, but glancing at her friend as she stood beside Tom with Rose and Charlie at their sides, Iris seemed to be marvellously and happily oblivious of the officious austerity.

The butterflies in Iris's stomach had stopped their nervous fluttering as she handed her bouquet to Rose and smiled happily up at Tom. She promised to love, honour and obey, to have and to hold, for better or worse, in sickness and in health until death 'do us part' and when he placed the plain gold band on her finger and bent to kiss his new wife, she saw the same light of love and joy reflected in his eyes.

'I love you, Tom Morrissey,' she whispered with a catch in her voice.

'I love you too, Mrs Morrissey,' he whispered back, gently taking her arm and preparing to lead the family group back outside.

Both Kate and Florence dabbed at their eyes and Rose thought of David Rhys-Pritchard and of how handsome he had looked at Elinore's engagement party and of how he had so kindly arranged for her to be present on this, the happiest day of Iris's life. She'd begun to think of him more often lately and of how kind he was to her. She realised that she missed him. She missed him a great deal.

Chapter Twenty-Five

The Christmas tree looked magnificent. It filled one entire corner of the hall and reached almost to the ceiling and Rose, Nancy and Nora stepped back to admire their handiwork. With the help of

Henry they'd spent over an hour decorating it. Ever since she'd returned after Iris's wedding Rose had been looking forward to spending Christmas at Plas Idris.

'You've done a great job, girls. Lovely it looks, very festive,' Mrs Mathews praised them.

'It certainly makes the hall look more welcoming,' Nancy enthused as she helped Henry to fold away the ladder and Rose collected the boxes that had contained the delicate coloured-glass decorations and tinsel and the little candles and their holders.

'We only ever had a tiny thing at home and we made the decorations ourselves from pipe cleaners and cardboard covered with silver paper from cigarette packets,' Rose told them. 'I'm really looking forward to my first Christmas here,' she added, thinking of the festivities that Miss Olivia had planned for the holiday. Ernest Williams would be coming over both on Christmas Eve for the large dinner party that had been planned, mainly for those who had not been invited to Elinore's wedding, and for the family lunch on Christmas Day. Another dinner party was being hosted on Boxing Day.

'Put those boxes away, Rose, and then you'd better see to decorating the tree in Mr David's drawing room. After you've done that make up the fire in the dining room and help Nancy with setting the table for supper,' the housekeeper instructed as she oversaw the safe removal of the ladder and the sweeping up of the pine needles that had dropped on to the floor.

Rose took the empty boxes away and fetched the

ones containing the decorations for the much smaller tree that had been placed in a corner of David's small drawing room. The room was empty for he was closeted with Evan Price, his land agent, in his study, something he did frequently these days. She admired the fact that he had begun to take an interest in the estate again. She felt it helped him to achieve a more normal outlook on life. She switched on the standard lamp and closed the shutters over the windows, then drew the curtains shutting out the bleak December afternoon, for although it was not yet four o'clock it was almost dark. She stirred up the fire and added more coal and wood and then started to take the ornaments and strands of tinsel from their boxes.

She was so engrossed with her task that she didn't hear him enter and he sat watching her for a few minutes as she carefully attached the red, green and gold glass baubles to the branches of the tree. The light from the fire caught her cheeks giving them a soft, pink glow and her dark hair beneath its white lace cap was thick and shiny. His heart turned over. She was completely unaware of how beautiful she was, he thought as she reached gracefully up to drape a strand of tinsel over the topmost branches. He moved forward a little and the faint humming of the wheelchair's motor made Rose turn suddenly.

'Oh, you startled me! I didn't hear you come in, I thought you were still with Mr Price,' she said, clutching the gold star that was to be the finishing touch in her hand.

'I'm sorry, I didn't mean to. Mr Price has gone. I have to say it looks lovely, Rose,' he said, moving closer to inspect her handiwork.

'It's not nearly as magnificent as the one in the hall, but it does look well,' Rose replied as she placed the stool beside the tree, preparing to put the star into place.

'Take care you don't fall, Rose,' he urged. If she did he could be of no assistance to her at all.

'There now, shall I light the little candles?' Rose asked, stepping down.

'No, leave them. Come and view your handiwork from this angle.' He had manoeuvred himself close to the fire and beckoned to her to sit beside him.

As there wasn't a chair situated near enough Rose knelt beside him and viewed the tree critically. 'It does make the room look festive. Do you think it should be brought a little bit further forward?'

'No, it's perfect. It's only the second time I've had a tree in here. I ... I wasn't very interested in Christmas and all its trappings when I first came home but then last year Livvie insisted I have some sort of festive decoration in here,' he said quietly.

Rose nodded; she could understand that. 'We always had a very small tree at home and even though money was tight, Mam made sure we all got an orange, a new penny, a bag of nuts and usually a penny toy. And we were very fortunate; there were children in our street who never got anything at all. Did you have lots of presents and parties when you were a child, David?'

He gazed into the fire, a smile playing around the corners of his mouth. 'We did. I suppose we were terribly spoilt by many people's standards. I remember the year I got my first pony. I was five. A sturdy little Welsh Mountain, he was, and I called him Merlin. It was snowing but I insisted on riding him and Father braved the weather to lead me up and down the drive while Mother and the girls waved from the windows. The house was always decorated with greenery and we had house guests and parties and Lewis always gave me a big bag of toffees but then after the ... accident, things ... changed. Christmas became a very quiet time.'

Rose looked up at him sadly. 'That must have been terrible for you. I ... I know how I felt when my father was killed.'

He nodded slowly, his eyes filled with pain. 'I was away at boarding school. The headmaster sent for me, to tell me. He was as kind as he knew how to be but it was still a very brief and awkward interview. And then I was sent home to a house that seemed so ... desolate and empty.'

Rose watched him, and in his expression and the loneliness in his tone, she suddenly caught a glimpse of the frightened, shocked and bereft child he'd been that day. She too had been away from home when her father had died but she had not been a child. Without really realising what she was doing she reached across and took his hand. 'It must have been far worse for you than it was for me, David. At least I was older.'

He held her hand tightly as he nodded. 'I hated this house. Every room held memories. I was so ... angry. But in time a sense of ... acceptance took the place of loss and resentment; the grief became more bearable. Then a semblance of normality seemed to return, Livvie took over the household and I went back to school and then war was declared, although I didn't have to go at once. I was too young.'

Rose looked at him pleadingly. 'Don't talk about it, David. Not if it upsets you. Those four years were the most terrible, tragic years everyone has ever known.'

He closed his eyes as he tried to dispel the memories of those days and months in the trenches. The unspeakably filthy, miserable conditions; the mud and the rats; the constant thundering of the heavy artillery; the terror that turned the stomach; and each heart-stopping, gut-wrenching moment when he'd led his men up the ladders and over the top, the whistle clenched so tightly between his teeth that his jaw ached yet he could not hear the noise it made. Not knowing if each second would be his last; not knowing how many of the lads who followed him – many of whom were the same age or even younger than he was – would survive for even an hour let alone a day. The terrible sights he'd seen, the sounds, the smells and the horror would remain with him for ever, his own wounds serving as a constant reminder. And he'd been fortunate, he hadn't had to endure years of it as some had, and he'd lived. He was unaware that tears were pouring down his cheeks and that his chest was heaving with suppressed anguish.

Gently Rose gathered him in her arms, her own eyes full of unshed tears. She was filled with guilt that she had unwittingly instigated such devastating memories. 'I'm sorry, David, so sorry. I know it must have been appalling. Charlie would never speak about it and there were so many lads I knew – grew up with – who died. They were all in the same regiment – the Liverpool Pals they called them. They were all friends. They'd grown up together, worked together and they...' She couldn't go on; memories of devastated families in every single street came flooding back and it was only four years since it had all ended.

She didn't know how long they clung together but at last he grew calmer and she released him, realising that she had overstepped the bounds of propriety. 'I ... I really am so very sorry, David. I didn't mean to... It was wrong of me.'

'I've never broken down in front of anyone or behaved like that, Rose. The fault is mine. We ... we were talking of Christmas but somehow...'

'I shouldn't have asked you about the past and I certainly shouldn't have...' She lapsed into awkward silence.

'Was it wrong to ... comfort me? Isn't it just what a friend would do?' He was fighting hard to control his emotions.

Rose was trying to gather her composure too, knowing that if either Mr Lewis or Mrs Mathews or, worse, Miss Olivia had come into the room she would have been instantly dismissed. 'I ... don't want ... anything to spoil our friendship, David.'

'Neither do I, and I feel that you at least try to understand.'

Rose nodded, getting to her feet. 'I hope I do. I'd best go now; Nancy will be wondering why I'm not working with her in the dining room.'

He remained silent as she collected up the boxes

and, with a last look at the tree, left. As he stared unseeingly at the tinsel and baubles David prayed that her spontaneous reaction to his despairing loss of control would not diminish her affection for him, would not cause her now to anticipate the time she spent with him with trepidation or, worse, regard him with pity. He loved her, he was certain of that now, but he was also certain that that love had no future. He would have to be content with her friendship.

Rose was very subdued as she helped Nancy but as Nancy chatted on happily about the Christmas festivities and Elinore's forthcoming wedding she didn't appear to notice. Rose was deeply disturbed by her emotions. She had felt so sorry for him; he'd suffered so much tragedy in his life that all she'd wanted to do was comfort him but now she had to admit to herself that as she had held him that feeling had changed. She'd grown increasingly fond of him over the months but now she knew that that affection had deepened to love – and that she could never tell him how she felt. Her mother's words of warning came back to her and she swallowed hard, fighting back the tears. *You are a paid servant in his house.* She didn't know how she was going to live with what she now felt, but of one thing she was certain: she would *have* to if she was to remain here.

As Christmas drew closer Iris felt that there were scarcely enough hours in the day. Both she and Tom were busy and despite the fact that Kate's arm was now out of plaster and much better, Iris insisted that her mother do as little as possible.

'I don't want to find you trying to put up the decorations, Mam. Tom and I will do it,' she had instructed, fearful that if Kate started climbing on chairs or stools she would fall.

'But you're both so busy, Iris,' Kate protested.

'And we're both much younger and fitter, Mam. Now, I'll go tomorrow afternoon and do the bulk of the shopping,' she said, frowning over the list she had made. The kitchen was tidy and warm and a large pan of thick mutton stew was simmering gently on the range. It was almost closing time and Tom would be in shortly.

'At least I can help with the preparations and we've already done the pudding,' Kate reminded her.

Iris smiled. 'Tom's going to bring home the tree tomorrow – nothing very grand – so you can decorate it, that's not too strenuous.' She knew it was hard for Kate to relinquish so many of the household chores and she tried to find things to make her mother feel she was useful. 'I bet they have an enormous tree where Rose works.'

'And I bet they are run off their feet too: they seem to be inviting half the county for dinner over Christmas, so Rose said in her last letter.'

Iris nodded, adding 'tinsel' to the list. The bits they had were looking decidedly tarnished and tatty she'd noticed when the box of decorations had been unearthed from the cupboard under the stairs. She'd get some in the market. 'I know. It's because Miss Elinore's wedding is going to be so quiet,' she replied, getting up and giving the stew a stir, sniffing its appetising aroma appreciatively.

'Which is more than can be said for our Charlie and Florence's, at least she's got Christmas to take her mind off it for a while,' Kate remarked dourly.

Iris sighed and replaced the lid on the saucepan; with only four months to go Florence was beginning to fuss in earnest now and despite her mother's instructions had begun to pester her father. At least Edward Taylor's retirement didn't look imminent, she thought, and Ethel seemed to have postponed plans to move until after the wedding, much to Florence's relief. 'Has our Charlie had any luck finding a place? What was the last one like?' she asked. Her brother and her friend seemed to have spent weeks viewing houses, none of which had suited them. She knew decent rented accommodation wasn't easy to find, but to her mind they were being far too choosy. The ones they'd viewed had been either too small, too big, too expensive or not in the 'right' area.

Kate raised her eyes to the ceiling. 'He didn't like the fact that there were kids playing around the streetlamp outside it. Said they were rowdy and could prove to be a nuisance.'

Iris shook her head. Charlie had often played around the streetlamp himself when he'd been young. He and his mates had attached a length of rope to one of the arms and used it as a swing, and he'd played football in summer, using the wall of the shop as the goal. 'He's got a very short memory, has our Charlie. Have you finished writing the cards? Tom offered to deliver them because if I take them I'll be gone hours; you know what they're all like for jangling.'

Kate nodded, indicating the small pile on the dresser. She had continued Bill's practice of sending one to the regular customers – most of whom were also neighbours – who although too poor to afford to buy cards themselves greatly appreciated the gesture. 'That's nice of him. He's a good lad.'

'I know, Mam.' Iris smiled, thinking that she'd never been happier in her life. Oh, they were busy but she enjoyed him being in the shop close at hand. Occasionally, if Charlie wasn't going out, they went to the music hall or the moving pictures for a treat. Yes, married life suited her very well. 'We're really looking forward to Christmas, our first together as man and wife.'

Kate's eyes misted a little as she thought of Bill. 'It will be nice to have you both here, and Charlie, although it will be his last in this house. I'll miss Rose but I know it will be better than last year. Sometimes I can't believe that your poor da has been gone for over a year now.'

Iris reached and took her hand. 'I still miss him too, Mam, but we'll all be thinking of him, I know, and Tom and I are going to make sure that we all have a really great day. Probably a better one than our Rose will have – she won't have the day off.'

Kate frowned. 'I sometimes worry about Rose.'

'Why? You know when Gwen called she said she's fine.'

'She also said she talks about David Rhys-Pritchard a great deal. She seems to spend a lot of her free time in his company, and that bothers me.'

'Oh, Mam! When she was home I thought Rose

had grown up a lot. She seems more ... sensible, less prone to daydreaming than she used to be. She won't go doing anything foolish.'

Kate sighed deeply. 'I hope so, Iris. I just hope so,' she replied.

Iris got up as Tom came through, rubbing his cold hands together. 'I'll put the kettle on, you must be frozen, luv. Supper's nearly ready and I've finished my shopping list for tomorrow.'

Tom kissed her on the cheek. 'We'll have a dinner fit for a king, won't we?'

She smiled happily at him. 'We will. It's going to be a great day.'

Chapter Twenty-Six

This Christmas had definitely been an improvement on last year, Iris thought as she helped Tom to arrange the fruit and vegetables he'd brought back from the market. It was hard to believe that it was a month ago now; tomorrow would be the first of February and they had escaped with little snow or ice so far, although there had been some quite wild and windy days. They'd indeed had a great lunch with a goose and all the trimmings. Afterwards Tom had helped her clear away while Mam had dozed peacefully in her chair and then they'd gone for a walk while Charlie went to Florence's house for tea.

She frowned as she swept up the loose soil from around the base of a sack of potatoes. With not very long now to go before the greatly anticipated wedding day Florence was becoming increasingly agitated, worrying incessantly about every single detail. She couldn't understand just what all the fuss was about or why her friend was putting herself through so much angst; in her opinion Florence should really be enjoying herself, happily looking forward to her big day.

Now her future sister-in-law was fussing over Kate's outfit for Ethel's was in the process of being made by a dressmaker in Bold Street.

'What's the matter, luv? You look as if you've lost sixpence and found a penny,' Tom asked, noticing his young wife's expression.

'I'm going to have to persuade Mam to come into town with me soon, Tom, to buy her outfit, and you know that's not going to be easy. She keeps telling me we've got weeks and weeks yet – and we *have* – but I don't think I can put up with Florence's nagging for much longer.'

Tom nodded. 'Why don't you both go on Wednesday afternoon?' he suggested.

'I suppose we could. She's adamant that she wants something she can get plenty of wear out of in the future. She's not wasting money on something she'll never wear again, which is sensible, but...'

'But what?' Tom queried.

'But I'm afraid that if we do get something soon, Florence will want to see it and maybe it won't come up to her expectations.'

'If you ask me, Iris, Florence is letting it all get out of control and is losing the run of herself.'

Iris smiled wryly. 'I have to agree with you, she

really is getting carried away but I don't want to go upsetting her by telling her so.'

'I'm beginning to feel sorry for your Charlie. I think he'll be glad when all the palaver is over and done with.'

'We all will,' Iris replied grimly.

Kate flatly refused to accompany her daughter into Liverpool city centre on the Wednesday afternoon, stating that firstly she'd heard that snow was on the way and secondly she wasn't having Florence dictate to her. 'It's not even February! There's plenty of time to buy an outfit. At least they've finally found a place to live but Charlie was telling me that Ethel Taylor is trying to put Florence off the place, saying that the neighbourhood is going down rapidly. I just hope she doesn't take any notice. Charlie confided that it is more than he wanted to pay in rent each week – almost eight shillings! – and they've got to furnish it. It just doesn't seem to occur to that woman that you have to live within your means and Charlie isn't making a fortune and never will from that shop. It's not the actual day itself, or what you wear, or where you have the reception that really matters, it's the commitment to spend the rest of your life together.'

'I know, Mam, but she's sort of let the whole thing ... take over,' Iris agreed.

'Grow out of all proportion in my opinion. That Miss Elinore Rhys-Pritchard didn't cause as much fuss over her wedding as Florence is. Ethel should sit her down and give her a good talking to.'

Iris sighed, nodding her agreement for Rose had written that although Elinore had worn a

291

beautiful dress of heavy white brocade, a silk tulle veil and headdress of tiny silk flowers and had looked lovely, it had all been very quiet and tasteful and as Miss Olivia had organised everything her sister had not got upset or worried about a single thing. She wondered if she should try to impress that fact upon her friend but doubted that Florence would take much notice.

Charlie too was getting a little impatient with all the fuss and although he was looking forward to getting married the actual day was beginning to look more and more like an endurance test. He'd been more concerned with finding a suitable house for them to live in. It certainly hadn't been easy but at last he'd found something – only for Ethel to start making adverse comments about the area. He was trying to keep Florence's enthusiasm bolstered up. She'd liked the house and the neighbourhood and they'd spent quite some time wandering from room to room and Florence had debated where they would put furniture and what colour curtains they should have and he'd felt content that they were both considering it as 'home'. He would be glad when the wedding was over and they could actually start their life together.

Christmas had passed in something of a blur, Rose thought as she made up the fire in the dining room while Nancy folded back the shutters and announced gloomily that it looked like snow. They had all been extremely busy over the Christmas and New Year holiday for there had seemed to be guests arriving and departing constantly. She hadn't spent any time alone with David Rhys-Pritchard over the holiday, in fact during the times when she had seen him there had always been company present. She'd missed reading to him.

They had all received a gift of money from him on Christmas Morning – apparently it was traditional – and after the family lunch had been served and the family had adjourned to the Blue Drawing Room, a cold collation had been prepared by Cook to be set out in the dining room for supper – another festive tradition to give the staff some leisure time. They had then all eaten their Christmas dinner together in the servants' hall, Mr Lewis carving the goose and Henry filling their glasses with either sherry or Madeira wine.

She had been tired but happy when she'd at last cycled back to Gwen's cottage to hear all about Gwen's day, which had been spent with Bob and Megan and the boys. And then there had been the preparations for Miss Elinore's wedding and the wedding itself and so the first month of the New Year had passed quickly.

'I hope it doesn't stick,' she replied, crossing to look out of the window at the flakes that had started to fall. She certainly didn't want to have to stay overnight and it wasn't just that that attic room was freezing. Whenever she was in David's company now she felt awkward and unhappy. The easy friendship they'd shared over the past months had somehow changed.

She had obtained a new crime novel, and they had started to read it but hadn't progressed very far. Now he seemed to spend more time dealing with Evan Price and matters concerning the estate and when she did read he seemed preoccupied and a little distant, although last time when she'd finished the chapter she'd looked up and had caught him looking at her with undisguised affection, which had suddenly changed to sadness. She'd quickly looked away.

Nancy's voice broke into her reverie. 'It might not. At least this is the last month of winter. Have you heard from your mam and Iris?'

'I had a letter yesterday and I'm glad I'm not there, Nancy. Florence seems to be driving everyone mad. Mam's digging her heels in over her outfit, Iris says, and they'll all be glad when it's over. Charlie has found a house for them to rent though, so I suppose that's a blessing.'

Nancy nodded and then smiled. 'Miss Elinore – I mean Mrs Williams – seems to be happy enough. I thought she looked very well when she was over last week.' She looked around and lowered her voice to a whisper. 'I think that it's got a lot to do with Miss Olivia not trying to "organise" her all the time.'

'Hush!' Rose hissed but Nancy just shrugged and went to help Beryl with the breakfast tray.

To her consternation it snowed heavily all morning and into the afternoon and it became clear that she wouldn't be able to get back to the village that evening. Nora had developed a heavy cold the previous day and was far from well, so the housekeeper insisted that she sit in the warmth of the kitchen with a hot toddy and instructed Rose to serve Mr Dai's tea in the parlourmaid's place. Rose had no option but to do so.

He was sitting staring out of the French doors at the blanket of white that stretched for as far as the eye could see.

'Nora isn't well, she's got a terrible cold,' Rose announced, placing the tray on a table and preparing to pour the tea from the silver pot.

David turned in surprise. 'Rose! I thought Mrs Mathews would have sent you home hours ago. The road to the village will be impassable by now. I telephoned Evan Price two hours ago and told him not to try to come up to the house today.'

'I'll have to stay then but I'm sure Miss Olivia will telephone Miss Roberts to let her know. I had to stay one night last year. It's not too much of an inconvenience,' she lied.

He smiled at her. 'Then perhaps after supper you could read to me?'

Rose nodded, smiling back as she handed him the delicate bone-china cup and saucer. If she had to stay at least it would be more interesting to read a few more chapters than sit in the servants' hall listening to Nancy, Cook and Beryl gossiping and complaining. Poor Nora, she was sure, would go to bed as soon as she could. 'I'd like that,' she agreed.

'It's inconvenient but it looks beautiful, doesn't it?' he said, his gaze turning back to the scene beyond the windows.

'It does. Snow seems to make even ugly things look pretty,' Rose replied, thinking how the snow softened the outlines of the narrow, soot-blackened streets of terraced houses and the ugly dock warehouses in Liverpool. 'I'll collect the tray later,' she added, for he continued to stare out across the terrace and the gardens, seemingly mesmerised by their tranquil beauty. She was unaware that his thoughts were not on the cold winter landscape but upon the brief time she would spend with him that evening: time that would be bittersweet because lately he had been refusing to allow himself the indulgence of her company on a regular basis. It was too painful; his feelings for her were too deep and he knew he would be cast into despondency after she'd gone back to the servants' hall, leaving him alone with his thoughts and turbulent emotions.

As she made her way back to the kitchen Rose thought sadly that before Christmas she would have been delighted to spend the winter evening with him but now it would be something of an ordeal to sit with him in that warm, comfortable, familiar room and have to hide her feelings. Oh, it was so hard, she thought, seeing him every day, knowing she loved him but knowing also that she could never betray by a word, a look or a gesture how she felt. It was making her life here so hard, so very hard to bear now, and tonight she would have to spend the night beneath the same roof as him. She had the feeling that she would cry herself to sleep. She wouldn't be able to stop the tears. Oh, why had it had to snow? she thought miserably as she pushed open the green baize door that led to the kitchen and the servants' hall.

Chapter Twenty-Seven

It wasn't possible for Rose to get back to the village for two more days. Gwen, knowing how much the girl disliked sleeping in that cold little room under the eaves, had asked her brother to go on his tractor to collect Rose that evening. It was the only vehicle that could manage the snow in the narrow lane.

Rose had spent two very cold and miserable nights, shivering beneath the blankets and trying not to think about David, so she was relieved when Henry informed her that Bob Roberts had arrived to take her back to the village.

'Make sure you wrap up warm, Rose, we don't want you going down with a cold too,' Mrs Mathews instructed for Nora had been confined to bed yesterday. Rose didn't look well, she thought and she had been very subdued these past two days, plus her eyes looked red and puffy which she viewed as an early symptom of Nora's cold. 'Beryl, get Mr Roberts a cup of tea while he's waiting,' she instructed.

'I'd be glad of one, Mona, thanks. It's still bitter out there but me having driven up and down that lane a couple of times will have made it more passable now. I'm afraid Rose will have to walk here in the morning though, I've the beasts to attend to, see. We've dried off most of the dairy herd so the milking doesn't take as long but a few of them have started to calve now so there's still plenty to do. This weather certainly doesn't help,' he informed the housekeeper. 'Still, I reckon it should have all melted by the end of the week if not sooner.' He took the mug from Beryl, cupping his cold hands around it.

When Rose reappeared, dressed in her heavy coat and wearing hat, scarf and gloves, he finished the tea and handed the mug back to the kitchen maid and then ushered Rose out. 'Soon get you home, luv, and Gwennie said to tell you she's got a beef stew with dumplings waiting which will warm you up.'

Rose nodded thankfully as he helped her up on to the tractor, at least she would be warm tonight, she thought, and hopefully she might get some sleep. She felt exhausted and emotionally drained.

Gwen quickly noticed that she wasn't her usual self although after they'd had supper Rose did look less pinched and weary. 'I gather you didn't get much sleep up there? Well, there's an extra quilt on the bed and I've put a hot-water bottle in it too to warm it up.'

Rose nodded her thanks, staring morosely into the fire.

'What's the matter, *cariad?* There's something wrong, isn't there, apart from you being tired out.' She hadn't failed to notice that Rose had hardly mentioned David Rhys-Pritchard these last couple of weeks.

'I'll be all right after a good night's sleep in a warm bed,' Rose replied rather unconvincingly. If she told Gwen what was really wrong she would sound such a fool, such a stupid little fool for falling in love with someone like him.

'Has something happened, Rose, between ... you and Mr Dai? You don't mention him at all now,' Gwen persisted. She was determined to get to the bottom of this. She hated to see Rose so unhappy.

'No. He ... he's been busy with Evan Price and estate matters and we've had all the extra work with Christmas and the wedding.'

'But that was weeks ago now, Rose,' Gwen reminded her. 'Things should have settled down again, surely? But I'm sure everyone will be pleased that he's getting more involved with the estate. It's been rather neglected these last years and Evan Price has been getting a bit too complacent, Bob says.'

Rose didn't reply.

'I think that in part you've been responsible for the improvement in him,' Gwen mused shrewdly.

Rose shook her head. 'Me? As Mam said I'm just a paid servant.'

Gwen frowned and poured herself another cup of tea. 'That's true but I thought you had become good friends as well.'

Rose was overcome by the realisation of just how that friendship had changed and the tears welled up in her eyes.

Gwen put down the cup and came and put her arms around the girl. 'Rose, what's happened? You're very unhappy, *cariad*, any fool can see that. You've changed this last month. You've fallen for him, haven't you?'

Rose could only nod. Her throat felt as though

it had closed over.

'Oh, Rose! You poor love! Does he know? Does he realise? Has he encouraged you?' Gwen gently stroked the girl's dark hair, thinking sadly that this was just what Kate had feared. She had foolishly told her friend not to worry, that Rose was more sensible now, but she hadn't reckoned on Rose's feelings and now the girl was bitterly hurt.

'No, he hasn't encouraged me and I ... I can't tell him. I can't let him even think ... but it's so hard, Gwen!'

Haltingly she told the older woman of the events of that afternoon before Christmas, of how she had come to realise that she loved him and of the way it had changed their friendship. 'I don't know what I'm going to do. I ... I can't go on like this,' she finished, wiping away her tears with the handkerchief Gwen produced.

Gwen sighed. That was true enough: she would make herself ill. 'You could go home, back to Liverpool. Your mam would welcome you and so would Iris, you know that, and with Charlie moving out in a couple of months they'll have plenty of room. You'd have to give them notice at Plas Idris and I don't suppose they'll be very pleased – and I'll miss you terribly, *cariad*, but I can't bear to see you so miserable. It will be a terrible strain for you to go on working up there and having to see him every day. Heart-breaking it would be and you'd not be giving yourself any chance to get over him.'

Rose didn't say that she wondered if she would ever get over him but she did feel a little calmer for sharing her secret and her sorrow. She was thankful Gwen hadn't reminded her of how foolish she'd been. 'But I love it here, you know that. I loved Tregarron from the first minute I arrived...'

'Sleep on it, Rose,' Gwen urged. 'After you come back tomorrow night we'll talk about it all again, you're exhausted and not just from lack of sleep.' She knew that Rose now looked on Tregarron as home but with the way things stood and virtually no prospect of Rose finding alternative employment she felt there was little chance that Rose could stay on.

Thankfully overnight it started to thaw and in the morning the snow had virtually gone when Rose set out for Plas Idris. She had slept well despite knowing that she had a very difficult decision to make and that she would have to make it soon.

After lunch was over Mrs Mathews instructed her to go and get some fresh air. The girl was still looking peaky, she thought. 'Take a walk around the garden, Rose, for half an hour. The weather is much milder today and it will put some colour back into your cheeks,' she'd instructed. Both Nancy and Beryl looked to have caught the parlourmaid's cold now and she didn't want Rose going down with it too or the household would go completely to pot.

Rose put on her coat and hat and wandered disconsolately towards the rose garden, drab and bare now, and made her way to the rustic bench. She sat staring miserably at the house and grounds that she'd come to love. She knew in her heart that she really didn't have a choice; she had to go home if she wanted to keep her sanity. But she would miss all this so much – and most of all she would miss *him*. If she had any hope of coming to terms with the fact that hers was a love that had no future, if she were to hang on to any shred of dignity and self-respect, she would have to hand in her notice. The thought of it was almost unbearable but she had to be resolute. She would speak to Mrs Mathews before she left this evening. She couldn't spend another day in this state of heart-breaking limbo.

She rose slowly to her feet, clutching her coat tightly to her, half blinded by tears, and began to walk back. She had reached the end of the pathway that led to the terrace when she saw him coming towards her. Her heart dropped like a stone. She couldn't face him but there was no alternative route back and, besides, he'd seen her.

'Rose, I was looking for you. Mrs Mathews said she'd sent you out for some fresh air. I thought perhaps that if you could be spared...' He suddenly noticed her distress. 'What's wrong, Rose? You've been crying.'

'It's nothing. I ... I think I've got dust in my eye,' she lied.

'No, Rose, you're upset. Let's go back to the bench; they won't mind you being out a little longer.'

Reluctantly she followed him back down the path and sat down again on the bench. Oh, this was going to be so hard but she had to do it. There was nothing else she could do.

'What is it, Rose? Has someone upset you?

Have *I* upset you? Please tell me!' He hated to see her so troubled.

Rose shook her head. She *had* to keep her emotions, her tears and her voice under control. 'I ... I'm afraid I'm going to have to ... leave Tregarron for ... for good.'

Her words shocked him profoundly. He'd tried to keep his feelings hidden from her. He had agonised over what he felt for her. He'd fought many battles against his heart using reason and common sense but they were battles neither of those faculties had won. He loved her but how could anyone as lovely, as compassionate, as vivacious love him? He was a cripple, he was a burden. He would always need someone to look after him.

'Why, Rose?' he asked, unable to keep the pain out of his voice. 'I ... I thought you liked Tregarron.'

Rose couldn't look at him. Tears were threatening to overwhelm her again. 'I do! I love the space and the beauty of the countryside, the ... peace, but I have to go. Really I do.'

'Is it your mother?'

Rose was too upset to seize the lifeline he had given her. She shook her head. 'No, Iris is caring for her.'

'Then why, Rose? Please tell me, perhaps I can rectify whatever is wrong,' he pleaded. He couldn't face the thought of never seeing her again.

'I ... I can't tell you, David. I can't!' She couldn't keep the sob from her voice as she looked at him, her eyes swimming with tears. The love she felt for him was clearly visible in that instant.

David felt as though he'd been physically struck. She'd ducked her head but he had seen the expression in her eyes. He reached out and took her hand in his. 'Rose, there is something I've wanted to tell you for weeks but I ... I was afraid to. I ... love you, Rose. I think I've loved you for quite a while but never realised it until ... that afternoon. Rose, if you love me then stay, please?'

'I do love you, David. I love you more than I can say, but how can I stay? I ... I work for you,' Rose whispered. Joy had surged through her at his words but had quickly been dispelled by the reality of her position.

He longed to take her in his arms and tell her that that was unimportant, what was important was that she loved him and he couldn't bear to lose her. His life would be unbearable without her, he had to ask her to be his wife, he had to keep her at his side. But what if she refused? What if she couldn't face a future tied to him – a cripple? He thought of the courage that had carried him through the months in the trenches, that had helped him survive the field hospital and the journey home to a world that had changed so much. 'Rose, will you ... marry me?'

Rose gasped aloud with shock. 'David ... I love you, I'll always love you but I can't...'

'Is it because of the way I am? A cripple?'

'No! I don't even think of you like that ... as being a cripple. David, I'm a servant. I'm a working-class girl from a humble home, I'm not even ... well educated. I ... I couldn't ... cope.'

'None of that matters to me, Rose. You have so many graces and wonderful attributes. I can't spend the rest of my life here without you. We'd lead a very quiet life. Livvie could continue to supervise the household, if that's what you would prefer. I don't have a title, so you wouldn't either. And, and … I promise it will be a "complete" marriage, there is no reason why we can't have children. I am not paralysed. Please don't go, Rose,' he begged, holding both her hands tightly in his now.

'But … the others. Mr Lewis, Henry…?'

He could see she was weakening. He'd fight tooth and nail to keep her. He didn't care what anyone thought or said – Olivia, Elinore, their relations and friends, the servants, convention, public opinion… He didn't care. All that mattered was that she would consent. 'Don't worry about anything, Rose. I'll discuss everything with them. It will be fine, I promise. And we'll be happy, Rose, that I promise too.'

She looked into his eyes and knew she couldn't refuse him. A great tide of happiness surged through her. 'Yes, I'll marry you, David,' she said shyly.

He leaned towards her and gently stroked her cheek before kissing her on the mouth. 'Oh, Rose, I love you so much. I never expected to love anyone, I never expected to be loved, not like this.'

She placed a finger on his lips, her eyes now shining with tears of joy. 'That doesn't matter to me. You are so … special. Oh, I do love you, David, and I'll be so happy to take care of you.'

'Then leave everything to me, Rose. You go and spend a few days with your family in Liverpool.

I'm sure your mother would like to hear the news first hand, rather than by telephone or letter,' he urged. It would be better, he judged, if she were not here when he broke the news to his sister for he had a good idea of what Olivia's reaction would be and he didn't want Rose to be upset or, worse, change her mind. 'Is there a bus tomorrow?'

She nodded, wondering how her mam and Iris and Charlie would react to her news. Hopefully they wouldn't be too dismayed because she would need Kate's permission.

'Then I'll arrange for someone to take you into Denbigh in the morning. Will you confide in Miss Roberts?' he asked, thinking that the news would spread like wildfire in the village.

Rose considered this, realising the amount of speculation and gossip it was going to cause. 'I'll ask her to say nothing about it until ... until I come back, David. Gwen can be very discreet,' she promised as she got to her feet. Life had changed so much in just a few short minutes, she thought as she looked towards the house. It dawned on her that very soon it would become her home and that her position would be drastically changed. She held tightly to his hand for it was a very daunting realisation.

Chapter Twenty-Eight

David wasn't disappointed by Olivia's reaction. He'd arranged for Rose to be collected from Gwen's cottage and driven to Denbigh to catch the bus and had spoken to Gwen Roberts on the telephone that morning. She'd sounded completely bemused, he'd thought, but had recovered herself enough to offer her congratulations and assure him of her discretion. He had then asked Lewis to inform Mrs Mathews that Rose had gone to visit her family for a few days. Lewis was acutely aware that something strange was going on but his years of training stood him in good stead and not even by the raising of an eyebrow did he betray his surprise. Then David had gone in search of his sister.

After he'd told her she stared at him blankly for a few seconds.

'Dai! David, you can't ... can't possibly be thinking of doing something so, so *crass*, so utterly stupid!'

'I don't see it like that, Livvie,' he replied curtly.

Olivia struggled for words. 'She ... she's a *servant!* She's ... she's...'

'Common? Working class? Yes, she is, but no one can say she's been ill mannered, loud or uncouth in any way while she's been here – just the opposite.'

'It's been her place to be well mannered!' Olivia

307

snapped back. 'Oh, I just don't believe this!'

'She's kind, gentle, intelligent and she ... she understands me. She's helped me to pick up the threads of my life again, to look forward instead of back. There will be no formal announcements, no engagement party, it will be an even quieter wedding than Elinore's.'

'I can't believe I'm hearing this, David! Mother and Father would be utterly mortified. Totally devastated.'

'They are dead, Olivia, and I have to live out the rest of my life as a cripple, dependent upon people. Do you think that prospect fills me with pleasure? I have little to look forward to and without Rose...'

Olivia could see he was determined. 'You do realise that the servants will all leave? How can we expect Lewis, Henry, Mrs Mathews, Cook to accept her as mistress of this house?'

David was becoming increasingly annoyed by her attitude. 'Are you more interested in what the servants will think than in my happiness?'

'That is unfair and uncalled for,' she snapped. 'But how can we expect them to accept her? And if they don't, how on earth is this household to continue to function? It will be disastrous! A complete shambles! Rose has no idea how to supervise staff, no idea of how to even communicate other than on the level to which she is now accustomed. You are putting the whole burden of the staff situation on my shoulders, David.'

'Leave that all to me, Olivia. Rose has no social ambitions whatsoever; she is happy for you to continue to supervise the household. And we intend to live very quietly, there will be no entertaining – except for Ernest and Elinore.'

'And what about her family? Will we be expected to entertain them?' Olivia was feeling quite faint at the thought.

'No. Her mother is a widow and has a medical condition which makes it unwise for her to travel. Her sister is married and runs a business and I believe her brother is to be married soon and he also has a business to attend to – shops, I gather.'

Napoleon's derogatory remark, 'a nation of shopkeepers', flashed through Olivia's mind, and then she pursed her lips. 'Well, I have to say I wash my hands of it entirely, David. On your own head be it! You'd better summon Lewis and ask him to inform the staff and be ready to try to find replacements. I want nothing at all to do with it.' She walked purposefully to the door and slammed it hard behind her.

He sighed heavily; it was what he had expected, which was why he'd sent Rose home.

Lewis had heard the door slam and had seen Olivia go upstairs with a grim, set expression on her face. She was obviously furious about something, he thought as he entered David's drawing room.

'I've upset Miss Olivia, I'm afraid, Lewis,' David informed him.

The butler inclined his head.

'I have just informed her that Rose has agreed to marry me. That's why she has gone home. To inform her family of the fact.'

It took all Lewis's years of training to keep his

composure and not reel with shock or utter a word.

'Olivia expects that the staff will resign en masse. Is that likely?' David asked quietly.

Lewis's emotions were in utter turmoil although his facial expression had hardly changed. 'I ... I don't think so, sir,' he managed at last. 'There will of course be ... comment.' There would of course be uproar, he thought, but the senior members of staff – including himself – had been with the family for years and knew no other life. Plas Idris was their home and when they retired it would be to David Rhys-Pritchard that they would look for a small pension; as for the maids, jobs for young girls were not easy to find in rural areas. However, it was a situation that would need a firm hand.

'Lewis, you've known me since I was four years old. It was you who amused me with those tricks involving bits of coloured paper. You gave me toffees at Christmas and a half-crown each time I went back to school; you taught me how to fish in the river. You were here waiting after the accident to try to ensure a semblance of normality prevailed and you saw me off to war with a handshake and cheerful words. You were waiting when I came back – like this. The damned war left me a cripple, unable to pursue any of the pastimes I once enjoyed. I had nothing to look forward to except years of loneliness and pain. I never expected to be loved or to find happiness.'

Lewis had recovered a little from the shock. Everything David had said was true, he thought, and he was fond of this young man whose life had been beset by tragedy. He wanted Mr David to be happy. Rose was a good girl: she was quiet, unassuming and thoughtful, but the fact remained she was not of his young master's class. He nodded slowly.

'Rose will need help, Lewis. Olivia will still supervise the household – I hope. We will live quietly; we will not entertain. There will be no formal announcements, a very quiet wedding but occasions may arise that she feels unable to ... cope with. I trust she can depend upon you for advice and support?'

Lewis nodded again as he digested all this. 'Rose seems to be taking a very ... sensible attitude, sir.'

David breathed deeply, feeling relieved. It appeared that Lewis was prepared to accept Rose and he hoped the rest of the staff would too. He hoped that in time Olivia would relent also.

As Charlie alighted from the tram and headed towards Cedar Grove he was thankful that the snow was rapidly melting. It had made life very difficult for everyone. Tom had struggled to get to and from the market and Iris had forbidden Kate to go over the doorstep in case she slipped; he hadn't been able to get to see Florence for a few days as the trams had virtually stopped running.

He was feeling very disgruntled for Florence had succumbed to Ethel's hints about the house they had and was now wondering if they should keep on looking. Well, he'd had enough. He intended to enlist Edward's help in putting a stop to this dithering. He'd paid a deposit to secure the house and he didn't intend to lose it.

When Florence had first told him – months ago now – that her mother intended that the business be sold and that they move away from Liverpool he'd been very upset. Getting rid of the business certainly hadn't been any part of his plan but thankfully Florence had caused such a fuss that Ethel had postponed everything, at least until after the wedding. Charlie frowned: that was something else that was getting completely out of hand. Well, he'd let her have her way over that – he wasn't paying for it – but he was going to put his foot down over the house, he thought as he knocked on the door.

Thankfully Florence was distracted about something else that appeared to have gone wrong and after giving him a quick kiss had ushered him straight into Edward's study and hastened back to her discussions with Ethel. Edward was at his desk, his shirt sleeves rolled up and a pile of papers in front of him.

'I take it the trams are getting back to normal now,' Edward greeted him.

'Yes, the snow has virtually gone. It's been nothing but a damned nuisance. I thought that bloke you took on was supposed to sort all those out?' Charlie indicated the cluttered desk.

'He is but like a lot of people he couldn't get to work. It's the coldest weather we've had this winter, my customers wanted and needed coal and my lorries have been stuck in the yard because the roads were so treacherous. Two of the drivers managed to make it in but then couldn't work because of the conditions,' Edward replied.

He looked harassed.

'Things should get back to normal in the morning. Do you want me to sort that lot out for you?' Charlie offered.

'No, Charlie, you've already done a day's work and it's what I employ Mellor for, except that he'll be short of a couple of days' pay this week.'

Charlie nodded his agreement. 'You've got more than enough on your plate as it is, but...' He hesitated.

'But what?' Edward asked. 'Not more fuss over this wedding?'

'No, not that – for a change. It's the house we're going to rent.'

Edward sighed heavily and leaned back in his chair. Charlie was being very tolerant with both Florence and Ethel, he thought, which was more than he could say for himself. 'I've heard the odd bit of conversation about it between Ethel and Florence. What's the matter with it?'

'Apparently it's not in the *right* area. I hate to ask this but ... I wonder if you could give me a bit of moral support on this. It's not a bad house, I doubt we'll get anything better for the rent they're asking and I've paid a deposit. The area seems reasonable enough to me, far better than some we've seen. It's in Walton, in one of those streets opposite the hospital gates.'

Edward nodded his agreement. 'I know them. It's convenient for all the amenities and they're quite substantially built houses. You know, we haven't always lived in this house, in fact we started married life in a small terraced property and Florence can't expect to–' Suddenly he leaned forward, his features contorted with pain, fighting for breath.

'Oh, my God! What's wrong?' Charlie cried, jumping to his feet. 'Is it your heart? What can I do? Edward! Edward!'

Edward was clutching at his throat. 'Pills ... pills...' he gasped.

'Where? Where are they?' Charlie cried, scattering the papers on the desk.

Edward tried to indicate a drawer and Charlie wrenched it open and rummaged around inside until he found the small round box. Charlie's hands were shaking for it was obvious that the older man was in agony and struggling to breathe. 'Damn! Damn!' he cursed as he finally got the lid off. The box was empty. He threw it down, hesitated for a second and then ran into the hall and burst into the morning room.

'Pills! His heart pills! The box is empty! For God's sake, he can hardly breathe!'

Florence screamed and Ethel went white and jumped to her feet and uttered, 'My bag!' in a strangled voice.

She ran from the room in search of her handbag and Charlie and Florence both dashed back to the study. Edward was lying face down across the desk and Florence started to cry hysterically as Charlie tried to lift her father.

Ethel, looking as if she were about to faint, stumbled in clutching the small pill box tightly in her hand. 'I ... I picked them up today but I ... I ... forgot...! Edward! Oh, Edward!' she cried for Charlie was sadly shaking his head.

'It's too late. He's gone,' he said. He'd seen

death often enough to know that pills would be of little use now. Edward Taylor had breathed his last and he felt a wave of sadness wash over him for he'd liked, respected and admired the man.

The trams had long since stopped running by the time Charlie was able to leave Cedar Grove. He'd called the doctor, who had arrived quickly and confirmed that Edward had died of a massive heart attack. He had assured Ethel that there was little anyone could have done, the pills would have been ineffective, and he'd administered a sedative to both Ethel and Florence. He'd then asked Charlie if he was able to manage the formalities. Charlie, although very shaken, had said he could and had contacted the funeral director's. Florence and her mother were both asleep when they arrived; they agreed with Charlie that it would be best if they took Edward to the mortuary.

'Much better if his wife ... widow ... and daughter see him tomorrow in the chapel of rest,' Mr Coyne had said gravely. 'Terrible shock for everyone. My deepest condolences,' he'd added respectfully.

Tom was already up and preparing to leave for the market when Charlie finally arrived home for he'd had to walk – the first tram had passed him at the bottom of the street. Taking in his brother-in-law's expression he knew something tragic had occurred. 'Mr Taylor?'

'He died in front of me, Tom. There was nothing I could do. It was his heart,' Charlie said, collapsing into an armchair. It had been a gruelling day and one that had brought back me-

315

mories of the shock of his father's death and the horror of his experiences during the war. Dealing with it all had drained him.

Tom immediately poured him a small brandy. 'Drink this. I'll go and wake Iris and Kate. Florence and her mam, are they all right? I mean how ... how are they coping?'

'They're both sleeping now, Tom. When the doctor came he gave them something. I'll grab a few hours then I'll go back. They're going to need me now. We're all going to have to manage ... somehow,' Charlie said, gulping down the liquid, which seemed to burn his throat. All thoughts of weddings, houses and businesses were far from his mind. He was just too exhausted now to think about anything.

Chapter Twenty-Nine

Kate and Iris were both deeply shocked and saddened by the news of Edward Taylor's sudden death.

'He was such a nice man! Oh, poor, poor Florence!' Iris cried, shaking her head and wiping away a tear. She had grown fond of her friend's father.

Kate nodded. 'I feel very sorry for them both. I liked him, he was a decent man with no side to him. And even though that doctor said there was nothing anyone could have done Ethel will never forgive herself for forgetting to make sure those

316

pills were close to hand when he needed them.' She sighed sadly. 'Even now I blame myself for insisting your da go to the bank that day.'

'I hope Florence doesn't start blaming herself because of all the fuss she's been causing lately. I wonder will she postpone the wedding now?' Iris mused aloud.

'It's still almost two months away,' Charlie reminded them wearily.

'But Ethel might insist on the year of formal mourning – you know what she's like. And it will have to be a much quieter affair too, but maybe that's not such a bad thing,' Kate added. 'You're taking on a lot of responsibilities, Charlie.'

Charlie nodded slowly. 'I'm becoming aware of that, Mam. Ethel can't run that business, she doesn't have a clue and I doubt she'll have either the interest or the heart to try. She'll need some-one to look after everything in the coming weeks and months too because she's in no fit state to cope. Edward did everything for her.'

'I'll go back with you, Charlie. Tom will see to the shop and it's the least I can do for poor Florence,' Iris offered.

'Thanks, Iris. I'll have to close for the next couple of days. Things are not going to be easy for anyone,' Charlie replied grimly.

'Go and get a few hours' sleep, lad, you look terrible,' Kate urged, thinking that you never knew what fate had in store from one minute to the next. She felt heartily sorry for Ethel Taylor: she knew how it felt to be so suddenly bereaved.

After Charlie had gone upstairs Iris put the kettle on. 'Mr Taylor's death is going to affect us all in time, Mam,' she said gravely.

Kate frowned. 'In what way, luv? Charlie and Florence will get married eventually. It will of course be very hard for Florence to have to get through that day without her da and they won't be able to hold on to that rented property, but they'll find somewhere else. You and Tom are managing well enough and I'm all right, as long as I'm careful and watch what I do.'

'But if our Charlie is going to take over Mr Taylor's business, which I'm sure he intends to do on a permanent basis, what will happen to the pawnbroker's? He can't be responsible for two businesses and Tom and I can't manage both shops.' Tom did most of the work now, she thought, leaving her free to look after her mother, but she did not remind Kate of that fact.

Kate looked perplexed. 'I hadn't thought of that and I don't think Charlie has either – yet. No one can divide their time in that way, it's a recipe for trouble. Eventually both businesses will start to suffer. Oh, if only I didn't have this damned condition!' she finished exasperatedly.

'Well, you have, Mam, so it's no use getting upset about it,' Iris said flatly, although she understood Kate's frustration.

'But if I was well enough we could easily manage the two businesses between the three of us and leave Charlie free to see to Ethel and Florence. Your grandfather started that business and your da worked in it all his life, I'd hate to have to let it go.'

Iris nodded. 'And I think that if they postpone the wedding, then when they do get married

Charlie intends to move into Cedar Grove.'

Kate considered this. 'Ethel might not be very happy with that arrangement, she's never really had much time for Charlie. It is a very big house, though, and she might find it lonely living there alone. She might decide eventually that she wants to sell the business. I presume it rightfully belongs to her now.'

Iris nodded, wondering if Charlie had thought of that.

'And she may feel she doesn't want to go on living in that house and look for something smaller. She was talking about moving out of Liverpool. These are all decisions she has to make but not for a good while yet, she's in no frame of mind to think clearly. She'll be dazed and confused; I know I was.'

Iris handed her mother a cup of tea. 'I think I know what our Charlie will suggest when he does realise that he can't be in two places at once. He'll say that there's no other option but to bring Rose home.' Indeed the way things were looking it seemed the only possible solution to the problem but she knew her sister would be far from happy, even though she wouldn't have to work in the greengrocer's. Iris would do that, Tom would take over in Charlie's shop and Rose could look after Mam.

Kate sighed heavily as she finished her tea. 'We'll have to let Rose know about Mr Taylor. I'll get Charlie to telephone Gwen and ask her to tell Rose the sad news but I don't think we should mention any of these ... problems to her just yet. It's very early days.'

Iris accompanied her brother when he returned to Cedar Grove later that morning. She was determined that beside trying to comfort her friend she would also think of the practical things, like contacting relatives and preparing a meal and trying to get Florence and her mother to eat. Charlie was going to spend the night if Ethel had no objections for he felt that they shouldn't be alone and would need someone to deal with any problems that might arise.

Both women were still very tearful and a little dazed and Charlie was very considerate with both his fiancée and her mother.

'Charlie, I ... I still can't believe he ... he's ... gone!' Florence said as she clung to her fiancé.

'I know, luv. It will be a while before it really sinks in. I speak from experience. But I'll be here to help you through it all. You know you can always rely on me,' he comforted her. He meant it for he had now realised that he did indeed love her. What had started out as ambition and affection had deepened into love and as he held her he vowed that he would always take care of both Florence and her mother. He owed it to the memory of a man he had come to feel great affection for as well as respect and admiration.

'I don't know how we would have managed without you and I just can't bear even to think about the ... future.'

'Then don't, Florence. You'll need time to get over everything and then ... well, we'll just take things as they come,' Charlie said firmly.

Florence confided to Iris that she felt as if she

were walking through a blanket of mist and that nothing seemed real.

'It's probably whatever the doctor gave you to make you sleep, Florence. It will wear off gradually but ... but I remember how unreal everything seemed when Da was killed. It all seems to get a bit better after ... after the funeral. I know that sounds improbable but things gradually do get back to something like normal, although they never really are again. Something – someone – is always missing. I still miss my da terribly.'

Florence sniffed and held tightly to her hand. 'I ... I ... feel I made things worse, Iris. I was fussing so much ... bothering him with trivial things...'

'Now stop that at once, Florence! You were just getting a bit overwrought, that's all. You wanted everything to be perfect – is that so wrong? The doctor said there was absolutely nothing anyone could have done. It was just his time to ... go.'

'I ... I can't even think about the wedding now. It ... it's all so ... unimportant,' Florence sobbed.

Iris put her arms around her friend. 'You'll be able to think more clearly in a few weeks and it's *not* unimportant, Florence. Your wedding day is the beginning of the rest of your life – yours and Charlie's – and it's what your da wanted for you; a happy life,' she said soothingly.

After some coaxing she managed to get both Florence and her mother to eat a little. Ethel had agreed that it would be best if Charlie stayed. There seemed to be so many things she didn't feel up to coping with; she just couldn't shake off this terrible sense of loss and guilt and the sedative had left her with a splitting headache. Before she left Iris persuaded the older woman to go and lie down, impressing upon her the fact that Charlie would look after everything – including Florence.

'It's a really horrible time, Mrs Taylor, I know. I remember how I felt. Try and rest, it might help,' she urged.

Florence was loath to see her leave but she gently reminded her friend that she had to keep her eye on her mother and that Tom would be looking for his evening meal after a long day in the shop. 'I'll come up for a couple of hours tomorrow, I promise, and Charlie will look after you, you know that.'

'I know. I don't know what I'd do without him, Iris, and I've been neglecting him lately too.' Florence wiped her eyes again.

'It's what fiancés and husbands are for, Florence, to depend on in times like this. Try to get some sleep tonight, you're exhausted,' she urged as she went out into the hall.

Charlie was standing staring at the telephone, his forehead creased in a frown.

'Have you phoned Gwen?' Iris asked.

He nodded. 'She's not there.'

'Who's not there? Gwen?'

'No. Our Rose.'

'Of course she's not there, Charlie. She'll be up at Plas Idris,' Iris reminded him a little impatiently.

'She's not. She's on her way home to Liverpool. Gwen said someone from Plas Idris drove her to Denbigh for the bus this morning and that she'll be staying a few days.'

Iris was startled to hear this. 'Someone from

the big house drove her to Denbigh! Oh, Lord, what's happened now? Didn't you ask Gwen why she's coming home?'

'All she said was: "Rose will tell you all about it herself." Well, at least she can make herself useful by seeing to Mam.'

Iris nodded slowly, wondering why her sister had suddenly decided to come home for Rose enjoyed her job and loved living in Tregarron. She prayed there was nothing sinister behind her sister's decision.

When she arrived home it was to find Rose sitting with Kate in the kitchen. As she'd gone through the shop Tom had informed her of this fact. She had asked him if her sister looked upset and he had shrugged and said far from it.

'Oh, Iris, I'm so sorry to hear about poor Mr Taylor. How are Florence and Mrs Taylor coping? Mam said you'd gone up there. I've only just arrived.' Rose got up and hugged Iris as she spoke.

'Mrs Taylor has gone to lie down and I've managed to get them both to eat something but they're both terribly upset and shocked.'

'I take it our Charlie is staying?' Kate asked distractedly. She was still getting over the surprise of seeing her youngest daughter walk into the kitchen unannounced and wondering what had happened at Tregarron to bring Rose home.

Iris nodded. 'This is a surprise, Rose. Charlie phoned Gwen to tell her about Edward Taylor and she said you'd left. It all sounds very sudden and mysterious. What's wrong?'

Rose smiled and sat down again. 'There's

nothing wrong. I've come home for a few days. I ... I've some news but it doesn't seem like the right time to tell you it, what with Mr Taylor...'

'This "news" must be very important to bring you all the way to Liverpool without a word of warning, Rose,' Kate demanded. 'Never mind Mr Taylor's death, why have you come home?'

'To ask your permission Mam, to ... to get married, as I'm under age.'

Both Kate and Iris stared at her dumbfounded but Iris regained her wits first.

'*Married!* Rose, you've never mentioned anyone, who on earth are you going to *marry?*' she cried.

Rose blushed and twisted her hands together nervously. 'David. He asked me yesterday afternoon and I agreed.'

'*David Rhys-Pritchard! You're going to be Mrs Rhys-Pritchard and live in that grand house!*' Iris shrieked, unable to contain herself.

Kate passed a hand over her eyes as her heart sank. As soon as Rose had mentioned marriage she had known it would be to him. 'Rose! Rose, do you really understand what you've done?' she pleaded.

'Yes. I love him, Mam, and he loves me,' Rose answered quietly.

Kate groaned. 'I tried to warn you. You're a servant, luv, you ... *we're* not of his class. We don't belong in his world; we don't know how to behave in it. Oh, Rose, how can it possibly work? I want you to be happy, luv, but you won't be.' Kate was close to tears, envisaging a future where her daughter would be rejected, ostracised and maybe openly sneered at for her lack of breeding, manners and accomplishments.

'I *will* be happy, Mam! It *will* work! I firmly believe that! David doesn't care about my background. At first I told him I couldn't marry him and he ... he thought it was because he is crippled but I don't care about that. I love him; I'll take care of him. We'll be happy! There will be no announcements in the papers, no engagement party, a very quiet wedding–'

'What about his sisters?' Kate interrupted. 'You can be sure they'll have something to say about it. That Miss Olivia for one won't take kindly to having you as a sister-in-law – and then there are the other servants. They won't accept you as their mistress, Rose, you've worked there long enough to know the way things are in those big houses. Oh, Rose!' Kate finished in despair.

Tears pricked Rose's eyes and she felt a tiny doubt enter her mind. Suppose Mam was right? What if Nora and Nancy and the others wouldn't accept her? What if Olivia refused to continue to supervise the household? She firmly quashed it and squared her slim shoulders determinedly. She loved David; they would be happy, despite everything. 'I'll cope, Mam. I can learn. We intend to live very quietly and we won't be entertaining. David is certain Olivia will be happy to continue to oversee the household and I think that will be for the best, and he will inform the staff himself. Oh, I was so miserable Mam, when I realised I loved him but that I'd have to leave ... him. I'd decided to come home, I couldn't go on working there, but I was at my wits' end. I just didn't know how I was going to face the future without him. We'll be happy, Mam, I know we will.'

Iris had finally regained her composure. 'You really do love him, Rose? You're not just ... dazzled ... by that big house and all their lands and money?' She was finding it hard to accept that her sister would be entering a world that was so totally different to her own.

'Iris, I'm not *dazzled!* I wouldn't care if he lived in a cottage and didn't have a penny to bless himself with. I love him and I'll take care of him for the rest of his life even if all the staff leave and I have to do the cooking and cleaning myself! All we want is a quiet life, time to be together, to ... share things. He's suffered so much in his life; he's lost his parents–'

'It's not just pity is it, Rose?' Kate demanded.

'No, Mam, it's not! At first I did feel sorry for him, but then as I got to know him and we grew ... closer, I knew I loved him for himself, not for who he is or what he has, and that's exactly how he feels about me. He doesn't care where I come from or what I do. He loves me.'

Kate sighed heavily. She'd never heard Rose speak so eloquently, sincerely or with such a depth of feeling.

'Mam, please do I have your permission?' Rose pressed quietly, glancing at Iris for support.

'Mam, if she loves him and is happy to devote her life to him, happy to embrace that kind of life, then...' Iris urged.

Kate at last nodded slowly but her heart was still heavy. 'You have my permission, Rose, but I give it with grave reservations.'

Rose smiled and her happiness transformed her. Iris smiled too: it was obvious that Rose truly loved David Rhys-Pritchard and she could see that love had increased her sister's confidence and maturity. Watching them both, Kate could not deny that her youngest daughter had grown into a quiet, poised and beautiful young woman. Rose would never be of the same class as her future husband and she might find it very difficult to adjust to his world, but she would not disgrace him.

Chapter Thirty

The following morning Rose took herself off into town, saying she had some things to purchase, while Iris prepared to visit Florence again. She hoped she would find her friend a little more composed. Kate had spent a restless night worrying about Rose's future, but had reluctantly come to the conclusion that she must let Rose live her own life and hope things would work out well and not prove to be the biggest mistake Rose had ever made.

It had been agreed that when Rose had finished in town she would call at Cedar Grove to see Florence and to telephone both David and Gwen to inform them of when she intended to return.

Rose had never ventured through the doors of

Hendersons, Cripps, the Bon Marché or De Jong et Cie, Liverpool's most exclusive and expensive stores, she'd only ever stood gazing into their windows, so it was with great trepidation that she now nodded her thanks to the uniformed commissionaire who held open the door of the Bon Marché for her. David had told her to inform them that she was his fiancée and stressed that she must buy whatever she needed, the family had an account to which her purchases would be added.

As she stood looking hesitantly around she was approached by the floor walker, a middle-aged gentlemen attired in a morning suit, to whom she rather timidly explained her position. She was immediately escorted to the second floor and handed over to the manageress of the Ladies' Haute Couture Department.

'I'm looking for something suitable for a quiet, country wedding – my wedding,' she replied upon being asked what she had in mind.

She was ushered into a dressing room which contained two delicate-looking chairs and a long mirror on an elaborate gilt stand. Within a few minutes half a dozen outfits were brought for her approval. She selected a pale blue fine wool crêpe dress with a matching coat, the collar and cuffs of which were trimmed with pale beige fur and as she stared at herself in the long mirror she thought that she'd never envisaged coming to buy her wedding outfit on her own. Somehow she'd always thought that Iris and her mam would have accompanied her and that the dress would be long and white but that had all been in her daydreams years ago. This was the reality and it was what she wanted, what she had chosen. She was about to enter a world where she would need more confidence, to rely more upon herself and to appear well dressed at all times. The outfit was simple, elegant and expensive, she thought, and as a small matching pale blue cloche was placed on her head she nodded slowly. It suited her perfectly and she was certain David would like it. She chose a further three wool day dresses, a heather-coloured tailored costume and a well-cut coat in black and white herringbone tweed. As she signed for her purchases she tried not to think of the enormous amount of money she had spent, but resolved to buy her shoes, gloves and stockings out of what she had managed to save. She did not wish David or Olivia to think she was being extravagant, although the accessories would not be purchased here.

'I thought you were only going for a few bits? How on earth are you going to get that lot back on the bus?' Kate remarked in astonishment as Rose struggled into the kitchen laden with boxes.

'I'll manage, Mam. I got them home on the tram,' Rose replied. 'I bought an outfit for my ... wedding.'

Kate smiled a little sadly. 'Why didn't you tell me that's what you were going for? I'd have come with you.' Then she caught sight of the wording on the boxes. 'Dear God! The Bon Marché!'

'David told me to buy what I needed, they have an account there,' Rose explained.

Kate shook her head. Only the very wealthy had accounts in shops like that but it was slowly beginning to sink in that soon Rose would be numbered amongst them. 'It's a good job you did go alone then, I'd have been a bag of nerves in a place like that.'

'I was a bit nervous, Mam, but they were very nice, very helpful. I could have had everything delivered here but...'

She shrugged. She'd wanted to show both Iris and her mother what she'd bought and she was also aware that had she given this address eyebrows would have been raised. 'I'll have a quick cup of tea and then I'll go up to see poor Florence,' she added, leaving her mother to try to guess how much she'd spent.

When she arrived it was to find Florence sitting with Iris and seemingly calmer although still pale, wan and grief-stricken.

'Florence, I'm so sorry about your father. How are you feeling today?' Rose asked, handing the girl the bunch of early spring flowers she'd purchased before boarding the tram, remembering how Florence had once brought her flowers. 'I thought you might like these,' she added.

'Thank you, Rose, that was thoughtful. I ... I don't feel quite as bad today,' Florence replied.

'Mrs Taylor has gone with Charlie to see the vicar, she's a bit more herself today too,' Iris informed her sister. 'Florence, why don't you put those in water while I make some tea?'

When Florence went in search of a vase Iris lowered her voice. 'I've told Charlie about you getting married but he's not exactly delighted. He was expecting you to come home and look after Mam while he takes over Mr Taylor's business. He's arranging the funeral and when that's over he'll take over the coal business full time and when he and Florence are married he'll move in here. He intended Tom to run the pawnbroker's, me the greengrocery and you to look after Mam. I have to admit that he's got a lot on his plate at the moment but he's not very happy, Rose, that he'll now have to think of some other solution. But don't say a word to Florence.'

'I won't,' Rose promised. 'I can understand that he's trying to do his best for everyone but I have my future to think of, Iris. Mine and David's.'

'Of course you do! *I'm* delighted for you, Rose, and I know Florence will be too.'

Rose was surprised. 'You haven't told her?'

'No, I left it to you. It's your good news and, let's face it, we could do with something good happening.'

As Iris had predicted Florence was cheered by Rose's news.

'That's wonderful, Rose, and it's to be in a few weeks? So, you'll both be married before me,' she added wistfully.

'It will be a very quiet ceremony, Florence. I'm going to ask David about having the Reverend Owen Williams conduct it, he's Bethan's husband and they are both so nice. It will be quieter even than Iris's wedding, just David's immediate family and Gwen and Iris and Tom, if they can manage a few days away?' She smiled enquiringly at Iris. 'And I'm going to have to get used to a very different life, which might be very difficult at first, but I love David and that's all that really matters.'

Florence nodded. 'It is. I'm beginning to understand that now,' she agreed with a note of remorse in her voice.

'Do you think your mother would mind if Rose used the telephone before she leaves? She needs to let both Gwen and David know when she's going back,' Iris asked.

'Of course not,' Florence replied, wondering vaguely how she would have to address Rose in the future. Would she be 'The Honourable Mrs Rhys-Pritchard' or maybe even something grander? However, she was still too confused to dwell for long on such thoughts.

Rose was preparing to leave when Ethel Taylor and Charlie arrived back, Ethel looking very pale and close to tears.

Rose offered her condolences which the older woman accepted before going into the morning room to compose herself. Charlie immediately turned to her.

'I hear congratulations are in order, Rose. You've done very well for yourself, very well indeed,' he said a little curtly.

'It is not a matter of "doing well for myself", Charlie. I am simply going to be David's wife. Just as Florence will be yours. I'm sorry if I've upset your plans. I know it's been a very difficult time for you but ... but everything happened so suddenly. I... We didn't plan it. When has the funeral been arranged for?'

'Wednesday morning,' he replied, wishing he could feel more enthusiastic but her news had simply added to his burdens.

'Then I will leave for Tregarron the day after.

There is a bus on Thursdays. I've asked Florence's permission to telephone both Gwen and David to inform them, so if you don't mind...'

'Help yourself, Rose,' Charlie replied, indicating the instrument on the hall table and thinking that already her manner of speech and her attitude had changed. This wasn't the Rose he was used to and he felt saddened but a little envious too. She was seemingly walking effortlessly into a position of wealth and status which he and so many others could only ever dream about. But he didn't envy her too much, it would be hard for her to fit into such a different world and he hoped she wouldn't come to hate it.

Later that evening Rose confided to Iris that she had been rather taken aback at being addressed as "Miss Mundy" by Lewis when he had answered the phone at Plas Idris. 'It made me realise that things have already changed, Iris.'

Iris nodded. 'I suppose everything will be done by the book from now on, Rose, you'll have to get used to it.'

'That's what Gwen said too,' Rose added. 'I'll go on staying with her until the wedding but it won't do for me to help out in the post office and when I go up to Plas Idris I have to use the front door now. That will seem strange at first.'

'You're not regretting it, are you?'

Rose shook her head and smiled. 'No, but I'm not looking forward to seeing the rest of the staff for the first time. I know things will be awkward.'

'At least no one's given in their notice so that's a start,' Iris reminded her for Rose had relayed most of her conversation with David to her.

'And then there's Olivia and Elinore. I know I'll have to see them both and I've got the feeling that as it's her home, Olivia in particular isn't going to be very happy.'

'She'll have to get on with it though, won't she?' Iris stated, thinking she didn't envy Rose much.

'I'd much prefer it … if we could at least be … pleasant to each other.'

'Give her time, Rose. She'll get used to it – to you. Now, I've already spoken to Tom and he is urging me to come and stand for you. He'll stay to keep his eye on Mam as our Charlie is going to have his hands full...'

'But I was hoping he might give me away, Iris?' Rose confided. 'Charlie will be much too busy.'

Iris could understand that but she was worried about leaving Mam. Charlie would be at the office and yard of Taylor's all day and probably spend a few hours at Cedar Grove too and if Kate fell with both herself and Tom away... 'We'll see, Rose, but I have to think of Mam.'

'I know. It was a bit selfish of me to ask. I'm sure Gwen's brother Bob would be quite happy to stand in.'

Iris sighed. 'Nothing is ever straightforward, is it? None of our lives are turning out the way we thought they would. Yours. Mine. Florence's. Only Charlie's seems to be running to plan.'

'I wonder will our Charlie finally be happy with that house and business?'

'For Florence's sake, I hope he is,' Iris answered quietly.

Chapter Thirty-One

The funeral had been quite a large affair, attended by not only Edward and Ethel's relations and friends but also by suppliers, employees, neighbours and many of Edward's customers, for he'd been greatly respected. As she and Iris followed the cortège out into the churchyard after the service Rose thought that both Florence and her mother had held up very well.

Iris had commented *sotto voce* that Charlie already looked the part of the respectful son-in-law and successful businessman as he supported Florence, he having purchased a new dark suit, Crombie overcoat *and* a bowler hat. He also carried a furled black umbrella for it had threatened rain. 'He'll be joining a Masonic lodge next,' had been her sister's final terse remark.

The following morning Rose had taken her leave of both her mother and sister, hugging them both.

'Let us know when you've got an exact date sorted out and I'll get myself organised. I'll see you in a couple of weeks with my wedding outfit,' Iris had promised. Tom had decided that only she would make the journey to Tregarron for he really could not be spared under the circumstances, although he would have liked to have seen Rose married and installed in the splendour of Plas Idris.

'You'll be in my thoughts and prayers, Rose, every day, and I wish you great happiness. I mean that. Just be yourself, luv. He's a thorough gentleman and I did like him so I feel he'll be protective of you,' Kate had said a little sadly, wishing it were possible for her to accompany Iris.

Gwen had welcomed her back warmly but warned her that although she had not breathed a word to a soul, the news had already reached the village, probably via one of the servants at the big house. Rose felt very apprehensive as she reached the top of the drive and the pale grey stone walls of Plas Idris rose before her. It *was* a beautiful house, she'd always thought so, she reminded herself, and in a few short weeks it would become her home. The March sunlight was reflected by the long windows and the stone urns on the terrace were filled with spring flowers.

She had dressed with care in her new heather-coloured costume with a pale lilac fine wool sweater beneath the jacket for it was still chilly. Her black shoes, gloves and bag were also new and a purple and black cloche hat covered her dark hair. The feeling of apprehension intensified as she slowly walked up the steps to the front door, but she was looking forward to seeing David again for they'd had so little time alone together before she'd left and she had so much to tell him.

Lewis opened the door to her and inclined his head formally. 'Good morning, Miss Mundy. Mr David is expecting you. He's in his drawing room.'

Rose managed a shy smile, clutching her bag

tightly to disguise the fact that her hands were trembling a little. 'Thank you, Mr Lewis.'

He leaned toward her and lowered his voice. 'Just "Lewis" from now on and if you are unsure about anything ... anything at all, I'll be here on hand to help. Don't hesitate to ask.'

Rose was very relieved. 'Thank you, that's very kind of you ... Lewis.' Encouraged by his generosity of spirit she continued: 'Can I ... can I ask how everyone else feels about...?'

He glanced around and then smiled at her. 'Surprised, of course, but I hope there won't be any ... remarks ... or ... unpleasantness from the staff, although I can't guarantee it. I will try to make sure things go as smoothly as possible, you have my word on that.'

'I have so much to thank you for and I have so much to learn... I dread making a fool of myself and – more importantly – David,' she confided.

'You'll be all right, don't worry. Now, follow me before he comes to find us both.'

David's face lit up in a smile as Lewis ushered her in. 'Rose, you look beautiful! Welcome back! That's a very becoming colour.'

Rose smiled back happily as she crossed and kissed him on the cheek. 'Thank you. I'm so happy to be back, David.'

David addressed the butler: 'Could we have some tea, Lewis, please? Say in about fifteen minutes? Miss Olivia is going to join us shortly.'

'Certainly, Sir. I'll instruct Nora to bring it up,' Lewis replied, wishing he could be a fly on the wall during that interview but feeling a little sorry for Rose just the same.

Rose sat beside David and he took her hand. 'Don't look so terrified, Rose. Livvie won't eat you, I promise.'

Rose managed a wry smile. 'What did she say? Was she upset? I really don't want to cause any trouble.'

'She was surprised and upset, I won't deny that, but I think she's getting used to it ... slowly. I haven't seen Ellie; Livvie drove over to see her but she hasn't seen fit to inform me of Ellie's reaction to our news.' He sighed, remembering Olivia's set expression when she'd returned, which he assumed meant that Elinore hadn't been nearly as outraged as her sister.

'Gwen says it's already common knowledge in the village although she vows she hasn't mentioned a word to anyone.'

He nodded. It was impossible to keep the servants from gossiping; he'd known that. 'And your mother is quite happy with your decision?'

Rose nodded. 'She wishes us every happiness although at first she was upset. Is ... is Olivia quite happy to continue to take charge of everything?' This had been worrying her for if Olivia flatly refused she would find it very difficult to manage.

'Stop worrying, darling. I'm certain she will. Now, I haven't been idle while you've been away. I've spoken to the Reverend Williams and he'll be delighted to marry us quietly in the chapel in the village. I thought you'd prefer it rather than the big church in town.'

Rose began to relax a little. 'I'd like that; I was going to ask you if he could marry us. He and

Bethan are so nice and Bethan was very kind to me when my father was killed.'

'We'll ask him to come up so we can discuss it further and you will have to discuss with Mrs Mathews if you wish the furniture in these rooms to be rearranged. This is going to be your home as much as mine, Rose. And, of course, you will have to think about the guests you'd like to invite and what we should have to eat after the ceremony.'

'I know. I'll ask her what she can suggest,' Rose replied, thinking that she had no idea what would be suitable fare for such an occasion.

Olivia was prompt, arriving five minutes before Nora appeared with the tea. She looked composed although she still considered this to be the worse misalliance in the history of the county and had no intention of greeting Rose with any degree of warmth. It hadn't helped that Elinore, although very surprised, hadn't been outraged at all. She'd commented that she'd always liked Rose and she was glad that poor Dai had found love and happiness; she'd also pointed out that times and attitudes were gradually changing. Marriage seemed to have changed *her* beyond all recognition, she'd fumed indignantly to Elinore.

'Good morning, Dai and ... Rose,' she greeted them rather curtly.

'Thank you, Livvie, for sparing us the time. I've asked for tea while we discuss the arrangements,' David informed her cordially.

Rose smiled, unsure of whether to speak or not. She had to remember not to get to her feet to help Nora when the parlourmaid entered. It didn't help that Nora hadn't even glanced at her.

Out of habit Olivia presided over the tea tray. 'And *have* you made any arrangements?' she asked in a clipped tone as she handed her brother a cup and saucer.

'Yes. Reverend Williams will marry us in the church in the village and while obviously he cannot forbid the members of his flock to attend, it will be made quite clear that we wish for as much privacy as possible. There will be just yourself and, I trust, Elinore. I intend to ask Ernest to be my best man.' He turned to Rose and smiled. 'Whom would you like to invite, Rose?'

'Mr Roberts has agreed to give me away and I'd like to invite Miss Roberts; I look on her as an aunt. Iris, my sister, is the only one who will be coming from Liverpool. Her husband has a business to attend to and Mam ... my mother,' she hastily amended for Olivia had visibly stiffened, 'needs ... care. Charlie has his hands full and I'm afraid I've upset his plans. He'd assumed that I'd go home to look after my mother so Iris could run the greengrocery while Tom took over the pawnbroker's, leaving Charlie to take over Mr Taylor's business. His future father-in-law died suddenly,' Rose explained.

Olivia closed her eyes momentarily. Dear God! A greengrocery and a *pawnbroker's!* she thought. 'That seems ... satisfactory,' she managed to reply.

'Rose was wondering if you will be happy to continue in your position as chatelaine?' David asked.

'I really would be very grateful ... Olivia. I have so much to learn,' Rose added timidly. She had never addressed David's sister as anything other than 'Miss Olivia' before.

If his sister was displeased she wasn't showing it, David thought thankfully.

Olivia inclined her head in a gesture of assent. She'd already decided that she couldn't possibly allow Rose to do so for the Lord alone knew what chaos would ensue and then there would be even more gossip and speculation. Lewis had informed her that regretfully there was indeed some degree of animosity towards Rose, particularly from Nora and Nancy, and that could not be allowed to escalate. 'I am ... prepared to do so,' she replied. She had been determined that she would not say she would be *happy* to.

'Then perhaps both of you could discuss with Mrs Mathews the menu for the wedding breakfast,' David suggested.

Olivia put her teacup down on the tray and got to her feet. This was something she had no intention of doing. 'I'm sure Rose is quite capable of doing that, David, after all there will only be a handful of people to accommodate. Now, if you will excuse me... I'll send Nora to collect the tray.'

Rose bit her lip as the door closed behind her future sister-in-law. 'She'll never accept me, David.'

David smiled at her. He was sorry Olivia had been so cold and abrupt but he could only hope that in time she would warm to Rose. 'At least she agreed to continue to supervise the household. Now, come here, I've missed you so much and we've not had more than a few minutes alone yet.' He held out his arms.

Rose hugged him tightly. There would be difficult days ahead but she was determined that she wasn't going to let Olivia mar her happiness.

The following afternoon, as she made her way to Mr Dai's drawing room, Mona Mathews thought that this was going to be the most unusual interview she'd ever experienced in all her years as a housekeeper. So far only Mr Lewis and Nora had seen Rose since her return and Nora had remarked grudgingly that Rose had looked very smart and seemed to be coping quite well; she was a bit quiet but wasn't that to be expected? She was aware that Rose's changed status had been discussed at great length by Nora, Nancy and Beryl and she'd overheard young Beryl stating that she thought it was just so romantic, which was just the sort of thing she'd expect from an empty-headed fifteen-year-old farmer's daughter. She, personally, thought young Rose Mundy was biting off more than she could chew and was going to find life far from easy, but she'd had a long discussion with Mr Lewis and they'd agreed that for Mr Dai's sake they would assist Rose all they could.

Rose was alone when she entered and she had to admit that the girl seemed to have gained in confidence and poise and her softly tailored green and navy checked dress was both smart and becoming.

'I believe there are some things you wish to

discuss with me, miss?' she said as Rose indicated that she should sit down.

'Yes, Mrs Mathews. Miss Olivia will continue to oversee the household and I am very grateful that's she's agreed to do so. I was hoping you would advise me on the wedding breakfast. There will be ten people in all, I hope, including the Reverend Williams and his wife. I'd like something that will suit ... everyone. As you are aware, I know very little about such things.' Rose was trying to sound calm but her embarrassment threatened to overwhelm her.

Greatly relieved that Olivia would continue to be in charge, Mona Mathews relaxed a little. 'If I could suggest a cold collation, something more elaborate than that provided at Christmas. It would be far less formal than a lunch as there will be a ... mixture ... of guests.'

Rose agreed, thinking it would be less work for the servants too. David had suggested that they all be given some time off to celebrate as well. 'There will, Mr Roberts is giving me away and Miss Roberts and my sister Iris will be my only guests. David is hoping Mr Ernest will be his best man.'

Mrs Mathews nodded. So, no other members of her family were to attend and none of the Rhys-Pritchard relations would be invited. It was going to be very quiet so a buffet would indeed be the best option. There would be no point in subjecting everyone to the formality of a sit-down lunch. 'Will your sister be staying with Miss Roberts?' she enquired, wondering if the girl was to be accommodated here during her short stay.

'Yes, Iris will only stay a few days. I ... I was also wondering if it is the custom for ... for me to present the staff with a token of some kind, in appreciation? Or would that be the ... wrong thing to do?'

She really was trying, the housekeeper thought, but then she'd always been a considerate girl. She smiled. 'I'm sure Mr David will attend to that but it's kind of you to mention it. I'll discuss with Cook which dishes she thinks will be suitable and you have no need to worry, everything will be prepared, presented and served satisfactorily. Mr David will no doubt discuss with Lewis what wines are to be served.'

Rose smiled. 'Thank you, Mrs Mathews. I really do appreciate your advice.'

Mona nodded. 'You only have to ask, you know that. Now, would you like some tea?'

'Yes, please, Mrs Mathews,' Rose replied, thinking a cup of tea would be very welcome. The interview had been a relief but also a bit of an ordeal.

It was Nora who brought the tray but as she placed it down on the table Rose noticed that she didn't look at her, let alone smile, and her heart sank.

'Shall I pour, miss?' Nora asked in a tight voice.

'No, thank you, Nora, I can manage,' Rose replied, deciding to take the bull by the horns. 'Nora, I ... I know this must have come as a great shock to you ... to everyone, but we didn't plan it. David ... David and I ... we just fell in love.' How hard it was to choose the right words!

Nora remained silent, her eyes downcast, her back rigid.

Rose soldiered on. 'I know things have ... changed and we can no longer be as friendly as we were, but I ... I hope we can still get on well together.'

Nora's reserve broke. 'We'll have to, miss, we haven't much choice, not if we want to keep our jobs!' Both Lewis and Mrs Mathews had made it quite clear to herself and Nancy and Beryl that if Rose were not treated with the deference and civility her position now demanded then they would have to find alternative employment, and they were all acutely aware that that would prove very difficult, especially as they would have to explain the reason why to prospective employers. Indeed it was very likely they would not be provided with a reference. Beryl hadn't been perturbed, Nora thought bitterly, but then she viewed the whole thing as romantic. Both she and Nancy felt angry and resentful and, if the truth be known, a little jealous. Rose had escaped their world of drudgery and servitude and it was extremely galling to now have to wait upon their former friend and companion.

'Nora, I'm sorry... I didn't know... I never wanted...' Rose felt at a loss. She'd never intended that they should be threatened in this way.

'I don't suppose you did. I don't suppose you even thought of Nancy and me – your friends – at all ... miss!'

Although Rose was hurt by her words she didn't show it; she did, however, nod slowly. She hadn't really thought how Nancy, Nora and

Beryl would take the news, she'd just thought collectively of the 'staff's' reaction.

'Well, I have to say that Nancy and me don't approve at all. The likes of us don't marry the likes of them!' Nora blurted out.

Rose was taken aback by this. 'And Beryl?' she asked quietly.

'Beryl is a little fool! But you'll not see much of her anyway from now on so what she thinks doesn't matter. Things have changed, miss. There's no going back. Now, if you'll excuse me, I have my duties to attend to.'

Rose nodded. It was obvious that it would take a long time to build up the degree of respect and amiability between herself and the two girls that had formerly existed. Maybe she never could. That saddened her but she comforted herself with the thought that she would keep on trying. She didn't regret her decision to marry David; his love was worth every sacrifice she would have to make.

When Nora had gone Rose turned and walked to the French doors that opened on to the terrace. The gardens and grounds stretched away before her, green and tranquil beneath the pale blue sky. She smiled. This would be the view she would see every day at David's side, and that made her feel happier. She would be quite content with the rooms he now occupied and the house was big enough that she need not encounter Olivia very often during the day. Thankfully, too, it appeared that most of the staff were prepared to accept and advise her, even though for now she could only expect bare civility from

Nora and Nancy. She now began to look forward to the day she would be married with more pleasure.

Chapter Thirty-Two

When Iris arrived in Tregarron, the Baltic blue coat and hat she'd worn for her own wedding packed carefully in her case along with her best dress, Rose was eagerly waiting for her.

'I have so much to tell you and so much to show you, Iris!' she exclaimed as she hugged her sister and escorted her into the cottage and up to the bedroom they would share.

'It's very ... quaint, but nice, Rose,' Iris remarked, glancing around the pretty, comfortable little room. Rose's pale blue coat and dress were hanging behind the door, ready for tomorrow.

'We'll have some tea and then we'll take the last of my things to Plas Idris and you can meet David and see the house. Gwen's nephew Aleric is coming with the car. David's taken him on to drive me whenever I want to go anywhere – and to drive David, of course. It's not fitting for me to walk, cycle or use public transport now – such as it is – and I can't drive. Aleric is delighted with his new job.'

Iris digested all this in silence, gazing out of the window at the fields beyond the garden. 'Wait until I tell our Charlie that you have a chauffeur now, he'll be green with envy!' she said, grinning impishly. 'Well, this is certainly all very different to Liverpool but I probably won't be able to sleep – it's so *quiet!*'

'You'd get used to it, Iris, if you were staying longer,' Rose said a little wistfully.

'You know I'd stay longer if I could, Rose. Besides, you don't want to spend the first few weeks of married life with your sister trailing along as well. Now, let me get my coat and dress on a hanger or they will be creased to death. I could murder a cup of tea and you can tell me all the arrangements for tomorrow.'

Rose sat on the bed and watched Iris hang up her outfit. Tomorrow would be the happiest day of her life and she was so glad that Iris would share it with her, but she wished she could have had the rest of her family around her too.

When young Aleric arrived, attired in a dark suit, white shirt, new tie and with a cap, both girls were ready and he helped them with Rose's luggage. As they drove slowly to Plas Idris Rose happily pointed out the village landmarks, including the little chapel where she was to be married next morning.

'You mean all this land belongs to him?' Iris whispered, glancing from side to side as they drove up the long curving drive. She'd only ever seen this much open space in the parks in Liverpool and of course the fields on the journey to Denbigh.

Rose nodded. 'And most of the surrounding farms too.'

Iris's eyes widened as she caught her first glimpse of the house and she completely forgot the presence of Gwen's nephew in the driving seat.

'Rose, it's the size of St George's Hall!' she gasped, thinking of the enormous, graceful, Grecian-style building in Lime Street.

'That's exaggerating a bit, Iris. It's not quite *that* big.'

'It's just as grand though. How do you find your way around?'

'I suppose I've become used to it now. I did think it was very large indeed when I first came here. David and I will use just a few rooms on the ground floor though, he can't manage stairs. They're lovely; the drawing room opens out on to the terrace,' Rose informed her as the car came to a halt.

'That paved bit with the big stone vases?' Iris asked but there was no time for further conversation as Lewis appeared followed by Henry, who helped Aleric with Rose's belongings while Lewis ushered them inside.

Iris was quite overawed by both the house and the fact that her sister now appeared not to have to lift a finger; there was someone on hand to do everything.

She liked David Rhys-Pritchard instantly and it was obvious from the way he looked at Rose that he adored her. She sipped her tea, very mindful of the opulent furniture, fabrics and ornaments, the delicate china and silver teapot, while Rose and her future brother-in-law discussed the final arrangements for tomorrow. Thankfully his sister hadn't put in an appearance, Iris thought when it was time to leave.

'Thank you so much for making the journey, Iris, we both do appreciate it, especially as circumstances are difficult. It's been a pleasure to meet you and I look forward to seeing you again in the morning,' David said, shaking her hand and smiling up at her.

He was very pleasant, she thought, and polite, but she still didn't envy Rose. She hadn't felt at all comfortable although she knew he had tried to put her at her ease. She'd felt more at home in Gwen's little cottage.

They both dressed with care the following morning and as Iris placed the pale blue hat over her sister's dark, shiny hair she gave her a kiss on the cheek.

'You look gorgeous, Rose. Every inch a lady and he'll be delighted with you. Mam would be so proud!'

'Oh, Iris, how I wish she could have been here.'

'I know, but it wasn't to be. She'll be thinking of you, you know that. Now, have I got this hat on at the right angle?'

Rose adjusted the brim slightly. 'I didn't think I'd be nervous, but I am.'

Iris smiled. 'I was nervous too when I got married, I suppose it's only natural, but you'll forget once you get to the church. Now, we'd better go down, collect our flowers and wait for Aleric,' she urged, glancing at the little clock on the bedside table.

Gwen was ready and peering intently out of the window for her nephew's arrival. She looked very smart, Iris thought, in her best navy costume with a pale pink blouse and a navy and pink hat.

'Oh, don't you look a picture, *cariad!* Like a fashion model in a magazine, you do!' Gwen enthused upon seeing Rose. 'See, I'm getting all emotional already,' she added, dabbing at her eyes and wishing that Kate could have been here to see her daughter. She was certain that neither Miss Olivia Rhys-Pritchard nor Mrs Ernest Williams would look as beautiful or elegant. 'Now, I'll fetch the flowers. Aleric will be here any minute now – he was picking Bob up first.'

It was a very short journey to the little chapel so it had been agreed that Rose's small party would travel together. The few people they passed waved. David was waiting with Ernest at his side; his two sisters were standing in the pew behind as was Bethan Williams. When Rose saw David all her nervousness vanished. She walked the few steps towards him on Bob's arm feeling happier than she'd ever done before and was surprised and touched when Elinore smiled pleasantly at her.

Rose made her vows in a quiet, steady voice but when the Reverend Williams pronounced them man and wife her eyes filled with tears of joy as she bent and kissed David on the cheek. Nothing mattered now, not even Olivia's barely concealed disapproval. She loved David and she loved Plas Idris and the years ahead stretched ahead like a beautiful dream come true.

Gwen had caught Iris's hand and squeezed it as Rose and David made their vows.

'Make sure you tell your mam every single detail,' she whispered, wiping away a tear.

With the brief ceremony over, the happy couple were congratulated by everyone, although

Olivia's tone was rather clipped, Iris noted, and the wedding party were driven back to Plas Idris by Ernest Williams and Aleric in the respective cars. Iris was astonished to see the entire staff assembled in front of the house, waiting to greet and congratulate their master and new mistress but she didn't comment, feeling a little sad. It was a very real reminder that Rose had now taken her first steps along a very different path to the one she would travel.

The buffet had been laid out in the dining room and Iris thought everything looked delicious and very elaborate. Lewis filled everyone's glass with champagne while Henry, assisted by a very subdued Nancy and Nora, were on hand to serve the food. The slightly tense atmosphere was dispelled by Ernest, who cleared his throat and proposed a toast to the bride and groom. After that, Elinore took her sister's arm and edged her towards the fireplace and engaged her in conversation to try to dispel some of Olivia's tenseness. Ernest, David, Bob and Owen began to discuss the merits of tractors over horsepower and Gwen and Bethan wondered if they could possibly prise the recipe for the cold game pie from Cook, via Mona Mathews of course.

Iris guided Rose towards the long sash windows as they sipped their champagne. 'I have to say I've never tasted wine like this, Rose, and things are going very well. Even Olivia is looking less frosty-faced than she was in the church.'

'I'm very grateful to both Ernest and Elinore, at least they are trying to put everyone at ease,' Rose confided.

Iris nodded. 'Well, the men are all getting on well but I suppose they have known each other for years even if they don't meet socially very often.'

'They've got farming in common,' Rose said, catching a glance from her new husband and smiling.

Iris lowered her voice. 'Will you be able to manage ... later? I mean ... at bedtime?'

Rose blushed but nodded. 'It's not as if David is paralysed. Either Lewis or Henry usually help him with his clothes but I'm his wife now...' Rose was feeling a little embarrassed but was determined not to show it. 'We'll be ... fine,' she added firmly as Lewis refilled their glasses.

When the guests had departed later that afternoon, Olivia informed them that Elinore and Ernest had invited her to spend a few days with them and that she would drive over when she had packed a small case. She had left instructions with Mrs Mathews, who was perfectly capable of seeing that things ran like clockwork during her brief absence.

Rose was very relieved to realise that she and David would have a couple of days alone, apart from the staff, of course, but their presence was something she was going to have to get used to.

They had a light supper after which they retired to the drawing room that overlooked the terrace and as daylight faded Rose sat on the floor, her head resting in David's lap. 'Happy?' he asked, gently stroking her hair.

'Happier than I've ever been in my life, David.'

'I thought everything went very well and at

least Olivia was civil to everyone.'

'Elinore was very good, David, she helped to smooth things and it was a lovely day. Even if things had been different, I wouldn't have wanted a big fuss or crowds of people. The chapel was just perfect, it felt so calm and peaceful, my nerves just vanished. When we got back I suddenly found I was very hungry. I'd hardly eaten any breakfast, and the food was delicious.'

'I think the champagne helped to keep everyone amiable. It's been a long day, Rose, shall we retire early?'

Rose got to her feet, holding his hand. 'There's no need to ask for Lewis or Henry tonight, David, I'll help you.'

'Oh, Rose, I wish—'

She placed a finger on his lips. 'Hush. I love you. It... Everything will be wonderful.'

David felt embarrassed and also resentful. 'It ... it might take time.'

'We have plenty of that, David. We have the rest of our lives.'

Her words dispelled his tension. She was right. 'I never thought I'd be happy again, Rose. You're my miracle and I love you.'

Chapter Thirty-Three

Kate folded Rose's letter and smiled. No longer were her daughter's letters written on cheap paper, she thought as she gently ran a finger over the thick cream vellum. Rose was happy and seemed to be settling into her new life well, although she wrote that Olivia was still very cool towards her whenever they met, occasions Rose tried her best to keep to the bare minimum. Kate frowned; she fervently hoped that in time Olivia's attitude towards her daughter would change. The maids Nora and Nancy seemed not to have entirely come to terms with the situation yet either. But there was good news too: David had suggested that Rose visit her at least once a month, driven by Aleric, and that Gwen should accompany her – if she wished to, of course. So, Rose was coming over on Sunday – in two days' time – with Gwen. She would be delighted to see them both, she thought. It was very thoughtful of him to have suggested it; it was a considerable distance.

When Iris arrived home from shopping Kate informed her of her sister's forthcoming visit

'That's great news, Mam. We can hear all Rose's gossip and I do like Gwen. Perhaps Florence could come for an hour or so too. She hasn't seen Rose since she got married and it might cheer her up a bit.' She glanced at the formal photograph of Rose and David that had pride of place on the dresser.

Kate sighed. Florence had taken her father's death hard. It had changed her, but for the better, or so she thought. Florence was now more serious and considerate, and far less frivolous. 'I'll tell Charlie to ask her would she like to come and I want to talk to both you and Tom and our Charlie after supper tonight.'

Iris nodded; she had a good idea what this was about. Charlie had been running Taylor's Coal Merchants for over a month now and somehow, between them and with the occasional help of Ada Marshall and Maggie Connolly, she and Tom had managed to run the two other shops. She felt proud of what she and Tom had achieved but it couldn't go on. She felt she was neglecting her mother's wellbeing and she had another reason she wanted the situation discussed and hopefully resolved. 'I'll put these groceries away and then I'll go and relieve Ada – she's her own chores to do at home. I know she likes the few hours in the shop as it's a welcome change to the daily drudgery but it's not fair to trade on her good nature.'

'Go on then, I'll be fine. I can peel the potatoes while I'm sitting here and then I'll do some baking. That shouldn't tax me too much and I'll need something to give Rose and Gwen,' Kate replied.

Before departing for home Ada popped into the kitchen to see Kate. 'I'm off now, luv. The kids will be 'ome soon an' iffen I don't watch them they'll 'ave the place destroyed, traipsing their mates in an' out an' all the dirt and muck of the street with them.'

'Thanks for all your help, Ada. You've always been a good friend and neighbour and I know our Iris is very grateful too, but I'm going to have to sort the whole situation out. We can't go on like this. I'm going to do it tonight,' Kate said determinedly.

'Well, luv, let me know 'ow it all goes. I'll see yer termorrer,' Ada said cheerfully as she went out the back way.

Iris cleared away after supper, assisted by Tom even though she told him she could manage. Kate relayed Rose's news to Charlie and asked him to invite Florence on Sunday afternoon for a couple of hours.

'You're right, Mam, it might take her out of herself although I think she's coming to terms with it all,' he mused aloud. Florence seemed to have matured a lot in these last few weeks, he thought. Now she never mentioned the wedding, for everything had been put on hold as Ethel had insisted that they observe the year of formal mourning. It was the least she could do for Edward, she had said, and he knew that she was still torturing herself with guilt. He had agreed wholeheartedly; he was beginning to understand Ethel more and to realise that underneath all her pretensions she had loved her husband and had only wanted the best for her daughter. Ethel had even thanked him for being so supportive to them through such difficult times and had expressed the hope that her daughter's future with him would be as happy and successful as hers had been with Edward. Florence had told him one evening last week that it wasn't

357

'occasions' that really mattered but 'relationships' and she wished she had fully understood that months ago. Yes, he felt that Florence had grown up a lot since Edward's death and he loved her more because of it. She even treated her mother in a different way, more as an equal, although she was still deferential towards Ethel.

'Well, I'm glad to hear it. Now, we've got to sort out what we're going to do in the future,' Kate said firmly. 'I've given this a great deal of thought and it hasn't been easy to make a decision. Charlie, I presume you intend to go on running the coal business?'

Charlie nodded. He'd had a long discussion with Ethel, who had agreed that he should take it on permanently. She had no interest in it at all, she had said, yet she hadn't the heart to sell it even though the damned business had been more than instrumental in sending Edward to an early grave. Edward had never been in favour of selling. Charlie had been very relieved and had promised he would do everything in his power to ensure it continued to be successful. He had plans for the future, although he'd kept that to himself. Once he and Florence were married he intended to go into property. In a small way at first: he'd buy a couple of terraced houses to rent out for in this city there was always a shortage of decent affordable housing. There were sufficient funds in the bank. Ethel had assumed that he would move into Cedar Grove next year. In fact Edward's death seemed to have left her very subdued and somewhat bewildered.

'I think it can be expanded too, there is always a

demand for coal and providing the miners don't keep going on strike, I can make a real go of it. I've got my eye on a couple of large contracts I'd like to tender for but I'll have to watch the profit margins carefully. It's hard work – I never realised just *how* hard nor the long hours that Edward had to put in.'

'You'll do well, Charlie. You've a good head on your shoulders and you've never been afraid of hard work,' Kate said, smiling. 'Then what I've decided is to keep the pawnbroker's, it's the longer-established family business and your da wouldn't want me to let it go. Tom, are you happy to take it on permanently? It will never be wildly successful, even though some round here say it must be a little gold mine, but it's a fairly steady income.'

Tom nodded. 'Of course, Ma-in-law, and it does provide people with a very necessary service.'

Kate agreed and Tom had the right temperament for it too, she thought. In some ways he reminded her of Bill and people liked and respected him for the very same reasons they had Bill. 'So, we'll have to sell the greengrocery. I've no idea how much we'll get but the goodwill should amount to something.'

'It's such a shame though, Mam. You worked so hard for years to build up that business,' Iris said sadly.

'I did but I'm stuck with this condition so there's no use getting upset about things we can't change. Whatever we get for it will help tide us over if times get hard,' Kate said resolutely.

Iris glanced questioningly at Tom and he

nodded, smiling. 'Maybe it's just as well, Mam, because I'm going to have my work cut out this time next year. I certainly won't have time to be trying to cope with a house, a business and a ... baby.'

Kate's eyes widened and then a smile of delight spread across her face. 'Oh, Iris, luv! You mean ... I'm going to be a granny?'

Iris nodded, her cheeks flushed and her eyes bright with happiness. 'You are, Mam.'

Kate suddenly looked stricken. 'Oh, and the way I've let you run around trying to see to the house *and* the shop! You'll have to take things easier now!'

Iris laughed. 'Mam, I'm expecting – I'm not ill!'

Charlie was looking a little bemused as he shook Tom's hand. 'Well, I never thought you'd make me an uncle quite so soon but congratulations!'

'We never intended to become parents quite so soon either but babies don't wait to be invited,' Tom replied, looking very proud just the same.

'And on Sunday you'll be able to inform Lady Rose of the fact that she's going to be an aunty, Iris. That'll bring her back down to earth,' Charlie added.

Iris shook her head reprovingly. 'Now, Charlie, she's not *Lady* Rose and you know it and she never set out to become Mrs Rhys-Pritchard.'

Charlie grinned. 'I know. But everything seems to be working out.'

Rose and Gwen arrived on Sunday after lunch and Kate thought that Rose had certainly blossomed.

'Rose, don't you look well!' she greeted her daughter.

'I brought you some farm butter and cheese, Kate, and Megan says they will do you good. She sends her regards, as do Bob and Bethan and Owen.' Gwen placed the neatly wrapped parcel on the table.

'What's the lad going to do with himself, Gwen? I suppose he could do with a cup of tea but if he leaves that car outside the door for long every kid in the street will be climbing on it,' Kate asked. A motor car was such a novelty in this neighbourhood the children wouldn't be able to resist but if it was damaged in any way Rose may not venture back to Liverpool again.

'He'd be grateful for a cup, Kate, but then he's going to have a drive around the city, see the sights. He's never been to Liverpool before, see, and there's not much traffic on a Sunday.'

Aleric was duly brought in and given a cup of tea and a slice of cake and as he departed Florence arrived.

'Oh, Rose, it's so lovely to see you,' Florence said sincerely before suddenly becoming flustered and clapping her hand to her mouth. 'Oh, I forgot! What should I call you now?'

Rose laughed as she hugged her. 'What you've always called me: "Rose". I'm going to be your sister-in-law, don't forget.'

Florence was still unsure and had no wish to offend anyone. 'But aren't you rather ... grand now?'

Charlie tutted impatiently. 'She may have married into the gentry but she's still just my

361

sister, Florence.'

Gwen's eyebrows rose and she glanced at Kate. Perhaps a bit of jealousy there? she thought.

'Charlie's right, Florence. I'm still just his sister. Sit down and have a cup of tea. I'll make a fresh pot, I certainly haven't forgotten how to, even though I did overhear Nora insinuating that I had. I quickly reminded her that I am perfectly capable of cooking a meal and even getting my hands dirty should the necessity arise.'

Kate nodded with some satisfaction. It looked as if Rose was capable of holding her own with those girls.

'For heaven's sake, relax,' Iris urged Florence. 'I've got some good news myself, Rose. I'm expecting a baby. You're going to be an aunty.'

Rose threw her arms around Iris. 'Oh, Iris! Tom! That's wonderful! You'll have to bring my niece or nephew out to Plas Idris to meet their Uncle David – as soon as he or she is old enough, of course.'

Gwen was helping Kate to set the table and the two women exchanged glances, both wondering if Rose would be blessed with children.

'Don't see why not. He's looking better, getting about more these days and has more energy,' Gwen whispered, making a clatter as she placed the teaspoons on the saucers.

'And we've decided to sell the greengrocery,' Kate informed her daughter and her friend. 'Tom's going to take over Bill's business as Charlie is now managing Taylor's Coal Merchants.'

'Sensible, that is, Kate, what with Iris expecting,' Gwen agreed.

Florence looked thoughtful as she sipped her tea. 'Isn't it strange how things have turned out?'

'Strange?' Iris probed.

'Well, both you and Rose are now married and you are going to be a mother, Iris. I always assumed that Charlie and I would be the first to be married. Oh, I'm not upset or anything, I can look at things more ... sensibly now.' She smiled at Charlie. 'I've even got a few ideas that may save us some money with regard to the business.'

Charlie looked at her in surprise. 'Really? I didn't think you were interested.'

'I do work in an accounts department, Charlie, and I did matriculate from school. I could be of some help to you. After all, I certainly don't want you working as hard as my poor father did or ending up the same way.'

Kate nodded her approval. Florence had every right to be involved for she was her parents' only child. The business was her inheritance.

Charlie could see Florence's point and it was beginning to dawn on him that his fiancée had a brain equally as good as his own. He smiled at Florence. Maybe they could work together – it would be in both their interests. A feeling of contentment crept over him. He had done well, he was now a successful businessman and the lads in the yard respected him. He had what he'd set out to achieve: a position in society and a healthy bank balance and soon he would have a loving and loyal wife and perhaps business partner.

'Now, Rose, tell us all about life at Plas Idris. We're dying to know how you are getting on,' Iris urged, thinking the conversation could benefit from taking a less serious turn.

Tom refilled Iris's cup and smiled at his wife. He was a very happy man, he thought. He had a beautiful, loving wife and he'd be a proud father in six months' time. When he'd first met Iris, on his first day at the market, he had never dreamed that he would one day be his own boss, the proprietor of a pawnbroking business. He'd just been grateful to have a job.

Kate leaned back in her chair and sipped her tea as she listened to the details of Rose's life. She was remembering a May morning two years ago when Rose had been confined to bed with rheumatic fever. She'd thought then that all she wanted for her children was a decent future, that if she lived to see them happy and settled she'd count herself very fortunate. Her gaze swept over them all fondly. All their futures looked rosy. Charlie had a thriving business which he intended to expand and it looked as if in Florence he had found an ideal partner. Iris and Tom wouldn't have nearly as much money but they had a good home, a strong marriage and now a baby on the way, and Iris had never wanted much more than that. And Rose ... well, she had never dreamed that Rose would marry a man like David Rhys-Pritchard and live in such style. Rose would never ever have to worry about money and, listening to her daughter, she knew that she'd found true love and happiness even if her marriage was viewed with disapproval by some. Yes, Rose was content.

Gwen reached across and touched her arm. 'A penny for them, Kate?'

Kate smiled at her friend. 'I was just thinking how fortunate I am, Gwen, they're all happy and I know that Bill would be proud of how they've turned out.'

Gwen smiled back. 'He would, *cariad*.'

Kate nodded, her eyes misting with tears. The years had not been easy, but together they had come through them. She missed Bill dearly every day, but as she looked lovingly at her family she felt an overwhelming sense of happiness. 'Yes,' she said, glowing with pride, 'we are truly blessed.'

The publishers hope that this book has given you enjoyable reading. Large Print Books are especially designed to be as easy to see and hold as possible. If you wish a complete list of our books please ask at your local library or write directly to:

Magna Large Print Books
Magna House, Long Preston,
Skipton, North Yorkshire.
BD23 4ND

This Large Print Book for the partially sighted, who cannot read normal print, is published under the auspices of

THE ULVERSCROFT FOUNDATION